NEW STORIES
FROM THE SOUTH

The Year's Best, 2010

The Series Editor would like to thank Ana Alvarez, for her incredible devotion and long hours and eagle eyes, and Brunson Hoole, for his continued careful and precise shepherding of this series over the years.

NEW STORIES
FROM THE SOUTH

The Year's Best, 2010

Selected from U.S. magazines
by AMY HEMPEL with
KATHY PORIES

with an introduction by Amy Hempel

Algonquin Books of Chapel Hill

Published by
ALGONQUIN BOOKS OF CHAPEL HILL
Post Office Box 2225
Chapel Hill, North Carolina 27515-2225

a division of
WORKMAN PUBLISHING
225 Varick Street
New York, New York 10014

Fic ‹S›

CONTENTS

INTRODUCTION
by Amy Hempel   ix

Adam Atlas, NEW YEAR'S WEEKEND ON THE HAND SURGERY WARD,
OLD PILGRIMS' HOSPITAL, NAPLES, ITALY
From *Narrative Magazine*   1

Rick Bass, FISH STORY
From *The Atlantic*   15

Brad Watson, NOON
From *The Idaho Review*   26

Danielle Evans, SOMEONE OUGHT TO TELL HER THERE'S
NOWHERE TO GO
From *A Public Space*   42

Ron Rash, THE ASCENT
From *Tin House*   64

Ashleigh Pedersen, SMALL AND HEAVY WORLD
From *The Iowa Review*   75

Wendell Berry, A BURDEN
From *The Oxford American*   93

Megan Mayhew Bergman, THE COW THAT MILKED HERSELF
From *New South*   106

George Singleton, COLUMBARIUM
From *Appalachian Heritage*   114

Bret Anthony Johnston, CAIMAN
From *AGNI Magazine*   121

Ben Stroud, ERASER
From *One Story*   126

Kevin Wilson, HOUSEWARMING
From *The South Carolina Review*   136

Dorothy Allison, JASON WHO WILL BE FAMOUS
From *Tin House*   151

Ann Pancake, ARSONISTS
From *The Georgia Review*   163

Aaron Gwyn, DRIVE
From *The Gettysburg Review*   181

Emily Quinlan, THE GREEN BELT
From *Santa Monica Review*   195

Stephen Marion, THE COLDEST NIGHT OF THE TWENTIETH CENTURY
From *Tin House*   203

Padgett Powell, CRY FOR HELP FROM FRANCE
From *Subtropics*   223

Kenneth Calhoun, NIGHTBLOOMING
From *The Paris Review*   226

Marjorie Kemper, DISCOVERED AMERICA
From *Southwest Review*   241

Elizabeth Spencer, RETURN TRIP
From *Five Points*   256

Tim Gautreaux, IDOLS
From *The New Yorker*   273

Laura Lee Smith, THIS TREMBLING EARTH
From *Natural Bridge* 297

Brad Watson, VISITATION
From *The New Yorker* 312

Wells Tower, RETREAT
From *McSweeney's* 331

APPENDIX 359

PREVIOUS VOLUMES 369

Amy Hempel

INTRODUCTION

Today the Saints won the Super Bowl. So I was thinking of what New Orleans novelist Nancy Lemann once said about the South: "There's a lot of human condition going around." There is a lot of human condition in the twenty-five stories that make up this anthology, and the authors go at it in immensely powerful ways. The power of humor, power of horror.

As series editor Kathy Pories and I read the stories that were up for consideration, I felt we were aligned in what we were looking for. What I wanted was, as Gary Lutz put it, "whatever I could never expect to get from anybody else." After making my selections, I looked up past years' contributors and found that thirteen of the writers here have been featured in the series before, and eleven of the writers are in *New Stories from the South* for the first time.

In 1996, the Algonquin staff, in conjunction with McIntyre's bookshop, threw a two-day party in Pittsboro, North Carolina, outside Chapel Hill, to celebrate *Best of the South,* a tenth-anniversary collection. I was the Yankee tagalong who took a train from New York City and justified her presence as a pal and fan of some of those being honored. The reading lists I have put together in nearly thirty years of teaching are top-heavy with writers from the South. Many of them were in Pittsboro that weekend. I remember asking

Mary Hood what she was doing in the class she was teaching that year as writer-in-residence at Ole Miss. "Life lies," she said. "What's that?" I asked. "You know," she said, "like, 'I thought my prime would last.'" Rick Bass was there, and Mark Richard. Bob Shacochis and Patricia Lear.

Rick Bass is back this year, his seventh appearance in the series, although other members of my personal pantheon, including Rick Barthelme, Allan Gurganus, and the late Barry Hannah, are not here, because they did not publish stories in 2009.

There were stories I adored but could not include, because those stories had already appeared in books published last year. Yet I chose to include "Retreat" by Wells Tower, a story that had already come out in his widely praised debut collection, *Everything Ravaged, Everything Burned.* "Retreat" was first published in *McSweeney's* in 2007; two years later it was published in *McSweeney's again;* the magazine ran a small-print apologia by the author on the copyright page, and it is worth looking up for its honest account of what it is to be a writer who doesn't feel a story is finished just because it has been published. I admire his attitude and what it says about revision. I have now read three different published versions of this story, and I felt the alterations from *McSweeney's* to book to the second *McSweeney's* incarnation were such that I could include it here. This anthology ends with "Retreat," and it is a comic dazzler.

Much of what I read from the contemporary South has a soundtrack. I hear Little Walter and Jimmy Reed and Carla Thomas, Ruby Johnson and Son Thomas. The blues legend I heard perform at the Hoka, in Oxford, Mississippi, when I was taken there by the late Barry Hannah and Willie Morris and Larry Brown. This was in another century (!), and in case I got too swoony over the scene, one of our party pointed out that he was "playing for his electric bill," said, "His wife shot him in the stomach last year."

I hear recordings made in the field in Yazoo City by Bill Ferris, then director of the Center for the Study of Southern Culture at Ole Miss. The album of these old bluesmen is titled *Bothered*

All the Time. There are visuals that sometimes go with these stories: photographs by Maude Schuyler Clay in Mississippi, and her cousin William Eggleston up in Memphis, the photographs of sacred landscapes—churches and cemeteries in the Delta—by Tom Rankin.

Then why is a story set in Italy the first in this year's Table of Contents? The author, Adam Atlas, was born and raised in Louisville, Kentucky; in "New Year's Weekend on the Hand Surgery Ward, Old Pilgrims' Hospital, Naples, Italy," we learn that events in Kentucky propelled the narrator to flee not only his home but his homeland, and fetch up in Naples, teaching English. This is only the second story Adam Atlas has published, and it is a pleasure to get to spotlight such a strong new voice. There are other stories here that struck me as distinctly Southern in character, stance, or voice, though they take place somewhere else: Padgett Powell's "Cry for Help from France," Brad Watson's "Visitation," and Megan Mayhew-Bergman's "The Cow that Milked Herself."

In addition to the human condition on display here, these stories have singular voices and striking language, the two things sure to win me over. The choices I made can be further understood this way: I don't have much interest in causality in fiction, but I do want to see accountability. Cleverness doesn't interest me, but humor—the darker the better—does. Menace is more interesting to me than violence. Blame doesn't persuade me, but a deep sense of "Life's like that" feels true. I prefer the natural world to the supernatural. I want effects, not just events. I look for stories that do not hide from real feeling behind irony, that are both of-the-moment and timeless, and that look at questions of loyalty, of what we owe one another. I want to see hard-barked people in retreat from the sweetness of their souls, and the collision of illusion and reality. I want yearning, not nostalgia. I want my breath to catch at a last line. I want "Not the surprise. The amazed understanding," as the poet Jack Gilbert put it. I want something that I didn't know I wanted.

•••

The people who are present in these stories include a child who robs the dead to help his parents ("The Ascent," by Ron Rash); a true coward's reaction to the phrase, "Go for it," in Padgett Powell's story; a kid who can't wait to get where he's going even if it's not really any place he wants to go (Ben Stroud, "Eraser"); an Iraq War veteran whose good intentions back home backfire publicly ("Someone Ought to Tell Her There's Nowhere to Go," by Danielle Evans). There are men attracted to evil, and women repelled by goodness. There is a giant catfish that refuses to die even after being skinned for a feast; we hear of it from the boy entrusted to keep the fish "hosed down with a trickle of cool water, giving the fish life one silver gasp at a time" (Rick Bass, "Fish Story"). "The facts kept dodging us," explains a woman in Elizabeth Spencer's "Return Trip."

Marjorie Kemper died last year before "Discovered America" was published in *Southwest Review*. I'm glad to have her story here for the voice that tells you in the first paragraph that while "People warned us we might hit bad weather" on a road trip across the country, "most of the heavy weather turned out to be inside the car . . ." In Kenneth Calhoun's "Nightblooming," a "shady neighborhood" means "it's leafy, not ghetto," and a young man hears the words of an old musician "driving into my head like pennies dropped from eight miles up." It's prisoners we hear from in Stephen Marion's ribald story, "The Coldest Night of the Twentieth Century," as they break into the women's cell block; later they will be "running from everything that could be run from." Flirtations with death revive a couple's erotic life in Aaron Gwyn's "Drive": ". . . and right before the truck coming toward them began flashing its lights, she glanced up, and then over." In Emily Quinlan's "The Green Belt," "It was hard to be a triplet," observes the father of a set; always there were "two copies of yourself who were doing correctly what you had just done wrong." In Bret Anthony Johnston's "Caiman," a father wanting to provide his son with a pet says, "On the drive home, I'd seen the man under the causeway and pulled over for a look. Our ice chest was still in the bed of the truck from when we'd gone floundering . . . And he had only one left . . ." A boy yearns for victimization as the surest route to celebrity (and uses "Tarantino" as a verb) in "Jason Who Will Be Famous," by Dorothy Allison. A man calls his father for help removing a dead deer from the pond in his yard ("House-warming," by Kevin Wilson), though this is not the most pressing problem the son's family faces. "Somebody started burning houses within a year after they blew up the first mountain," writes Ann Pancake in "Arsonists," set in West Virginia coal country. A sixty-three-year-old man inherits a grand but dilapidated mansion on his great-grandfather's property, and sets out to bring it back to its glory—"It had shamed him to long for the house, and now he owned it" ("Idols," by Tim Gautreaux). Laura Lee Smith gives us the Okefenokee Swamp as safe haven for a young man who "knows its secrets" ("This Trembling Earth"). "The swamp is a national preserve, but that doesn't mean much to those of us who have always lived here." In Ashleigh Pedersen's "Small and Heavy World," a community "moved up into the trees when the neighborhood flooded that April," the folks looking down at water "the color of peanut butter." The last two lines of Brad Watson's "Noon."

There's more. George Singleton's "Columbarium" features a woman's refrain, as recalled by her son: "For at least fifteen years she substituted 'No,' 'Okay' or 'I'll do it if I have to,' with 'I could have gone to the Rhode Island School of Design . . .'" A veterinarian examines his pregnant wife with an ultrasound probe in his clinic, says, "I think we cleaned this after the Rottweiler" ("The Cow That Milked Herself"). In Wendell Berry's "A Burden," a friend of the elderly, drunken Uncle Peach recalls having seen him "drink all he could hold and then fill his mouth for later."

So. Why was a Chicago-born writer who grew up in Colorado and California and has lived in New York City for the past many years asked to select the stories for this important anthology of short fiction from the South? *I was too thrilled at the invitation to ask!*

Though one's sense of geography is keen, it's hard to feel there is much that separates us after reading the stories collected here. And I don't get tired of hearing one of the truest things I've ever heard about writing, about life—William Faulkner's famous observation that "The past is not dead. It's not even past." My sense of connection to the South has something to do with—not just being haunted, but as Jack Gilbert wrote, being "haunted importantly."

Nancy Lemann wrote that "a place is different when you love someone in it."

And when you read someone from it.

In memory of Barry Hannah

Adam Atlas

NEW YEAR'S WEEKEND ON THE HAND SURGERY WARD, OLD PILGRIMS' HOSPITAL, NAPLES, ITALY

(from *Narrative Magazine*)

O utside, the neighbors were firing a pistol and setting off firecrackers in honor of the coming New Year. I decided to make a lasagna so I began chopping onions and I cut off the end of my thumb.

In Italy the emergency number is different for police and ambulances. I couldn't remember which emergency number was which so I called a pediatrician to whom I had been giving English lessons and she called the ambulance.

The dispatcher started calling me, she kept asking me which building was mine and I kept telling her which one it was. I eventually realized the ambulance guys didn't want to walk up all the stairs to my apartment, so I called my neighbor, Norma, to ask her to go down and meet them, but I accidentally called my ex-girlfriend on the speed dial. I don't know if I hung up before it started to ring. The fourth time the dispatcher called, she said the ambulance guys were waiting at the bottom of the stairs. We began to argue. I told her I understood that they wanted me to go down but I was in one room and my thumb was in the kitchen. I kept saying, my thumb is on the cutting board! My thumb is on the cutting board with the onions in the kitchen!

Shut up, the dispatcher told me, just shut up.

When the ambulance guys finally came, they were put out and winded. They asked me if I had a plastic bag for the piece of thumb and they watched with their arms folded while I stumbled around and found them a plastic bag.

In the emergency room, a doctor began cleaning the wound using a silver cauterizing pen to stop the bleeding. Two delinquents with tanning-salon tans and blood on their shirts wandered in and started to watch. Their skin around their eyes was white from the goggles they use in the tanning booths and they kept staring at me and the place where the end of my thumb used to be.

While she was talking to a colleague about changing her clothes, the doctor pressed down into the wound with the pen. It felt like lightning going into my hand. Another doctor from the university where I teach English arrived, a pediatric allergist. He came in and put his hands behind his back and watched silently. The doctor cleaning the wound suddenly got serious and told the delinquents to go away. After she finished, the doctor said to come back the next day when there would be a hand surgeon on duty who could examine me. Then she said that the piece of thumb was useless. She pointed to a yellow trash can and told me to throw it away so I went over and threw it away.

The hand surgeon on duty said they would need to operate, and that even though my surgery couldn't be scheduled until New Year's Eve, three days off, I should admit myself the following morning, since there would be an open bed: "A bed opens up and you stay in it until it's your turn to be operated on, that's the way it works around here." On New Year's Eve, he told me, the Hand Surgery Ward would fill up with the Neapolitan delinquents who buy boxes of contraband fireworks to celebrate.

"Dozens of them will blow off their hands at midnight," he said.

•••

When I checked into the hospital, there was a family in the room. Their boy, Giovanni, was there because of a large firecracker he'd found on the ground. He just picked it up and it exploded in his hand. His father was a little shorter than me, barrel-chested with thick hands, a strong, straight nose, balding with straight hair on the sides of his head. He was wearing a green plaid shirt and jeans, very neat and clean. Giovanni's hand was wrapped in a gigantic bandage and there were no fingers poking out of it. He said his fore- and middle fingers were just bones underneath the bandages, they didn't have any skin on them anymore. His thumb had been blown out of its socket, all the muscles shredded. His pinky and ring fingers were okay though. On Saturday, just me and Giovanni and his father were in the room (there were four blue linoleum beds in that room, and four blue linoleum chairs, and there was a blue linoleum table). Giovanni and I had to have the same pre-op exams, the blood work, EKG, anesthesiology exams, and so on, so we went to those together. When we saw the anesthesiologist, Giovanni went in first. I waited outside while the orderlies looked at his X-rays and shook their heads and said, *"Mamma mia"* and, "What a shame."

After dinner, Norma came to visit and we all talked. Giovanni and his father were from Vico Equense, a small town on the Amalfi Coast, near Sorrento. Norma mentioned her dog, Pasquale, and the boy's eyes lit up, he said they had seven dogs, five for the boar hunt and two for hunting birds. Norma said she didn't know that they hunted wild boar on the Amalfi Coast, and then Giovanni explained how clever and conniving the boars were and how they had killed a number of their dogs by tricking them into falling off a certain cliff. Giovanni was fourteen. He was a country kid like so many I had known back in Kentucky, tall and skinny, with bright eyes always watching everyone and everything in the room. The father was a bricklayer and they had some land. Giovanni was his only son.

We smelled cigarette smoke in the room but didn't know where it was coming from. Norma started to talk about how she didn't like to eat meat and we made fun of her. She left and really there wasn't much to say, but Giovanni offered me a little cake. I told him I didn't need it, that he and his father might need a snack, but Giovanni threw it onto my bed with his good hand and told me to have it for breakfast. He said that breakfast in the hospital wasn't very good. Every time the orderlies came around with our meals, they also had one for Giovanni's father. He had to help everyone else in the room cut their meat before he could allow himself to eat.

An orderly came by at eight that evening and warned us to hide our wallets, our watches, our phones. On Saturday nights, delinquents hid inside the hospital and roamed the halls, sneaking into the rooms and stealing whatever they could find. "Saturday nights are sad in the hospital," the orderly said, "real sad." After the orderly left, Giovanni's father lay down on one of the empty beds. Fireworks were going off outside. In the dark, waiting for the delinquents, we saw the flashes. We heard a boom. A flare went up and I saw Giovanni in silhouette. He was looking out the window.

"Firecrackers," he said.

The next morning, at about six-thirty, they brought in a guy who was moaning. He had gotten his hand stuck in a machine that cut off three of his fingers. He was from a place called Cassino, which is about halfway between Rome and Naples. He didn't say much that morning because he had been in surgery for seven hours while they sewed his fingers back on. He was awake the whole time during the surgery. His thumb was still black with oil from the machine. The man slept and cigarette smoke seeped into the room. Giovanni's father cleaned his son's head with a Wet-Nap. He made his way down to his good arm and then he started to weep. Giovanni looked at the ceiling and tried not to cry.

A couple of hours after the man from Cassino came, the orderlies wheeled in a delinquent from Secondigliano, the notorious slum outside Naples, the epicenter of the clan wars around here. He had been playing with some fireworks and one went off in his hand. As soon as they brought him in he wanted to know when lunch was going to be served. He was taller than me with a large head and chin. Maybe he was a bit retarded or maybe he was the typical idiot-delinquent—he had just lost the upper digits of his middle and ring fingers but he didn't even seem to care. His bandages were bloody and he was with the two friends who had driven him to the hospital. Then his mother arrived. Secondigliano started yelling at her, "What are you doing here, what are you doing here?" His mother slapped him on the head and said, "What the fuck have you done? What the fuck have you gotten yourself into?"

"Ma," he said, "when do they serve lunch around here? Get me some smokes, get me some water, get me some decent food." His mobile phone kept ringing and ringing.

The surgeon walked in, the surgeon who would be operating on me and Giovanni and Secondigliano. The surgeon first went to Giovanni and looked at the X-rays. Giovanni's mother and sister were there too. The surgeon was very curt with the family. When the father asked if they could save the boy's fingers, the surgeon said, "Save? Save? Excuse me, is there something you didn't understand? Did I not explain myself well enough?" And the father who spoke only dialect and not real Italian didn't say anything else. The surgeon had combed-back white hair, wore spectacles, and was extremely tan, probably from skiing. Because I was American, the surgeon was more respectful to me, giving me the formal *Lei*, and treating me with something that could be called tolerance, like tolerating a toothache. When Secondigliano's case was explained to him, the surgeon told Secondigliano that at least the boy had the excuse of being young, but at Secondigliano's age there was no excuse for playing around with fireworks. "Doc," Secondigliano said, "is it possible to have a smoke in here every once in a while?" The surgeon said no, no smoking was permitted inside the hospital. Finally, he looked at the hand of the man from Cassino. The surgeon who had been on duty had operated on him. One of the fingers didn't look so good. It might have to come off. Again.

The surgeon told Giovanni to follow him to another room so he could see what was underneath the bandages. Secondigliano chimed in, asking what time they would serve dinner and the surgeon didn't answer. He just turned around and walked out. Later, I was outside the room, sitting in the hallway. I heard the white-haired surgeon saying to Giovanni's family, "What happened to your son is an utter disaster. Despite our best efforts, we may not—" and then I stopped listening.

Norma visited me again that evening. We sat out in the hall and she asked if I had called my psychologist. I told her no, she was out of town and anyway it wasn't such a big deal. I said the only hard part had been watching Giovanni's father begin to cry, and while I was speaking I suddenly choked up and couldn't talk anymore so we just sat there not saying anything. Eventually, a man came out from behind a door. The man was visiting his mother. By this time, Giovanni and his father had come out into the hall too, probably just to get out of that hot, blue room for a second. The man looked at my thumb and asked, "Firecrackers?" I said that I had cut myself while chopping onions. "Ah, a moment of distraction," he said. "You should have been more careful." He was one of these bald, macho types almost feminine in the machismo, the fastidiousness of the pressed jeans, the dramatic gestures with the hands on the hips, and then the hands in the air, gesturing. Giovanni and his father were standing there near us, not really part of the circle of conversation, but not apart from it either. The man started speaking, pontificating, "Idiots, whoever hurts themselves playing with firecrackers. They deserve what they get. There isn't a person more stupid than the person who plays with firecrackers." He went on and on. "I tell my son here never to touch firecrackers. Would you ever pick up any firecrackers, son?" "No, Dad, never." "That's right, son. I brought my only boy, my only son here with me tonight not just to visit his grandmother but so he could see what happens to idiots who play with firecrackers." The man's son must have been nine or ten. He was short, plump, and really hairy. He had glasses and a clubfoot and a little mustache. Giovanni and his father were standing there looking desperate. The man turned to Giovanni and said, "And you? What about you? Firecrackers?"

"Firecrackers," Giovanni said.

"Firecrackers," the man said, and looked at the ceiling dramatically.

I couldn't listen to the man anymore. But five minutes later I saw him touch Giovanni's chin and tilt it up. "Took a little bit of it in the face, did you?" He looked at the cuts and scrapes on that smooth, porcelain cheek.

Earlier that day, the man's "companion," a black-haired girl with gray teeth, wandered into our room. She saw me, asked me what had happened. I told her I had cut off the end of my thumb. She said, "You cut off your thumb?" My thumb was wrapped in gauze but it was pretty obvious I hadn't cut the whole thing off. I told her no, just this part here, just the end, and I showed her on my good thumb about how much I had cut off. She looked at me with her empty eyes. "You cut the whole thing off?" she said.

Secondigliano walked around the Hand Surgery Ward as if he were on holiday, going out and smoking, horsing around. After visiting hours were over, some friends of his arrived, two more delinquents. One of them was dressed preppy in blue jeans, a blue button-down shirt, and a navy blue sweater. The other one had an extremely oval-shaped head, which was shaved, a tanning-booth tan, and a big overbite. He was wearing a backward baseball hat and athletic gear. They brought a girl into the room too, a bleached blonde, and Giovanni stared at her and I stared at her, and even if she was big, even if she was tawdry, even if everyone around here knows female delinquents are the worst delinquents of all, she still embarrassed us, she devastated us, us in our pajamas and bandages and everything we didn't have underneath those bandages. All of them went out to the stairwell and smoked, and the man from

Cassino with three fingers cut off woke up and began to talk. He had a big store in Cassino. He had land with thirteen thousand olive trees on it. In the afternoon, his family and his brothers and sisters had called him, they told him it was time to stop working, time for him to retire. He was fifty-seven but had been working since he was fifteen and his brothers and sisters had told him it was time to stop. "We're all getting older," his brother had told him on the phone. "At our age we can only get ourselves into trouble." The man from Cassino said he didn't care anything about the finger that might have to come off. "When all this is over," he said, "I just want to be able to eat again with two hands."

Secondigliano and the two delinquents came back without the girl. The two delinquents pulled up their chairs next to his bed and began talking, sometimes screaming, mobile phones ringing constantly. While Secondigliano was out of the room, Giovanni offered me another kind of cake. I told him I didn't want it and he rolled his eyes and said *"Madonna però,"* and threw it on my bed. "We've got to eat," he said, "we've got to eat a lot. After midnight we can't eat anymore." I ate the cake. Giovanni's father said his back hurt. He had fallen thirty feet in September and broken nine ribs. One of the ribs had punctured a lung. He rested his head at the foot of Giovanni's bed and tried to sleep a little bit. The man from Cassino said he should take a night off from watching over Giovanni. There was a long pause. "A night off?" Giovanni's father said, looking at his boy, his voice cracking.

The two delinquents stayed in the room. Secondigliano kept saying he still heard the firecracker ringing in his ears, he kept making a whistling sound like a bomb falling. The delinquent with the shaved head began telling Secondigliano how much the operation was going to hurt. The man from Cassino said, "What do you know?" and the delinquent held up his own hand. It was missing two fingers.

"Seven years ago I was playing around with some firecrackers, see . . ." he said and then he began *to laugh.*

• • •

The delinquents stayed until past midnight. At a certain point, Secondigliano's mother called and Secondigliano said, "I'm sleeping, call me tomorrow," and the delinquents laughed. We wanted to sleep, but the way the delinquents positioned themselves around Secondigliano's bed was the classic way of the organized criminals, even the ones who aren't organized criminals—a delinquent is wounded and the others sit next to him, they protect him and show off their loyalty. We knew better than to say anything. We didn't want to make things worse. The night before, a guard had passed by every so often, but that night no guard passed by. The delinquent with the shaved head began talking to Giovanni's father. They went through the various prognoses. If they can save this finger, if there's enough of that bone left. The delinquents went away. We all went to sleep. At three a.m., Secondigliano's phone rang. He spoke loudly. We all woke up and we didn't say anything. Two hours later it rang again.

The next morning, Giovanni was the first one to be operated on. Then they called Secondigliano, and fifteen minutes later they called me. I was in the waiting area outside the operating room when I heard Secondigliano scream. He screamed three or four times and then nothing. I saw a man in a white coat and a beard run out of the room. It was scary, really scary. Then it was my turn and they wheeled me into the operating room. As they wheeled me through the doors I saw Secondigliano on a gurney, asleep. It was the anesthetic that had made him scream. They hadn't even touched him yet.

There were two surgeons. One was the white-haired surgeon from the day before. The other I'd never seen. They asked me where I worked. I said I gave English lessons at the medical school. They asked me why I didn't go there for the surgery and I said that I lived five minutes away from their hospital and thirty minutes away from the medical school and, anyway, most of the doctors I knew were pediatricians. They said those were good reasons. They wondered aloud if I was there as a kind of "favored" case. I told them I hadn't asked anyone for any favors. Then they began to discuss if I were a "signaled" patient, which is to say someone who is less than "favored" but better than "normal." Finally one said to the other, "Anyway, he told us he worked at the university, so he signaled himself." I told them that they had asked me where I worked and I had answered honestly. The chief surgeon, the one with the white hair, asked me who I worked for at the university. I told him. He asked me who the director of my department was. I told him. He asked me what my role was and I pretended not to hear him. I heard the clicking of whatever they were using to shave a layer of skin from my thumb. I felt them transferring the skin onto my wound. He said he wanted me to say hello to the director of my department on his behalf. He repeated his request. "Do you know who I am?" he asked, "Do you know my name?" He was sewing the layer of skin into place. I said I had to admit that I didn't know his name (and he had never bothered introducing himself, but I didn't remind him of that). He told me his name, but I couldn't understand what he was saying. He had his mask on and I had a sheet over my head to block the view of my hand. I'm the director of this ward, he finally said.

The pediatric allergist, the one who'd watched over me in the emergency room, had told me he knew the wife of the director of the ward. They'd worked together years before. The pediatric allergist even tried to call her, but her phone was off. "Must be on vacation," he'd said. I asked the surgeon if he knew the pediatric allergist. "I know everyone," the surgeon said, "and everyone knows me."

The white-haired surgeon explained what he had done using Italian anatomical terms. He asked if I had understood what he had said. Then he explained it to me using a simpler terminology. He walked out of the room for a second and I asked the other surgeon how it had gone. The other surgeon told me that the goal of their work is to save as much as they can. He said that if the thumb is "three" and it's been cut down to "two," there's no way it can ever be three again. While they were wheeling me out, I saw they were getting ready to move Secondigliano into the operating room. He began to scream again.

Back in the room, Giovanni was asleep, but he opened his eyes when I came in. While I was in the operating room, the orderlies had placed a *pandoro* next to each of our beds. Later, the surgeon entered our room and told Giovanni's family what he had done. Giovanni's arm was in a gigantic Ace bandage–type sling. His hand had been sewn into his gut in hopes that some skin would form around his fingers. The surgeon talked about prosthetics. The sister, speaking for the family since she spoke proper Italian, asked the doctor something about the kinds of movements her brother would be able to make. The surgeon said, "Did I not explain myself well enough? Was I unclear? Your brother will never make those movements! What he has lost will never be recovered." The surgeon turned his back on her and looked me in the eye, "You, sir, have been lucky enough to be the beneficiary of a perfect reconstruction of the left thumb."

When he got to Secondigliano, he said they had sewed the wounds shut and performed various skin grafts. As the surgeon was leaving, Secondigliano asked him if they had reconstructed his fingers and the surgeon looked at him and said, "A bomb exploded in your hands, young man. There was nothing to reconstruct," and walked out. It was the first question Secondigliano had ever asked about his wounds. The nurse who had been in the operating room told Secondigliano that he had lost the upper segments of his middle and ring fingers. The nurse told me I could leave later that day. Giovanni stayed in his bed, he had never complained once, not about anything. He turned his head to me and said, "Does it hurt?" I said it hurt a little, but it was tolerable. I asked him how he was doing. He said it hurt, but it was tolerable. Meanwhile, Secondigliano kept trying to convince everyone that he had it worse than Giovanni. But Giovanni was so dignified that it wasn't embarrassing, just sad. Secondigliano wanted to eat as soon as he came back in the room, but they told him not to. He acted like an ass until his anesthetic started to wear off, then he writhed and moaned and cried until they gave him an injection and he fell asleep. After he fell asleep, they brought us dinner, the traditional New Year's dinner with a seafood salad and a "strengthening" salad, a total of four heat-sealed boxes of food for each patient. Giovanni's father took a metal knife he'd brought from home and began doing for us what some of us would have to learn from scratch how to do for ourselves—he took that knife and slit open our boxes of hospital food and cut it up into little pieces.

When I was released from the hospital, they called me to the nurse's room to sign all the papers. I told the head nurse what had gone on the night before, the delinquents, the phone calls. The on-duty surgeon was there, the one who had operated on the man from Cassino. He was out on the balcony, smoking, finishing one cigarette, and then lighting another, waiting for all those people to come in without their hands. Even if it was only early evening, it was New Year's Eve, the firecrackers were already going off one after the other, the windows were shaking and flashes of light and flares were diffused in the soft, curling cigarette smoke. The head nurse and the on-duty surgeon listened to me, nodding. They said they would alert the guards, but I don't think they did anything. New Year's Eve was the busiest night of the year on the Hand Surgery Ward at the Old Pilgrims' Hospital in Naples. I read in the newspaper that ten came that night, to that hospital, to that ward.

Norma helped me with my bags and we called a cab and went outside to wait for the cab, and it was New Year's Eve and there was chaos in the streets, people were shooting off fireworks and firecrackers everywhere, from their balconies, from their windows, even from right down on the street in the middle of everyone. The cab pulled up and we went home, the cabbie cursing Naples, saying that Vesuvius needed to take care of things, Norma saying she agreed but hoped some of us would be spared, and the cabbie finally declaring that what was needed was a Vesuvius intelligent enough to distinguish the good from the bad or the bad from the good, and the cabbie left us there on the corner instead of at our building's door like Norma had asked. It would have been too hard for him to turn around, he said, so we ended up having to walk a couple blocks up the hill to the top where our building sits. We met some other neighbors along the way and we walked up with them, and some kids shouted, *"Auguri!"* from a window, and a few seconds later a gigantic boom came upon us from behind, a firecracker they had dropped nearly on top of us, and the kids began to laugh.

The parents of these kids are the ones with the pistol. Around the neighborhood they say this family used to be dirt-poor. Now they own a restaurant and have four cars that they drive and a pistol that they fire into the air. I'm waiting for those bullets to come in through my windows, to come up through my floor, to come down through my ceiling, to hit me in the head. It's time for me to get out of here. I don't claim that any of this is so traumatic but Norma is after me to call the psychologist. I already talked to the psychologist. The psychologist said that me cutting off the end of my thumb wasn't an accident. She said it was a conclusion, that there was a "before the thumb" and now there is an "after the thumb."

I sit here wondering if something drove me to do this to myself, if something inside me acted on its own so that I would finally end this self-imposed exile, so that I would finally just go home.

Like Giovanni, I too am someone's only son. My father is eighty. Ten years ago, when I was in college, he divorced my mother and he wanted me to become responsible for my mother in his place. She is often a patient in mental hospitals from which she always seems to escape. That is why I fled to Italy. Now my father has cancer, and my mother has disappeared again, and he calls me to ask me once more to come home. I tell him about my thumb, and when I tell him I had to throw part of it away, he cries.

Stop crying, I tell him. It was an accident.

———

Adam Atlas was born in Louisville, Kentucky. He lives in New York City.

*M**ost of the text has its origins in a long letter I wrote to an uncle of mine. My uncle told me I ought to do something with the letter, and this story was the result.*

MICHAEL ATLAS

Rick Bass

FISH STORY

(from *The Atlantic*)

In the early 1960s my parents ran a service station about sixty miles west of Fort Worth. The gas station was in the middle of the country, along a reddish, gravelly, rutted road, on the way to nowhere. You could see someone coming from a long way off. Pumping gas was a hard way to make a living, and my father was never shy about reminding me about this. Always waiting.

When I was ten years old one of my father's customers had caught a big catfish on a weekend trip to the Colorado River. It weighed eighty-six pounds, a swollen, gasping, grotesque netherworld creature pulled writhing and fighting up into the bright, hot, dusty world above.

The man had brought the fish, wrapped in wet burlap, all the way out to my father's service station in the back of his car. We were to have a big barbecue that weekend, and I was given the job of keeping the fish watered and alive until the time came to kill and cook it.

All day long that Friday—in late August, school had not yet started—I knelt beside the gasping fish and kept it hosed down with a trickle of cool water, giving the fish life one silver gasp at a time, keeping its gills and its slick gray skin wet: the steady trickling of that hose, and nothing else, helping it stay alive. We had no tub large enough to hold the fish, and so I squatted beside it in the dust, resting on my heels, and studied it as I moved the silver stream of water up and down its back.

The fish, in turn, studied me with its round, obsidian eyes, which had a gold lining to their perimeter, like pyrite. The fish panted and watched me while the heat built all around us, rising steadily through the day from the fields, giving birth in the summer-blue sky to towering white cumulus clouds. I grew dizzy in the heat, and from the strange combination of the unblinking monotony and utter fascination of my task, until the trickling from my hose seemed to be inflating those clouds—I seemed to be watering those clouds as one would water a garden. Do you ever think that those days were different—that we had more time for such thoughts, that time had not yet been corrupted? I am speaking less of childhood than of the general nature of the world we are living in. If you are the age I am now—mid-fifties—then maybe you know what I mean.

The water pooled and spread across the gravel parking lot before running in wandering rivulets out into the field beyond, where bright butterflies swarmed and fluttered, dabbing at the mud I was making.

Throughout the afternoon, some of the adults who were showing up wandered over to examine the monstrosity. Among them was an older boy, Jack, a fifteen-year-old who had been kicked out of school the year before for fighting. Jack waited until no adults were around and then came by and said that he wanted the fish, that it was his father's—that his father had been the one who had caught it—and that he would give me five dollars if I would let him have it.

"No," I said, "my father told me to take care of it."

Jack had me figured straightaway for a Goody Two-Shoes. "They're just going to kill it," he said. "It's mine. Give it to me and I'll let it go. I swear I will," he said. "Give it to me or I'll beat you up."

As if intuiting or otherwise discerning trouble—though trouble followed Jack, and realizing that did not require much prescience— my father appeared from around the corner, and asked us how everything was going. Jack, scowling but saying nothing, tipped his cap at the fish but not at my father or me, and walked away.

"What did he want?" my father asked.

"Nothing," I said. "He was just looking at the fish." I knew that if I told on Jack and he got in trouble, I would get pummeled.

"Did he say it was his fish?" my father asked. "Was he trying to claim it?"

"I think he said his father caught it."

"His father owes us sixty-seven dollars," my father said. "He gave me the fish instead. Don't let Jack take that fish back."

"I won't," I said.

I can't remember if I've mentioned that, while not poor, we were right at the edge of poor.

The dusty orange sky faded to the cool purple-blue of dusk. Stars appeared and fireflies emerged from the grass. I watched them, and listened to the drum and groan of the bullfrogs in the stock tank in the field below, and to the bellowing of the cattle. I kept watering the fish, and the fish kept watching me, with its gasps coming harder. From time to time I saw Jack loitering, but he didn't come back over to where I was.

Later in the evening, before dark, but only barely, a woman I thought was probably Jack's mother—I had seen her talking to him—came walking over and crouched beside me. She was dressed as if for a party of far greater celebration than ours, with sequins on her dress, and flat leather sandals. Her toenails were painted bright red, but her pale feet were speckled with dust, as if she had been walking a long time. I could smell the whiskey on her breath, and on her clothes, I thought, and I hoped she would not try to engage me in conversation, though such was not to be my fortune.

"Thass a big fish," she said.

"Yes, ma'am," I said, quietly. I dreaded that she was going to ask for the fish back.

"My boy and my old man caught that fish," she said. "You'll see.

Gonna have their pictures in the newspaper." She paused, descending into some distant, nether reverie, and stared at the fish as if in labored communication with it. "That fish is prolly worth a lot of money, you know?" she said.

I didn't say anything. Her diction and odor were such that I would not take my first sip of alcohol until I was twenty-two.

Out in the field, my father was busy lighting the bonfire. A distant *whoosh,* a pyre of light, went up. The drunk woman turned her head slowly, studied the sight with incomprehension, then said, slowly, "Wooo!" Then she turned her attention back to what she clearly thought was still her fish. She reached out an unsteady hand and touched the fish on its broad back, partly as if to reestablish ownership, and partly to keep from pitching over into the mud.

She had no guile about her; the liquor had opened her mind. I could see she was thinking about gripping the fish's toothy jaw and dragging it away, though to where, I could not imagine. As if, given a second chance at wealth and power, she would not squander it. As if this fish was the greatest luck that had happened to them in ages.

"You don't talk much, do you?" she asked. Wobbling even in her sandals, hunkered there.

"No, ma'am.'

"You know my boy?"

"Yes, ma'am."

"Do you think your father was right to take this fish from us? Do you think this fish is worth any piddling sixty-seven dollars?"

I didn't say anything. I knew that anything I said would ignite her, would send her off on some tangent of rage and pity.

"I'm gonna go get my boy," she said, turning and staring in the direction of the fire. Dusk was gone, the fire was bright in the night. She rose, stumbled, fell in the mud, cursed, and labored to her feet, then wandered off into the dark, away from the fish, and away from the fire. As if she lived in the darkness, had some secret sanctuary there.

I kept watering the fish. The gasps were coming slower and I felt that perhaps a fire was going out in the fish's eyes. Lanterns were lit, and moths rose from the fields and swarmed those lanterns. Men came over and began to place the lanterns on the ground all around the fish, like candelabra at a dinner setting. I hoped that the fish would die before they began skinning it.

Moths cartwheeled off the lantern glass, wing-singed, sometimes aflame—like poor, crude, awkward imitations of the fireflies—and landed fuzz-busted on the catfish's glistening back, where they stuck to its skin like feathers, their wings still trembling.

A man's voice came from behind me, saying, "Hey, you're wasting water," and turned the hose off. Immediately, or so it seemed to me, a fine wrinkling appeared on the previously taut gunmetal skin of the fish—a desiccation, like watching a time-lapse motion picture of a man's or woman's skin wrinkling as he or she ages, regardless of the man's or woman's wishes to the contrary.

The heat from the lanterns seemed to be sucking the moisture from the skin. The fish's eyes seemed to search for mine.

The man who had turned off the water was Jack's father, and he was holding a Bowie knife. My heart stopped, and I tried to tell him to take the fish, but found myself speechless. Jack's father's eyes were red-drunk also, and he wavered in such a manner as to seem in danger of falling over onto the dagger he gripped.

He beheld the fish for long moments. "Clarebelle wants me to take the fish home," he said, and seemed to be studying the logistics of such a command. "Shit," he said, "I ain't takin' no fish home. Fuck *her*," he said. "I pay my debts."

He crouched beside the fish and made his first cut lightly around the fish's wide neck with the long blade as if opening an envelope. He slid the knife in lengthwise beneath the skin and then ran a straight incision down the spine all the way to the tail, four feet distant. The fish stopped gasping for a moment, opened its giant mouth in shock and outrage, then began to gasp louder.

In watering the fish all day, and into the evening, I had not noticed how many men and women had been gathering. Now when I straightened up to stretch, I saw that several of them had left the fire and come over to view the fish—could the fish, like a small whale, feed them all?—and that most of them were drinking.

"Someone put that fish out of its misery," a woman said, and a man stepped from out of the crowd with a pistol, aimed it at the fish's broad head, and fired.

My father came hurrying over from the fire, shouted, "Stop shooting, dammit," and the man grumbled an apology and retreated into the crowd.

The bullet had made a dark hole in the fish's head. The wound didn't bleed, and the fish, like some mythic monster, did not seem affected by it. It kept on breathing, and I wanted very much to begin watering it again.

Jack's father had paused only slightly during the shooting, and now kept cutting.

When he had all the cuts made, two other men helped him lift the fish. They ran a rope through its mouth and out its gills and hoisted it into a tree, where roosting night birds rustled in alarm, then flew into the night.

The fish writhed, sucked for air, and, finding none, was somehow from far within able to find, summon, and deliver enough power to flap its tail once, slapping one of the men in the ribs with a *thwack!* The fish was making guttural sounds now—that deep croaking sound they make when they are in distress, right before they die—and Jack's father said, "Well, I guess we need to cook him." He had a pair of pliers in his pocket—evidently part of the debt reduction required that he also do the cleaning and cooking—and he gripped the skin with the pliers up behind the fish's neck and then peeled the skin back, skinning the fish alive, as if pulling the husk or wrapper from a thing to reveal what had been hidden within.

The fish flapped and struggled and twisted, swinging wildly on the rope and croaking, but no relief was to be found. The croaking was loud and bothersome, and so the men lowered the fish, carried it over to the picnic table beside the fire, and began sawing the head off. When they had that done, the two pieces—head and torso—were still moving, but with less vigor. The fish's body writhed slowly on the table, and the mouth of the fish's head opened and closed just as slowly: still the fish kept croaking, though more quietly now, as if perhaps it had gotten something it had been asking for, and was now appeased.

The teeth of the saw were flecked with bone and fish muscle, gummed up with cartilage and gray brain. "Here," Jack's father said, handing me the saw, "go down and wash that off." I looked at my father, who nodded. Jack's father pointed at the gasping head, with the rope still passed through the fish's mouth and gills, and said, "Take the head down there, too, and feed it to the turtles—make it stop that noise." He handed me the rope, the heavy croaking head still attached, and I took it down into the darkness toward the shining round pond.

The full moon was reflected in the pond, and as I approached, the bullfrogs stopped their drumming. Only a dull croaking—almost a purr, now—was coming from the package I carried at the end of the rope. I could hear the sounds of the party up on the hill, but down by the pond, with the moon's gold eye cold upon it, I heard only silence. I lowered the giant fish head into the warm water and watched as it sank quickly down below the moon. I was frightened—I had not seen Jack's mother, and I worried that, like a witch, she might be out there somewhere, intent upon getting me—and I was worried about Jack's whereabouts, too.

Sixty-seven dollars was a lot of money back then, and I doubted that any fish, however large, was worth it. It seemed that my father had done Jack's family a good deed of sorts, but that no good was coming of it; I guessed too that that depended upon how the party went. Still, I felt that my father should have held out for the sixty-seven dollars, and then invested it in something other than festivity.

The fish's head was still croaking, and the dry gasping made a stream of bubbles that trailed up to the surface as the head sank. For a little while, even after it was gone, I could still hear the raspy croaking—duller now, and much fainter, coming from far beneath the water. Like the child I was, I had the thought that maybe the fish was relieved now; that maybe the water felt good on its gills, and on what was left of its body.

I set about washing the saw. Bits of flesh floated off the blade and across the top of the water, and pale minnows rose and nibbled at them. After I had the blade cleaned, I sat for a while and listened for the croaking, but could hear nothing, and was relieved—though sometimes, for many years afterward, I would dream that the great fish had survived; that it had regenerated a new body to match the giant head, and that it still lurked in that pond, savage, betrayed, wounded.

I sat there quietly, and soon the crickets became accustomed to my presence and began chirping again, and then the bullfrogs began to drum again, and a peace filled back in over the pond, like a scar healing, or like grass growing bright and green across a charred landscape. Of course the world has changed—everyone's has—but why?

Back in the woods, chuck-will's-widows began calling once more, and I sat there and listened to the sounds of the party up on the hill. Someone had brought fiddles, which they were beginning to play, and the sound was sweet, in no way in accordance with the earlier events of the evening.

Fireflies floated through the woods and across the meadow. I could smell meat cooking and knew that the giant fish had been laid to rest above the coals. I sat there and rested and listened to the pleasant night-bird sounds.

The lanterns up on the hill were making a gold dome of light in the darkness—it looked like an umbrella—and after a while I turned and went back up to the light and to the noise of the party.

In gutting and cleaning the fish, before skewering it on an iron rod to roast, the partygoers had cut open its stomach to see what it had been eating, as catfish of that size were notorious for living at the bottom of the deepest lakes and rivers and eating anything that fell to the bottom. And they had found interesting things in this one's stomach, including a small gold pocket watch, fairly well preserved though with the engraving worn away so that all they could see on the inside face was the year, 1898.

The partygoers decided that, in honor of having the barbecue, my father should receive the treasure from the fish's stomach (which produced, also, a can opener, a slimy tennis shoe, some balingwire, and a good-sized soft-shelled turtle, still alive, which clambered out of its leathery entrapment and, with webbed feet, long claws, and frantically outstretched neck, scuttled its way blindly down toward the stock tank—knowing instinctively where water and safety lay, and where, I supposed, it later found the catfish's bulky head and began feasting on it).

Jack's father scowled and lodged a protest—his wife was still not in attendance—but the rest of the partygoers laughed and said no, the fish belonged to my father, and that unless the watch had belonged to Jack's father before the fish had swallowed it, he was shit out of luck. They laughed and congratulated my father, as if he had won a prize of some sort, or had even made some wise investment, rather than simply having gotten lucky.

In subsequent days my father would take the watch apart and clean it piece by piece and then spend the better part of a month, in the hot middle part of the day, reassembling it, after drying the individual pieces in the bright September light. He would get the watch working again, and would give it to my mother, who had not been in attendance at the party; and for long years, he did not tell her where it came from—this gift from the belly of some beast from far below.

That night, he merely smiled and thanked the men who'd given him the slimy watch, and slipped it into his pocket.

The party went on a long time. I slept for a while in the cab of our truck. When I awoke, Jack's mother had rejoined the party. She was no less drunk than before, and I watched as she went over to where the fish's skin was hanging on a dried, withered mesquite branch meant for the fire. The skin was still wet and shiny. The woman turned her back to the bonfire and lifted that branch with the skin draped over it, and began dancing slowly with the branch, which, we saw now, had outstretched arms like a person, and which, with the fish skin wrapped around it, appeared to be a man wearing a black-silver jacket.

In that same detached and distanced state of drunkenness— drunk with sorrow, I imagined, that the big fish had slipped through their hands, and that their possible fortune had been lost—Jack's mother remained utterly absorbed in her dance. Slowly, the fiddles stopped playing, one by one, so that I could hear only the crackling of the fire, and I could see her doing her fish dance, with one arm raised over her head and dust plumes rising from her shuffling feet, and then people were edging in front of me, a wall of people, so that I could see nothing.

I still have that watch today. I don't use it, but keep it instead locked away in my drawer, as the fish once kept it locked away in its belly, secret, hidden. It's just a talisman, just an idea, now. But for a little while, once and then again, resurrected, it was a vital thing, functioning in the world, with flecks of memory—not its own, but that of others—attendant to it, attaching to it like barnacles. I take it out and look at it once every few years, and sometimes wonder at the unseen and unknown and undeclared things that are always leaving us, constantly leaving us, little bit by little bit and breath by breath. Of how sometimes—not often—we wake up gasping, wondering at their going away.

Rick Bass is the author of twenty-five books of fiction and nonfiction, including, most recently, a novel, *Nashville Chrome*. He was born in Texas and has worked as a biologist in Arkansas and a geologist in Mississippi and Alabama. He lives with his wife and daughters and divides his time between Yaak and Missoula, Montana.

ELIZABETH BASS

*F*ish Story," which received much-appreciated editing assistance from
Michael Curtis, Maria Streshinsky, and Ross Douthat, comes partly
from family lore and the hard times when to my father's family in north
Texas a single big fish was a windfall, a respite from the long echo of the
Great Depression. The confining seam of space inhabited by those who skated
at the edge of poverty, coupled with the seemingly paradoxical liberation
when those inhabitants encountered windfall, and the way they felt a need,
like a summons, to celebrate that brief escape from those boundaries, struck
me as being as rich as the idea that a fish could be kept alive—for a while—
on dry land, if only tethered to the ceaseless administrations of a boy and a
hose. In my mind I saw and still see a slender seam of life—as thin as the
glinting stream of water from that hose—between the three mediums, water
and earth and sky, with all of the partygoers hunkered there, briefly, as if
effectively sealed but still stirring between the laminae of those three worlds.

Brad Watson

NOON

(from *The Idaho Review*)

The doctors had delivered Beth and Tex's only child still-
born, in breach, and the child had come apart. Their voices
seemed to travel to her from a great distance and then open up
quietly, beside her ear. She felt the strength leave Tex's grip on her
hand as if his heart had stopped, the blood in his body going still.
She looked up at him, but he turned away. Then the drugs took
over, what they'd given her after so much reluctant labor, and she
drifted off.

They'd allowed the funeral home to take their child, and to fix
her, though they'd never had any intention of opening the casket
or even having a public service. And neither did they view the
man's work at all, despite his professional disappointment. He understood they wouldn't want others to view her, but seemed to
think they'd want to see her themselves. He was a soft and pale
supplicant, Mr. Pond, who kind of looked like a sad baby himself,
with wet lips and lost eyes. They explained, as best they could, that
they'd wanted only to have her as whole again as she could possibly be, never having been whole and out in the world. But Beth
couldn't bear to see it, to see her looking like some kind of ghoul-
ish doll. They'd named her Sarah, after Beth's mother, who'd died
the year before. Beth found a fading black-and-white photograph
of her mother as an infant on a blanket beside a flowering gardenia

bush. She placed it in her pocketbook's secret compartment. This was what her Sarah would have looked like.

They'd made him decide what to do, and he'd decided to save her more risk. She made him tell her about it, next day. He stood beside her hospital bed, hands jammed into the pockets of his jeans, hair lopsided from sleep.

"It was getting a little dangerous for you," he said. "It was either pull her out somehow or cut you, and they asked me what we wanted to do. You were kind of out of it.

"I understood what they meant," he said. "You were having some problems. It was dangerous. I said to go ahead and pull her out, to get it over with as quickly as they could.

"I was afraid for you," he said. "Something in the doctors' voices made me afraid. I told them to get it over with and to hurry. So they did."

What he was saying moved through her like settling, spreading fluid.

"I don't want to dwell on it," Tex said after a moment. He sounded angry, as if he were angry at her for wanting to know. "There wasn't anything they could do. She was already gone and it was an emergency. There was nothing anyone could do about that."

He stood there looking at the sheet beside her as if determined to see something in it, words printed there in invisible ink.

"She broke," she whispered. Her throat swollen and too tight to speak.

He looked at her, unfocused. She understood he could not comprehend what he'd seen.

"It doesn't mean anything," he said. "She was already gone."

"It means something," she said. "It means the world is a horrible place, where things like that can happen."

They went home. They arranged the funeral and attended it with his parents and her father, who came with her two sisters. No one had very much to say and everyone went home that afternoon.

In the house over the next few weeks they seemed to walk through one another like shadows. One night she woke up from a dream so far from her own life she couldn't shake it and didn't know herself or who slept beside her. A long moment of terror before she returned to herself with dizzying speed. She lay awake watching him as calm was restored to her bloodstream, quiet to her inner ear. Her heartbeat made an aspirant sound in her chest. She gently tugged the covers from beneath his arms. Their skins were a pale, granular gray in the bedroom's dim moonlight, which failed in silent moments as if an opaque eyelid were being lowered over its surface. She gathered his image to her mind swiftly, as if to save it from oblivion. But he seemed a collection of parts linked by shadows in the creases of his joints, pieces of a man put together in a dream, escaping her memory more swiftly than she could gather it in. In a moment he would be gone.

Julie Verner and May Miller had lost theirs, too, at about the same time. Miscarriages. They were all in their middle to late thirties, friends for close to ten years now, ever since they were young and happily childless.

It was May's first, but Julie and Beth had each lost two, so they were like a club, with a certain cursed and morbid exclusivity. Their friends with children drew away, or they drew away from the friends. They speculated about what it was they may have done that made them all prone to lose babies, and came up with nothing much. They hadn't smoked or drunk alcohol or even fought with their husbands much while pregnant. They'd had good obstetricians. They hadn't even drunk the local water, just in case. It seemed like plain bad luck, or bad genes.

On Friday nights the three of them went out to drink at the student bars near the college. They smoked, what the hell. Julie smoked now anyway but Beth and May smoked only on Fridays, in the bars. They smoked self-consciously, like people in the movies. Saturdays, they slept in and their husbands went golfing or fishing or hunting. Tex was purely the fisherman, and he would rise before dawn and go to the quiet, still lakes in the piney woods, where he tossed fluke-tailed artificial worms toward largemouth bass. When he returned in the afternoons he cleaned his catch on a little table beneath the pecan tree out back. He kept only those yearlings the perfect size for panfrying in butter and garlic. On days he didn't fish he sometimes practiced his casting in the backyard, tossing lures with the barbs removed from their hooks toward an orthopedic donut pillow Beth had bought and used for postpartum hemorrhoids.

On the mornings he went fishing Beth rose late into a house as empty and quiet as a tomb. Despite the quiet she sometimes put in earplugs and moved around the house listening to nothing but the inner sounds of her own breathing and pulse. It was like being a ghost. She liked the idea of the houses we live in becoming our tombs. She said to the others, out at the bar:

"When we died they could just seal it off."

Julie and May liked the idea.

"Like the pharaohs," May said.

"Except I wouldn't want to build a special house for it," Beth said. "Just seal off the old one, it'll be paid for."

"Not mine," May said. She tried to insert the end of a new cigarette into a cheap amber holder she'd bought at the convenience store, but dropped the cigarette onto the floor. She looked at the cigarette for a moment, then set the holder down on the table and pushed her hands into her hair and held her head there like that.

"And they shut up all your money in there, too," Beth said. "Put it all in a sack or something, so you'll have plenty in the afterlife, and they'd have to put some sandwiches in there. Egg salad."

"And your car," Julie said, "and rubbers, big ones. Nothing but the big hogs for me in the afterlife."

"Is it heaven," May said, "if you still have to use rubbers?"

"Camel," Beth said.

"Lucky," May said.

Julie doled them out. When they were in the bars, when they smoked, it was nonfiltered Camels and Luckies.

•••

They went to the Chukker and listened to a samba band, the one with the high-voiced French singer. Beth danced with a student whose stiff hair stood like brown pampas grass above a headband, shaved below. Then a tall, lithe woman she knew only as Gazella cut in and held her about the waist as they danced, staring into her eyes.

"What's your name?"

"Beth."

Gazella said nothing else, but gazed frankly at her, without flirtation or any other emotion Beth could identify, just gazing at her. Beth, unable to avert her own gaze, felt as exposed and transparent as a glass jar of emotional turmoil, as if the roil and color of it were being divined by this strange woman. Then the song stopped. Gazella kissed her on the cheek, and went back to the bar. Watching her, Beth knew only one thing: she wished she looked like Gazella, a nickname bestowed because the woman was so lithe, with a long neck and an animal's dispassionate intelligence in her eyes. Powerful slim hips that rolled when she moved across the room. And like an animal, she seemed entirely self-reliant. Didn't need anyone but herself.

She looked around. The pampas grass boy was dancing with someone else now, a girl wearing a crew cut and black-rimmed eyeglasses with lenses the size and shape of almonds. Beth went back to the table. Julie and May raised their eyebrows, moved them like a comedy team, in sync, toward Gazella. May had the cigarette holder, a Lucky burning at its end, clamped in her bared teeth. Then the two of them said the name, *Gazella,* in unison, and grabbed each other by the arm, laughing.

Beth said, "I was just wondering when was the last time y'all fucked your husbands?" May and Julie frowned in mock thought. May pulled her checkbook from her purse and they consulted the little calendars on the back of the register. "There, then," Julie said, circling a date with her pen.

May spat a mouthful of beer onto the floor and shouted, "That's 1997! A fucking year!"

• • •

"I'm not going home now," Julie said. "Let's go where there's real dancing."

Because she'd been drinking the least, Beth drove them in the new Toyota wagon she and Tex had bought for parenthood. They went to Seventies, a retro disco joint out by the interstate. There they viewed the spectrum of those with terminal disco fever, from middle-aged guys in tight white suits to young Baptist types straight from the Northend Laundry's steam press, all cotton creases and hairparts pale and luminous as moonbeams. Beth watched one couple, a young man with pointed waspish features and his date, a plumpish big-boned girl with shoulder-length hair curled out at her shoulders. They seemed somehow designed for raucous, comic reproduction. The man twirled the woman. She was graceful, like those big girls who were always so good at modern dance in high school, their big thick legs that rose like zeppelins when they leapt. Beth indulged herself with a Manhattan, eating the cherry and taking little sips from the drink.

May now drooped onto the table in the corner of their booth before the pitcher of beer she and Julie had bought. Julie whirled in off the dance floor as if the brutish, moussed investment banker type she'd been dancing with had set her spinning all the way across the room. She plopped in opposite Beth and said, breathless, "Okay, I think I'm satisfied."

"Not me," May intoned.

"Words from a corpse," Julie said. "Arouse thyself and let's go home."

"Oh," May said then, and spread her arms as she sat up, then slumped back against the seat. She was crying. Too late, Beth thought, she's hit the wall.

"Better gather her in," she said to Julie.

"No, no," May said, shucking their hands off her arms. "I can get out by myself. Stop it."

"All right, but we'd better go home, honey."

"I just keep thinking something's wrong with me."

"Come on, none of that," Beth said.

"Oh, I'm sorry!" May said. "I know! It's not as bad as what happened to you. Shit. I'm sorry."

"Okay," Beth said.

"'Cause, like, *no* one had it worse than *Beth*."

"May, shut up," Julie said.

"I have to shut up, I know that," May said, and let them guide her out to the car. They managed to tumble her into the backseat. Julie, drunker than Beth had realized, tossed a match from the flaming end of her Lucky Strike, spat tobacco flecks off the tip of her tongue, and said, "Let her sleep, let's go over to the L&N and sip some Irish whiskey. Leave a note in her ear, she can wake up and follow us inside if she wants to."

"She'll throw up in the car," Beth said.

They reached in and rolled May onto her belly.

"Okay, I'm all right," May mumbled.

"Good enough," Julie said. "She won't choke."

They drove to the L&N and plowed into the deep pea gravel covering the parking lot. The streetlights cast a dim, foggy light onto the building, an old train station that stood on the bluff above the river like a ruined cathedral. May's voice came as if disembodied from the backseat, "I'm sorry, Beth, goddamn I really am sorry for that," and Beth was about to say, That's okay, but May said, "I need to talk about all that. But y'all won't talk about it. Y'all won't say shit about all that. Tough guys." She laughed. "Tough gals."

Julie said, "May, I don't want to hear it."

"See, like that," May said, trying to sit up. "The strong, silent type. John Wayne in a dress. No, who wears a dress anymore? Why, only John Wayne. John Wayne with a big fat ass. John Wayne with a vagina and tits. John Wayne says, 'Rock, I'm havin' your baby—but there's complications.'" She got out of the car and fell into the pea gravel, laughing. "It's so soft!" she said, rolling onto her back. "Like a feather bed! Look, it just molds to your body!"

Julie said something in a low voice to May but Beth had gotten out of the car, leaving the door open, and started down the road. She called back, "I'm going to take a walk," and headed down the hill toward the river, the sound of Julie now speaking in an angry tone to May and May's high-pitched protests pinging off the assault becoming distant, the beeping sound of Beth's keys still in the ignition behind it all.

At the boat landing behind the Chevrolet dealer's lot the river was broad and flat and black beneath a sky gauzy with the moon's veiled light. Like old location Westerns where they'd shot night scenes during the day using something like smoked glass over the lens. She stood there listening to the faint gurgling of the current near the bank, seeing ripples from the stronger current out in the middle.

She waded in to her waist, feeling her way with her old sneakers, and stood feeling the current pull gently at her jeans and the water soaking up into her faded purple T-shirt. The river was warm like bathwater late in the bath. She leaned forward and pushed out, swimming with her head above the water, and turned back to look at the bank now twenty feet behind her. She felt the need to be submerged for a moment, to shut out the upper world. She dunked her head in and pushed the sneakers off with her toes, then swam a few strokes underwater before coming up again, where she heard a shout, "There she is!"

She threw a hand up. "Here I am!"

It was Julie shouting again. "Beth, that's too dangerous! Come back to the goddamn bank, you idiot!"

"Beth!" May shouted. "I'm sorry! Come back!"

"Oh, for Christ's sake," Beth said to herself. The water was still warm, though she passed here and there through columns of cool. She called out to them, "I'm just going to float along here for a while!"

More shouted protests, but she was farther out now, and moving downstream. She saw them start trotting along the bank, then came a crashing of leaves and branches, a jumble of cussing and some shouting, and then she couldn't see them anymore. She was maybe thirty yards off the bank, mostly floating or treading water, moving with the current. The moon was beautiful overhead, its light on the water and the trees on either bank silver and weightless. The river was almost silent, giving up an occasional soft gurgling burp, and she could feel a breeze funneling through the riverbed, cooling her forehead when she turned her face back upstream. Nothing out there but her. There could be barges. This thought came to her. But she was lucky, none of that just then. Some large bird, a massive shadow, swooped down and whooshed just over her head, then flapped back up and away toward the opposite bank. "My God," she shouted. "An owl!"

"Beth!" she heard from the near bank again, and she saw them, jogging along in a clearing atop a little bluff no more than a few feet above the water level.

"Here I am!"

"Swim in!"

"Beth, please!" May struggled to keep up with Julie's long strides, and Beth heard them both, between shouting, panting, *Shit . . . Shit . . . Shit.* "Fucking cigarettes," she heard Julie say. They disappeared into a copse of thick pines. There must be a trail, Beth thought. From the pines she heard Julie's voice come up again, "Goddammit, Beth! Are you still floating?"

Their voices carried beautifully across the water, with the clarity of words transported whole and discrete across the surface, delivered to her in little pockets of sound.

"Still floating!" she called back. Then, "I'm not going to be able to hear you for a while. I'm going to float on my back. Ears in the water!" And then she turned over onto her back and floated, the water up over her ears to the corners of her eye sockets. Wispy clouds skimmed along beneath the moon, or was she moving that swiftly down the river? There was a soft roaring of white noise from the water beneath her. So much water! You couldn't even imagine it from the bank. You couldn't imagine it even here, in it, unless maybe you were a fish and it was your whole world. She heard a clanking, a moaning like whale soundings that could've been giant catfish she'd heard about, catfish big enough to come up and take her in one sucking gulp. Some huge, sleek, bewhiskered monster to swallow her whole, her body encased within its own, traveling the slow and murky river bottom for ages, her brain growing around the fish's brain, its stem lodged in her cerebellum.

Half ancient fish, half woman with strange, submerged memories. She senses Tex on this river, in the early morning before first light, casting his line out into the waters. She follows some familiar current to where she hears the thin line hum past trailing the little worm, fluke tail squibbling by. It's an easy thing to take it in, feel the hook set, sit there awhile against the determined pull on the line, giving way just enough to keep him from snapping it. Rising beside the little boat and looking walleyed into his astonished face, wouldn't she see him then as she never had?

She remembered Tex fucking her the night she knew Sarah was conceived, their bodies bowed into one another, movements fluid as waves. Watching his face.

Tex saying two weeks after it happened, We could try again, Beth. But it was almost as if he hadn't meant to say it, as if the words had been spoken into his own brain some other time, recorded, and now tripped accidentally out. He sat on the sofa, long legs crossed, looking very tired, the skin beneath his eyes bruised, though she marveled at how otherwise youthful he was, his thick blond hair and unlined face, a tall and lanky boy with pale blue eyes. Though younger, she was surpassing his age.

"I had this dream," he said, "the other night."

In his dream he was talking to one of the doctors, though it wasn't one of the doctors who'd been there in real life. The doctor said that if they had operated and taken Sarah out carefully, they could have brought her back to life. *But she was dead,* Tex said in the dream. *Well, we have amazing technology these days,* the doctor said.

Tex's long, tapered fingers fluttered against his knee. He blinked, gazing out the living room window at the pecan tree in the back-yard.

"I woke up sobbing like a child," he said. "I was afraid I'd wake you up, but you were as still as a stone."

"I'm sorry," Beth said.

Tex shrugged. "It was just a dream."

In a minute, she said, "I just don't think I could do it all again." Her voice quavered and she stopped, frustrated at how hard it was to speak of it at all.

"We're not too old," he said. "It's not too late."

But she hadn't said just that.

"I didn't mean that," she said.

She turned herself over in the water and came up again into the air, and her knees dragged bottom, and she saw the current had taken her into the shallows along the bank. She floated there and then sat on the muddy bottom, the water lapping the point of her chin. She wished she could push from herself everything that she felt. To be light as a sack of dried sticks floating on the river. She heard the thudding weary footsteps of the others approaching through the clearing at this landing, breath ragged, and they came and stood on the bank near her, hands on knees, heads bent low, dragging in gulps of air. "Oh, fuck, I'm dying," Julie gasped. "Are you all right?" Beth raised a hand from the water in reply. May fell to her knees and began to throw up, one arm held flat-handed generally toward them. They were quiet except for the sound of May being sick, and when she was finished she rolled over onto her back in the grass and lay there.

Beth and Julie carried May, fortunately tiny, with one of her arms across each of their shoulders, back along the river to the downtown landing and then back up the hill to Beth's car. They left her in the backseat and struggled to walk through the deep pea gravel of the lot into the bar and borrowed some bar towels for Beth and then sat at a table drinking Jameson's neat and not talking for a while. May dragged herself in and sat with them and the bartender brought her a cup of coffee. She lay her head beside the steaming cup and went to sleep again.

Julie reached out and took Beth's hand for a second and squeezed it.

Beth squeezed back, and then they let go. Julie looked down at the floor and held out one of her feet, clad in a ragged dirty Keds.

"Pretty soon I'll need a new pair of honky-tonk shoes," she said sadly.

"I like them," Beth said. "My mother had a pair just like that. She wore them to work in the yard."

"I didn't cut these holes out, baby, I wore 'em out. I got a big old toe on me"—she slipped her toe through a frayed hole and wiggled it—"like the head of a ball-peen hammer."

"My God," Beth said. "Put it up."

"Billy says I could fuck a woman with that toe."

"Put it back in the shoe."

"I'm 'on put it up his ass one day," Julie said.

Somehow they'd become the only patrons left in the place. The bartender leaned on an elbow and watched sports news on a nearly silent TV above the bar. Julie looked at the sleeping May and said to Beth, "Don't worry about all that, that shit May was saying. She's just drunk. She doesn't know what she's talking about."

"No," Beth said. "I know what she's talking about. She's right."

Julie stared at her blankly, then sat up and sighed.

"I can't even remember what all she was saying. Forget it. You should forget it."

"I don't want to forget it," Beth said, and set her shot glass down on the table harder than she'd meant to. "What do you mean?"

Julie didn't answer.

"It changes you," Beth said. "It's changed me. It's different," she said. "It is worse, Julie. It's not like the other time. It is worse. A real child."

So then she'd said it. Julie had started to say something, then turned her head away, toward the wall. Neither said any more after that. The bartender roused himself, flicked off the TV, and his heels clicked through the tall-ceilinged old station as he went from table to table, wiping them down.

They drank up, paid, and left, hefting May's arms again onto their shoulders, and put her into the car. Beth drove them to May's house, and they helped her to the front door, got her keys from her pocket, and let themselves in. Her husband, Calvin, was at the hunting camp building stands. They took her to the bed and undressed her, tucked her in, put a glass of water beside the bed and a couple of ibuprofen beside it, and left. They pulled into Julie's driveway. Julie started to get out.

"You okay to drive home?" She sat with one leg out the open door, in the car's bleak interior light.

"Sure, I'm fine," Beth said. She caught herself nodding like a trained horse and stopped. Julie looked at her a long moment and then said, "Okay," and got out. Beth watched her till she got inside and waved from the window beside the door. And then she drove home through the streets where wisps of fog rose from cracks in the asphalt as if from rumbling, muffled engines down in the bedrock, leaking steam.

She was prone these days to wake in the middle of the night as if someone had called to her while she'd slept. A kind of fear held her heart with an intimate and gentle suppression, a strange hand inside her chest. She was terrified. Soft and narrow strips of light slipped through the blinds and lay on the floor. Their silence was chilling.

Just after 4 A.M. she woke and Tex was already gone. He hadn't moved when she'd come in, his face like a sleeping child's. She'd lowered her ear to his nostrils, felt his warm breath. He slept with arms crisscrossed on his chest, eyebrows lifted above closed lids, ears attuned to the voices speaking to him in his other world. She hadn't heard him rise and leave.

The covers on his side were laid back neatly as a folded flag.

One crumpled dent marked the center of his pillow. He had risen, she knew, without the aid of an alarm, his internal clock rousing him at three so that he would be out on the lake at four, casting when he couldn't even see where his bait plopped into the water, playing it all by ear and touch. He knew what was out there in the water. If a voice truly whispered to him as he slept she hoped it spoke of bass alert and silent in their cold, quiet havens, awaiting him. She hoped it was his divining vision, in the way some people envisioned the idea of God.

For her the worst had been prior to the delivery, after she'd learned what she feared, that the child had died inside her and she would have to carry her until they could attempt a natural delivery, and that would be at least a month, maybe two. That had been worse than the delivery, because sometimes in her distraction she almost thought the delivery had not really happened, it had been only a nightmare that would momentarily well into her conscious-ness and then recede. This was not so with Tex, because he'd seen it all happen, it was imprinted in his memory as surely as Sarah had been implanted in her womb. It was what his mind worked to obscure, awake and asleep, in its different ways.

She lay in bed as dawn suffused the linen curtains with slow and muted particles of gray light. The room softened with this light, and she slept.

It was noon. The front that had kept them under clouds and in light fog was moving, the same clouds she'd seen beneath the river moon scudding rapidly, diagonally, to the northeast, and oc-casional rafts of yellow light passed through the bright green leaves and over the weed-grown lawn.

From the living-room picture window she could see Tex in the backyard cleaning his catch in the shade of the splayed pecan tree. He worked on the plain wooden table he had built for that. His rod and reel leaned against the table's end, his tackle box on the ground beside it. A stringer of other fish lay on the ground beside the box, and Beth could see, every few seconds or so, a fish tail rise slowly from the mess—as if the tail had an eye with which to look around, stunned—and then relax. Tex wore a baseball cap and a gauzy-thin, ragged T-shirt. The muscles on his neck and shoulders bunched as he worked away at one of the fish, his back to the house. He left them gutted but whole, heads on. He hadn't always. When he slit their undersides to gut them, he did it carefully with just the tip of his sharp fillet knife. He gently lifted out the bright entrails with a finger, the button-sized heart sometimes still beating. Then he pulled them free of the body with a casual tug, as if distracted, an after-action.

She watched now from the picture window as he almost reverently palmed a cleaned fish into the pail of water. He rinsed his hand before sliding another one off the stringer. The shadows of patchy clouds moved across the yard and over him with the slow gravity of large beasts floating by. She still felt the effects of sleep, of the drinking and smoking, and a mild vertigo, as if she'd stood up too quickly. That hungover sense of having waked into a life and body that were not her own. She reached out to the window and steadied herself.

As if he'd heard her, Tex turned to look, fish and knife poised in his hands, interrupted so deeply into his task he seemed lost, either not seeing or not recognizing her image behind the windowpane.

She had dreamed, reentering the waking dream she'd had of the catfish in the river. Her sight in the dream through the eyes of the fish. Tex had lifted her into the boat, taken her home, lain her on the old plyboard table, and carefully slit the fish skin covering the length of her belly, worked it away from her own true form. But he was unable to detach the fish's brain from her own. Her words, some gurgly attempt to say she loved him, bubbled out and then she died.

It was a whole world, the way dreams can be.

He buried her in the yard, with a stone on top to keep the cats from digging her up to sniff at the bones. But over time she drifted in the soil. The grass grew from her own cells into the light and air. She watched him when he passed over with the lawn mower. The times between mowings were ages.

Brad Watson's books include *Last Days of the Dog-Men*, *The Heaven of Mercury*, and *Aliens in the Prime of Their Lives*. A native of Mississippi who also spent most of his adult life in Alabama, he now teaches at the University of Wyoming. He does not yet know how to write about Wyoming.

OWEN WATSON

*N*oon" *grew out of a strange and disorienting experience that happened just days before my second son's mother was to deliver. We were talking to a tired, hardened ob-gyn in her office at the hospital. For some reason, no reason I suppose, she told us the story of a couple who'd had an experience in the delivery room just like the one Beth and Tex experience with their child in this story. We were horrified, or terrified. Both. We couldn't believe she'd told us about this when my wife was about to go into the delivery room herself. I never could shake the story. I tried to imagine what it must have been like for the couple to whom it actually happened. It took a while to get there. If I did.*

Danielle Evans

SOMEONE OUGHT TO TELL HER THERE'S NOWHERE TO GO

(from *A Public Space*)

Georgie knew before he left that Lanae would be fucking Kenny by the time he got back to Virginia. At least she'd been up-front about it, not like all those other husbands and wives and girlfriends and boyfriends, shined up and cheesing for the five o' clock news on the day their lovers shipped out, and then jumping into bed with each other before the plane landed. When he'd told Lanae about his orders, she'd just lifted an eyebrow, shook her head, and said, "I told you not to join the goddamn army." Before he left for basic training, she'd stopped seeing him, stopped taking his calls even, said, "I'm not waiting for you to come home dead, and I'm damn sure not having Esther upset when you get killed."

That was how he knew she loved him at least a little bit; she'd brought the kids into it. Lanae wasn't like some single mothers, always throwing their kid up in people's faces. She was fiercely protective of Esther, kept her apart from everything, even him, and they'd been in each other's lives so long that he didn't believe for a second that she was really through with him this time. Still, he missed her when everyone else was getting loved visibly and he was standing there with no one to say good-bye to. Even her love was strategic, goddamn her, and he felt more violently toward the men

42

he imagined touching her in his absence than toward the imaginary enemy they'd been war-gaming against. On the plane he had stared out of the window at more water than he'd ever seen at once, and thought of the look on her face when he said good-bye.

She had come to his going-away party like it was nothing, showed up in skintight jeans and that cheap but sweet-smelling baby powder perfume and spent a good twenty minutes exchanging pleasantries with his mother before she even said hello to him. She'd brought a cake that she'd picked up from the bakery at the second restaurant she worked at, told one of the church ladies she was thinking of starting her own cake business. *Really?* he thought, before she winked at him and put a silver fingernail to her lips. Lanae could cook a little, but the only time Georgie remembered her trying to bake she'd burnt a cake she'd made from boxed mix and then tried to cover it up with pink frosting. Esther wouldn't touch the thing, and he'd run out and gotten a Minnie Mouse ice cream cake from the grocery store. He'd found himself silently listing these non-secrets, the things about Lanae he was certain of: she couldn't bake, there was a thin but awful scar running down the back of her right calf, her eyes were amber in the right light.

They'd grown up down the street from each other. He could not remember a time before they were friends, but she'd had enough time to get married and divorced and produce a little girl before he thought to kiss her for the first time, only a few months before he'd gotten his orders. In fairness, she was not exactly beautiful; it had taken some time for him to see past that. Her face was pleasant but plain, her features so simple that if she were a cartoon she'd seem deliberately underdrawn. She was not big, exactly, but pillowy, like if you pressed your hand into her it would keep sinking and sinking because there was nothing solid to her. It bothered him to think of Kenny putting his hand on her that way, Kenny who'd once assigned numbers to all the waitresses at Ruby Tuesday based on the quality of their asses, Kenny who'd probably never be gentle enough to notice what her body did while it was his.

It wasn't Lanae who met him at the airport when he landed back where he'd started. It was his mother, looking small in the crowd of people waiting for arrivals. Some of them were bored, leaning up against the wall like they were in line for a restaurant table, others peered around the gate like paparazzi waiting for the right shot to happen. His mother was up in front, squinting at him like she wasn't sure he was real. She was in her nurse's uniform, and it made her look a little ominous. When he came through security she ran up to hug him so he couldn't breathe. "Baby," she said, then asked how the connecting flight had been, and then talked about everything but what mattered. Perhaps after all of his letters home she was used to unanswered questions, because she didn't ask any, not about the war, not about his health, not about the conditions of his honorable discharge or what he intended to do upon his return to civilian society.

She was all weather and light gossip through the parking lot. "The cherry blossoms are beautiful this year," she was saying as they rode down the Dulles Toll Road, and if it had been Lanae saying something like that he would have said *Cherry blossoms? Are you fucking kidding me?* but because it was his mother things kept up like that all the way around 395 and back to Alexandria. It was still too early in the morning for real rush-hour traffic, and they made it in twenty minutes. The house was as he'd remembered it, old, the bright robin's egg blue of the paint cheerful in a painfully false way, like a woman wearing red lipstick and layers of foundation caked over wrinkles. Inside, the surfaces were all coated with a thin layer of dust, and it made him feel guilty his mother had to do all of this housework herself, even though when he was home he almost never cleaned anything.

He'd barely put his bags down when she was off to work, still not able to take the whole day off. She left with promises of dinner later. In her absence it struck him that it had been a long time since he'd heard silence. In the desert there was always noise. When it was not the radio, or people talking, or shouting, or shouting at him, it was the dull purr of machinery providing a constant background soundtrack, or the rhythmic pulse of sniper fire. Now it was a weekday in the suburbs and the lack of human presence made him anxious. He turned the TV on and off four times, flipping through talk shows and soap operas and thinking this was something like what had happened to him: someone had changed the channel on his life. The abruptness of the transition overrode the need for social protocol, so without calling first he got into the old Buick and drove to Lanae's, the feel of the leather steering wheel strange beneath his hands. The brakes screeched every time he stepped on them, and he realized he should have asked his mother how the car was running before taking it anywhere, but the problem seemed appropriate—he had started this motion, and the best thing to do was not to stop it.

Kenny's car outside of Lanae's duplex did not surprise him, nor did it deter him. He parked in one of the visitor spaces and walked up to ring the bell.

"Son of a bitch! What's good?" Kenny asked when he answered the door, as if Georgie had been gone for a year on a beer run.

"I'm back," he said, unnecessarily. "How you been, man?"

Kenny looked like he'd been Kenny. He'd always been a big guy, but he was getting soft around the middle. His hair was freshly cut in a fade, and he was already in uniform, wearing a shiny gold name tag that said Kenneth, and beneath that, Manager, which had not been true when Georgie left. Georgie could smell the apartment through the door, Lanae's perfume and floral air freshener not masking that something had been cooked with grease that morning.

"Not bad," he said. "I've been holding it down over here while you been holding it down over there. Glad you came back in one piece."

Kenny gave him a one-armed hug, and for a minute Georgie felt like an asshole for wanting to say *Holding it down? You've been serving people KFC.*

"Look man, I was on my way to work, but we'll catch up later, alright?" Kenny said, moving out of the doorway to reveal Lanae standing there, still in the T-shirt she'd slept in. Her hair was pulled back in a head scarf, and it made her eyes look huge. Kenny was out the door with a nod and a shoulder clasp, not so much as a backward glance at Lanae standing there. The casual way he left them alone together bothered Georgie. He wasn't sure if Kenny didn't consider him a threat or simply didn't care what Lanae did; either way he was annoyed.

"Hey," said Lanae, her voice soft, and he realized he hadn't thought this visit through any further than that.

"Hi," he said, and looked at the clock on the wall, which was an hour behind schedule. He thought to mention this, then thought against it.

"Georgie!" Esther yelled through the silence, running out of the kitchen, her face sticky with pancake syrup. He was relieved she remembered his name. Her hair was done in pigtails with little pink barrettes on them; they matched her socks and skirt. Lanae could win a prize for coordinating things.

"Look at you, little ma," he said, scooping her up and kissing her cheek. "Look how big you got."

"Look how bad she got, you mean," Lanae said. "Tell Georgie how you got kicked out of day care."

"I got kicked out of day care," Esther said matter-of-factly. Georgie tried not to laugh. Lanae rolled her eyes.

"She hides too much," she said. "Every time they take the kids somewhere, this one hides, and they gotta hold everyone up looking for her. Last time they found her, she scratched the teacher who tried to get her back on the bus. She can't pull this kind of stuff when she starts kindergarten."

Lanae sighed, and reached up to put her fingers in her hair, but all it did was push the scarf back. Take it off, he wanted to say. Take it off, and put clothes on. He wanted it to feel like real life again, like their life again, and with him dressed and wearing cologne for the first time in months, and her standing there in a scarf and T-shirt, all shiny Vaselined thighs and gold toenails, they looked mismatched.

"Look, have some breakfast if you want it," she said. "I'll be out in a second. I need to take a shower, and then I gotta work on finding this one a babysitter before my shift starts."

"When does it start?"

"Two."

"I can watch her. I'm free."

Lanae gave him an appraising look. "What *are* you doing these days?"

"Today, nothing."

"Tomorrow?"

"Don't know yet."

"I talked to your mom a little while ago," Lanae said, which was her way of telling him she knew. Of course she knew. How could Lanae not know, gossipy mother or no gossipy mother?

"I'm fine," he said. "I'll take good care of her."

"If Dee doesn't get back to me, you might have to," said Lanae. She walked off and Georgie made himself at home in her kitchen, grabbing a plate from the dish rack and taking the last of the eggs and bacon from the pans on the stove. Esther sat beside him and colored as he poured syrup over his breakfast.

"So what do you keep hiding from?" he asked.

"Nothing." Esther shrugged. "I just like the trip places better. Day care smells funny and the kids are dumb."

"What did I tell you about stupid people?" Georgie asked.

"I forget." Esther squinted. "You were gone a long time."

"Well, I'm back now, and you're not going to let stupid people bother you anymore," Georgie said, even though neither of these promises was his to make.

Honestly, watching Esther was good for him. His mother was perplexed, Kenny was amused, Lanae was skeptical. But Esther could not go back to her old day care, and Dee, the woman down the street who ran an unlicensed day care in her living room, plopped the kids in front of the downstairs television all afternoon and could only be torn away from her soaps upstairs if one of them hit someone or broke something. It wasn't hard for Georgie to be the best alternative. He became adequate as a caretaker. He took Esther on trips. They read and reread her favorite books. He learned to cut the crusts off of peanut butter and jelly sandwiches. Over and above her protests that the old sitter had let the kids stay up to watch *Comic View,* he made sure she was washed and in bed and wearing matching pajamas by the time Lanae and Kenny got home from their evening shifts.

"Are you sure it doesn't remind you . . ." his mother started once, after gently suggesting he look for a real job, but she let the thought trail off unfinished.

"I wasn't *babysitting* over there, ma."

"I know," she said, but she didn't.

The truth was Esther was the opposite of a reminder. In his old life, his job had been to knock on stranger's doors in the middle of the night, hold them at gunpoint, and convince them to trust him. That was the easiest part of it. They went at night because during daytime the snipers had a clear shot at them, and anyone who opened the door, but even in the dark, a bullet or an IED could take you out like that. Sometimes when they got to a house there were already bodies. Other times there was nothing—a thin film of dust over whatever was left—things too heavy for the family to carry and too worthless for anyone to steal.

The sisters were sitting in the dark, huddled on the floor with their parents, when Georgie's unit pushed through the door. Pretty girls, big black eyes and sleepy baby-doll faces. The little one had cried when they first came through the door, and the older one, maybe nine, had clamped her hand tightly over the younger girl's mouth, like they'd been ordered not to make any noise. The father had been soft-spoken—angry, but reasonable. Usually, Georgie stood back and kept an eye out for trouble, let the lieutenant do the talking, but this time he went over to the girls himself, reached out his hand and shook their tiny ones, moist with heat and fear. He handed them each a piece of the candy they were supposed to give to children in cooperative families, and stepped back awkwardly.

The older one smiled back at him, her missing two front teeth somehow reminding him of home.

They were not, in the grand scheme of things, anyone special. There were kids dying all over the place. Still, when they went back the next day, to see if the father would answer some more questions about his neighbors, and the girls were lying there, throats slit, bullets to the head, blood everywhere but parents nowhere to be found, he stepped outside of the house to vomit.

When Georgie was twelve, a station wagon had skidded on the ice and swerved into his father's Tercel, crushing the car and half of his father, who had bled into an irreversible coma before Georgie and his mother got to the hospital to see him. Because his mother had to be sedated at the news, he'd stood at his father's bedside alone, staring at the body, the way the part beneath the sheet was unnaturally crumpled, the way his face began to look like melted wax, the way his lips remained slightly parted.

Georgie hadn't known, at first, that the sisters would stick with him like that.

"What's fucked-up," Georgie said to Jones two days after, "is that I wished for a minute it was our guys who did it, some psycho who lost it. The way that kid looked at me. Like she really thought I came to save her. I don't want to think about them coming for her family because we made them talk. I don't want to be the reason they did her like that."

"What's the difference between you and some other asshole?" Jones said. "Either nobody's responsible for nothing, or every last motherfucker on this planet is going to hell someday."

After that, he'd turn around in the shower, the girls would be there. He'd be sleeping, and he'd open his eyes to see the little one hiding in the corner of his room. He was jumpy and too spooked to sleep. He told Ramirez about it, and Ramirez said you didn't get to pick your ghosts, your ghosts picked you.

"Still," he said. "Lieutenant sends you to talk to someone, don't say that shit. White people don't believe in ghosts."

But he told the doctors everything, and then some. He didn't care anymore what his file said, as long as it got him the fuck out of that place. And the truth is right before the army let him go, sent him packing with a prescription and a once-a-month check-in with the shrink at the VA hospital, it had gotten really bad. One night he was sure the older girl had come to him in a dream and told him Peterson had come back and killed her, skinny Peterson who didn't even like to kill the beetles that slipped into their blankets every night, but nonetheless he'd held Peterson at gunpoint until Ramirez came in and snapped him out of it. Another time, he got convinced Jones really was going to kill him one day, and ran up to him outside of mess hall, grabbing for his pistol; three or four guys had to pull him off. Once, in the daytime, he thought he saw one of the dead girls, bold as brass, standing outside on the street they were patrolling. He went to shake her by the shoulders, ask her what she'd been playing at, pretending to be dead all this time, but he'd only just grabbed her when Ramirez pulled him off of her, shaking his head, and when he looked back at the girl's tear-streaked face before she ran for it like there was no tomorrow, he realized she was someone else entirely. Ramirez put an arm around him and started to say something, then seemed to think better of it. He looked down the road at the place that girl had just been, and shook his head.

"The fuck you think she's running to so fast anyway? Someone ought to tell her there's nowhere to go."

Sometimes Esther called him *Daddy*. When it started out, it seemed harmless enough. They were always going places that encouraged fantasy. Chuck E. Cheese's, where the giant rat sang and served pizza. The movies, where princesses lived happily ever after. The zoo, where animals who could have killed you in their natural state looked bored and docile behind high fences. Glitter Girl, Esther's favorite store in the mall, where girls three and up could get manicures, and any girl of any age could buy a crown or a pink

T-shirt that said ROCK STAR. What was a pretend family relationship, compared to all that? Besides, it made people less nervous.
When she'd introduced him to strangers as her babysitter, all six
feet and two hundred and five pounds of him, they'd raised their
eyebrows and looked at him as though he might be some kind of
predator. Now people thought it was sweet when they went places
together.

"This is my daddy," Esther told the manicurist at Glitter Girl,
where Georgie had just let Esther get her nails painted fuchsia. She
smiled at him conspiratorially. He had reminded her, gently, that
Mommy might not understand about their make-believe family,
and they should keep it to themselves for now.

"Day off, huh?" said the manicurist. She looked like a college
kid, a cute redhead with dangly pom-pom earrings. Judging by the
pocketbook she'd draped over the chair beside her, she was working there for kicks—if the logo on the bag was real, it was worth
three of Georgie's old army paychecks.

"I'm on leave," he said. "Army. I was in Iraq for a year. Just trying to spend as much time with her as I can before I head back."
He sat up straighter, afraid somehow she'd see through the lie and
refuse to believe he'd been a soldier at all. When they'd walked
in, she'd looked at him with polite skepticism, as if in one glance
she could tell that Esther's coordinated clothes came from Target,
that he was out of real work and his gold watch was a knockoff
that sometimes turned his wrist green, like perhaps the pity in her
smile would show them they were in the wrong store, without the
humiliation of price tags.

"Wow," she murmured now, almost deferentially. She looked
up and swept an arc of red hair away from her face so she could
look at him directly. "A year in Iraq. I can't imagine. Of course
you'll spend all the time you can with her. They grow up so fast."
She shook her head with a sincerity he found oddly charming in a
woman who worked in a store that sold halter tops for girls with
no breasts.

"Tell you what, sweetheart," she said to Esther. "Since your daddy's such a brave man, and you're such a good girl for letting him go off and protect us, I'm going to do a little something extra for you. Do you want some nail gems?"

Esther nodded, and Georgie turned his head away so the manicurist wouldn't see him smirk. Nail gems. Cherry blossoms. The things people offered him by way of consolation.

When Esther's nails were drying, tiny heart-shaped rhinestones in the center of each one, and the salesgirl had gone to wait on the next customer, a miniature blonde with a functional Razr phone but no parent in sight, Esther turned to him accusingly.

"You're going away," she said.

"I'm not," he said.

"You told the lady you were."

"It was pretend," he said, closing his eyes. "This is a make-believe place, it's okay to pretend here. Just like I'm your pretend daddy."

He realized he had bought her silence on one lie by offering her another, but he couldn't see any way out of it. So they wouldn't tell Lanae. So the salesgirl would flirt with him a little and do a little something extra for Esther next time. He *had* made sacrifices. Esther deserved nice things. Her mother worked two jobs and her real father was somewhere in Texas with his second wife. So what if it was the wrong things they were being rewarded for?

At the counter, he pulled out his wallet and paid for Esther's manicure with the only card that wasn't maxed out. Esther ignored the transaction entirely, wandering to the other end of the counter and reappearing with a purple flier. It had a holographic background, and under the fluorescent mall light seemed, appropriately, to glitter.

Come see Mindy with Glitter Girl! exclaimed the flier. Mindy was a tiny brunette, nine, maybe, who popped a gum bubble and held one hand on her hip, and the other extended to show off her nails, purple with gold stars in the middle.

"Everybody wants to see Mindy," said the manicurist. She winked at them, then ducked down to file his receipt.

"Maybe we could go," he said, reaching for the flier Esther was holding, but the smile that started from her dimples faded just as quickly.

"I don't really wanna," she said "It's prolly dumb anyway."

He followed her eyes to the ticket price, and understood that she'd taken in the number of zeros. He was stung, for a minute, that even a barely five-year-old was that acutely aware of his limitations, then charmed by her willingness to protect him from them. It shouldn't be like that, he thought, a kid shouldn't understand that there's anything her parents can't do. Then again, he was not her father. He was a babysitter. He had less than a quarter the price of a ticket in his personal bank account—what was left of his disability check after he helped his mother out with the rent and utilities. He spent most of what Lanae paid him to watch Esther on Esther herself, because it made Lanae feel good to pay him, and him feel good not to take her money. He folded the *Mindy* flier into his pocket, and gently pulled the twenty-dollar glittering tiara Esther had perched on her head off to leave it on the counter. "Mommy will come back and get it later," he lied, over and above her objections. Even the way he disappointed her came as a relief.

Of course, the thought had crossed his mind. He never thought Kenny and Lanae were the real thing, didn't even think they did, really. Things had changed between her and Kenny in the year Georgie had been gone, softened and become more comfortable than whatever casual on-again, off-again thing they had before she and Georgie had dated, but he wasn't inclined to believe it was real. He pictured himself and Lanae as statues on a wedding cake—they were a pair. Kenny was a pastime. How could Georgie not hope that when she saw the way he was with Esther, she'd see he belonged with both of them?

But it wasn't like that was the *reason* he liked watching her.

Not the only reason. Esther was a good kid. He thought it meant something, the way she didn't act up with him, didn't fuss and hide the way she'd used to at day care. But yeah, he got to talk to Lanae some. At night, when Lanae came home, and Esther was in bed, and Kenny was still at work for an hour, because being manager meant he was the last to leave the KFC, they talked a little. Usually he turned on a TV show right before she came in, so he could pretend he was watching it, but mostly he didn't need the excuse to stay. It was Lanae who had sat with him that week after his father had died, Lanae, who when she found out she was pregnant with Esther, had called him, not her husband or her best girlfriend. There was an easy kind of comfort between them, and when she came home and sat beside him on the couch and kicked off her flats and began to rub her own tired feet with mint scented lotion, it was only his fear of upsetting something that kept him from reaching out to do it for her.

When Lanae came home the day he'd taken Esther to the mall, he wanted to tell her about the girl, the way she'd smiled at him, and scan her face for a flicker of jealousy. Then he remembered he'd earned the smile by lying. So instead he unfolded the Mindy flier from his pocket and passed it to her.

"Can you believe this shit?" he asked. "Five hundred a pop for a kids' show? When we were kids we were happy if we got five dollars for the movies and a dollar for some candy to sneak in."

"Hey," Lanae grinned. "I wanted two dollars, for candy *and* a soda. You were cheap." She held the flier at arm's length, then turned it sideways, like Mindy would make more sense that way. "Esther wants to go to this?"

"The lady at Glitter Girl said all the girls do. She said in most cities the tickets already sold out."

"That whole store is creepy anyway. And even if it was free, Esther don't need to be at a show where some nine-year-old in a belly shirt is singing at people to *come pop her bubble*. Fucking perverts," Lanae said.

"Who's a pervert?" asked Kenny. Georgie hadn't heard him come in, but Lanae didn't look surprised to see him standing in the doorway. He was carrying a steaming, grease-spotted bag that was meant to be dinner, which was usually Georgie's cue to leave. As Kenny walked toward them, Georgie slid away from Lanae on the couch, not because they'd been especially close to begin with, but because he wanted to maintain the illusion that they might have been. But Lanae stood up anyway, to kiss Kenny on the cheek as she handed him the flier.

"These people," said Lanae, "are perverts."

Kenny shook his head at the flier. Georgie silently reminded himself of the sophomore Kenny had dated their senior year of high school, a girl not much bigger than Mindy, and how Kenny had used to joke about how easy it was to pick her up and throw her around the room during sex.

"Esther ain't going to this shit," Kenny said. "This is nonsense."

"She can't," said Georgie. "You can't afford it."

Kenny stepped toward him, then back again just as quickly.

"Fuck you man," said Kenny. "Fuck you and the two dollars an hour we pay you."

He pounded a fist at the wall beside him, and then walked toward the hallway. A second later Georgie heard the bedroom door slam.

"Georgie," said Lanae, already walking after Kenny. "You don't have to be an asshole. He's not the way you remember him. He's trying. You need to try harder. And this Mindy shit? Esther will forget about it. Kids don't know. Next week she'll be just as worked up about wanting fifty cents for bubblegum."

But Esther couldn't forget about it. Mindy was on the side of the bus they took to the zoo. Mindy was on the nightly news, and every other commercial between kids' TV shows. Mindy was on the radio, lisping, *Pop my bub-ble, pop pop my bub-ble.* What he felt for Mindy was barely short of violence. He restrained himself from shouting back at the posters, and the radio, and the television:

Mindy, what is your position on civilians in combat zones? Mindy, what's your position on waterboarding? Mindy, do you think Iraq was a mistake? He got letters, occasionally, from people who were still there—one from Jones, one from Ramirez, three from guys he didn't know that well and figured must have been lonely enough that they'd write to anyone. He hadn't read them.

He went back to the mall alone on the Saturday after he'd pissed Kenny off. He told himself he was there to talk to the manicure girl, pick up a little present for Esther and meanwhile maybe get something going on in his life besides wet dreams about Lanae, who'd been curt with him ever since the thing he said to Kenny. But when he got to the store, the redhead was leaning across the counter, giving a closed-mouth kiss on the lips to a kid in a UVA sweatshirt. He looked like an advertisement for fraternities. Georgie started to walk out, convinced he'd been wrong about the whole plan, but when the boyfriend turned around and walked away from the counter, the redhead saw him and waved.

"Hey!" she called. "Where's your little girl?"

"I came to pick up something to surprise her," he said. "She's been asking for a princess dress to go with the crown her mom got her."

He was pleased with the lie, until the redhead, whose name tag read Annie, led him over to the dress section and he realized he'd worn suits to weddings that cost less.

"Come to think of it," he said, "I'm not sure of her size. Maybe I oughta come back with her mother. Meantime, maybe she would like a wand."

"That's a good idea," said Annie. "All the kids are into magic these days."

Annie grabbed the wand that matched the crown and led him back to the register. The Mindy fliers had been replaced by a counter-length overhead banner. Mindy's head sat suspended on a background of pink bubbles.

"What's this Mindy kid do, anyway?" he asked.

"She sings."

"She sing well?"

"It's just cute, mostly. She has her own TV show, and her older sister sings too, but sexier. You get tickets for your daughter?"

"Nah," he said. "Bit pricey, for a five-year-old. Maybe next year."

"They ought to pay you people more. It's a shame. It's important, what you do."

She said this like someone who had read it somewhere. It would have seemed stupid to disagree and pathetic to nod, so he stood there, waiting for his change.

"Hey," said Annie. "We're having this contest to win tickets to the show. Limo ride, dinner, backstage passes, the whole shebang. All you have to do is make a video of your daughter saying why she wants to go. I bet if your daughter talks about how good she was while you were gone, she'd have a shot. It's right here, the contest info," she said, picking up a flier and circling the website. "Doesn't have to be anything fancy—you could do it on a camera phone."

"Thanks," he said, reaching to take the bag from her.

"Really," she said. "I mean it. Who's got a better story than you? Deadline's Tuesday. It'd be nice, if they gave it to someone who deserved it."

He liked to think that Annie's encouragement was tacit consent. He liked to think that if he'd had longer to think about it, he would have realized it was a bad idea. But as it was, by Sunday he'd convinced himself that it was a good idea, and by Monday he'd convinced Esther, who, after hearing the word *limousine,* needed only the slightest convincing that this was not the *bad* kind of lie. And when she started the first time, it wasn't even a lie, really. "Hi Glitter Girl," she began, all on her own, "for a whole year while he was in Iraq, I missed my daddy." Okay so he wasn't her father, but he liked to think she *had* missed him that much. When she said how much she wanted for him to take her to the show now that he was back, he thought it was honest: she wanted not just to see the show but to see it with him. He had downloaded the video from his phone and played it back for her, and was ready to send it like that, when Esther decided it wasn't good enough.

"Let's tell how you saved people," she said. "We have more time left."

He hesitated, but before he could say no, she asked him to tell her who he'd saved, and looking at her, the hopeful glimmer in her eyes, her pigtails tied with elastics with red beads on the end, matching her jumpsuit and the ruffles on her socks, he realized her intentions had been more sincere than his. How could they not be? Esther didn't doubt for a second that he had a heroic story to tell. He closed his eyes.

"Two girls," he said, finally. "A girl about Mindy's age. She was missing her two front teeth. And her little sister, who she loved a lot. Some bad men wanted to hurt them, and I scared off the bad men and helped them get away."

"Where'd they go then?"

"Back to their families," he said. He opened his mouth to say something, but nothing came out.

"Start the movie over," Esther said. "I'm going to say that too."

Somehow, he was not expecting the cameras. It was such a small thing, he'd thought. But there was Esther's video, labeled, *Contest Winner!: Esther, age 5, Alexandria, VA,* right on the Glitter Girl website. It was only a small relief that this was the last place Lanae would ever go herself, but who knew who else might stumble upon it? He'd named himself as her parent, given his name and phone and authorized the use of the images, and now he had messages, not just from Glitter Girl, who'd called to get their particulars, but from *The Washington Post,* and Channels 4 and 7 News. Even after the first few, he thought he could get this back in the bottle, that Lanae would never need to know. In his bathroom mirror, in the morning, he practiced what to say to the journalists to make them go away. He tried to think of ways to answer questions without making them think to ask more.

Listen, he told the Channel 4 reporter, I'd love to do a story, but Esther's mother has this crazy ex-boyfriend who's been threatening her for years, and if Esther's last name or picture were in the paper, we could be in a lot of trouble. Look, he told the Channel 7 reporter, the kid's been through hell this year, with me gone and her mom barely holding it together. It was hard enough for her to say it once. Please contact Glitter Girl for official publicity.

It was the *Post* reporter that did them in, the *Post* reporter and the free makeover Esther was supposed to get on her official prize pickup day. He figured it was back page news, and anyway, Esther was so excited about it. They would paint her nails and take some pictures and give them the tickets, and that would be the end of it. When they walked into the store a week later, there was a giant pink welcome banner that proclaimed CONGRATULATIONS ESTHER! and clouds of pale pink and white balloons. All of the employees and invited local media clapped their hands. Annie was there, beaming at them when they walked in, like she'd just won a prize for her science fair project. The CEO of Glitter Girl, a severe-looking woman with incongruous big blond hair, hugged Esther and shook his hand. Mindy's music played on repeat over the loudspeakers.

There was cake, and sparkling cider. The CEO gave a heartfelt toast. Annie gave him a hug, and slipped her phone number into his pocket. One of the other employees led Esther off. She came back in a sequined pink dress, a long brown wig, fluttery fake eyelashes, pink lipstick, and shiny purple nails. People took pictures. He was alarmed at first but she turned to him and smiled like he'd never seen a kid smile before, and he thought it couldn't be so bad, to give someone exactly what she wanted. Finally, the CEO of Glitter Girl handed them the tickets. She said Esther had already received some fan mail, and handed him a pile of letters. He looked at the return addresses: California, Florida, New York, Canada.

"Is there anything you'd like to say to all your fans, Esther?" shouted one of the reporters.

"I want to say," said Esther, "I am so happy to win this, but mostly I am so happy to have my daddy."

She turned and winked at him. She smiled a movie star grin. There was lipstick on her teeth. For the first time, he realized how badly he'd messed up.

It was two days later the first story ran. Esther had told the *Post* reporter her mommy worked at the Ruby Tuesday on Route 7, but when the reporter called her there to get a quote, Lanae had no idea what she was talking about, said she did have a daughter named Esther, but her daughter's father was in Texas and had never been in the army, and her daughter wasn't allowed in Glitter Girl or at any Mindy concert.

She called him on her break to ask him about it, but he said it must have been a mix-up, he didn't know anything about it.

"You'd damn well better not be lying to me, Georgie," she said, which meant she already knew he was.

That night he called the number Annie had given to him, wondered if she could meet him somewhere, pictured her long legs wrapped around his.

"Look," she said softly, "I'm sorry. I was being impulsive the other day. You're married, and I'm engaged, and I'm really proud of you, but it's just better if everything stays aboveboard. Let's not hurt anyone we don't have to."

Georgie hung up. He went downstairs and watched television with his mother, until she turned it off and looked at him.

"You know I watch the news during my break at the hospital," she said.

"Uh-huh," said Georgie. "They're not still shortchanging you your break time, are they?"

"Don't change the subject. Other day I coulda swore I saw Esther on TV. Channel 9. All dressed up like some hoochie princess, and talking about her *daddy,* who was in the *army.*"

"Small world," said Georgie, "A lot of coincidences."

•••

But it was a lie, about the world being small. It was big enough. By the time he drove to Lanae's house the next morning, there was a small crowd of reporters outside. They didn't even notice him pull up. Kenny kept opening the door, telling them they had the wrong house. Finally, he had to go to work, walked out in his uniform. Flashbulbs snapped.

"Are you the one who encouraged the child to lie, or does the mother have another boyfriend?" yelled one reporter.

Georgie couldn't hear what Kenny said back, but for the first time in his life, Georgie thought Kenny looked brave.

"Did you do this for the money?" yelled another. "Was this the child's idea?"

All day, it was like that. Long after Kenny had left, the reporters hung out on the front steps, broadcasting to each other. Lanae had already given back the tickets; beyond that, she had given no comment. He could imagine the face she made when she refused to comment, the steely eyes, the way everything about her could freeze.

"How," the reporters wanted to know, "did this happen?"

Their smugness made him angry. There were so many things they could never understand about how, so many explanations they'd never bother to demand. How could it not have happened?

At night, when no one had opened the door for hours, the reporters trickled off, one by one, their questions still unanswered. Lanae must have taken the day off from work; her car was still in its parking space, the lights in the house still on. Finally, he made his way to the house and rang the doorbell. She was at the peephole in an instant. She left the chain on and opened the door as wide as it could go without releasing it.

"Georgie," she said. She shook her head, then leaned her forehead against the edge of the door so that just her eyeball was looking at his. "Georgie, go away."

"Lanae," he said. "You know I didn't mean it to go like this."

"Georgie, my five-year-old's been crying all day. My phone number, here and at my job, is on the internet. People from Iowa to goddamn Denmark have been calling my house all day, calling my baby a liar and a little bitch. She's confused. You're confused. I think you need to go for a while."

"Where?" he asked.

He waited there on the front step until she'd turned her head from his, stepped back into the house and squeezed the door shut. He kept standing there, long after the porch light went off, not so much making an argument as waiting for an answer.

Danielle Evans's work has appeared in magazines such as *The Paris Review, A Public Space, Callaloo,* and *Phoebe,* and was featured in *The Best American Short Stories 2008.* Her short story collection, *Before You Suffocate Your Own Fool Self,* is forthcoming, and she is currently at work on a novel titled *The Empire Has No Clothes.* She grew up in Virginia, Washington, D.C., New York, and Ohio; received an MFA in fiction from the Iowa Writers Workshop; was a fellow at the Wisconsin Institute for Creative Writing; and is now teaching fiction at American University in Washington, D.C.

SEAN HILL

*T*his story started as an image I had of a man in uniform carrying a little girl on his shoulders. I knew that he was not her father and not quite her stepfather, and I was interested in the dynamics of that relationship, perhaps because I was just barely old enough to be on the other side of the equation—to wonder about negotiating boundaries with children of people you might date instead of being a child second-guessing the intentions of your parents' suitors. I knew that Georgie had come from Iraq and some of it had come home with him, but for a year or so, the story was just those two figures in my head. I wrote the first few pages of the story in graduate school and was immediately pleased and charmed by Lanae, but while I knew the emotional arc of the piece, I was stuck on the mechanics of plot. I kept trying to nudge

SOMEONE OUGHT TO TELL HER 63

Georgie and Kenny into a melodramatically violent confrontation, and the story, quite sensibly, kept refusing to go there. A few years later I read a news story about a mother inventing her husband's death so that her child could win a contest. I never did come up with an answer for what the woman in the real-life story was thinking, but it seemed immediately clear to me why Georgie might lie under similar circumstances, and the story finished itself from there.

Ron Rash

THE ASCENT

(from *Tin House*)

Jared had never been this far before, over Sawmill Ridge and across a creek glazed with ice, then past the triangular metal sign that said Great Smoky Mountains National Park. If it had still been snowing and his tracks were being covered up, he'd have turned back. People had gotten lost in this park. Children wandered off from family picnics, hikers strayed off trails. Sometimes it took days to find them. But today the sun was out, the sky deep and blue. No more snow would fall, so it would be easy to retrace his tracks. Jared heard a helicopter hovering somewhere to the west, which meant that after a week they still hadn't found the airplane. They'd been searching all the way from Bryson City to the Tennessee line, or so he'd heard at school.

The land slanted downward and the sound of the helicopter disappeared. In the steepest places, Jared leaned sideways and held on to trees to keep from slipping. As he made his way into the denser woods, he wasn't thinking of the lost airplane or if he would get the mountain bike he'd asked for as his Christmas present. Not thinking about his parents either, though they were the main reason he was spending his first day of Christmas vacation out here—better to be outside on a cold day than in the house where everything, the rickety chairs and sagging couch, the gaps where the TV and microwave had been, felt sad.

He thought instead of Lyndee Starnes, the girl who sat in front of him in fifth-grade homeroom. Jared pretended she was walking beside him and he was showing her the tracks in the snow, telling her which markings were squirrel and which rabbit and which deer. Pointing out a bear's tracks too and Lyndee telling him she was afraid of bears and Jared saying he'd protect her.

Jared stopped walking. He hadn't seen any human tracks, but he looked behind him to be sure no one was around. He took out the pocketknife and raised it, making believe that the pocket-knife was a hunting knife and that Lyndee was beside him. If a bear comes, I'll take care of you, he said out loud. Jared imagined Lyndee reaching out and taking his free arm. He kept the knife out as he walked up another ridge, one whose name he didn't know. Lyndee still grasped his arm as they walked up the ridge. Lyndee told him how sorry she was that at school she'd said his clothes smelled bad.

At the ridge top, Jared pretended a bear suddenly raised up, baring its teeth and growling. He slashed at the bear with the knife and the bear ran away. Jared held the knife before him as he descended the ridge. Sometimes they'll come back, he said aloud.

He was halfway down the ridge when the knife blade caught the midday sun and the steel flashed. Another flash came from below, as if it was answering. At first Jared saw only a glimmer of metal in the dull green of rhododendron, but as he came nearer he saw more, a crumpled silver propeller and white tailfin and part of a shattered wing.

For a few moments Jared thought about turning around, but then told himself that someone who'd just fought a bear shouldn't be afraid to get close to a crashed airplane. He made his way down the ridge, snapping rhododendron branches to clear a path. When he finally made it to the plane, he couldn't see much because snow and ice covered the windows. He turned the passenger-side door's outside handle, but the door didn't budge until Jared wedged in the pocketknife's blade. The door made a sucking sound as it opened.

A woman was in the passenger seat, her body bent forward like a horseshoe. Long brown hair fell over her face. The hair had frozen and looked as if it would snap off like icicles. She wore blue jeans and a yellow sweater. Her left arm was flung out before her and on one finger was a ring. The man across from her leaned toward the pilot window, his head cocked against the glass. Blood stains reddened the window and his face was not covered like the woman's. There was a seat in the back, empty. Jared placed the knife in his pocket and climbed into the backseat and closed the passenger door. Because it's so cold, that's why they don't smell much, he thought.

For a while he sat and listened to how quiet and still the world was. He couldn't hear the helicopter or even the chatter of a gray squirrel or caw of a crow. Here between the ridges not even the sound of the wind. Jared tried not to move or breathe hard, to make it even quieter, quiet as the man and woman up front. The plane was snug and cozy. After a while he heard something, just the slightest sound, coming from the man's side. Jared listened harder, then knew what it was. He leaned forward between the front seats. The man's right forearm rested against a knee. Jared pulled back the man's shirtsleeve and saw the watch. He checked the time, almost four o'clock. He'd been sitting in the backseat two hours, though it seemed only a few minutes. The light that would let him follow the tracks back home would be gone soon.

As he got out of the backseat, Jared saw the woman's ring. Even in the cabin's muted light, it shone. He took the ring off the woman's finger and placed it in his jeans pocket. He closed the passenger door and followed his boot prints back the way he came. Jared tried to step into his earlier tracks, pretending that he needed to confuse a wolf following him.

It took longer than he'd thought, the sun almost down when he crossed the park boundary. As he came down the last ridge, Jared saw that the blue pickup was parked in the yard, the lights on in the front room. He remembered it was Saturday and his father had gotten his paycheck. When Jared opened the door, the small red glass pipe was on the coffee table, an empty baggie beside it. His father kneeled before the fireplace, meticulously arranging and rearranging kindling around an oak log. A dozen crushed beer cans lay amid the kindling, balanced on the log itself three red-and-white fishing bobbers. His mother sat on the couch, her eyes glazed, as she told Jared's father how to arrange the cans. In her lap lay a roll of tin foil she was cutting into foot-long strips.

"Look what we're making," she said, smiling at Jared. "It's going to be our Christmas tree."

When he didn't speak, his mother's smile quivered.

"Don't you like it, honey?"

His mother got up, strips of tin foil in her left hand. She knelt beside his father and carefully draped them on the oak log and kindling.

Jared walked into the kitchen and took the milk from the refrigerator. He washed a bowl and spoon left in the sink and poured some cereal. After he ate, Jared went into his bedroom and closed the door. He sat on his bed and took the ring from his pocket and set it in his palm. He held the ring under the lamp's bulb and swayed his hand slowly back and forth so the stone's different colors flashed and merged. He'd give it to Lyndee when they were on the playground, on the first sunny day after Christmas vacation, so she could see how pretty the ring's colors were. Once he gave it to her, Lyndee would finally like him, and it would be for real.

Jared didn't hear his father until the door swung open.

"Your mother wants you to help light the tree."

The ring fell onto the wooden floor. Jared picked it up and closed his hand.

"What's that?" his father asked.

"Nothing," Jared said. "Just something I found in the woods."

"Let me see."

Jared opened his hand. His father stepped closer and took the ring. He pressed the ring with his thumb and finger.

"That's surely a fake diamond, but the ring looks to be real gold."

His father tapped it against the bedpost as if the sound could confirm its authenticity. His father called his mother and she came into the room.

"Look what Jared found," he said, and handed her the ring. "It's gold."

His mother set the ring in her palm, held it out before her so they all three could see it.

"Where'd you find it, honey?"

"In the woods," Jared said.

"I didn't know you could find rings in the woods," his mother said dreamily. "But isn't it wonderful that you can."

"That diamond can't be real, can it?" his father asked.

His mother stepped close to the lamp. She cupped her hand and slowly rocked it back and forth, watching the different colors flash inside the stone.

"It might be," his mother said.

"Can I have it back?" Jared asked.

"Not until we find out if it's real, son," his father said.

His father took the ring from his mother's palm and placed it in his pants pocket. Then he went into the other bedroom and got his coat.

"I'm going down to town and find out if it's real or not."

"But you're not going to sell it," Jared said.

"I'm just going to have a jeweler look at it," his father said, already putting on his coat. "We need to know what it's worth, don't we? We might have to insure it. You and your momma go ahead and light our Christmas tree. I'll be back in just a few minutes."

"It's not a Christmas tree," Jared said.

"Sure it is, son," his father replied. "It's just one that's chopped up, is all."

He wanted to stay awake until his father returned, so he helped his mother spread the last strips of tin foil on the wood. His mother struck a match and told him it was time to light the tree. The kindling caught and the foil and cans withered and blackened.

The fishing bobbers melted. His mother kept adding kindling to the fire, telling Jared if he watched closely he'd see angel wings folding and unfolding inside the flames. Angels come down the chimney sometimes, just like Santa Claus, she told him. Midnight came and his father still wasn't back. Jared went to his room. I'll lay down just for a few minutes, he told himself, but when he opened his eyes it was light outside.

As soon as he came into the front room, Jared could tell his parents hadn't been to bed. The fire was still going, kindling piled around the hearth. His mother sat where she'd been last night, wearing the same clothes. She was tearing pages out of a magazine one at a time, using scissors to make ragged stars she stuck on the walls with tape. His father sat beside her, watching intently.

The glass pipe lay on the coffee table beside four baggies, two with powder still in them. There'd never been more than one before.

His father grinned at him.

"I got you some of that cereal you like," he said, and pointed to a box with a green leprechaun on its front.

"Where's the ring?" Jared asked.

"The sheriff took it," his father said. "When I showed it to the jeweler, he said the sheriff had been in there just yesterday. A woman had reported it missing. I knew you'd be disappointed, that's why I bought you that cereal. Got something else for you too."

His father nodded toward the front door where a mountain bike was propped against the wall. Jared walked over to it. He could tell it wasn't new, some of the blue paint chipped away and one of the rubber handle grips missing, but the tires didn't sag and the handlebars were straight.

"It didn't seem right for you to have to wait till Christmas to have it," his father said. "Too bad there's snow on the ground, but it'll soon enough melt and you'll be able to ride it."

Jared's mother looked up.

"Wasn't that nice of your daddy," she said, her eyes bright and gleaming. "Go ahead and eat your cereal, son. A growing boy needs his breakfast."

Jared ate as his parents sat in the front room passing the pipe back and forth. He looked out the window and saw the sky held nothing but blue, not even a few white clouds. He wanted to go back to the plane, but as soon as he laid his bowl in the sink his father announced that the three of them were going to go find a real Christmas tree.

"The best Christmas tree ever," his mother told Jared.

They put on their coats and walked up the ridge, his father carrying a rusty saw. Near the ridge top, they found Frazier firs and white pines.

"Which one do you like best?" his father asked.

Jared looked over the trees, then picked a Frazier fir no taller than himself.

"You don't want a bigger one?" his father asked.

When Jared shook his head no, his father knelt before the tree. The saw's teeth were dull but his father finally broke the bark and worked the saw through. They dragged the tree down the ridge and propped it in the corner by the fireplace. His parents smoked the pipe again and then his father went out to the shed and got a hammer and nails and two boards. While his father built the makeshift tree stand, Jared's mother cut more stars from a magazine.

"I think I'll go outside a while," Jared said.

"But you can't," his mother replied. "You've got to help me tape the stars to the tree."

By the time they'd finished, the sun was falling behind Sawmill Ridge. I'll go tomorrow, he told himself.

On Monday morning the baggies were empty and his parents were sick. His mother sat on the couch wrapped in a quilt, shivering. She hadn't bathed since Friday and her hair was stringy and greasy. His father looked little better, his blue eyes receding deep into his skull, his lips chapped and bleeding.

"Your momma, she's sick," his father said.

Jared watched his mother all morning. After awhile she lit the pipe and sucked deeply for what residue might remain. His father crossed his arms, rubbing his biceps as he looked around the room, as if expecting to see something he'd not seen moments earlier. The fire had gone out, the cold causing his mother to shake more violently.

"You got to go see Wesley," she told Jared's father.

"We got no money left," he answered.

Jared watched them, waiting for the sweep of his father's eyes to stop beside the front door where the mountain bike was. But his father's eyes went past it without the slightest pause. The kerosene heater in the kitchen was on, but its heat hardly radiated into the front room.

His mother looked up at Jared.

"Can you fix us a fire, honey?"

He went out to the back porch and gathered an armload of kindling, then placed a thick oak log on the andirons as well. Beneath it he wedged newspaper left over from the star cutting. He lit the newspaper and watched the fire slowly take hold, then watched the flames a while longer before turning to his parents.

"You can take the bike to town and sell it," he said.

"No, son," his mother said. "That's your Christmas present."

"We'll be all right," his father said. "Your momma and me just did too much partying yesterday is all."

But as the morning passed, they got no better. At noon Jared went to his room and got his coat.

"Where you going, honey?" his mother asked as he walked toward the door.

"To get more firewood."

Jared walked into the shed but did not gather wood. Instead, he took a length of dusty rope off the shed's back wall and wrapped it around his waist and then knotted it. He left the shed and followed his own tracks west into the park. The snow had become harder, and it crunched beneath his boots. The sky was gray, darker clouds farther west. More snow would soon come, maybe by afternoon.

Jared told Lyndee it was too dangerous for her to go with him. He was on a rescue mission in Alaska, the rope tied around him dragging a sled filled with food and medicine. The footprints weren't his but of the people he'd been sent to find.

When he got to the airplane, Jared pretended to unpack the supplies and give the man and woman something to eat and drink. He told them they were too hurt to walk back with him and he'd have to go and get more help. Jared took the watch off the man's wrist. He set it in his palm, face upward. I've got to take your compass, he told the man. A blizzard's coming, and I may need it.

Jared slipped the watch into his pocket. He got out of the plane and walked back up the ridge. The clouds were hard and granite-looking now, and the first flurries were falling. Jared pulled out the watch every few minutes, pointed the hour hand east as he followed his tracks back to the house.

The truck was still out front, and through the window Jared saw the mountain bike. He could see his parents as well, huddled together on the couch. For a few moments Jared simply stared through the window at them.

When he went inside, the fire was out and the room was cold enough to see his breath. His mother looked up anxiously from the couch.

"You shouldn't go off that long without telling us where you're going, honey."

Jared lifted the watch from his pocket.

"Here," he said, and gave it to his father.

His father studied it a few moments, then broke into a wide grin.

"This watch is a Rolex," his father said.

"Thank you, Jared," his mother said, looking as if she might cry. "How much can we get for it?"

"I bet a couple of hundred at least," his father answered.

His father clamped the watch onto his wrist and got up. Jared's mother rose as well.

"I'm going with you. I need something quick as I can get it."

She turned to Jared. "You stay here, honey. We'll be back in just a little while. We'll bring you back a hamburger and a Co-Cola, some more of that cereal too."

Jared watched as they drove down the road. When the truck had vanished, he sat down on the couch and rested a few minutes. He hadn't taken his coat off. He checked to make sure the fire was out and then went to his room and emptied his backpack of schoolbooks. He went out to the shed and picked up a wrench and a hammer and placed them in the backpack. The flurries were thicker now, already beginning to fill in his tracks. He crossed over Sawmill Ridge, the tools clanking in his backpack. More weight to carry, he thought, but at least he wouldn't have to carry them back.

When he got to the plane, he didn't open the door, not at first. Instead, he took the tools from the backpack and laid them before him. He studied the plane's crushed nose and propeller, the broken right wing. The wrench was best to tighten the propeller, he decided. He'd straighten out the wing with the hammer.

As he switched tools and moved around the plane, the snow fell harder. Jared looked behind him and on up the ridge and saw his footprints were growing fainter. He chipped the snow and ice off the windshields with the hammer's claw. Finished, he said, and dropped the hammer on the ground. He opened the passenger door and got in.

"I fixed it so it'll fly now," he told the man.

He sat in the backseat and waited. The work and walk had warmed him but he quickly grew cold. He watched the snow cover the plane's front window with a darkening whiteness. After a while he began to shiver but after a longer while he was no longer cold. Jared looked out the side window and saw the whiteness was not only in front of him but below. He knew then that they had taken off and risen so high that they were enveloped inside a cloud, but still he looked down, waiting for the clouds to clear so he might look for the blue pickup, making its way through the snow, toward the place they were all headed.

Ron Rash's latest story collection is *Burning Bright.* His previous collection of short stories, *Chemistry and Other Stories,* was a finalist for the PEN/Faulkner Award. He teaches at Western Carolina University.

*I*n 1998 an airplane crashed in the Nantahala *National Forest. Six years passed before a bear hunter found the wreckage. I thought that having a child instead of an adult find the lost plane would be an interesting opening to a story, so I started there, and the rest of the story slowly came into focus.*

Ashleigh Pedersen

SMALL AND HEAVY WORLD

(from *The Iowa Review*)

We moved up into the trees when the neighborhood flooded that April—blue plastic tarps slung up with belts and ropes, splintered plywood floors, dinghies or canoes bumping up against the tree trunks. Makeshift hammocks hung from the branches, swaying in the breeze. The water was the color of peanut butter. It roiled below our branches, churning up a soup of all the things we'd lost: spatulas, dolls, romance novels, Tupperware, spools of colored thread, porn magazines, textbooks, bicycle tires, empty picture frames. Once a miraculously airtight bag of minimarshmallows, which my younger brothers fished out and gave to our mother, six months pregnant with her fourth child and hungry in every way.

My mother spoke to the neighborhood physician often, describing her latest cravings or a cramp in her lower back. Dr. Adair was not actually a physician at all, but a professor of linguistics at the local community college, new to the neighborhood just that March, not long before the rain started up. His neighbors promptly appointed him physician when the local doctors' offices were swept away with everything else, and he took to his new role with stoicism and an endless reserve of ambiguous homeopathic remedies. Because he was a single parent, and good-looking, Dr. Adair was a rich source of gossip. He was also slightly darker-skinned, a smooth shade of caramel, and although American-born he was considered by most to be foreign, to be exotic. It was rumored that he had moved south from Boston not long after his wife—beautiful, we were sure—left him for another man. It was rumored he had lived in South Africa as a boy and discovered a new species of beetle, and also that he was a huge snob. His freshly painted house washed away with the rest of the neighborhood, and Dr. Adair now lived with his son, Peter, in the ancient oak that had marked the edge of their property line.

Shortly after our new living arrangements were made, my mother rigged the first neighborhood telephone: two empty soup cans linked from tree to tree with a long, yellow string. Dr. Adair was on the other end.

"Sahd," she would say, lying flat on her back. "I haven't felt it kick in hours."

His voice rising up through the can sounded thin and weary. "Annie, Annie," he'd reply. "The baby is probably just resting. As should you."

"Still. I worry."

"Ring me in an hour. If nothing by then, I'll row over."

By mid-May, we began to settle in. My father hung a rope swing from a thick branch. It struck me as boyish and primitive—I was never a strong swimmer, anyway—but my brothers, Charlie and Jackson, loved it.

"Watch out for water moccasins," my mother would call, lying in the shade, one hand rubbing her ripening belly. She glowed blue in the light filtered through the tarp. "When an alligator eats you, don't come crying to me."

In truth, the local wildlife seemed to have abandoned our town. Birds were scarce, and we had not seen so much as a catfish since the water rose. I wondered about the alligators that had haunted our swamps, if after the rain they swam towards sea, mistaking this boundless new space for freedom. Something less easily identified had replaced the usual dangers, and so my brothers busied themselves all day, swinging like monkeys and dropping into the muck below. When I grew bored watching them, I found other ways to occupy myself—painting my toenails with the gold polish Charlie found among the debris, or closing my eyes and thinking about Mr. Janice, my Advanced Algebra teacher, whom I'd harbored a secret crush on for the entirety of the school year. My mother and I, though often inches apart, said very little to one another. There seemed little *to* say, even when I thought I might want to say something.

On days when she expected Dr. Adair, my mother straightened up our living space as best as she could, stacking the cans of food in neat pyramids, stretching the tarp rooftop taut or rolling it back to illuminate us in dappled light. Once, on a sultry morning early on in the summer, she asked me to braid her hair.

"I don't know how," I lied. I was sprawled out on a branch, my limbs dangling to either side, as Charlie and Jackson fought for turns on the rope swing. It was the first truly hot day that season. Steam curled off the water and perspiration frosted our foreheads, though it was long before noon.

"Yes you do, Rayanne. I've seen you do it to your own hair a million times. I'm no good at doing it myself."

I climbed down from my perch and sat behind her, tugging the plaits hard with each fist.

"Ouch," she said, and reached behind her to pinch my thigh. "You're hurting me."

I tied the ends with bits of leftover yellow string and my mother rested cross-legged against the tree trunk, pretty and bathed in sweat. When Dr. Adair appeared at the edge of our wooden platform, glasses fogged, my mother smiled. "Hello," she said.

He hoisted himself over the edge and took her hand. "Annie," he said, and even I, then thirteen and resentful, could hear that the word was filled with love.

This was the Deep South, the houses clung low to the flat earth. The weathermen had not predicted this flood. It came fast, and from all sides: from the river that ran to our east and the canals threading through the neighborhood and from the granite sky overhead. The rain beat an angry chorus on our rooftops until the shingles slid off in defeat.

Our town was small and surrounded by farmland and easily forgotten. Rescue boats never came. We saved what we could—chaining our dinghies and canoes to the trees, carrying food and extra clothes in plastic garbage bags—and then we sought shelter in the crude tree houses the neighborhood men had desperately, fearfully constructed, and we watched the water rise. We saw corpses float past, already bloated, the color of hardboiled eggs. There was a horse—a colt—struggling to swim, or to find footing. We watched his head dip under and then come back up, his eyes black and frantic. I saw our house float away in a torrent of foamy water, although my family does not remember it that way. But I saw it rise up off the earth and drift some yards, turning and bowing in the rapids, before pulling apart with a long and awful moan.

My father was often gone for days at a time. He rowed out with the other dads, searching for houses on higher land, some of which still stood, their third stories or attics peeking out over the water like islands. They returned with armfuls of canned fruits and vegetables, soggy chocolate bars, hammers, nails, tarps, or oftentimes nothing at all.

Whatever my father brought, my mother seemed to resent. One afternoon in early June, we watched him unload his share of the goods, squatting on two legs and spreading his findings across the plywood floor like a proud salesman. A rusting corkscrew, a broken sports watch, a few cans of dolphin-safe tuna. The water gave off a sour stench, and we slapped away the mosquitoes gnawing at our arms and necks. Charlie and Jackson were down below, playing pirates in the dinghy. Their whooping sounded distant, and their feet stomped out erratic rhythms on the metal. I watched the corners of my mother's mouth turn down, down, as my father squatted there, and I wished I was young enough to join them.

"That's all," my father said. His face and bald patch were sunburned, his eyes creased.

"Well," my mother said.

"We found one house, but it had already been looted. This we fished out of a half-sunk boat, turned over on its side. Dave Johnson found a radio, but it didn't work. Probably no reception out here anyway."

My mother turned her gaze out past the branches, squinting in displeasure. A web of multicolored string stretched across our neighborhood—her idea with the soup cans, borrowed from a television show she remembered from her childhood, had grown popular. The string quivered even in the stagnant air.

"There's tuna," Dad tried. "I know you love tuna."

Across the way, Dr. Adair's tree house was reinforced with rafters and a mobile wall to block wind and rain, regardless of the direction it blew. None of these details were visible from my mother's vantage point, but I wondered if she wasn't thinking of them, envying them.

My mother sighed. "I can't eat tuna," she said. "The mercury's bad for the baby."

I picked up the black rubber watch. Its digital face was blank and filled with water. "I like this," I said.

"You take it then, Ray." Dad stood and brushed his hands off on his shorts. They were frayed at the bottom and he looked a little like Robinson Crusoe, I thought. "It's about as useful as a working clock, these days."

The next evening, the sky pink and orange, Dr. Adair came over. He greeted my father with a handshake and asked my mother questions about her appetite and dreams. I hugged my knees to my chest, and my brothers played war with a deck of crumpled playing cards. My father stood, his hands on his hips, his back towards us all.

Dr. Adair was fond of dream interpretation as a means of diagnosis, and although none of us knew where such authority originated, we accepted it as truth. Peter had come with his father and sat on the far edge of the platform, looking embarrassed. From the corner of my eye I could see him staring at me, but when I looked over he ducked his head.

My mother said she had dreamed that she gave birth to a raccoon instead of a child, with sharp yellow teeth and an absurdly long tail. As she spoke, Dr. Adair prodded her stomach with his long steady fingers, examining.

"That's a good sign, Annie. Promising. It only seems like a nightmare." He handed her a can of pears, her favorite fruit. "Pears have restorative properties. They're good for the heart, yours and the baby's."

My father made a coughing noise. "I've never heard of that," he said.

My mother rolled her eyes and laughed. "You're not a doctor, Jim."

"Neither is he," Dad said, and turned around to face us. He laughed without smiling.

Dr. Adair stood and said, "I think we'd better be going."

"Oh, don't be silly, Sahd."

Peter stood as well, his face blotched red. He and his father had to stoop low so their heads wouldn't hit the tarp overhead. My father shook hands with Dr. Adair. His lips looked thin and white. "Thank you for all you've done for my wife," he said.

"I'm doing my best, Jim." Dr. Adair's voice was low and serious. He had lines jutting from the corners of his eyes, and the start of a promising beard. Standing across from him, my father looked small, almost elfin, his head clearing the roof by several inches despite his upright posture. He looked nothing like the Robinson Crusoe—the rustic hero—I had seen the previous day, and I felt an inexplicable pang.

He nodded and then let both hands fall to his side. "Yes," he said. "I guess we all are."

My mother heaved herself to her feet and linked one arm around my father's elbow. "We'll be seeing you soon, Sahd. Stop by anytime."

I looked towards Peter, but he was already climbing down towards their boat, his dark head disappearing over the edge of the platform.

I lay awake late that night, curled on one side, my brothers breathing soft and deep from their hammocks nearby. My parents whispered a long while. I caught bits and pieces only. At one point my father started to speak too loud. "I can't stand that he calls you—"

"Shh!" my mother said. "You'll wake the kids."

My father lowered his voice, but not by much. "—that he calls you Annie," he said. "That's my name for you. Mine."

I heard a great sigh, and then only the lapping of the water, the creaking of the branches.

Peter was my age. He was over six feet tall and bony, with bad acne and shaggy dark hair that he flipped out of his face all the time. He shared only his height and his black hair with his father; in every other way he was almost wholly opposite. At school he had always seemed sulky and alone, and I sat far from him on the bus and ignored him in the cafeteria. After the flood, I found myself both hating him and craving his attention. When he came by with his father, I hoped to catch him looking at me. Some days, while my mother napped and my brothers played Marco Polo, I lay on my stomach and peered through the branches, through the sifting clumps of Spanish moss, towards the Adair oak. Occasionally I caught Peter climbing down into the boat with his father, headed off on some appointment or another—stomach aches, snake bites, allergies. Once, on a hot, cloudy morning, I saw him dive into the water. He was shirtless and seemed, in that instant, to fly from the tree like some enormous and graceful bird. He swam for some time, doing backstroke and breaststroke with ease, venturing further from the tree than I would have ever dared to go. Against the muddy landscape, his body was pale as ice.

I had grown tall myself, too tall. Both my parents were fairly short, but that year I had sprouted upward with alarming force.

My feet were long and flat and I no longer knew what to do with my hands or arms. They felt superfluous, gorilla-like. When Peter came by, I made myself small. I squeezed my knees to my chest, or folded my arms and slumped against a branch.

A week after bringing back the watch, Dad left again. He shouldn't be too long this time, he said. They were headed in a direction they had already explored, in hopes that they may have missed something. My brothers and I watched our father row off, his friend Tom rowing a canoe alongside him, and supplies and food tied in plastic bags at their feet. I waved. Jackson bit his lip, eyes watery, and Charlie stood with his arms crossed and his brow furrowed. Both boys had streaks of blond in their messy brown hair, with lean, tan limbs. They looked more and more like two of the Lost Boys in the illustrated copy of *Peter Pan* I had so loved, that I still loved, although of course it too was lost in the flood.

"It's all right, Jack," I said. "Don't cry."

"I'm not." He wiped at his eyes.

"He'll be back soon enough," my mother said. She had rolled back the tarp and was doing yoga moves, arms stretched to the sky, eyes closed. She wore one of my father's button-down shirts, and had tied it in a knot at the top of her belly. Her breasts were voluminous, and through the white of the shirt I could see her nipples.

That morning, I had pointed this out. *"Mom,"* I said. "You should put on a bra."

She laughed. "What for?"

"Because they're"—I was embarrassed, and nodded towards her chest—"they're *showing*."

She had cupped a hand around each breast and given them a thoughtful squeeze. Then she laughed. "No one will see," she said. "And it doesn't matter up here, anyway."

"Dr. Adair could see," I said.

She narrowed her eyes at me, and then, in the next instant, rolled them as if I'd told her a bad joke. "He's a doctor," she said. "He's seen it all before."

I had imagined Dr. Adair teaching linguistics to a room of lithe, bare-chested college girls, furiously scribbling in their notepads. The thought had made me giggle, and I no longer felt like arguing. Now, my brothers upset, and our father's boat sliding past a grove of unoccupied trees and then out of sight, I grew angry. Who did she think she was, exposing herself this way, so self-satisfied? Hardly batting an eyelash as my father left, and yet bound to resent him for his absence? I moved past her and opened a can of roasted potatoes for my brothers, who plopped down with it and made bets about the treasures Dad would bring home. When my mother finished stretching, she inhaled deeply and climbed into her hammock to rest. I watched her from a tree branch and wondered what had sprouted inside of her, in the wake of this flood, to make her seem so free.

My father and Tom had not yet returned, and we were growing nervous. My brothers began keeping watch through fists stacked like telescopes, and I watched through the foliage in hopes I might see him rowing towards us, his reddened head, his sideways grin. Tom's wife rigged up a telephone between her tree and ours, and began calling us several times a day, speculating about reasons things may have gone awry. "I'm sure they're fine," my mother told her each time. "They're perfectly capable, Marian."

My mother, too, seemed concerned, although she sought solace with Dr. Adair. "I think you need to get out more," he told her, patting her hand. "Get your mind off the waiting."

He began taking her out in his boat, helping her climb down the ladder, going first and promising to catch her should she slip. Then they would row off, past the neighborhood trees, the oars making water ripple back towards our tree and lap at its trunk. My mother sat in the basin of the boat, leaning back against the bow, her belly full and tumid. Oftentimes they left at night, my mother kissing my brothers' foreheads, asking me to look after them. Then the two of them, gliding off in the moon-drenched water.

My brothers were lost in their own world, but my mother's relationship with Dr. Adair was affecting me in ways I couldn't seem to explain. I was aware of an energy between them that didn't exist between my parents. I tried to recall a time when it *had* existed.

When my mother was pregnant with the twins, my father had sung to her, pressed his lips against the globe of her stomach and sang Aretha Franklin, Willie Nelson, Frank Sinatra—whatever came to mind. He sang badly and his voice cracked and it made my mother laugh. Sometimes she rested a hand on top of his head, as she might do to a child, to me.

With this new baby, though, he was often visibly tense, his jaw rigid, his silence more disturbing than whatever inexplicable anger he seemed to be experiencing. He did not sing, although I had heard her plead with him to do so on more than one occasion. When my mother had morning sickness that February and vomited up her breakfast into the kitchen sink, my father seemed angry at the sound of it, at the very fact that she was nauseated. She went into the bedroom to clean herself up, and my father ran the water in the sink, slamming the faucet handles on and off with unnecessary force.

Charlie and Jackson had looked at me, nervous, and I left my bowl of cereal and went into the bedroom to check on my mother. She was sitting on the edge of their bed, her back to the door, staring out the window towards the white winter sky.

"Mom?" I had called from the doorway. "Do you feel okay?"

She waved a hand behind her and said, "Oh, I'm fine," but her voice trembled.

Crying was not something my mother often did. I had only seen her cry once before, and it was when *Brian's Song* played on television sometime that year, before the pregnancy. My father had sat beside her on the couch, his arm wrapped around her neck. I was drifting in and out of sleep next to them, glad for the time with just them, my brothers asleep in the bedroom they shared. Then, her tears were sweet, almost funny. Now it scared me, her crying. My father so angry at something I could not comprehend.

When I went and sat next to her on the bed, she pulled me close to her with both arms. "Rayanne," she said, crying hard now, her back shaking with the effort of it.

"Yes?"

She pulled away, wiping at her eyes even as new tears welled up in them. "It's just the hormones," she said.

I took a deep, shaky breath and then blurted, "Is Dad mad at you?"

She shook her head. "No. Dad isn't mad at me."

"He seems mad."

"He's just worried," she said, and took a blue tissue from the nightstand, blowing her nose hard.

I said I didn't understand.

"Babies mean a lot of responsibility," she said. "This one—we didn't plan for it to happen. It just happened. And it means we need more money, and a bigger house, and things we just don't have right now. That's all. Dad is just worried. Okay?"

"Okay." I rubbed her back, glad, in some way, to act as her sole confidant, as a source of comfort. I said I understood, that it would be okay.

But I still didn't understand, not then, and not when I thought back to this moment from my perch in the tree, trying to comprehend my mother and father, my mother and Dr. Adair. I could not understand, not really, and I would not until I had my own children, my own bills, my own household, an entire small and heavy world of my own.

There had not been rain in over a month, and the water seemed to be slowly receding. This would have been good news, but my father and Tom were nowhere to be seen, and my mother's due date was approaching faster than the water could diminish entirely.

"I'm going to have a tree baby," I heard her say to Dr. Adair one evening. He had not brought Peter with him; he rarely did, since my father left. My mother shook her head. "A fatherless tree baby."

"Annie," Dr. Adair said, offering my mother a hand up from

her seat against the trunk. They were getting ready to leave again. "Don and Larry are out looking for them. I'm sure they're fine, just fine. Probably stranded on high ground somewhere, what with the drought, waiting for a good rain to come our way."

Don and Larry, two neighbors with families of their own, had left the day before in Larry's sports cruiser. Larry, retired from the Coast Guard, brought flares and promised to shoot them off should they run into trouble. "Which they won't," it was said, and then said again, into the makeshift phones, across the gulf of water.

It was twilight, the clouds pulled in plush ribbons of deep violets and pinks and blues. Heat lightning flashed over the horizon. Charlie and Jackson had gone to sleep even before sundown, and lay shirtless and brown in their hammocks. My mother leaned over them and kissed each boy on the cheek, then began tying her hair in a low knot at the nape of her neck. Dr. Adair stood with his back to me, his cotton shirt stained with sweat, watching the bursts of lightning. He seemed to rarely know what to say to me, and with my father gone we stayed out of each other's way.

"I'll just be a moment, Sahd," my mother said, and then she turned to me. In the strange light she looked much younger than her thirty-five years—almost a teenager, but with a lushness that no girl my age could have possessed, no matter how much we tried. "Watch your brothers, Rayanne. I'll be back later, of course."

I was standing, too, my long arms tucked into the pockets of my cut-off denim shorts. "Why do you have to go?" I asked.

"I'll be back," she said again. Her eyes gleamed, cat-like. "This is good for my health, good for the baby."

But I was feeling bold, my breath quickening. "Why?" I asked. "What exactly do you two do that is so good for the baby?"

Dr. Adair stepped forward. "Annie and I have—" he started, but I was too angry to hear him out. Something in me had been growing taut these last weeks—even before, maybe—and it had snapped, just then, in one sudden and unexpected motion.

"Dad is gone," I said, the volume of my voice rising. "He's

gone, and you keep leaving, and Charlie and Jackson are worried, and—"

"You watch your tone, young lady," my mother said.

"—and Dad doesn't even *like* him calling you Annie, but you keep going off with him and doing who knows what—"

My mother slapped me, hard, across the face. Dr. Adair, in silhouette behind her, said, "Annie, that's really not . . ." and then, "Perhaps we shouldn't . . ." I held a hand to face, my mouth hanging open. From the branches behind me, my brothers snored and murmured in their sleep. A knot swelled in my throat.

"Rayanne," my mother started. "You don't—you can't understand. You can't—"

She turned back towards Dr. Adair, as if looking for help, and then back to me.

She shrugged. "I'm sorry," she said, and the words sounded so sincere I wanted, more than anything, to accept them. I wanted her to hold me the way she held Charlie when he broke his wrist from a bike fall, or the way she had held my father's head when he sang to my unborn brothers.

Instead I turned and made for the upper branches of the tree, the place I often climbed towards when I wanted solitude, or to spy on Peter, or to watch for my father. After a moment of murmuring, I heard them climb down into Dr. Adair's boat. I watched as they rowed away, heard Dr. Adair's low and soothing voice. When my back grew stiff and my eyelids felt heavy, I climbed back down to the platform and lay on my back. Through the dark mesh of branches and leaves, the sky was alight with stars.

I had just started to drift off when I heard water splashing, and then the creaking of the ladder rungs nailed into our tree. I wondered if my mother was back already. I watched the edge of the platform as a long, white figure climbed up over it.

"Peter?" I whispered, and made my way to my feet.

Peter stared at me, his bare chest slick in the moonlight, his hair plastered back from his face. He was drenched, water dripping off his shorts and staining the plywood in a dark constellation. His shoulders looked broader than I remembered, his muscles firmer. Standing there, waiting for him to speak, I didn't slouch. I didn't try to make myself small. I stood upright, as though I had expected him somehow.

"I know what it is they do," he said, and reached for my hand.

We swam east, out past the trees.

Before plunging in, I told Peter that I wasn't a strong swimmer, that I was afraid of alligators and debris and dead bodies. I stood on the ladder, hugging the rungs close, while he treaded water below.

"All that's gone," he had said. "There's nothing here anymore."

"But I can't swim well," I repeated.

He said, "I was on swim team at my old school. If you get tired, I'll help you along."

So we glided through the warm water, pushing aside an occasional piece of driftwood with our sweeping breaststrokes. Peter coached me in how to kick my legs like a frog, to take steady breaths through my nose. Beyond the threshold of our neighborhood was mostly open water, the highway and tobacco fields sunk ten, fifteen feet below us. After some time, my muscles burning, Peter whispered, "There. Slow down."

We came to a slow tread. Up ahead some fifty feet or so glinted metal. Across the open water, the sound of voices.

Peter moved in front, and together we crept, crept along the surface of the water until we got so close I was afraid they would hear us breathing. The boat was rocking, groaning, and in the silver light I saw my mother and Dr. Adair. They were naked and facing one another, only inches of night air between them. I saw the curve of my mother's stomach, the arch of Dr. Adair's back as he leaned towards her. His toffee skin glowed even in the dark.

Maybe it was the water, so warm and calm, or my own heartbeat pounding away like wings in my chest, or the moonlight pouring out over this endless lake. Or perhaps it was the sight of my mother, so undeniably naked, her breasts hanging heavy and huge, her long dark hair curling over her shoulders, looking like some small god, or a ghost. Whatever the reason—as I watched them there, Dr. Adair reaching out to press his hand to my mother's stomach—I felt only a sharp and inexplicable yearning.

We need to leave, I thought, we should go—though for what reason I couldn't place. Moving as quietly as I could, I began backing away from the boat, back towards our neighborhood, but Peter caught me by the wrist. He held his other finger to his lips, and wrapped one arm around my waist, pulled me closer. A rush of currents from his kicking legs pushed below the surface of the water, churned around us. He used his free arm to continue treading, and held me flush against his body with the other.

"Listen," he whispered, and wet lips pressed against my ear.

With Peter holding me, my body relaxed. I watched, and listened. The doctor was kneeling in the basin of the boat, now, between her legs, and she said something to him and they both laughed. Then he dropped his head forward, towards her stomach. His hands still rested on it, as if holding an enormous and tender piece of fruit. I could hear some murmuring, but I could not make out what he was saying. After several moments, though, his voice grew a little louder, and then louder. He kept his eyes down. His voice rose loud and steady now, and in the same instant I realized I was crying, I realized Dr. Adair was singing.

The next morning, Don and Larry's boat came cruising through a cloudy dawn, the four men—Don, Larry, Tom, and my father—standing at its hull, hands on hips, grinning towards the trees in anticipation of our welcome.

Later, my brothers pressed at his sides, my mother and I sitting cross-legged nearby, he told us what had happened: they found ground that had not been evident before, when the water was higher. It was a thick brown muck, too sticky to walk on, so they skirted around its shore for days. It was littered with objects, with canned food. If the sun heated the surface enough, it would firm up the ground, and they could collect a treasure trove of food and supplies for their families, for the neighbors. As they waited, though, the water levels continued to sink, so that by the time they awoke the next morning, their boats were stranded in a sea of mud. When they tried stepping across it, they sank in up to their thighs. "We had plenty of food," my father said, his face streaked with mud, "but nowhere to go, no way of moving."

After some days, the ground did firm up, grew hard enough to walk on, and they abandoned their boats and headed back in the direction of the neighborhood. When the land sloped down and met the water again, they decided to wait for rescue, with their sacks full of canned food, full of rusting tools, and prayed it would not rain.

"And I kept thinking," my father said, staring at my mother, "about what a great story this would make to tell the baby. You know, 'When your mother was pregnant, and we lived in trees, I was stranded on this muddy shore. . . .' This is a story I've got to tell, I kept thinking. I've got to make it back and tell this story."

My mother stood and waddled to our food supply. She took a rag and poured water over it and began, as my father answered my brothers' endless questions, to wipe the dirt from his forehead, from his sunburned and peeling cheeks.

When my mother went into labor—a seven-hour process that sent her screams echoing through the trees, my brothers and I crying and trembling in both terror and excitement as we waited in the dinghy below—it was Dr. Adair who delivered the baby, a slick little boy with a domed head and reddish blond hair, like my father's. That was the last I knew of them together, Dr. Adair and my mother. And as if because of Jonah's birth, the water dropped quickly after that. Peter stayed with his father, hidden behind the foliage, the water too shallow to dive into. Eventually it was all mud, no water, and each family stayed high in the trees until the wasteland below looked hard enough to support our weight, to allow us to move about on the slab of its surface.

Some years later, visiting home with my first husband, I sat with my mother and drank cold root beers on the porch of our new home, a larger version of our old house, in our reconstructed neighborhood. Jonah squatted on the driveway, drawing pictures of enormous-headed creatures in green chalk, talking to himself or to some imaginary friend, shaded by the same oak we had lived in during those months. Charlie and Jackson were out with their girlfriends; they were teenagers now, and no less inseparable. My father and husband were somewhere else, my husband trying hard to appease his in-laws, to impress them with his attentiveness.

Across the street, a young family lived where the Adair house had once stood. The Adairs moved back to Boston the autumn following the flood, where it was rumored Dr. Adair remarried, and that Peter went on to Harvard Law. The tree in which the Adairs had resided had been cut down long ago, and, for all the people of our town had experienced, the only reminders of the flood were the occasional rusted soup cans that dropped to the ground after a bad storm, bits of discolored string still attached.

My mother finished her soda and then set the bottle next to her lawn chair.

I said, "Mom?"

She swept back her graying hair with two hands and then over one shoulder, waiting for me to speak. I had planned to tell her I was pregnant, two months along, but that was not on my mind now. I was thinking instead of her and of Dr. Adair in the boat, of his voice in the dark. I wanted, in that moment, to ask her about the affair. I wanted to ask not what started it, or ended it, or anything like that. What I wanted to know was what she had been seeking, and if she had found it.

But I turned back towards the lawn, towards the sweltering greenness of our neighborhood, sweat trickling down the backs of my outstretched thighs. I bit my lip. I remembered the currents of warm water, Peter's mouth against my ear. The silvery darkness outspread around us, endless, like an untold secret.

Ashleigh Pedersen recently earned her MFA from the University of Pittsburgh. She currently lives in Austin, Texas, where she writes, works, swims, and soaks up all the outstanding dive bar honky tonk.

GEORGIA CARR

*W*hen I was a kid my family spent a week or two each summer on a beach off the coast of South Carolina, not far from the Georgia border. After a ten-hour haul in a crowded, brown, wood-paneled minivan, we turned onto a narrow two-lane road that stretched beneath a canopy of live oaks, their branches ashy with Spanish moss. I have felt fond of these trees my whole life. It was recalling the image of them, I think, that first sent me heading toward "Small and Heavy World."

Wendell Berry

A BURDEN

(from *The Oxford American*)

"Me and Teddy Roosyvelt, we rode through hair, shit, blood, and corruption up to here." Uncle Peach used the stick he was whittling to mark a level about an inch above his nostrils.

"You did not," Wheeler said, but all the same he was laughing. He was seven years old, and sometimes just looking at Uncle Peach made him laugh.

"The hell you did!" said Andrew, who was Wheeler's brother and five years older, because to Uncle Peach he could say anything he wanted to and he did. Andrew, as Wheeler understood, was practicing to be a grown-up. An ambitionless boy would not say "the hell you did," even to Uncle Peach.

The boys supposed, because everybody else appeared to suppose, that Uncle Peach had been somewhere in the Army during the war with Spain. But they knew from their own observation that Uncle Peach's shotgun, "Old Deadeye," was an instrument of mercy to all creatures that ran or flew as well as to some that were sitting still.

The three of them, the two boys and their Uncle Peach, who was their mother's baby brother, were sitting in the shade of the tall cedar tree in front of the house. Uncle Peach was whittling a small cedar stick, releasing a fragrance. His knife was sharp, and he was making the shavings fine for fear he would use up the stick and have to go look for another. One of his rules for living was "Never stand up when you can set down," and he often quoted himself.

None of the three of them wanted to get up, for the day was already hot, and the shade of the old tree was a happiness. It was all the happier for being a threatened happiness. A sort of suspense hung over them and over that whole moment among the old trees and the patches of shade in the long yard. Maybe that was why Wheeler never forgot it. They had not seen the boys' father since breakfast. They did not know how come he had forgotten them. They knew only that if Marce Catlett came back from wherever he was and found them sitting there, they would all three be at work before they could say scat.

"Yeees saaah," Uncle Peach said, drawing out the words as if to make them last as long as his stick, "them was rough times, which was why we was called the Rough Riders. Hair, shit, blood, and corruption up to the horses' bits, and you needed a high-headed horse to get through it atall. When it was all over and we was heroes, Teddy says to me, 'Leonidas, looks like one of us is pret' near bound to be the presi-dent of the United States, and if it's all the same to you, I'd just as soon it would be me.' And I says, 'Why, Teddy, by all means! Go to it!'"

"The hell you did!" Andrew said again. "You couldn't tell the truth if it shit on your hat."

And that made Wheeler laugh so much he had to lie down in the grass.

At the age of seven, Wheeler was already aware that his loyalty was divided between his father and Uncle Peach, and he felt the strain. He loved Uncle Peach because he was funny and was interesting in the manner of a man who would do or say about anything he thought of, and because Uncle Peach loved him back and treated him as an equal and was always kind to him. Uncle Peach's trade was carpentry, which he was more or less good at, more or less worked at, and more or less made a living from. When he made more than a living from it, sooner or later he spent the surplus on whiskey and what he called "hoot-tootin'" in Hargrave or Louisville or wherever he could get to before he got down and had to be fetched home.

Uncle Peach was, in fact, a drunk, which at the age of seven Wheeler pretty well knew and easily forgave. Once, thinking to change his life after a near-lethal celebration of the heroism he had shared with by-then President Roosevelt, Uncle Peach had gone so far as to emigrate to Oklahoma, and had persevered there for one year that he ever afterward referred to as "my years in the Territory." While there he had been adopted into a tribe of Indians, he said, with whom he had lived and hunted and fought, and about this Wheeler had decided to have some doubts. Uncle Peach called Indians Eenjins. His Eenjin name was "See-we-no-ho," meaning in English "Friend of Great Chief." Though Wheeler suspected that Uncle Peach was just storying, he could nevertheless in his mind's eye see Uncle Peach all feathered and painted, riding his Indian pony named "Wa-su-ho-ha," which in English was "Runs Like Scared Rabbit." Uncle Peach loved to tell how he had hunted buffalo with his Eenjin brothers, how well he had ridden, how accurately he had shot with his bow.

And Andrew would say, "You got enough damn wind in you to blow up an onion sack."

Uncle Peach had about him the ease of a man who had never come hard up against anything. All his life he had been drifting. All his life he had followed the inclination of flowing water toward the easiest way, and the lowest. Wheeler may always have known this, for he was an alert boy who could pick knowledge out of the air without asking. And with a boy's love for even the appearance of freedom, he loved Uncle Peach for his drifting.

He loved his father, as eventually he knew, for precisely the opposite reason. Marce Catlett was a man who lived within limits that he had accepted. He did not drift. Year after year, he had been hard up against the demands of farm and family, of weather and the economy. As a farmer in a world that mainly took farmers for granted, and gave them not a thought, he had known more hard times than good ones. In the fall of that year when Wheeler was seven, his father sold his tobacco crop for just enough to pay the commission on its sale.

But he was not a one-crop farmer. His rule was "Sell something every week." This, as Wheeler would come to know, meant economic diversity; it required a complex formal intelligence; it was good sense. Marce was a man driven to small economies, which his artistry made elegant. He once built a new feed barn exactly on the site of the old one, tearing down the old one, reusing its usable lumber as he built the new one, and his work mules never spent a night out of their own stalls. His precise fitting of force to work, his neat patches and splices, his quiet transactions with a saddle horse or a team of mules—Wheeler learned these things as a boy, and all the latter part of his life he thought and dreamed of them, as of precious possessions lost.

As he grew in understanding, Wheeler more and more consciously chose his father over Uncle Peach. He chose, that is, his father's example, not his life. When the time came for Wheeler to choose his work, there was not a living for him at home and he could not afford to buy a place, and so out of economic necessity he went to school and became a lawyer. And yet he never abandoned his inheritance from his father. Marce Catlett's love of farming lived on in his son, as later it would live on in his grandsons. And all his life, Wheeler felt his father's good ways aching in his bones. He remembered them in palpable detail and loved them, though in his own life he had given most of them up for others less palpable.

Because after law school Wheeler did not go to any place offered him as "better," but returned to set up his practice at home, he came into an inheritance that was desirable, but it was also complex and in some ways difficult. That he had deliberately made himself heir to his father's example did not prevent him as well from inheriting Uncle Peach, as an amusement but also as a responsibility and a burden.

Uncle Peach, in fact, was amusing enough, He always had been—

"in his way," as his sister, Dorie Catlett, often felt called upon to add.

As a boy, wanting to "do like the old mule" who drank directly from the water trough, he tried to drink buttermilk from a stone churn and got his head stuck. Dorie had to break the churn to get him loose.

"Damn him, I would have left his head right where he put it," Marce would say. He would be growling, also laughing.

He would pause then, to allow her to say, "Yes, I reckon you would have let him drown."

And then Marce would say, "Something gone, nothing lost."

Once, exasperated by his daily resistance to washing and going to school, Dorie told her brother, "I ought to let you grow up in ignorance."

And he replied, "That's it, Dorie! Let me grow up in ignorance."

As Wheeler would tell it much later, his Uncle Peach did grow up in ignorance. And even before he had finished growing up, he shifted from buttermilk to whiskey, which he drank, while it lasted, as freely as the old mule drank water. He seldom had enough money to make it last very long. "And that," Dorie would say, "was his only good fortune, poor thing."

But his surpluses of money, seldom as they were, gave him a sort of fame. His reputation as a drinker far exceeded his reputation as a carpenter, and stories of his exploits were still told in Port William and Hargrave half a century after the beginning of television.

One afternoon, Burley Coulter came upon Uncle Peach in front of a roadhouse down by Hargrave. Uncle Peach had evidently been drinking a lot of whiskey and evidently eating a lot of pickled food from the bar. He had just finished vomiting upon the body of a dead cat, at which he was now gazing in great astonishment.

"Well, what's the matter, old Peach?"

"Why, Burley," Uncle Peach said, "I remember them pigs' feet and that baloney, but I got no recollection whatsoever of that cat."

Sometimes Uncle Peach found drunkenness to be hard work. Dancing to keep standing, he would pronounce solemnly, "Damn, I'm tard! My ass is draggin' out my tracks."

Sometimes he found himself in a moral landscape difficult to get across: "I got a long way to go and a short time to get there in."

Wheeler's own favorite story was about, so far as he knew, Uncle Peach's only actual fight.

Standing at the bar of a saloon in Louisville, Uncle Peach discovered, to his great disgust, that the man standing next to him was drunk.

"If they's anything I can't stand," Uncle Peach confided to the man, "it's a damn drunk."

At which the man confided back to Uncle Peach: "You ain't nothing but a damn drunk yourself."

Upon which Uncle Peach, grievously offended, took a swing.

"It is generally understood," Wheeler would say, "that when one man aims a violent blow at another, he had better hit him."

But Uncle Peach missed. Whereupon the previously offended flew at Uncle Peach and thrashed him not hardly enough to kill him, but thoroughly even so.

When Wheeler came later to rescue Uncle Peach from the Stag Hotel—where he lay, bloodied, defiant, and unable to stand—Uncle Peach was already referring to his opponent, in what may have been a mere flaw of perception, as "them gentlemens."

"Them gentlemens sholy could fight. They sholy was science men."

When, after his adventures in Oklahoma, Uncle Peach had decided to become a carpenter and showed some inclination to settle down, Marce Catlett helped him to find and buy a place with a few acres for pasture, a garden, and a little tobacco crop over by Floyd's Station. It was ten miles away, a distance that ought to have kept Uncle Peach "weaned," as Marce conceived it, from Dorie. But when Uncle Peach was on the downslope of a binge and in need of help, he would show up, intending to stay until he wore his welcome out—and longer, if he could.

On a certain night in Wheeler's childhood, perhaps not long after their conversation under the cedar tree, Uncle Peach showed up and, to the immense happiness of Wheeler and Andrew, drank copiously from a pan of dirty dishwater, complaining all the while of the declining quality of Dorie's soup. He proceeded to get sick, and then, shortly, to disappear. There must have been a passage of strict conversation between him and Marce at that time. Uncle Peach continued to show up now and again, but he never again showed up except sober.

Wheeler inherited Uncle Peach from his mother, who had inherited him from her mother, who had died soon after his birth. Dorie had pretty much had the raising of him, and it was she who named him "Peach," because it was handier than "Leonidas Polk" and because he was so pretty a little boy. That this Peach may have been a born failure did not mitigate Dorie's sense that he was her failure. With exactly the love that "hopeth all things," she did not give up on him.

Marce, on the contrary, gave up on his brother-in-law as a condition of his tolerance of him. It was a tolerance that worked best at a distance. With Peach in view, it was limited. After Uncle Peach had met the limit, he was always sober when in view. For Peach Wheeler drunk there was no longer a place within Marce Catlett's horizon.

And so Wheeler Catlett inherited, along with Uncle Peach, two opposite attitudes toward him, and was never afterward free of either. As he grew into the necessary choice between his father and his uncle, and made the choice, Wheeler found that he had not merely chosen, but, by choosing his father, had acquired in addition his father's indignation. Wheeler could at times look upon his uncle as an affront, as if Peach had, at conception or birth, decided to be a burden, specifically to his as-yet-unborn nephew.

But as he grew in experience and self-knowledge, Wheeler also grew to recognize in himself a sort of replica of his mother's love and compassion. He was never able quite to anticipate and prepare himself for the moment at which the apparition of Uncle Peach as nuisance would be replaced by the apparition of Uncle Peach as mortal sufferer. This change was not in Uncle Peach, who never changed except by becoming more and more as apparently he had been born to be. The change was in Wheeler. When the moment came, usually in the midst of some extremity of Uncle Peach's drinking career, Wheeler would feel a sudden welling up of love, as if from his mother's heart to his own, and then he would pity Uncle Peach and, against the entire weight of history and probability, wish him well. Sometimes after telling, and fully delighting in, one of his stories about Uncle Peach, Wheeler would fall silent, shake his head, and say, "Poor fellow."

Andrew, the firstborn son and elder brother, despite all his early practicing to be a grown-up, did not manage to grow much farther up than Uncle Peach. Andrew, as it turned out, did not inherit attitudes toward Uncle Peach so much as he inherited Uncle Peach's failing. Andrew in his turn became a drinker, and he too would say or do about anything he thought of. He would do so finally to the limit of life itself, and so beyond. As Andrew's course declared itself as more or less a reprise of Uncle Peach's, that of course intensified and complicated the attitudes of the others in the family toward Uncle Peach. Their stories all are added finally into one story. They were bound together in a many-stranded braid beyond the power of any awl to pick apart.

When Wheeler came home and started his law practice, he bought a car, because his practice involved distances that needed to be hurried over. But the automobile was a fate that, as it included distance, also included Uncle Peach. The automobile made almost nothing of the ten miles from the Catletts' house to Uncle Peach's. Because of the automobile, Dorie could more frequently go over to housekeep and help out when Uncle Peach was on one of his rough ascents into sobriety, when, she said, he needed her most.

Uncle Peach most needed Wheeler when he was drunk and sick and helpless and broke and far from home. The automobile made this a reasonable need. No power that Wheeler had acquired in law school enabled him to argue against it, though he tried. Because he had the means of going, he had to go.

If Uncle Peach had the money to get there, his favorite place of resort was a Louisville establishment that called itself the Stag Hotel. From the time of Wheeler's purchase of the automobile until the time of Uncle Peach's death, Wheeler, who would not in any circumstances have taken Uncle Peach to the Stag Hotel, went there many a time to bring him home.

At the Stag Hotel and other places of refreshment, Uncle Peach would encounter commercial ladies of great attractiveness and charm. Sometimes when Wheeler would be bringing him home, and despite his pain and exhaustion, Uncle Peach would still be enchanted, and he would confide as much to Wheeler: "Oh, them eyes!" he would say. "Oh, them eyes!"

Many a good and funny story came of Wheeler's missions of mercy, and also many a story of real pain and suffering that moved Wheeler to real pity, and also many moments of utter exasperation at the waste of time and effort when Wheeler, half mocking himself and yet meaning every word, would cry out against "the damned Stag Hotel and every damned thing involved therein and pertaining thereto." Or he would say of Uncle Peach indignantly, "He's got barely enough sense to swallow." And then he would laugh. "Burley Coulter told me he'd seen Uncle Peach drink all he could hold and then fill his mouth for later." He would laugh. And then, affection and hopelessness and sorrow coming over him, he would shake his head and say, "Poor fellow."

In his turn, young Andy Catlett, namesake of his doomed Uncle Andrew, also inherited Uncle Peach, who was bequeathed to him by his grandmother's lamentation and his father's talk. From those sources, from trips with his father to see that their then-failing uncle was alive and had enough to eat, and from various elders who remembered with care and delight Uncle Peach's sayings and doings, Andy gathered up a sort of legendry that belonged intimately to his childhood and would remain with him all his life.

One Christmastime, when he was about six, Andy overheard his father tell Uncle Andrew, just home for the holidays, that Uncle Peach, "sleeping one off in his front yard," had frozen several of his toes, which had then needed to be amputated.

"Toes!" Uncle Andrew said, laughing his big laugh. "Anybody can spare a few toes. He better be glad he didn't freeze his pecker off." In the midst of his sadness and exasperation Wheeler also laughed, and they went away, leaving Andy, whom they had not noticed, with a possibility he had never considered before.

Andy had gone with his father to visit Uncle Peach after the surgery. Uncle Peach was sitting by the drum stove in his bare little house with his foot wrapped in a soiled white bandage. He was talking in his old, slow voice about the hospital in Louisville, which he pronounced "Louis-ville," Uncle Peach had enjoyed his stay in the hospital. He had admired the nurses. "Damn pretty, some of 'em," he said to Wheeler.

And then, studying Andy, he said, "This boy'll be looking at 'em, 'fore you know it."

When Uncle Peach died in Andy's seventh year, Andy overheard his father and mother saying what a story it had been. His father said with regret and sorrow and amusement and, instead of indignation, perhaps relief, for Uncle Peach had died sober in his sleep in bed at home: "Like Jehoram, poor fellow, he has departed without being desired." Wheeler was capable of feeling some things simply, but he never spoke of Uncle Peach with unmixed feelings.

And then when they were all in Wheeler's car, driving home from the graveyard on the hill outside Port William where they had laid Uncle Peach to rest, they were silent until Wheeler said, "Well!"

He let the silence come back, and then he said, "The preacher takes a very happy view of Uncle Peach's prospects hereafter."

Wheeler was lining out a text that would be clearly printed in his son's memory, where it would gather commentary for a long time.

Nobody was talking except Wheeler. Andy understood that his mother wasn't saying anything because she felt that the continuation of Uncle Peach's story hereafter was none of her business, and his grandfather wasn't saying anything because he didn't want it to be his business, and his grandmother wasn't saying anything because it was her business. It came to Andy then, for the first time, that his father was still a relatively young man.

The preacher had said Uncle Peach was going to Heaven, or was there already, because his soul had been saved when he gave his life to Jesus and was baptized at the age of twelve. His baptism, so many years ago, in another century, was still in force. Andy imagined that baptism had left on Uncle Peach's soul a mark like a vaccination scar to show that he had been saved. When he got to Heaven, he was to be let in.

Andy had stood in church beside his mother, had heard her singing with the others,

> While I draw this fleeting breath,
> When mine eyes shall close in death,
> When I rise to worlds unknown,
> And behold Thee on Thy throne,
> Rock of Ages, cleft for me,
> Let me hide myself in Thee,

and he had thought, "*She? She* will?" And so he knew that in the soul's bewildering geography there was a Rock of Ages. In his mind it looked like the Rock of Gibraltar, cleft like a cow's foot, and you could hide in the cleft and be all right.

But from other songs they sang he knew that this geography had a shore, too, from which the dead departed to cross a wide river, and another shore beyond the river, a beautiful shore, that was Heaven. He had seen in his mind a picture of people on the far shore waving to people coming across who were waving back.

They were calling one another's names and they were happy. The picture meant that in Heaven, love would last as long as it wanted to and have as much room as it needed.

But Wheeler wasn't finished. He was always concerned with fittingness, which was maybe a kind of honesty. Those were words he used: fitting and honest. He was always trying to get the scattered pieces to fit together in a pattern that made sense. He wanted to find the right words and to say things right. Right was another of his words. His effort often made him impatient. This also Andy took in and remembered.

"If Uncle Peach is in Heaven," Wheeler said, "and Lord knows I hope that's where he is, then grace has lifted a mighty burden, and the preacher ought to have said so."

And then he said, as if determined in his impatience to capture every straying piece, "And as an earthly burden, it wasn't lifted just by grace"—meaning it was a burden he too had borne. Even at the time, Andy caught that.

So did his grandmother. She said one syllable then that Andy never forgot, and that later he would know had at least four meanings: that his father would have done better to be quiet, that she too had borne that earthly burden and would forever bear it, that Uncle Peach had borne it himself and was loved and forgiven at least by her, and that it was past time to hush.

She said, "Hmh!"

Wendell Berry was born in 1934 and has belonged all his life to the place where he still lives. He has been married since 1957 to Tanya Amyx Berry. They have two children and five grandchildren. His most recent books are *Andy Catlett: Early Travels* (a novel), *Leavings* (poems), and *Imagination in Place* (essays).

GUY MENDES

*F*or me, the question of how something of mine got written is always embarrassing, because I am never sure. By now, I have known a lot of people, have a lot of memories of my own, and have a lot of memories of other people's memories. I also have a collection of imaginings. All I'm pretty sure of is that you can't make a story either by thinking it up or by remembering. If you live long enough, sometimes, somehow, you will see how the single thread of a story may connect—as here, the childhood of Peach Wheeler to that of Wheeler Catlett to that of Andy Catlett. The question of how things hang together is fascinating. To be able to imagine one possible way is a privilege and a pleasure.

Megan Mayhew Bergman

THE COW THAT MILKED HERSELF

(from *New South*)

First, he showed me his kidney.

This, Wood said, is the cranial pole. He pointed to the C-shaped edge of his organ.

My turn, I said.

He moved the ultrasound probe to my belly, rolling the small tip across my hardening stomach.

I think we cleaned this after the Rottweiler, he said. He squinted at the probe.

Don't drop it, he said, handing me the probe while he dimmed the exam room lights and warmed the transmission gel. Twenty thousand dollars.

We were sitting in the veterinary clinic after hours, Wood still in his white coat, stethoscope around his neck. I was seated on a steel table, the metal cold against the backs of my knees. Wood had missed my last OB/GYN appointments and wanted to see the fetus for himself.

I was lonely at my OB appointments, but there were dogs with shattered elbows, cats with failing livers, cows with mastitis. Crying women in the waiting rooms cradling arthritic shih tzus, one-eyed ferrets. Malamutes with slipped discs, terriers with severe allergies to carpet cleaner. I believed they needed him more than I did.

He pressed the probe into my abdomen.

Here is the gestational sac, he said. And this flash here—this is the heart.

We were speechless then, watching the beginnings of our child thrive onscreen. Two freshly neutered Labradors whined from their cages outside.

Every week there was a patient at the clinic Wood forbade me from seeing. Last week it had been a cancer-stricken lemur, a golden-crowned sifaka who was the last of his kind in captivity. He had been gentle with his keeper, raising his bony arm so she could stroke his side, a gesture that seemed to comfort him.

This week it was Cerulean, a tripod Rottweiler.

Too hard on the heart strings, Wood said, knowing I'd be unable to resist.

Take me to see her, I said.

She's not pretty, he said. She's been self-mutilating. Down there.

He raised his eyebrows.

Cerulean had come in that morning with a deaf man. Wood was an ultrasound specialist, and they had hoped he would be able to reveal a tumor or kidney stones—something specific.

You don't want it to be behavioral, Wood said. Always harder to treat the mind than the body.

But they had found nothing. Her scan was clean.

No mineralization, no masses, Wood said.

Cerulean sat on the concrete floor and leaned against the cinderblock wall. Her black fur shone in the fluorescent lights. Her ears were small. I could not bring myself to look at her eyes. She had mussed the towels into piles. Her feet made me want to cry, the pads of her three remaining paws plump and worn.

At three months I just looked fat. Like I had four sandwiches instead of one, I told my mother. I could cup my belly in one hand, swing my forearm underneath the slight mound the book said should be the size of a grapefruit. I couldn't bring myself to say the word *womb*.

Wood came home in his white coat, smelling of formaldehyde and anal glands. He asked "what's for dinner" but did not listen for the answer. Instead, he stuck his head inside the refrigerator.

How was your appointment? he asked, peeling off his white coat, pulling off his left shoe with the heel of his right.

I made three-bean chili, I said, shooing the cat from the stove.

I wiped buttered paw prints from the glass.

Wood cracked open a beer.

I was palpated today, I said. Like that thing you do to cows, when you feel for lumps in their abdomen.

I can tell when a woman is pregnant by finding the ridge of her uterus, my OB had bragged. I touch a thousand tummies a year, for godssake.

On the screen, the fetus had doubled over, then stretched, a sun salutation with no sun.

I couldn't help thinking, I told Wood, that the nub of his or her vestigial tail looked a lot like the end of a cocker spaniel.

Incessant waggers, he said. Submissive urinators.

Loving, I said. Warm on your lap.

The picture of my fetus, taped to the kitchen cabinet, made my niece cry.

I'm scared, too, I said.

I meant it.

The black-and-white photograph showed our child's skull and vertebrae, eye sockets like moon craters.

Later that evening, Wood rubbed my back, sutured the dress straps I had snapped with my swelling bosom. I could feel his breath on my scapula, his needle stitching cotton like skin.

Friends came over for dinner that night bearing presents, pop-up books and sock monkeys. I put out a plate of crudités, noticed dog hair wound into the broccoli heads.

Wood spoke of his upcoming conventions, the paper he'd co-authored on using ultrasound to monitor the morphology of female jaguar reproductive tracts. It was hard to trump frozen jaguar sperm.

In captivity, the jaguar mother is capable of devouring her own cubs, he said.

I blushed. I took this as a sign of Wood's lack of faith in mothers.

Here, Wood, I said. Open this package from your aunt. It isn't just my baby, you know.

Wood slipped his finger underneath the wrapping paper.

A breast pump is an awful lot like a vacuum milking cup, my husband said, untangling the gifted contraption. He held the suction cups to his chest.

Soon she will be the cow that milked herself, he said.

Our friends howled.

Cerulean came back to the clinic a week later for observation.

She smells like pepperoni pizza, Wood said over the phone. I can't explain it.

I hated the thought of her on the cold cement floor, the cage bars in front of her view, the indignities of her mysterious sickness.

Can I bring you lunch? I asked.

I drove to the clinic with sandwiches and a bag of soft dog toys.

What is this? Wood asked, holding a headless hedgehog.

Let me put one in, I said.

Wood placed one hand over his eyes and left me alone with Cerulean.

Hi, I said.

She looked at me from the corners of her eyes, shy and damaged. I sat on the floor and tucked my legs underneath my body. I wanted to massage lotion into her feet, stroke her back.

Here, I said, handing her the hedgehog through the bars of the cage, then the stuffed cat.

I want to mother the world, I thought. I have so much love.

Then—I have no business being a mother. I am a selfish woman.

Then—I can do this. Millions of women have been mothers.
Then—I feel very alone. I do not know what I'm capable of.

My fetus grew arms, carried a yolk sac like a balloon.
These, the OB had said, pointing to a white Cheerio on the
screen, are the sex cells of your grandchildren.
Tell them I'm sorry about all the weed I smoked in high school,
I said. And that time . . . well, there were a lot of times.
I wondered if I would fill the shoes of the mythical matriarch,
if suddenly my pancakes would become legendary, my dresses tai-
lored, my back rubs soothing.

When I first told Wood I was pregnant, he had taken off his
sweatshirt and placed the cockatiel he was administering medica-
tion to on the exam room counter.
I think Nathan Scott Phillips pooped in my hood, he said.
Wood's cheeks were flushed. I touched his shoulder. It was a
Saturday morning and I was helping him with his early morning
rounds. I liked those mornings when the clinic was quiet and it
was just the two of us feeding schnauzers and ferrets in between
sips of coffee and exclamations about the morning paper.
I am excited, he clarified, minutes later. He wrapped his arms
around me and kissed the crown of my head.
I wanted to be as interesting to Wood as a urinary bladder wall
tumor, labwork. I wanted to be pored over, examined by his fingers, researched, discussed, diagnosed. I wanted to keep him up
late, bring him in early.

Cerulean likes the stuffed cat, Wood said on the way to our
birthing class.
I have to leave early, he reminded me. Gall bladder infection in
a Chesapeake Bay Retriever.
The instructor wore fleece leggings and a purple spaghetti strap
top.

Some women, she said, hands cupped as if she was holding a beach ball, achieve orgasm during birth.

I may have to poke out her third eye, I said.

Wood did not understand my anxieties—miscarriage, autism, premature delivery.

I wish it would come out like a goat, I told him. Sturdy, hooved, walking.

Every spring we helped the veterinary school calve and foal. The meat goats bloated with twins, the petrified sheep with their petrified lambs, limp and gentle on the mud floor.

You'll do fine, he said, patting my stomach. Rugged stock.

But I knew how I would do. I would take my maternity leave and he would come home for dinner at night, late. My milk would let down when the cat cried at the moon from the staircase window. I would wake up sticking to the sheets. I would love and complain with equal vigor.

I'm sorry I missed the asexual revolution, I said. Aphids, bees, captive hammerhead sharks—they know they're on their own. They don't expect understanding.

What the cape bee gains in martyrdom, she loses in genetic potential, Wood said.

Self-reliance, I began.

Take last week's lemur, Wood said. His was the last of his kind. He needed others.

I'd been thinking about nativity scenes. Camels leaning over the manger, like my cat nesting in the crib. The way Joseph pretended his hands were tied, that he wasn't responsible in the first place.

The birthing class instructor passed around a wooden bowl of mixed berries. Wood held up one hand in protest.

In your last weeks of pregnancy, the instructor said to the class, the cervix softens like ripe fruit.

These women don't know much about birth, Wood whispered.

I'd like to take the class on a field trip. I'd like to take these girls to a farm during calving season.

This is different, I said. Your child will not be a ruminant.

Remember, the instructor said. It may take days to fall in love with your newborn.

The next Saturday Cerulean's cage was abandoned. The stuffed cat, overturned in the corner, was missing an eye.

Don't tell me how this ends, I said to Wood.

Later, as the sun rose, Wood rolled me onto my side and warmed the transmission gel. The exam table was cold.

He pressed the probe into the taut skin stretched across my womb like canvas. In the treatment room his fingers were deft and comforting. His eyes focused on the baby beneath my skin. I could feel his anticipation. It washed over me like love.

The ultrasound excels at imaging the heart, Wood said. The heart is a fluid-filled organ.

States away, a woman gave birth to octuplets like pups. Perhaps another arched her back in ecstasy as a head fourteen inches in diameter emerged from her cervix. An endangered lemur picked at her barren womb in the confines of the zoo hospital. Me, I watched a heart, small but fast, beat between the shadows of our daughter's ribs. I hope you never break, I said, though I knew it would, again and again.

With his finger, Wood traced the outline of our daughter's organs on the screen.

Tell me again about jaguar reproduction, I said.

The baby gestates for a little over ninety days, Wood said. If her cubs are taken from her in the wild, the mother will chase them down for hours, roaring continuously.

I would do that, too, I said. I promise.

———————

Megan Mayhew Bergman was born in Gaffney,
South Carolina, and was raised in Rocky Mount,
North Carolina. After thirty Carolina-bound
years, she has recently moved to rural Vermont
with her veterinarian husband, Bo, her daughter, Frasier, five dogs, four cats, two goats, and
a horse. Her work has appeared in *The Kenyon
Review, Shenandoah, Oxford American, Gulf Coast,*
and elsewhere.

BO BERGMAN

*When I began "The Cow That Milked Herself," my father-in-law
and mother-in-law were both veterinarians, and my husband was
about to graduate from veterinary school. I was four or five months pregnant, and cancer was spreading aggressively through my mother-in-law's
body—so any time she got to "see" the baby was significant. One evening, as
the business day was drawing to a close, the three vets whipped out the ultrasound machine usually reserved for bloated dogs and blocked cats, plopped me
onto the examination table, and found my daughter's heartbeat. The rest
of the story reflects my pregnancy anxiety, or stolen bits of dinner table talk.
(Ever tried to eat dinner with a table of veterinarians? Everything on your
plate looks like something they see in a dog's abdominal cavity.)*

George Singleton

COLUMBARIUM

(from *Appalachian Heritage*)

Not until my father walked into the post office—or perhaps it was a few days earlier at the bastardized crematorium— did I understand how much he despised my mother's constant reminders. For at least fifteen years she substituted "No," "Okay," or "I'll do it if I have to," with "I could've gone to the Rhode Island School of Design" or "For this I gave up the chance to attend Pratt" or "When did God decide that I would be better off stuck with a man who sold rocks for a living, than continuing my education at Cooper Union?" I figured out later that my parents weren't married but five months when I came out all healthy and above-average in weight, length, and lung capacity. To me she said things like, "I should've matriculated to the Kansas City Arts Institute, graduated, and begun my life working in an art studio of my own, but here I am driving you twenty miles to the closest Little League game," or "I had a chance to go to the Chicago Art Institute on a full scholarship, but here I am trying to figure out why the hell x and y are so important in a math class," or "Believe you me, I wouldn't be adding pineapple chunks, green chiles, and tuna to a box of macaroni and cheese for supper had I gotten my wish and gone to the Ringling School of Art."

I went through all the times my mother offered up those blanket statements about her wonderful artistic talents—usually by the

fireplace while she carved fake fossils into flat rocks dug out of the
Unknown Branch of the Saluda River—there at the post office
while my dad and I waited in line. She sold these forgeries down
at the Dixie Rock and Gem Shop, or to tourist traps at the foot of
Caesar's Head, way up near Clingman's Dome, or on the outskirts
of Helen, Georgia. My mother's life could've been worthwhile and
meaningful had she not been burdened with motherhood; had she
not been forced to work as a bookkeeper/receptionist/part-time
homemade dredge operator at the family river rock business; had
she not met my father when her own family got forced to move
from Worcester, Massachusetts, because her daddy was in the tex-
tile business and got transferred right before my mother's senior
year in high school. There were no art classes in the schools here;
she could only take advanced home ec and learn how to make
fabric and dye it, just as her father knew how to do at the cotton
mill, more than likely.

"I could've gone to the School of the Museum of Fine Arts in
Boston had I not been forced to take an English class that I'd already taken up in Massachusetts, and sit next to your father who
cheated off my paper every time we took a multiple choice test on
The Scarlet Letter. I blame all of this on *The Scarlet Letter*, and how
your dad had to come over on more than one occasion for tutor-
ing," my mother said about once a week.

I didn't get the chance to ever point out to her how Nathaniel
Hawthorne lived in Massachusetts. A year after her death I figured
out the math of their wedding date and my birth, and didn't get
to offer up anything about symbolism, or life mirroring art, et
cetera.

My mother died of flat-out boredom, disdain, crankiness, ennui,
tendonitis from etching fake fossil ferns and fish bones into rocks,
and a giant handful of sleeping pills. Her daily allotment of hemlock leaves boiled into a tea probably led to her demise, too, if not
physiologically, at least spiritually.

According to my father, the South Carolina Funeral Directors
Association didn't require normal embalming and/or crematorial

procedures should the deceased have no brothers or sisters, and should said dead person's parents both be dead. Looking back, I understand now that my father made all this up. At the time, though, I just sat on the bench seat of his flatbed, my mother in back wrapped up in her favorite quilt inside a pine coffin. "We're going up to Pointy Henderson's, and he'll perform the cremation. Then we'll scatter your mother down by the river so she can always be with us."

Mr. Henderson was a potter, and president of the local Democratic Party. About once a year he came down from the mountains and enlisted young democrats—and we all joined seeing as once a year, too, he held a giant shindig that included moonshine for everyone willing to either vote right or, if under aged, at least put yard signs up.

"Cremation takes two to three hours at 1400 to 1800 degrees," Mr. Henderson said when we got there. "I did the research long ago." He got his two daughters to heft my mother off of the truck and carry the box to the groundhog kiln, which appeared to be dug into the side of an embankment. "My fire reaches near two thousand degrees on a good day," he said. "After Mrs. Looper cools, I'll go to ashing down the hard bones, if that's all right."

My father nodded. He'd done his crying the night before, as had I. "We'll come back in a couple days," my father said.

"You and me's kind of in the same business, I guess," Henderson said. "You take rock and sell it to people who want paths to their front doors and walls to keep them out, and I take clay and sell it to people who want bowls on their tables."

I didn't get the connection. I guessed that clay was kind of like ground-down rocks, to a certain extent. I looked at Mr. Henderson's daughters, who were my age, and were so inordinately beautiful that no one spoke to them in school. If Homer came back to Earth and met the potter's daughters, he'd've had to rewrite the Siren section of *The Odyssey*. One of them said, "Sorry."

I said, "I'm a democrat," for I could think of nothing else. "I'm thinking that some laws need changing."

The other daughter said, "Sorry."

My father and I drove back home, as they say, in silence. Right before my mother slumped over in her chair dead at the age of thirty-three, she had set her last pancake-sized rock, a fake millipede etched into it, down on the stool. For her carving tool she'd been using a brand-new single-diamond necklace my father bought her. I don't know if her engagement ring, which she normally used for such forgeries, had worn out or not. My father had bought the necklace as a way to celebrate a new account he'd won—as the sole river rock supplier for an entire housing tract deal down in Greenville that would include a hundred patios, and driveway-to-front-door paths.

I sat at the kitchen table reading a book about three out of the four ancient elements. My mother had just gotten up to go to the bathroom, I assumed. She said, "I could've gone to the Maryland Institute College of Art. Here I am walking to the bathroom one more time."

Those were her last words, as it ended up. "Mom's last words were 'Here I am walking to the bathroom one more time,'" I said. My father, without offering a reason, performed a U-turn in the middle of highway 108 and drove back to Mr. Henderson's. I said, "I guess she didn't know those would be her last words."

"Maybe she was a visionary. Maybe Heaven's just one giant toilet, Stet. I don't mean that in a bad way." I knew that he did mean it that way, though. My father didn't cotton to there even being a Heaven or Hell. In the past he had said, "If there was a Hell in the middle of the planet like some idiots believe, I think I'd've seen a flame or two shoot out from as deep as I've dug for rocks over the years."

We drove back up Mr. Henderson's rocky driveway not two hours since we first arrived. He had already shoved my mother into the chamber. My father told me I could sit in the truck if I wanted, which I did at first until I realized that I had something important to say to the potter's daughters, something that might prod them into seeing me as special, something that might cause both of them to be my dates at the prom in a few years. I got out and stood there. Mr. Henderson explained something about the firing process, about the wood he used, something about how he can perform cremations cheaper than making his own pots because there's no glaze involved. His daughters walked up and stood with us twenty feet from the kiln door. I said, "My mother was an artist."

They said, in unison, "Sorry."

Smoke blew out of the kiln's chimney, and my father said, "Well I don't see any smoke rings going skyward. Which means I don't see a halo. Come on, son."

Not until I had graduated from college with a few degrees—my father had told me to get my fill of education before coming back to run the family river rock business—and married my wife did I understand the backtracking to Mr. Henderson's makeshift crematorium: My father wanted a sign from the Otherworld, just in case his final plan bordered on meanness or immorality.

I'm not sure what we spread down by the Unknown Branch of the Middle Saluda River. It's not like I shadowed my father for two days. I imagine he flung plain hearth ash down on the ground. At the post office, though, my father told Randy the post office guy, "They all weigh the same. You can weigh one, and the postage will be the same on all of them."

There were six manila envelopes. Randy said, "Don't you want return addresses on these?"

"I trust y'all," my father said. "I trust the postal service."

To me, Randy said, "You applying to all these colleges?" He sorted through the envelopes. "I guess you are, what with all these admissions departments."

I said, "Sorry," like a fool, for the words of the Henderson girls rang in my ears still. I'd learned long before not to contradict my father. A man with a river rock business doesn't keep many belts around. I could go throughout life saying my father never spanked me, but I couldn't say that I'd never been stoned, in a couple of ways.

Driving back home my father said, "She got her wish. She finally got to attend all those art schools." Then he pulled off to the side of the road, past a short bridge. Beneath it ran a nameless creek. I got out, too, and together we took drywall buckets out of the back of the truck, trampled our way down the embankment, and scooped up smooth rounded mica-specked flagstone, each one the size of an ice cube, each one different in glint.

George Singleton has published four collections of stories, two novels, and a book of advice. His fiction has appeared in a number of magazines and literary journals. This is his tenth appearance in *New Stories from the South*. He was a 2009 Guggenheim fellow, and he teaches fiction writing at the South Carolina Governor's School for the Arts and Humanities.

GLENDA GUION

In the old days, one took the SAT test once, applied to two or three colleges, chose one of them, then went there and suffered through it all for four years. I have noticed lately that high school students' parents make their kids take the SAT and ACT tests innumerable times, starting in about the third grade. Then the students apply to, say, forty colleges. They spend most of the first semester of their senior years writing various quirky and/or awe-inspiring essays of questionable validity. Come April, they have gotten into a few prestigious colleges, plus all of their "safety" schools.

Then their parents say, "You know, we think you should go to any of those safety schools, because they're free. Even with scholarships and loans and FAFSA paying half the costs, we can't afford to come up with the other $30,000 per year."

Maybe if the parents hadn't spent all that money on taking standardized tests, hiring tutors, et cetera . . .

So then the student goes to a midlevel state university, remains bored, takes a year or two off, and maybe graduates with a degree, eventually, that he or she isn't really interested in. These perpetually depressed individuals go around for the next fifty years saying to friends, relatives, and strangers alike, "I could've gone to NYU! I could've gone to USC film school! I could've gone to Brown! I could've gone to Duke!"

And then they die.

I thought of this while writing the story.

Bret Anthony Johnston

CAIMAN

(from *AGNI Magazine*)

Your mother wouldn't let me bring the ice chest into the house, so I left it in the garage. Earlier, I'd knifed four holes into the styrofoam lid. One of them looked like half a star, which I remember liking. This was years ago, a windswept Sunday. This was Texas.

When I returned to the kitchen, she pointed at the sink. She said, "Wash your hands. With soap."

She was breading flounder. She'd been listening to radio reports about that little girl who'd been abducted. So had I. Probably I pulled over and gave that man eighty dollars because I thought it would keep you safe. He was parked under the causeway, a hand-lettered sign propped against the tire of his van, as if he were just selling pecans.

Your mother had flour dust on her neck. She'd already fried okra, boiled potatoes. Soon we would call you to the table and you, our little man, would bolt in like you'd heard a starter pistol. You were seven, a boy who liked bedtime stories with fantastic monsters and twisty, unexpected endings. You liked sneaking up on us. You hid behind closed doors and in the laundry hamper, then jumped out screaming and laughing. You loved the word "maybe." (*Maybe I'm a kid who's a million years old. Maybe we should be a family with a pet. Maybe someday my eyes will turn blue.*) Your mother swiped her forehead with her wrist. The kitchen was gummy with the day's heat, the windows open. Before leaving that morning, I'd mowed the yard—you helped me rake, you wore your cowboy boots—and now, with dusk coming on, the cut-grass smell was rising and trying to cool everything off.

"She's still missing," your mother said. "Now they think the uncle did something."

I nodded. I'd heard that, too, and if it was true, I thought he'd get killed in prison. But I didn't want to talk about such things. Instead, I asked, "How's our little man?"

"Worn out," your mother said. "He's napping in his room."

I'd been all day at the job site, drawing overtime. On the drive home, I'd seen the man under the causeway and pulled over for a look. Our ice chest was still in the bed of the truck from when we'd gone floundering. I took that as a sign. And he had only one left, which also seemed lucky. I was excited to surprise you, to hear what you'd name it.

Now I said, "I wonder what he'll name it."

"He asked for a dog."

"A pet," I said. "He asked for a *pet*."

"Right, a dog. A cat. A goldfish. Pets have fur and show affection. Pets aren't deadly."

"Goldfish don't have fur," I said. I didn't think she was angry, not really. I took three glasses from the cabinet. "And it's not deadly."

She fixed me with her eyes. "It's an alligator."

"It's a caiman. There's a difference. It's the size of a shoe."

"Not for long," she said. She turned back to the stove. She laid one piece of fish in the skillet, then another. Grease started snapping.

"They're smart," I said, repeating what the man had told me. "They won't mate until the river is high. They make sure there's enough water for their offspring. They build nests."

"They're cold-blooded. They have scales."

"Danny can take it for show-and-tell."

"They bite. They escape. They escape into sewers and terrorize neighborhoods. They eat regular pets."

I laughed at that, but your mother said, "They do."

She flipped the fish in the skillet. The sound of frying started up again like distant applause. She blew hair from her eyes, stood with her hip cocked, holding the spatula. The applause quieted. She slipped the fish onto a plate she'd covered with a paper napkin to soak up grease. She put two more pieces in the pan and watched them sizzle.

She said, "Why would that man take that little girl?"

"We don't know that he did."

"But you think he did?"

"Yes," I said. "I do."

"I do, too," your mother said. "You know she's Danny's age."

"They could still find her."

"But you don't think they will?"

"I don't know, honey," I said.

"I don't think they will."

She lowered the flame on the stove and turned to stare out the window. She was touching her fingertips to her thumb, one after the other, something she did when she was concentrating. The air in the room shifted.

"What would we do if something—"

"It won't," I said. "Not to him."

She nodded, pressed the heel of her palm to her eyes. She said, "We're still getting a dog."

"I know."

"And you owe me a new ice chest," she said.

I poured milk for you but returned our glasses to the cabinet and opened up two bottles of beer. The meal was starting to feel like a celebration, like one of us had gotten a raise or was having a birthday. I found some cocoa mix, stirred it into your glass.

"An alligator," your mother said, shaking her head.

"Caiman," I said.

"You know some husbands bring home candy, right? Or roses or diamonds."

"Their poor wives," I said. "They probably—"

"Tell Danny you caught it," she said. "Tell him you were fishing and you saw it and you caught it just for him."

"You want me to lie to our son."

"I want you to make up a story for him, something with a happy outcome," she said and turned off the stove. She went to the refrigerator and took out the tartar sauce and a salad she'd been chilling. The wind lifted the curtains over the sink and sent a few paper napkins gliding off the counter. Your mother closed the window, and the kitchen went quiet as a secret.

And then, with the wind shut out, we could hear your boots on the floor in the hallway. You were stalking toward us, planning one of your sneak attacks. Your mother sipped her beer. The flour was on her neck—it looked like snow, like a smeared galaxy—and she was smiling a little. I understood what she didn't: you'd been awake the whole time, listening to us. You already knew about the caiman, about the flimsy hopeful story I'd tell, about everything else. The only surprise left was that I *did* believe they could still find that girl. I thought her uncle might prove everyone wrong. Maybe he cooked her favorite meals, played her favorite movies, never touched her. Maybe such extravagant misguided love was still possible. As a baby, you liked putting your feet in my mouth. You'd laugh until you got the hiccups and your toes would move behind my teeth as slow as growing coral, and sometimes, I swear, I wanted to bite down, to crush your perfect bones and swallow your body whole.

Your mother knelt to pick up the strewn napkins. You were just on the other side of the door now, trying not to giggle and preparing your ambush. Maybe you knew we were onto you, maybe not. I joined your mother on the floor. I felt like we were praying or giving thanks or mourning. The kitchen tile was cool, hard. We were listening to you breathe, waiting for you to strike. We were on our hands and knees, our bodies low to the ground like strange and ancient creatures.

Bret Anthony Johnston is the author of *Corpus Christi: Stories* and the editor of *Naming the World and Other Exercises for the Creative Writer.* His stories have previously appeared in *New Stories from the South: The Year's Best, 2003, 2004, 2005,* and *2008.* Currently, he teaches in the Bennington College Writing Seminars and is the director of creative writing at Harvard University. More information can be found at www.bretanthonyjohnston.com.

*O*riginally, this story had a very funky and metafictional ending, a long and dense and syntactically snazzy final paragraph that commented on the uniquely human act of writing stories. It would have blurred the line between fiction and autobiography; it would have pitted the slipperiness of memory against the traditional reader's desire for a reliable narrator and a satisfyingly consequential narrative arc; it would have, I felt not one doubt, made you think, "That BAJ, he's one smart puppy!" It was just awful.

So I went back through the story, taking inventory, retracing not my steps but the characters'. I paid attention to where they were in their hearts and fears and desires (and where they were in their house), and only then did I realize the son had been listening in on his parents. I was surprised and relieved to find him there, as I knew his parents would be, as I hoped the reader would be.

Thanks go to Julie Barer and Daniel Menaker, and to Sven Birkerts and Bill Pierce at AGNI, and to the woman in a pet store who said Pets aren't deadly as I was buying a thirty-pound bag of Eukanuba low residue dry dog food. I remember being struck by the woman's assertion, remember walking to my truck thinking, Really? Really? I didn't rush home to write the story, I never do that, but as I drove away I knew a story was out there, knew I was heading in its general direction.

Ben Stroud

ERASER

(from *One Story*)

Two Deadly Fish

I lift up the lid of the livewell and look inside. A couple fish—bass, largemouth—sit in place, not really swimming.

"What's up, fish?" I say.

The fish open their mouths and close them, which is about all they do. You can't tell by looking at them, but they're poisoned—like, if you eat too many, you go blind, or crazy, or you become sterile or someshit. They've got signs at the pier and boat ramp, no more than two fish a week. It's the fish's revenge, I guess, even though it's really the big power plant that sits on the side of the lake that does it.

"Fish don't need hassling," my stepfather says to no one, meaning me.

I close the lid.

Usually, whenever my stepfather wants to tell me something, he'll make some general comment or filter what he's got to say through my mom instead of just talk to me. Not that I'm complaining.

I go sit behind the steering wheel and look at the screen mounted there. It shows how deep the lake is below the boat, and the size of any fish passing below. I wonder if it would show a dead body, if there's a picture programmed in it for that. *See, son,* a dad'll say, tapping on the screen, *that's a child. We only need the small net.*

"Monster off the port bow!" I shout when a large fish swims on screen, to be helpful.

My stepfather ignores me.

My mom reads her book.

The fish swims away.

A Choice of Ends

I don't like to fish. I just don't. Maybe it's genetic. My dad never fished, and we were never big on any of the typical father-son stuff. Like the one time I dragged him outside to play catch, the ball missed my glove on the first throw and bounced off my skull and over the fence.

Instead, my dad used to take me to Civil War battlefields, re-enactments, history talks where minié balls and pottery shards were passed around the audience of old people and us. He left three years ago, when I was nine. He got a new job in Shreveport and told my mom he needed to start over in the city. Which is pretty funny. I mean, have you seen Shreveport?

Once, before I discovered I don't like to fish, I was baiting my hook with a cricket. A *live* cricket. I, who was never one of those boys that likes torturing insects or cats or anything, could not get around the central fact of this action: the sticking of the hook through the cricket's (live!) abdomen. The cricket jumped in my fingers, twitching its legs. I brought the hook to its side, pushed a little, then my fingers loosened and the cricket got away. Chasing it, I knocked over the carton of crickets, a dozen more got out, and the one I was chasing jumped into the lake. So there you go. Drowning versus impaling.

If given the choice, I think I'd do the same.

Exhibit A

A while back my stepfather was cooking dinner when he told me to drop a piece of chicken into the Fry Daddy.

"Gotta learn how to cook," he said, and so like an idiot I went over and took a drumstick and dropped it in. When the oil popped I jerked my hand back and he said, "Scared?"

Right then I knew I'd screwed up, that I should have just kept walking out of the kitchen. He hummed something menacing—a hash-up of *Jaws*—and grabbed my wrist, forcing my hand to the hot oil until it was just an inch from the fizzing surface. When I finally pulled my hand loose, he said, "Lighten up."

I didn't say anything, just laughed like I'd been in on the joke from the beginning.

There's still a round brown scar on the back of my hand from where the oil spattered.

The Water's Return

My stepfather moves the boat over to the bridge to fish for perch. From here you can see the dam. Little orange buoys mark out where you're not supposed to cross. I imagine a boat accidentally drifting in there, its outboard burning against the strain, a whole family with their rods and lunchmeat sandwiches being pulled in, under and through the turbines.

"Kids, I'm so, so sorry," the father says, on his knees. "I'm sorry, too," the mother says. "We are full of regret," they both say as they weep.

My mom says, "Why don't you fish a little?" She puts down her book and picks up her rod.

I tell her there's no way I'm putting another cricket on a hook.

My stepfather casts his line out. He and my mom married two years ago. When he came into the family, it's like he saw us as a bunch of softies he needed to toughen up. "Y'all need to get outside more," he'd say, "see the sun." But where he tanned, we burned, and even though he took us camping and fishing and paid for us to go on horse rides, none of it stuck. My stepfather must have been surprised when he got me. All along he must have wanted a son to teach all this crap to, and there I was—a chubby kid who'd rather watch *The Price Is Right* while downing a bag of Cheetos than gut an animal. I can't say I blame him for being disappointed.

"Put a worm on it then," my mom says.

I say OK and get one of the rubber worms from the tackle box. I pick a green one with sparkles. Then I cast and the line actually goes out a respectable distance. I take my time reeling it in, stopping and starting the line in erratic jiggles to make my worm more life-like. It probably makes my worm look like it's got epilepsy. All part of the plan, I say half aloud. What fish could resist the easy prey of an epileptic worm?

While I'm reeling in, I watch the lake. It's pretty new, only about ten or fifteen years old. There aren't any real lakes in Texas—they're all built with dams. People used to live on the bottom when the lakes were still farms and ranches. It must be awkward for their ghosts, I think. To find fish swimming in and out of where they used to sleep.

My science teacher, Mr. Homeniuk, says Texas was covered by a sea in prehistoric times. So maybe all these new lakes do belong here. Maybe we're the ones in the wrong place.

A Bad Habit

At school, I get good grades. Like, really good grades. I mean, I've still got five years to screw up, but my grades are good enough that some of my teachers are already talking college.

In math class I don't have to listen too much because the work comes easy. One day I was bored and playing around with my textbook and accidentally marked one of the pages with my pen. So I took my pencil and—careful, hiding what I was doing from Mrs. Pickett so I wouldn't get into any trouble—erased the pen mark. It came off, but so did the lower half of a fraction. Where the ink and denominator had been, there was just blank page. I erased the other numbers. They disappeared. Without a trace.

At first I was scared. This was *tampering with school property*, the thing our principals are always getting angry about. But then it was like, hey, they'll never catch me. They still don't know who set the practice field on fire.

During class I erase more numbers. Not too many—not enough to tip off the next poor kid who gets the book, whose little world won't add up. And you have to do it right. Like if the number's 14, you don't erase the 4. That's just stupid. You erase the 1. Sometimes I turn to the answers and erase a couple numbers there, too.

Exhibit B

A month ago we were at a barbecue at one of my stepfather's friends' houses. These people breed Rottweilers in their backyard, and while we were there the barking never stopped. "You get used to it," my stepfather's friend said. He was a short man without a neck, like a movie gangster, and he called all of the dogs Beauty. He was showing them off when one of the dogs, Beauty #4, bit at me through the cage, her teeth snagging my shirt.

I could already hear my stepfather's comment. *Guess she don't care for lean.* So I acted like I didn't even notice and picked up a stick and poked at the dog through the cage's wires, just to mess with it, to show I knew which side of the cage I was on. It was the kind of thing my stepfather would do, I thought, but before I could even touch Beauty's side he came and grabbed the stick out of my hand and asked what the hell I was thinking. Then he shook his head like I was stupid and walked away.

Later, when no one was looking, I grabbed a hotdog and set it outside the cage where Beauty couldn't reach it. I watched as she pressed her nose against the wires and whined, like that would make the hotdog roll closer. She strained and strained and I didn't do anything to help her.

The Train to Nowhere

My line catches and for half a second I think I've got a fish. But then there's no pull and I reel the line in, dragging up a beard of hydrilla. I tug it off the hook and throw it back into the lake.

Hydrilla's like seaweed, except it grows in the lake. So lakeweed, I guess. It's not supposed to be here. It accidentally came in on someone's boat, or someone brought it here to kill off something else, and now it fills the lake, wrapping itself around outboards, fishing lures, your legs and arms if you actually go for a swim in this toxic dump. It's green and slimy and looks almost sentient.

"OK. I fished," I say.

"You see that," my stepfather says to my mom. And through her to me, of course. At first I think he's talking about my defeatism, as he calls it, and going to say something about how kids today (meaning me) need more discipline, but then I see he's pointing at the shore. He does this a lot, wherever we go. Spots wildlife like he's our hunting guide. Part of that whole toughening us up scheme, I guess. So if me and my mom ever have to survive on our own in the woods or something, we can spot animals. Which will comfort us, I suppose, as we die of starvation.

"I don't see it. What?" my mom says. She's got this stupid pink hat on—like a baseball cap but with an oversized bill—that ties in the back with a bow, and the bow jiggles as she jerks her head looking up and down the shore.

"A nutria," my stepfather says. "By that log. Now it's gone into the water."

I don't even know what a nutria is.

"Oh, shoot," my mom says. She's always disappointed when she doesn't see something my stepfather points out, like it's this big deal. And for half a second I think, hey, maybe she's right. Maybe I'm the idiot for not paying attention. Maybe I should be staring at nutrias after all.

Not long after my dad moved to Shreveport, he quit his job and started selling belt buckles and canteens at reenactments. He said it was his dream. He grew a beard, started dressing up like he was in a tintype and working on a book about some guy named Corporal Edwards who fought in the Civil War. He told me all this in a letter, said he was going to Xerox the book himself and sell it for five dollars. But I haven't seen it yet.

Behind me I hear a whistle and I turn to look at the power plant. A little train runs from the plant to somewhere else—I don't know where—and brings back coal. Maybe there's a coal mine nearby, though in school when they gave us maps with little pictures showing Texas's natural resources, I didn't see a coal nugget. An oil derrick, yes. A cow, yes. A cotton boll, yes. But no coal nugget. So maybe it's just a stockpile of coal this train goes to. Anyway, the train only runs back and forth from the plant to wherever the coal comes from. It does this all day and all night too, I guess. Right now it's headed to the power plant, its cars filled to the top with coal.

I point to the train. "You see that?"

No one looks.

The Wind in My Hair

My favorite part of a fishing trip—yes, I do have a favorite part—is when we speed across the lake to find a spot to fish or speed back to the boat ramp. I sit up front and let the wind hit me. I like going places fast, even if it's not really any place I want to go.

Sometimes I imagine rolling off the boat when we're speeding across the lake. Balling up my legs and wrapping my arms around them, then tumbling off. It would hurt, I know. I've gone tubing before, and every time I fell off the tube it was like someone slapping me in the gut, hard, before I sank into the water.

But my fear isn't how it'll hurt when I land on the water. It's the propeller. What if I somehow roll the wrong way, get sucked under the boat and shredded by the propeller? It's a small propeller, sure, but it scares me enough.

Still, it would be nice to hear my mom scream in worry. It would be nice for my stepfather to stop the boat to save me.

Exhibit C

Just last week we were at a different lake, camping, when my step-father said, "Heads up!" and pushed me underwater. I flailed, the murk flooding my nostrils and my mouth as I tried to scream.

"Don't be such a pantywaist," he said when he let me up. "I was just horsing around."

I told him I wasn't scared, that he was too quick, I didn't have enough time. Which was a big lie, of course. I went after him to grab him, to pull him under. This was a rare sight: me trying. But he just looked at me and said it was too late. And it's like I finally knew. Of course I could never win. So I said I didn't give a shit. His back was turned, and I muttered it, but I meant it. I swam some more, my feet catching at tree roots, and didn't give a shit.

A Narrow Escape

In math class, I was erasing more numbers when Mrs. Pickett called my name. I'd been taking too many chances. Like, I'd erase a whole problem, which is just stupid because it shows my hand. I mean, when you look from problem eight to problem ten and see this huge blank space in between, it doesn't take a genius to figure out something's off.

I started to sweat. Mrs. Pickett was looking at me, and the class was quiet.

"Could you come up to the board and help Jason with this problem?"

Oh. That's all. "Sure," I said.

At the board, Jason breathed in my ear and whispered "pussy-licker" at me while I finished his problem.

I whispered, "You wish," and only when I sat down did I realize the perfect comeback. *You fucking bet I am.* I said it now under my breath—"You fucking bet I am"—and Jenna Blalock, who's already thirteen, flirts with everyone, and has the third biggest tits in our grade, turned around, her eyes wide in mock horror.

Later, during lunch, I thought of what I'd say if Mrs. Pickett ever did catch me. It's perfect. It's in every after-school special and probably every teacher's student psychology handbook. "What is this?" she'll say, pointing to some empty spaces. "That," I'll say, "is a cry for help."

Back to Port

I've got a sunburn now, so there's that. My stepfather puts another fish in the livewell, ripping the hook out of its jaw like it's nothing, and then decides it's time to go home. My mom's been ready for a few minutes. I've been ready for hours.

I help prepare the boat, though no one asks me, taking down the raised fishing seats so they screw in level with the deck. Then I sit in the one up front.

My stepfather heads us back toward the boat ramp, opening up the motor when we get to the part of the lake where the hydrilla isn't so bad. The boat bounces a couple times when we cross someone else's wake, and then we round a bend and come in sight of the beach, where the Army Corps of Engineers trucked in sand so people can swim and play in a lake that poisons fish.

"You're going to help me clean these bass," he shouts up to me, and all of a sudden I'm sick of it, I'm so sick of it. He knows I hate cleaning fish: the dead scales sticking to my fingers, the fish blood on my hands. And of course my mom's just sitting there, saying nothing.

Once, when I wrote to my Dad and told him how crappy things were and begged him to let me stay with him, he wrote back that life is about adjustment. I couldn't tell if he was talking about me or himself. He went on about Corporal Edwards, saying how when he returned home from the war, he found chickens roosting in his cabin, his wife run off to New Orleans. *But I'm not dead,* I thought, *and I'm not going to be in some book.*

The shore's rushing toward us, and I'm about to mouth off when it comes to me, the daydream from my other fishing trips. Me tumbling over the side, my mom and my stepfather seeing it all and springing into action to save me. I picture how they'll worry, the quick sad flash in their faces. And then it's like, why not? I mean, what if this is the thing, the one thing that'll make everything else OK? And then it's like I can't not do it. I look around. The lake's clear. I think about it, and then I stop thinking about it. I ball my legs and grip my knees, and I go.

Halfway over, I hear my mom shriek. I'm in the air, and my stepfather's killed the engine. For a split-second it's like it's all falling into place. They're watching, I know they're watching, and I want to keep this moment forever, the quiet, the smell of the lake below me, the wind twisting in my hair, everything belonging, me belonging, just like I wanted.

Then I glance back, and it's all lost. They haven't seen me. That pink hat has flown off my mom's head. That's why my stepfather stopped the boat. They're looking the other way, watching as the hat floats on a breeze. And it's like, really? Really? I take a breath, but before I can shout to them, the lake reaches up to slap me and pull me in, and I'm gone.

Ben Stroud's stories have appeared or are forthcoming in *One Story, The American Scholar, Subtropics, Boston Review,* and other magazines. He has received residencies from Yaddo and the MacDowell Colony, and while a graduate student at the University of Michigan won three Hopwood Awards: for short story, novel, and essay. Originally from East Texas, he has most recently been living in Wiesbaden, Germany.

MARISSA BASS-STROUD

*F*ishing *always seems to be treated as this wondrous, spiritual event in fiction. I guess we have Hemingway to thank for that. I've got nothing against fishing itself, but I've never been very good at it, and part of me thinks of this story as my "anti-fishing-story" story. It grew out of memories of my own fishing trips with my parents, but I didn't get the idea for the story until a few years ago when I attended a reading by Jim Shepard. I was inspired by the energy of his voice—something about hearing other people read their work always helps me with my own. With this story, it all came at once: the fishing trips, the landscape of that lake (based on the actual Martin Creek Lake), the kid's voice. By the end of the reading I more or less had the story blocked out—though it took me several years to get it right.*

Kevin Wilson

HOUSEWARMING

(from *The South Carolina Review*)

Mackie's son needed help with the deer. "It's in our pond," Jackson said to his father, "and we've got a housewarming party tomorrow afternoon and this damn deer is in our pond. It's dead, by the way. I don't remember if I told you that."

"I assumed that," Mackie said. "This is the first I've heard of a housewarming."

"It's just some people from work," his son said without pausing, "It's no one you would want to be around."

"How did it die?" he asked.

"Well, it drowned, I guess. It's floating in our pond. I don't know what else to tell you."

"You want me to come up there?" Mackie asked.

"Why do you think I'm calling?" his son replied, and both of them hung up the phone without saying another word.

Mackie had driven the route from his own house to Jackson's cabin over a dozen times in the last month. Since Jackson and his wife, Cindy, had bought the house in November, Mackie had been coming by to help renovate, make it livable.

Two weeks after closing, his son called during his break at the factory, and told him, "Cindy says we should put new tile in the kitchen before we move in, since we're doing all these other projects at the same time." Mackie showed up at the empty cabin,

Cindy was staying with her sister until the repairs were finished, and found the boxes of tile waiting in the kitchen, the old lino-leum pulled up and curled in the corner of the room. He started mixing mortar, snapped on his kneepads, and got started. The house smelled of new paint and wood chips, and Mackie wished he'd brought a mask for his face. When his son got off of work, his truck winding down the long driveway, headlights flicker-ing through the trees, Mackie was cutting tile with a wet saw he'd brought from his own house. With each cut, the water shot into his face like sparks, his eyebrows dripping wet. "We're mak-ing good progress," Jackson said, peering inside the house at the kitchen floor.

"We are," Mackie replied, drying the reformed tile with a towel, touching the new shape along the smooth edges.

Mackie's knees ached from the constant kneeling, fitting the tile into place. His son was standing over him, his pockets filled with foam dividers to place between the tiles. It was good to work together, Mackie feeling his son's eyes on his hands, learning how to make things work. Another piece had to be cut and he did not want to stand again, to walk to the front porch and lean against the saw. "Jackson," he said, "hand me a tile." Jackson walked gin-gerly to the box and brought one back. Mackie took out his red pencil and marked off the section, handing the tile back to his son. "Make that cut," he said. Jackson went outside and Mackie listened to the whine of the saw as it started, the sound of metal touching ceramic, and then he heard his son shouting, "Goddamn it all." Mackie shot up, immediately blaming himself for not doing it to begin with. He was already hoping for the best of the worst, just a finger, not his thumb.

"Motherfucking, son of a bitch," his son was screaming, down on one knee, facing away from Mackie. The wet saw was turned over, the dull gray water pooling around it. When Mackie knelt by his son, Jackson stood up and pushed past his father, back into the house. Mackie looked around for a digit, blood, but he didn't see anything. He ran back to the house and found Jackson in the bathroom, water running, examining his face. "A goddamned piece of tile popped up and hit me in the face." Mackie looked at his son's reflection in the mirror; a small cut was bubbling blood just under his right eye. "I could've been blinded," Jackson said, staring angrily at Mackie. "Don't we have any son of a bitching goggles?" Mackie shook his head. Jackson turned off the water, took out his handkerchief and pressed it against the cut. "Well I'm driving to the Wal-Mart to get some then." His son was out of the house, into his truck, and pulling out of the driveway, while Mackie stood on the porch, lifting the wet saw upright. He worked until midnight, waiting for Jackson to return, and finally gave up. He rolled out his sleeping bag and slept in his clothes, waiting for morning, listening to the house settle around him.

The next day, Jackson showed up with a bandage covering the wound, a pair of goggles resting on top of his head. "Got to be safe," he said. "We can't get hurt anymore." Mackie nodded and they worked into the evening, finishing the job.

When he got to the house, Cindy was waiting on the porch. "He's waiting for you," she said. "It's awful, that deer. You can see it from the house, just floating in the water. Its eyes are open." She hugged him and then pointed towards the trail, which led down to the pond. "Don't let him get too angry," she said. "He takes everything so personally. This isn't his fault, of course." Mackie nodded. "I know," he said.

Jackson was throwing rocks at the deer, which was floating about ten or fifteen feet from the shore, its swollen belly rising above the surface of the water, a small island. Mackie stood and watched his son for a few seconds without making his presence known. His son had surprisingly good aim, the rocks cutting through the cold air and thumping against the belly of the deer. "Fucking deer," his son said to no one. Mackie wondered if Jackson was trying to sink the deer, trying to get it fully underwater and hidden. He stepped out from the trees and waved to his son.

Jackson nodded, then threw another rock. "This isn't going to be pleasant," Jackson said. "I know," Mackie responded.

Jackson had come back to Tennessee last year, to stay, Mackie hoped. After high school, Jackson had left to work as a mechanic in Hunstville, and then moved around the southeast for the next eight years, never staying long in any one place, Mackie's letters to him bouncing back with no known forwarding address. He would wait until Jackson's next phone call, locating his son for the time being. Sometimes he would get calls from prison, Jackson asking his father to post bail and Mackie would be in the car, driving for hours to Louisville or Mobile or Daytona Beach to retrieve his son. This particular time, Jackson had shot out the tires of his neighbor's car. "He'd cut me off a few days before," Jackson had told his father on the drive back from the police station. "Cut me off and nearly made me slam into him. I yelled at him and the son of a bitch smiled. Smiled." Mackie could feel his son's anger vibrate within the car, as if the event was happening all over again. "Well," Mackie said, "he probably don't remember that." Jackson smiled, his face white from an oncoming car's headlights. "I know that," he said. "That's why I shot his tires. To remind him."

"We need a boat," Jackson said. Mackie agreed with him, but they didn't have a boat. He walked toward the edge of the woods and dragged a fairly long branch back to the shore, something to work with, a tool. He sat down on the ground, which was wet from the melting frost, and took off his shoes and socks, rolling up his pant legs. Jackson was still staring out at the deer, as if waiting for it to show signs of life, to swim to the shore and jump into the woods. "Okay," said Mackie, but Jackson still didn't move. "Okay," he said again, "here's what we'll do." Jackson turned and saw Mackie, barefooted. "Good lord, dad, it's thirty degrees out here."

"We have to get in there, Jackson. We have to wade out there and get that deer. Then we'll take it somewhere else. Hell, we'll just toss it on the side of the road if it comes to that, but we need to get it out of your pond. That's why you called me."

Jackson looked at Mackie's feet again, then back at the deer. "Maybe we should call animal services or something," he offered. "It might be diseased. We should get an expert out here."

"Son, they're not going to come on a weekend. This housewarming you're having for your friends? It's tomorrow. If you don't want them to see this deer in your pond, we're going to just get in the water and fish it out. Now take your shoes off, so they don't get wet."

Jackson kicked at the ground. "Let me hear the rest of the plan first."

"It's pretty simple. We'll wade into the pond, and I'll take this stick and move away from you. Then I'll direct the deer towards the shore and you get a hold of it and then you drag it in. Then we'll both pull it onto land and get rid of it."

"Maybe I should be the one with the stick," Jackson said.

"Son," Mackie said quickly, a flash of irritation striking his voice, "just take off your shoes and let's go get the damn deer."

Jackson had last been in Raleigh, painting houses or working at a guitar store. Mackie had received a postcard. *Got a job and a girl,* it read, *and my probation for the dog thing is done.* A few weeks later, his son called. Mackie had been slightly shocked to hear his son's voice, "Hey, Dad," without the usual mechanized voice intoning the particular jail where he'd been locked up which usually opened any phone call he received from Jackson. "You okay, son?" Mackie asked. "Better than okay," Jackson answered. "Much better than that." Mackie was glad to hear it, but he still would not allow himself to believe it was true.

"Amy's pregnant," Jackson said.

"Who?" Mackie asked, worried again.

"Amy. The girl I told you about in the postcard," Jackson said, his voice rising. "She's pregnant. We're going to have a baby."

"Did you marry her? Are you already married?"

"You don't have to be married to have a baby," Jackson answered, the connection fading and then coming back.

"I know that," Mackie said, feeling stupid for having asked, complicating things. "I just wanted to know if I'd missed anything. Congratulations."

"If it's a girl, we're going to name it Carla, after mom."

"That's a nice name," Mackie said, remembering his wife. His son was just a boy when she died, and it made him happy to hear that he still thought of her. "What about a boy?"

"Jackson Junior," Jackson said, "Jackson Junior for sure."

Mackie asked to speak to Jackson's girlfriend, but she was taking a nap. "I'll wake her," Jackson said, and before Mackie could stop him, the phone was set down and there was silence, humming. Less than a minute later, a voice, barely a whisper, a sore throat, answered. "Jackson said you wanted to speak with me?"

"I just wanted to say hello and to tell you congratulations."

"Thank you," the woman said, her voice still quiet. When she didn't offer anything, Mackie continued, "And I want you to call me if you need anything. If you need anything at all, you give me a call, okay?"

"I'll do that," she said, and then hung up.

It wasn't working. The branch he'd found, substantial enough to steer the animal towards Jackson, was too heavy and Mackie couldn't control it, the water up to his armpits, the shock of the cold taking away every other breath. Jackson was shivering, waist deep in the water. "I'm gonna have to get out of the water soon," he shouted, and Mackie understood that he hadn't planned this well. He felt the situation falling out of his control, into a place where Jackson's anger would surface and take over. Mackie tossed the stick into the water and began swimming towards the deer, kicking his legs under the water, his clothes weighing him down. "I'm going to push it towards you," he shouted to his son over the sound of the water splashing around him. "Wade out a little further and grab it." He finally reached the deer and touched its fur, which was unexpectedly colder than the water. It was heavy, but he'd anticipated the weight of this dead animal. The bad things he'd carried in his life had always been just as heavy as he'd expected, always measuring up to his worst expectations.

"Keep swimming," his son instructed. "Just swim a little further to me and we'll be done. C'mon, Dad."

Jackson's girlfriend called Mackie three weeks later, at two in the morning. When Mackie answered, he immediately said, "Jackson?" anticipating another phone call from jail, another thing to fix. "It's Amy," the soft voice replied. "Jackson's girlfriend?" she offered helpfully. "What's wrong?" Mackie asked. "I lost it," she said, crying. "I lost the baby."

"Oh god," Mackie said. "I'm sorry, honey."

"And Jackson," she continued, "he thinks I did it on purpose. He says I did something wrong. He keeps hitting me."

Mackie sat up in bed, felt his neck stiffen and jerk to the left, a tic he'd had since childhood, as if the danger was just over his left shoulder. "He hit you?" he asked, to be certain.

"He hits me," she answered.

"Put him on the phone."

"He won't talk to you. He doesn't want to talk to anybody."

"Amy, you need to go to a motel, or go to a friend's house. We'll figure this out, but you cannot have him hitting you. That's got to stop."

"I don't want to call the police, but I might have to."

"Amy, call them if you need to. Let me think and I'll call you back."

"I don't want him here anymore," she said. "I don't love him now."

Mackie hung up the phone and was already out of bed, putting on his clothes, grabbing his keys off the dresser. Before he knew it, he was in the car, on the interstate, going to see his son.

•••

"I've got it," his son announced, the weight of the dead animal shifting from father to son. He watched Jackson tug the deer by its legs towards the shore, a tiny wake trailing behind it. He watched the white tail of the deer and then saw a jerk in the movement, a hesitation and then there was a splash. Jackson was under the water, flailing, the deer spinning just slightly, and Mackie waded through the water to reach his son.

Jackson was thrashing around in the water, his feet and arms surfacing and then submerging, splashing water everywhere. When he realized how shallow it was, he stood up again, soaking wet, the leg of the deer in his hand. "The fucking leg fell off," he screamed. "You told me to just drag it in," he said, staring at Mackie, "but it's decayed."

"Let's get it to the shore," Mackie said. "Then we can get angry at each other." Jackson stared at his father a little longer and then turned and threw the detached leg onto the shore.

"I'm grabbing the antlers this time," Jackson said. "Pull his damn head off." Mackie pushed the hind end of the deer towards the shore. "Let's just get it out of here," he whispered.

Eight hours and he was in North Carolina, staring at his son's house, the car idling on the street in front. He saw his son look through a window and then quickly close the blinds. A few seconds later, Amy looked out the window, shaking her head. Mackie thought about what he would say to his son, how he could fix the situation. He felt foolish for driving this far without having a plan, some way to help. His son was now coming down the steps of the porch, pointing at him. Mackie still couldn't think of anything to say. He got out of the car.

"Go home, Dad," Jackson said. "I'm sorry Amy called you and that you had to drive all this way, but go home."

"Could I talk to Amy?" he asked. He could see her in the window, but her hand was shading her eyes.

"Go home, Dad. Please go home."

"Did you hit her, Jackson?"

"She lost the baby, Dad."

"Did you hit her?"

"Please go home."

Mackie punched his son in the mouth and then placed his interrwined fingers behind his son's head, pushing Jackson's face into his own knee. Jackson fell to the street, and Mackie was already pulling him into the car, placing his body across the backseat. His son was unconscious, his mouth bleeding, and Mackie slammed the door and walked up to the house. He knocked on the door and Amy opened it.

"I need some rope," Mackie said.

"He really did hit me," Amy said. Her throat showed pale purple fingerprints where he had grabbed her, and there was a deep cut above one eye. She looked so young, barely out of her teens, and Mackie felt sick all over again.

"I know," Mackie finally said. "I'm going to take him back to Tennessee. Is that okay with you? He won't come back here and bother you."

She thought about this and then nodded. "I'll get you some rope," she said.

He drove ten miles above the speed limit, his son tied up in the backseat, groggy, shouting obscenities. He stopped only for gas, pissing in a bottle, letting his son wet himself rather than untie him. His son kept struggling against the ropes, lying on his stomach, his ankles tied to his bound wrists, but Mackie had fashioned the knots well, the added pressure only cinching the knots tighter. "Well, I'm gonna shit in my pants, you asshole," his son yelled from the backseat. "I'm your son and you're going to let me shit in my pants." He let his son shit in his pants.

After five hours, his son fell asleep and Mackie had the rest of the drive to think about what he'd done. He thought about it for five minutes and then focused on the road, counting billboards, watching for highway patrol cars. He knew when they reached Tennessee, he couldn't keep his son there. He couldn't keep fighting his son, knocking him out and hoping he'd awaken a better person. He'd do what he could, help him find a job, get him an apartment. He'd fix his son and then hope it stuck.

Back home, in the garage, when he dragged his son out of the car, reeking of sweat and piss and shit, Mackie told him about his plan. "You stay here and we find something for you to do and you get yourself straight." His son fell into a corner of the garage. "I don't do drugs," he said. "It's not like that." Mackie shook his head. "I know that. I wish it were that easy. You're a good boy, Jackson; you just get too angry. You need to understand that things happen and they're usually bad, and you just figure out how to deal with it without beating somebody up or killing their dog or setting their tree on fire. Do you understand?"

Jackson slid a finger into his mouth and spit blood. "One of my teeth is loose."

"Will you try?" Mackie asked his son. Jackson nodded and went inside to take a shower while Mackie climbed back into the car, pressed his face against the steering wheel, and kept himself from crying.

"Fucking deer," Jackson kept saying. "Fucking dead, three-legged, no account deer." They were on dry land now, both cold, getting colder in the wind. They had stripped out of their wet clothes, father and son now in their wet boxer shorts, shivering, their hair dripping cold water down their bodies. Neither had thought to bring a change of clothes. "This," Jackson said, "is getting worse."

The deer, sans leg, was still beautiful. It was an eight-point buck, the cold having preserved the skin except for a small wound at its chest and the exit wound near its right back leg. A hunter must have shot it and chased it into the pond, then decided it wasn't worth the effort, or perhaps never even found it. Either way, it was here now, dead, glassy-eyed, lying in the grass between Mackie and Jackson.

"We should bury it," Jackson said. "Cindy said to bury it." It was a nice idea, but the ground was too cold for that. The county dump was closed until Monday. "Well, we can't leave it here," Jackson shouted, "Fucking deer." Mackie thought if they could get a tarp under the deer, they could drag it to Jackson's truck and dump it on the side of the highway. "Someone from the city will come get it," Mackie told his son. Jackson seemed reluctant to agree. "Fucking deer." He finally nodded and Mackie went to find a tarp, to wrap up this deer, and to get through the day, freezing cold, soaked to the bone, but otherwise undamaged.

Two months after he brought Jackson back home, his son now servicing and setting up video poker machines at strip clubs and gas stations, the phone rang again in the middle of the night. It was Amy, her voice as soft as the first time he'd talked to her.

"Is he okay?" she asked.

"Are you okay?" he asked her. "I want to know that first, because if you aren't, I'll go make him worse."

She started to cry. "I'm okay, I think," she said. "I'm better without him here."

He told her that Jackson was trying harder to be a good person.

"I had hoped that he would turn out to be a good person," she said, "but I couldn't stay with him long enough to find out."

Mackie couldn't think of a response that would help anything and so he stayed silent.

"I wanted to thank you," she said, still whispering, as if concerned that Jackson might be listening to them. "You helped me and I wanted to thank you for that."

Before he could answer, she hung up the phone. He kept the receiver against his ear, listening to the dial tone, waiting for her to come back on the line.

Mackie was in the shed, nearly naked, looking for a tarp, when Cindy nudged the door open. "This must not be going well," she said, avoiding eye contact with Mackie.

"Do you have a tarp?" Mackie asked.

"We have extra clothes," Cindy said. "You don't have to use a tarp for that."

"No, I need a tarp to wrap up the deer. Extra clothes would be nice though."

"You can't bury the deer?"

"No." He felt unable to explain any further and she didn't push the issue. He found himself liking Cindy more and more.

After he located an orange tarp, wrapped up like a sleeping bag, Cindy waved him into the house, and he stepped into the warmth, a fire going. She handed him some clothes for both himself and Jackson and he put on an ill-fitting shirt, pants that were too tight and left unzipped, and squeezed his feet into shoes two sizes too small for him. "How is he doing?" she asked him. "He's doing fine. We just got a little wet trying to get the deer."

"Anything could set him off, I've learned," she said. "The smallest thing; you never know."

"He's fine," he said. "I'll bring him the clothes and he'll be fine."

At his son's wedding, waiting off to the side of the altar, groom and best man, Mackie rehearsed his toast in his head. Jackson put his hand on Mackie's shoulder and said, "Thank you for all this. You made this happen." Mackie shrugged. "I didn't do much," he said. "You knocked me out, tied me up, brought me back here, and helped me get a job. You did a lot." Mackie told him that he didn't want any thanks, that he was just happy he'd cleaned himself up, had found a nice woman, was settling down.

"You saved me from that woman," Jackson said.

"You mean Amy?" Mackie asked.

"Yeah, she was a bad influence. She made me think things would always be happy, nothing but good times, but that's not reality. She really had me off the rails, and you came and got me away from all that, and I want to thank you."

"I don't want any thanks for that."

Jackson pulled the flask out of Mackie's coat pocket, his gift to his father for being the best man. He took a swig of whiskey. "I filled it before I gave it to you," Jackson told his father. "So that's two gifts I gave you."

When Mackie got back to the pond, Jackson was beating the deer with his raised boot, shouting curses, now totally naked, his strikes stripping wet chunks of fur from the animal's body. Mackie dropped the tarp and the clothes and charged after his son. "Stop," he shouted. "Jackson, that don't help a goddamned thing. Just stop."

Jackson pushed his father and kept hitting the deer with the boot. "A perfect day before this fucking deer showed up," he screamed. Water was dribbling from the deer's mouth, its eyes wide open.

"Calm down, Jackson," Mackie shouted again, pulling his son away from the deer. Yanking his arm free, Jackson whirled around and punched Mackie, catching his right cheekbone, which caused Mackie to wince and release his son. Jackson ran away from Mackie and the deer, through the woods, making sounds that seemed like sobbing.

Mackie lay out the tarp and rolled the deer onto it, the water still deep in the deer's body. He knew better than to wait for his son to return. He pulled the corners of the tarp together and dragged the deer as best as he could through the woods, stopping every few minutes when his hands got too sore. He thought to leave the deer on his son's front lawn, but realized it would be cruel to the deer, the further abuse Jackson would inflict upon it. Mackie knew he would just have to take responsibility for this dead thing, until he could find a way to put it to rest.

He could see Cindy through the window of the house. She was frowning, continually looking over her shoulder at what Mackie imagined was Jackson, hiding until he was gone. He lifted the deer into the backseat of his car, shoving it into the spaces that it would go, trying to make it fit. The passenger seat was now folded forward to accommodate the head and neck of the animal, the mouth of the deer now peeking out from the tarp. There was still frost on the deer's whiskers. He waved to Cindy, who did not wave back, and drove down the mountain, the air conditioner on to keep the deer from thawing out too much, to keep the smell of decay away from his senses.

Back home, in the garage, Mackie tried to think of what to do about the deer. The options were just as limited as they were at Jackson's house. He did not want to bury this deer, the hours upon hours of breaking through the frozen earth, no matter how much better he thought it would make him feel. It wouldn't change anything. He would dig a hole and fill it back, and everything would be the same.

His teeth were chattering. His nose wouldn't stop running. He checked the rearview mirror and noticed the skin under his right eye was starting to swell from where Jackson had punched him. He opened the tarp and stared at the deer's dead eyes. He rubbed the condensation from its snout. He knew he had to get out of the car, to get the deer out of the car, but he couldn't do it, not just yet. He sat in his garage, the deer beside him, and tried to catch his breath. He waited for the muscles of his heart to send blood throughout his body, to make him warm again.

Kevin Wilson was born, raised, and still lives in Tennessee. He is the author of the short-story collection *Tunneling to the Center of the Earth*. His stories have appeared in *Ploughshares, Tin House, One Story,* and elsewhere. He currently lives with his wife, the poet Leigh Anne Couch, and his son in Sewanee, Tennessee, where he teaches fiction at the University of the South. This is his fourth appearance in *New Stories from the South*.

LEIGH ANNE COUCH

When my wife and I first moved into our house, a cabin in the woods, I found a dead deer in our pond in the middle of winter. The deer was retrieved through ridiculous means, wading into freezing-cold water, pulling it to shore. It was an unpleasant experience, but I have used the event in several works of fiction and nonfiction, so I feel that it was worth it.

My father, who is the most kind and capable man I have ever met, served as the inspiration for Mackie, though I hope I am a more decent person than Mackie's son.

Dorothy Allison

JASON WHO WILL
BE FAMOUS

(from *Tin House*)

Jason is going to be famous, and the best part is that he knows
he will be good at it.

He has this real clear picture of himself, of him being inter-
viewed—not of the place or even when it happens, but of the event
itself. What he sees is him and the interviewer, a recording so clear
and close up, he can see the reflections sparking off his own pu-
pils. It's hi-def or Blu-ray or something past all that, a rendering
that catches the way the soft hairs just forward of his earlobe lift
and shine in the light reflecting off his pale cheeks. All he has to
do is close his eyes and it begins to play, crisp and crackling with
energy as the microphone bumps hollowly against the button on
his open collar.

"A lot of it, I can't tell you," he says, and the interviewer nods.

Jason is sitting leaning forward. His features gleam in the
bright light, his expression is carefully composed, focused on the
interviewer. Jason nods his head and his hair swings down over
his forehead. One auburn strand just brushes across the edges of
his eyebrows. The interviewer is so close their elbows are almost
touching. He is an older man with gray in his hair and an expression of watchful readiness—a man Jason has seen do this kind

151

of thing on the news before, someone to be trusted, someone serious.

That is the word. Serious. The word echoes along Jason's nervous system. He is being taken seriously. Every time he imagines it again, the thought makes him take a deep breath. A little heat flares in his neck as the camera follows his eyes. He looks away from the interviewer, and his face goes still. He looks back and his eyes go dark and sad.

"I'm sorry to have to ask you about something so painful," the interviewer says to him.

"It's all right," Jason says. "I understand." He keeps his expression a mirror of the other man's, careful and composed. He can do this. Piece of cake.

Behind the cameraman, there are other people waiting to speak to Jason, others are standing close by to hear what he has to say. Everyone has questions, questions about what happened, of course, about the kidnapping and all the months in captivity. But they also want to ask him what he thinks about other things, about people, and events. In the interview as Jason sees it, he always has answers—surprising and complicated, wonderful answers.

"That boy is extraordinary," he hears the serious man tell another.

Extraordinary. The heat in his neck moves down into his chest, circles his diaphragm, and filters out to his arms and legs. He hopes it does not show on his face. Better to remain pale and impassive, pretend he does not hear what they say about him. How extraordinary he is, that everyone says so, some kind of genius. He half-smiles and then recomposes his expression. Genius. Jason is not sure what his genius is exactly, but he trusts it. He knows it will be revealed at the right time, in the right circumstances. It is simply that those events have not happened as of yet. But they will.

He opens his eyes. He has stopped at the edge of the road. Dust, white-grey and alkaline, has drifted up from his boots, and he can taste eucalyptus and piney resin. He looks up the road toward the next hill and the curve down into the shade of the redwood stand there. Should have brought a bottle of water, he thinks. Then, extraordinary. How would you know if you were extraordinary? Or a genius? He's pretty good at math, and music—though nothing that special. If he worked more, put more of himself into the work, no telling what he might not do. His dad told him that, once, when he was still living with them. His teachers have said something of the same thing. All of them though, his dad, teachers and his mom, they say it like it's a bad thing—his talents and his waste of them.

"If you worked more. If you worked harder."

They don't understand. No one does.

Jason wipes dust off his mouth and rocks his head from side to side. He knows the problem. It's not that he's lazy or stupid or even scared. No. The problem is that he never has had enough time or focus. There's just always so much that has to be done, and how does anyone do that kind of kung fu stuff anyway? How does anyone become extraordinary? Like Uma Thurman in the Tarantino movie? Years going up and down staircases. It's like that. You do some stupid thing over and over and over, and sometime along in there, you discover you have achieved this enormous talent.

He glares up the road and resumes his pace, boots kicking dust and his hands gripping the straps of his backpack. He could do extraordinary stuff. Given the right circumstances, he has everything in him to do stuff that will startle everyone. It just takes the right circumstances—getting everything out of the way. He nods to himself. He can feel that coming toward him—the opportunity, the time, and the focus.

He has dreamed it so often, he knows it is coming—though he doesn't know all of how it will happen. That too, he sees like a movie, the movie of his life going on all the time. Step in and it is already in motion. Like that. He grins and speeds up slightly. Might be, he will be walking home along the river road from Connie's on a day just like this one. He'll have something in his backpack, after working for Connie all day, doing what he does so well, little baby buds his specialty. Connie always tells him how good he is. He knows exactly how to clip and trim and harvest only what is ready to come away, leave what should be left behind. That shows talent. That shows aptitude. Bonsai killer weed work, he does that all the time. Connie knows she can trust him. Some people she strings along, but him she always pays with a ready smile and a touch along his arm or one quick knuckle push at his hip. Cash or buds, she pays him, and that's all good. Just as it is good no one knows what Jason has in his backpack. No one knows his business.

Still, he knows, the day is coming. Someone is going to snatch him up right off the road or outside the liquor store downtown—some old guy maybe, or even one of them scary old dykes from out the bay side of the Jenner beach. Those bitches are dangerous and he can barely imagine what they would do with a piece of work like him. Everyone knows they all got stuff, guns and money and stuff. Bitches like that stick together. But maybe it will be someone from nowhere nearby, some bunch of crazies with some plan he will never fully understand, that no one will understand.

He nods slowly, his hands gripping the straps tight as he imagines it—the snatch, the basement, the months alone and everything that comes after. He has been seeing it for a long time, the story in his head, the way it will happen. It was a dream the first time, a nightmare, grabby hands and the skin scraped off his knees—a nightmare of sweaty basement walls and dirt in his mouth. But by the third or fourth time he dreamed it, everything receded and it was not so nightmarish. He was fighting back and able to think. Then it was magical how he started thinking about it in the daytime, daydreaming it, planning what he would do, how he would handle things. Then what came after the snatch became more and more important. He had started imagining the person he would be afterward. He didn't think so much about the kidnapping then, or even the kidnappers. It was all about him and the basement and what he did down there, who he would become, who he was meant to become. It was set and in motion. It was coming, Jason was sure of it. Not that he thought he was psychic or anything, it was just that this big thing was coming, so big he could feel it, and he had thought it through and whatever happened, he was going to be ready.

He stumbles and stops. He is almost gasping, smelling the sweat on his neck, the dust on the road, the acrid breeze from the eucalyptus trees past the stand of old-growth stunted apple trees around the curve. He leans forward, stretching his back, and straightens to watch a turkey buzzard circling the hill to his left. No hurry. It is only half a mile to his mom's place, two twists in the road and an uphill grade. Jason shakes his head. He knows this road in its whole length, two and a half miles and every decrepit house along the way, every crumbling garage and leaning fence. Of course, everyone here also knows him, which is sometimes more than he can stand. But somewhere someone who does not know him is coming along, and they will change everything. He nods and resumes a steady pace. Everything will be made over—and he will never know when or why. It will be a mystery.

He thinks of the basement room, that dim space with the windows boarded over. Nothing much will be down there, but he won't need much. He would love a piano, of course, but a guitar is more the kind of thing you might find in a basement. Nothing fancy. Some dented old acoustic. Jason thinks about it, the throwaway object he will use. God knows what he will have to do to tune the thing. Not likely to be any help in the junk people keep in basements. But there will be paper or notebooks. The notebooks will have pages marked up, of course, but he can work around that, use the backs of pages or something. It is what he creates in the silence that will need to be written down, the songs or poems. Lyrics. He will write it all down—easy to imagine that—him singing to himself in the quiet. The pencil marks along the pages. Of course his music notation sucks. He's never been too good at that. He sighs and stops again.

Maybe there will be a recorder—some old thing probably. A little old tape recorder, not a good digital. But hey it will get the job done. He smiles and hears above him the turkey buzzard's awkward call. Ugly sound from an ugly bird. He watches a big white pickup truck drive slowly up and past him. Big metal locks clamp down on the storage bin at the front of the truck bed.

Connie's boyfriend, Grange, told Jason you could bust most of those locks with the right chisel and mallet. "It's all in the angle. Got to hit it right."

Jason has a chisel in his backpack but no mallet. He licks his lips and resumes his slow hike between the ditch and the road. You got to have the right stuff to get anything done. Unless you are lucky or have an edge.

Famous is the way to go, he thinks. You get stuff once you are famous.

Jason wipes sweat off his neck as he walks and imagines it again—the reporter, the camera, the intensity of the lights, the intensity of his genius. It will take time, but he will figure it out. Maybe it won't be music. Maybe it will be words. He's damn good with words, not like those assholes at school who talk all the time. He knows the value of words, keeps them in his head, not always spilling them out like they mean nothing. He doesn't have to tell what he knows. He just knows—lyrics and poetry and all that stuff. Good poetry, he tells himself. Not that crap they want him to read in school. Kind of stuff makes your neck go stiff, that kind of poetry, that's what he likes. He looks at the dust on his hand, sweat-darkened and spotted with little grey-green bits. Little nubbins of weeds and grass flung up with the dust as the trucks pass. He'll get on the computer tonight, look up all the words for grey-green. Emerald, olive-drab, unripe fruit, something or the other. Nothing too hard about getting the words right.

Jason wipes his hands on his jeans, enjoying the feel of the fabric under his palms. Truth is more important than how you tell it, he thinks. And he knows stuff, lots of stuff, secrets and stuff. He has stories.

Maybe that will be it, the stories he tells himself to pass the time. Movie scripts, plays, dialogues between characters that come and go when he is all gaunt and feverish. In the basement, they won't feed him much, so he will get all dramatic skinny and probably have lots of fever dreams. He'll write them down, everything. His hands will cramp and he'll go on writing, get up and pace back and forth and write some more. Pages on pages will pile up. He'll bathe his face in cool water and walk some more. He'll drink so much water his skin will clear up. His mom is always telling him that if he washed his face more, drank more water and yeah, and ate more vegetables, his skin would do that right away. Maybe she has a point. Maybe in the basement that's all they will give him. Vegetables and water—lots of water, 'cause you know they ain't gonna waste no greasy expensive stuff on no captive. No Coke, no potato chips, no Kentucky Fried Chicken.

Pure water and rivers of words. Jason grins and lengthens his stride. Maybe after a while he won't care what he eats, or he will learn to make an apple taste like a pie. That would be the kind of thing might happen. He could learn to eat imaginary meals and taste every bite—donuts and hot barbecue wings—and stay all skinny and pure. That would be something. He could teach people how to do that afterwards maybe. Some day he might run an ashram like the one his mama used to talk about.

The turkey buzzard swoops low and arcs downhill toward the river. Jason stops to watch its flight. A moment in time and the bird disappears. Things can change that fast. Anything could happen and you can't predict what might come along. But what he knows is that there won't be any distractions down in the basement, anything to get in the way. Cold walls and dim light and maybe just a shower. Might be it will only run cold water, but he can handle that. What he hates is tub baths, sitting in dirty water. No way there is not gonna be a shower in the basement, or, all right, maybe only a hose and a drain in the floor. But he knows he will bathe himself a lot 'cause what else will there be to do? 'Cept write what he knows and use the weights set. He laughs out loud. Maybe there won't be no weights, though every shed or garage he knows has some stacked in some corner or the other. If there's nothing like that in his basement, still there will be stuff, something he can use.

He grabs his backpack straps again and begins the uphill grade. His steps slow and he focuses on the notion of making do, figuring out what he will use. Stuff like old cans of paint or bundles of rebar or bricks left lying around. He'll Tarantino it all, laying on the concrete floor and pushing up and down over and over till his arms get all muscled, and his legs too. He'll push off against the wall or doorjamb or something. He's gonna be bored out of his mind. He'll get desperate. He'll be working out, running in place and lifting heavy things—whatever he finds. Yeah, he'll get pretty well muscled. He grins. That is how it will be. He's going to come out just amazing.

Jason looks up the road, quarter of a mile to his mom's turnoff. He's right at the spot where the old firebreak cuts uphill, right up to his dad's place. He can almost see around the redwoods along the hill up to the house. He won't be like his dad, he thinks, he won't waste his chances. He'll grab what comes and run with it. When he comes out of that basement, he'll be slick. That is what it is all gonna be. Slick and sure, and he will know how to manage it, not wind up house-sitting for some crappy old guy wants you to carry stuff and keep an eye on the dogs.

Fuck it. Jason says it out loud. "Fuck it!" He's gonna come out of that basement Brad-Pitt handsome and ready for anything. He'll be ready, all soulful and quirky like that guy from the White Stripes, only he won't take himself too seriously. Everyone else will do that for him. He'll know how to behave.

Jason laughs out loud again. "Yeah," he says. Yeah.

Serious. Yes. That's the word. He is going to be seriously famous.

That's when his mom will realize how shitty she has treated him. Then his dad will hear about it, for sure—and maybe let him come back up to the house and hang out. Of course that creep that owns the property will be around too, but Jason knows it won't be scary like last time. He'll have all those muscles, and he will have gotten past being scared of small shit like grabby old guys and dads that don't give a shit.

It will be different. It will all be different. His mom and his dad will work it all out. His dad will be his manager, his mom will take over the press stuff. You got to have someone handle that stuff, and if the creepy guy comes round to stake some kind of claim, it won't be no big deal. Everyone will know how to handle him—what to believe and what to laugh at. He can almost hear his dad talking loud in his growly hoarse voice. He can hear him finally saying what he wanted him to say before.

"Jason didn't take nothing off you, old man. Look at him. What would he need off you?"

Yeah.

But maybe he will let the old guy hang around. Jason thinks about it, looking uphill and remembering. He gnaws at the nail on his left little finger.

Maybe not.

Why would he want that old bastard around?

He thinks about his dad, what he looks like now, all puffy and grey around the eyes with his hair so thin on top. His dad had this belly on him that he tries to hide under loose shirts, and he's always worried about money and stuff. That kind of old is embarrassing. After the basement though, his dad will be all different. He'll be old, but not so gross. He'll be more like Clint Eastwood old, craggy and wise. That's the notion, and his dad will have figured stuff out all that time worrying about Jason. Things will be different once he sees his son clear. Maybe he'll even own the property by then. The old guy can't live forever. Maybe he'll just give his dad the top of the hill as a kind of death tip. Might be it will turn out like that guy in Forestville a few years back, that black guy who got the thirty acres in the will of the man he worked for all that time.

That could happen. And then if his dad needs someone to help him with things, Jason will be there. That bad leg will hurt his dad a lot by then, even though he will try not to show it. Jason could do stuff—carry things for him and give him a hand. Maybe that is how they work it out—all the anger and guilt and shame and resentment. He can see that too, hear how it will go, them finally talking.

"You had no business running off like that, leaving Mom and me, I was just a little kid."

"You don't know how it was, how desperate I had gotten. I couldn't take care of you the way I wanted to, and you know your mom. She was always telling me I was lazy and the world wasn't gonna wait for me to get myself together."

That was just the kind of thing his mom said all the time. Jason nods. His mom can be a real pain in the ass. He sees himself looking at his dad and trying to imagine how he had felt when he had left. Maybe his dad had left in order to get himself together, to try and make something of himself so he could come back and take good care of them. After all that time cold and miserable and hungry in the basement, he will be able to feel stuff differently. Even standing in the dust of the road he can imagine his dad looking at him with an open face. Maybe they could talk finally, and it would shift all the anger around.

Maybe his dad will get to the point where he can look at him and see Jason clearly, see how he became so strong in that basement. Maybe he will finally see himself in his son. Of course, like everyone, his dad will know the story, how the kidnappers beat him, and starved him, and how Jason endured everything and stood up to them. It will make stuff in his dad shift around. He will get all wet-eyed and ashamed of himself. Jason can see that—the moment between them as real as the interviewer and the cameras, the moment burning him right through to his backbone. He almost sobs out loud, but then stops himself. His eyes are closed. The wind is picking up the way it always does as the afternoon settles toward evening. There is a birdcall somewhere up in the trees, but Jason is inside seeing into what is coming, what has to come.

They will touch each other like men do. Men. Yeah. Maybe his dad will embrace him, say his name. Jason can see that. It is as clear as anything. That is how it is in stories, how it is in his head, how it could be.

Jason sways a little there by the side of the road in the sun's heat. His ears are ringing with electric cricket sounds, the buzzard's cries, and the movement of the wind. Still, he hears a vehicle coming and the sound of its tires on the gritty tarmac. Rock and redwood debris grinding into dust and crackling as the wheels turn into the bend. Jason can see that, the wheels revolving and grinding forward. He imagines the kidnapper's truck, white and thick like one of those big Dodge Fat Boys, but one with a camper on the back—just the thing for snatching a guy off the road. Slowly Jason lets his face relax into a lazy smile. He doesn't look back. He keeps his eyes forward. His mom is always telling him to stop living in a dream, to be in the real world. But this is the real world, the road and the truck and everything that is coming toward him.

Anything can happen any time.

Everything can change, and it is going to, any time now.

Any time.

Any time.

Now.

Dorothy Allison was born in Greenville, South Carolina, but these days she lives just outside Guerneville, California, with her partner, Alix Layman, and teenage son, Wolf Michael. Her books include the novels *Bastard Out of Carolina* (1992) and *Cavedweller* (1997); a book of essays, *Skin: Talking about Sex, Class, and Literature*; and a book of poetry, *The women who hate me*; as well as a collection of short stories, *Trash* (2003). A novel, *She Who*, is forthcoming.

BRETT HALL

*T*his story started when I was stopped at the main intersection in the little town where I live and found myself watching the boys who were hanging around the gas station, hands in pockets and hoods pulled forward.

They were working hard at appearing tough and grown-up, but I knew enough of them to be sure none was more than sixteen.

One of the boys suddenly turned and stalked off alone, his backpack hanging over one shoulder and his muddy shoes almost coming off with every step. The slump of his shoulders seemed impossibly sad, but as he turned to head for the bridge he threw one hand up and shot out a middle finger as if he were cursing not any particular person but the whole world. "Boy needs someone to shake him hard," I thought but then flushed with heat. He was no one I knew, a child in the world and for all I knew someone had already shaken him hard. I started imagining him, who he was, what he was thinking, that long walk across the river and up into the hills.

A few weeks before I had heard another writer say that he was sure he could finish his new book if only he could connive a stay in jail. "Too many distractions out here," he told me. I had laughed and nodded.

"But jail is pretty noisy," I told him. "You wouldn't get as much time to think as you imagine. What you need is to be shipwrecked somewhere with an empty notebook."

"Tuna fish," he said pensively. "A stack of notebooks and a case of tuna fish. I could get everything done."

I had laughed again, but his fantasy was no so far off my fantasy. Maybe we all imagine what might be if only. If only. This is that story, the one about living in hope if only.

ARSONISTS

(from *The Georgia Review*)

The phone rings just as he's zipping his suitcase shut, even
though he hasn't seeped a word to anyone in town, but Dell
is not surprised. Kenny always knows. Five years ago, Dell would
have let it ring; ten, he would have cussed it, too. Now he cups
the back of his head with one hand, shuts his eyes, and says hello.

The first call is Becky, gobbling desperate—"Dell, you got to
get up here, get him to himself"—before the receiver is grabbed.
Dell hears the scuffle, and the connection thumbed off. Within
fifteen seconds, it rings again, Kenny this time—"You just stay
where you're at, boy, I don't need nothing from you"—before that
call goes dead, too. Dell waits until the glow of the number pad
darkens in his hand, then calls them back.

"Listen, Becky." He says his words like flat creek rocks laid. "I'm
sorry. I am. But it's my little granddaughter's birthday. I'm just out
the door to northern Virginia."

"Oh, Dell, I'm sorry, too, I'm just as sorry as I can be, but I've
been trying to talk sense to him for two hours. It's the them-
coming-to-burn-us-out again, only now he's saying he's got a
bomb strapped to his wheelchair and's gonna blow us all up when
they get here, Dell, I don't know where else to turn."

Dell tips the receiver away from his mouth. The birthday present
lies beside him on the bed. "Can't you at least try?"

"He don't want me in there, you know that better'n I do, *please,* Dell."

The wrapping is twisted sloppy, the white undersides of the birthday paper showing. It was Carol always took care of that. Dell shuts his eyes again, his middle and first fingers forked below his brows. "All right," he says. "I'll be up."

"Oh, I thank ye, Dell" . . . the gobbling again, "I thank ye, if it weren't—"

"Put him on first."

He waits. When enough time has passed for Kenny to lift the phone to his ear, Dell speaks to the silence. "They ain't yet burned one with people still in it, Kenny."

The nothing on the other end lasts so long Dell wonders if Kenny hasn't hung up and he's just not heard. Then a mutter comes.

"Boy. You just don't get it." The voice rasps to whisper. "This house is worth so much they don't got the money to put an offer on it."

Although it'll take at least a half hour to crawl the busted-to-pieces road to Kenny's place, Dell does not rush. Kenny'll never touch Becky, and anything he's ever owned that can shoot or blow up is locked in Jason's old room in the upstairs of Dell's house. He gets Carol's Geo Metro started, his truck sitting with a bad alternator, and goes to scraping the windshield with a spatula. He had called Jason as soon as Kenny hung up on him the second time.

"I don't suppose you could hold it a day, could you, son?" He winced at his selfishness soon as he spoke, so it was mostly relief he felt when Jason said no.

"All her little friends are coming over. I'm sorry, Dad."

"I understand," Dell cut in quick. "Don't you worry, I understand." And while Jason talked on, Dell felt, as he always does, the surprise and then the pride: his youngest son, at twenty-four, speaking into his own phone, sitting in his own condo, surrounded by things he's provided for his wife and two kids. Jason already that kind of man. He built houses in northern Virginia, went up there at first thinking the job was temporary and then found himself plunged happy over his head in the construction boom, earning overtime every week and sometimes even more than that.

"We'll do something, too, when you get here, Dad," Jason was saying. "Manda'll like that. Make her birthday two days long."

He's forgotten to turn on the defrost, and the coffee he stowed on the dash has steamed the windows good. Dell smears holes where he needs them. Then he is stuttering past the padlocked beige trailer that was the Tout post office, past the old gas station/ grocery store with its window shattered into webs, and—here and there, rotten teeth among the sound ones—the burned-down homes. Dell sips his coffee careful, his eyes narrowed on the road. Some of the houses are just scorched, their windows like blackened eyes. Others went full blaze, gaping open now, their charred rooms exposed—a pitiful vulgarity to it, Dell can't help but feel. Others are nothing but steps climbing to rubble-cluttered concrete slabs. The kudzu already covering. Overhead, the flattened hills roll in dead slumps, like men's bodies cold-cocked. That's how Dell sees them when he brings himself to look—like men knocked out. The humps of their twisted shoulders, their arms and legs drunk-flung. Sprouting their sharp foreign grass.

The company is finished with Tout, West Virginia, now.

Somebody started burning houses within a year after they blew up the first mountain. More than a decade ago, Jason still a boy, Carol still with them. In the worst of the blasting, dust stormed the hollow so thick Dell couldn't see Sam Sears's house across the road, and everybody'd had to burn their headlights, their house lights, right through the middle of the day. A few people'd even videotaped it—Lorenzo Mast had, and Sibyl Miller—back when some believed bearing witness could make a difference. That year there was no summer green, no autumn red. Everything ever-gray and velvet.

Sam got him and his wife gas masks from an army surplus store, but Dell made do with a scarf. Standing on his front porch, a winter muffler wound round his face, watching the horizon dissolve in linked eruptions like the fire-cracker strings him and Kenny'd a couple times got hold of as kids. Blasts thunder-clapped the wishbone of his chest, and the rock dust taste was familiar in his mouth. Dell looked on at first in disbelief and even awe—it was nothing fancy they used, ammonium nitrate and fuel oil, exactly how Tim McVeigh bombed Oklahoma City at about the same time—but quick that turned to outrage and frustration and, finally, helplessness and grief. Which was at last, Dell understood now, a different kind of awe. *Brimstone*—the word would come to Dell, he couldn't help it. It came on its own in the taste of the rocks. And through it all, the hole opening in him. The hole small at its mouth, but boring deeper, deeper. Craving always to be filled.

Six months into that gray blizzard, the company started offering the buy-outs. By then, a lot of the properties were good and blast-busted, with walls cracked, ceilings dropping, foundations split. Wells knocked dry. By the time the offers came, the homeowners had been told by the Department of Environmental Protection that they couldn't prove the damage hadn't been there before the blasting started, and no one had the lawyer money to argue with them, so many people sold, even at the pathetic prices offered them. If their houses weren't shot, their nerves were, and those who could start over, did.

Dell and Carol talked about it, too. Discussed it, argued it, full-on fought. Lying in bed of a night in the silver glitter of the lights on the mine, Carol crumpling Dell's hand under her chin. Pressing her lips there. Shouting at each other once while they were power-washing the dirt crust off their house–that comes back to Dell too often now, the splatty roar of the spray, the expense of the rental, and still the dust sticking like paint. How hard it was when you got nowhere else to put it not to take it out on who you loved. Sometimes Dell'd take the leave side and Carol'd take the stay, then by next time, they'd have traded places on it. Bottom line was, Dell was pushing sixty, had taken early retirement, and where were their life savings? Right there in the house. Like a big pile of money blowing away littler and littler with every explosion, every dust cloud, every coal truck crashing through town.

They reached the final decision one afternoon while they were reframing family photos and Carol's needlepoint, fixing them sturdier to the walls. They simply couldn't begin again on what the house would fetch now. Dell remembers how they weren't even sitting when they decided it, they were standing in the living room, finished with rehanging the last picture. He remembers the gray cast to Carol's face, the afternoon having just reached that moment when it's time to turn on the lights. The minute they made it definite, there came in Dell a peculiar painful rightness that he recalled from when he was a kid, back when he used to bang his head against his bed frame, against walls, usually out of anger, occasionally to salve a shame. And for a day or two, the little hole hushed its yearning.

In the meantime, the other houses were bought up; the families packed; the homes darkened. And then, when the machines finally began to retreat, still blowing up ridges but farther away, and just when Dell and Carol thought the dust might lay . . . the smoke came.

The Williamses' house went first. They'd been gone for several months, and it sat there at the far end of town, no neighbors on its one side, and Dell and Carol and Jason slept right through the fire. Woke in the morning to the odor of smolder. Slept through because although everyone left in that end of Tout had called it in, no fire trucks showed. The second fire came about three weeks later, then the third, both in abandoned company-bought houses. Then they burned regular, about once a month, the glows of the closer fires quavering Dell and Carol's window, choking them awake on their trash smoke stink. Sometimes the firefighters came. Other times Dell rushed out with the neighbors and their sorry garden hoses, trying to contain the flames. But what has stayed with him tightest, longest, is not the panic or the odor or the colors of blaze. It's the noises. The pops of little things blowing up in the houses, the whoosh-roar of bigger, the shuddering, wrenching cracks, then the crashes as roof parts cave in. It is the ripple sound of flames moving good. The "I'm coming" like sheets of canvas flapping in wind.

For over a year, they burned. Still, even living in the middle of it, no one, no matter how close they watched, could figure out how they were lit or by who. The arsonists couldn't be caught, even though there was a clear design, never did a lived-in house ignite, always the deserted company-owned ones, and usually those houses targeted were some distance from inhabited homes; only once did a fire jump to a place where people lived. The mysteriousness of it all terrorized everyone even worse, and more people sold, just like the company wanted. If they couldn't shake them out, they'd burn them out—Dell suspicioned this at the first one, and by the third one, he knew. But every house burned was company property, just like county law was company property, just like state law was. When some official finally arrived to investigate, the company was behind that, too.

They pronounced it vandalism. Local boys. The locals, the officials reminded them, had a long history of vandalizing company property.

By this time, the holdouts were patrolling with shotguns in pairs. Kenny came down off the mountain to help, him and Dell doing their turns together. Jason begged in on it, too, and for nonschool nights Carol finally said yes, although Dell never let him go farther off than reaching distance. They'd stake out the houses most likely marked and, if they had enough people, post two men at each one. If they didn't, they rotated between them. Houses burned anyway, but never on Kenny and Dell's watch.

"I know what's going on," Kenny started grinding. "Somebody ain't got the balls to hang in there, face who it is. Or else somebody's lazying off. Sneaking home for a nap."

"I believe you're right," Dell eventually agreed. "I believe you're right."

After August, they didn't say that anymore.

Five men were on duty that night, Dell and Kenny and Jason

covering the rancher that had been Lorenzo Mast's, Charlie Blizzard and his cousin Burl on the other house across town. Dell and
Jason were hunkered down in lawn chairs in the brush behind the
Masts' backyard, Kenny guarding the front from his own chair in
the blackened house frame across the road.

Dell pulled his undershirt away from his skin, him sticky with
sweat and Off and the bugs still biting. Beside him, Jason slept
in an upright slump would have left a six-day crick in Dell's neck.
The Coke can was already warm and slippery in Dell's hand, and
he wrangled a colder one from the stash in his old lunch cooler,
his fifth of the night, its sizzle like another layer of locust shriek.
The core of his body was pulling down hard toward sleep, but his
skin and his mind rode the caffeine current, memories and images
roiling up like drift. First him and Carol, at their beginning, and
that led further back to a wild girl who'd been his high school love.
And then the pictures were of him and Kenny, who'd come before
any woman, those images, too, moving in reverse: the first day
of their first real job, working underground; the night they got
arrested, running the roads drunk at seventeen; the shared frustration of second-string in junior high basketball. Then clear back to
a time in grade school Dell had almost forgot, both of them sent
to Mr. Dickens' office for a paddling. Dell couldn't remember for
what, and the paddling hurt, but being watched by each other was
worse, which is what Mr. Dickens made them do. Dell didn't cry.
Kenny did. At least that's how it comes to him now.

He drained the last of that Coke and shoved the can under
his chair. Stepped deeper into the weeds to take a piss. When he
turned back around, he saw the light.

At first he didn't believe it, but quick it went from a winking
glimmer to a blaze, ripply but constant. Dell snatched up his
twelve-gauge, thumbed off the safety, jerked Jason awake. And
then he was straining on the balls of his feet, every inch of him
taut, him twenty years younger, thirty pounds lighter, not an achy
place in him save the effort of his eyes. The loud part of his body
hollering, *Go,* Dell, *Run,* close in and *grab* him, while his head

hissed, *Hold* your place, *hold* it, you take off now and you'll never see him if he flies out the other end, Dell's eyes searing the over-grown juniper bushes against the house, the single back door over its three-stepped stoop, the five shutterless windows in their neat row. The fire was accelerating now, furying from the middle of the house into both ends until the whole building was puking flame, every window sheeted with it, flames battering out the roof, and Dell knew the burner had to have been flushed. Couldn't no one survive that hot, that high.

"Kenny's got him!" he yelled at Jason, and his boy took off so fast he slipped down on one knee. Then they were tearing through the yard toward the side of the house, Dell as fast as Jason was, not feeling his body, not feeling the house heat, all the while knowing— Dell did not expect, he *knew*—that Kenny'd either be chasing the arsonist or have him at gunpoint.

When Dell careened around the corner and into the front, he at first couldn't find Kenny, what with the neighbors streaming in, faces red-lit, them still in the commotion of what to do. Dell finally spotted Kenny because he was the only person standing still. Kenny paralyzed in the road, taut-frozen, a mirror of how Dell'd been out back, Kenny's gun stock in his armpit, the barrel resting in his left hand, and not a soul at the end of it. Dell rushed up to his side, and as Kenny recognized him, Dell saw from his face that just as much as Dell'd expected to see two there, Kenny'd expected them to come as three.

Kenny slammed his shotgun to the ground. Dell jumped back, pushing Jason behind him. "Goddamn you, Kenny," he heard somebody yell even though the gun didn't trigger. "Watch your-self! Watch yourself!"

Not long after that, Carol got diagnosed and Dell turned his attention there. A couple more abandoned houses were torched that year, but as the machines gutted the mountains in the middle distance and then pulled even farther away, the fires stopped, too.

After Dell quit, Kenny only kept it up a month or two more. By then, they were closing in on his own place.

It had been on one of those watch nights before the Mast house burned, Jason not with them, that Kenny had said it. Coming on toward dawn, and them meeting up to share a cigarette after guarding separate houses all night, they heard the clunk of the monster bucket in the distance overhead, and the hish of dead earth poured over the hillside. Kenny said it just once, and in the dark. Said it not as a question, didn't risk contradiction or conversation. "What we did, Dell," he said. "It wasn't like this here."

Through Dell, a cold gust flashed, from his groin to the top of his chest. He wet his mouth to speak back, to agree. Then he stopped and let it go.

Now he takes the turnoff to Kenny's leery and slow, the road cratered dirt with asphalt stumps rearing up out of it until it breaks down to no pavement at all. Dell straddles the worst of it best he can, eases the car into the holes when he has to, the jolts up his body so bad he can't tell if his bones are scraping together or pulling apart. Used to be a creek run down along this road, the same creek that used to run by Kenny's house. They played in it as boys, back when both him and Kenny lived down in Tout and it was Kenny's grandma on the place. When Kenny got too worked up—oh, that temper, how he'd beet like a redhead, windmilling punches at air—his grandma'd screech, "You all get outta here! Go getcha in the creek!" And she was right. Even back then, water worked.

He drives by the barred haul road to the shutdown part of the mine, the guard shack plywooded over, the sign beside it peppered with pellets: COAL KEEPS THE LIGHTS ON. The last couple places him and Kenny worked, they passed every shift a sign that said that, too. Right beyond that fork, the road returns to mostly hardtop, and Dell leans into the gas. Not long after, he hits the first of the NO TRESPASSING signs Kenny's hung all along the borders of his property and right up to his front door—some store-bought, some homemade—and finally, Kenny's house swings into view.

It's a big four-bedroom. Single-story, but rangy and imposing, built against the steep hill with a grand high deck on two sides. Painted a two-tone blue, baby for the walls, navy for the trim, and a full basement, a two-car garage. It makes the house that was up here before, the one Kenny's grandma lived in, look like a goat shed. Makes the houses him and Kenny grew up in down in Tout in the forties and fifties look that way, too. But Dell can see, if he squints through the half-leaved autumn trees, the mine, crunching away to the horizon like Satan's gravel pit. The house, the bit of woodland around it, the sweep of yard that Becky cuts with the ride mower, Becky and Kenny themselves—they are surrounded on three sides. Living inside a nutcracker's vee.

Dell pulls up beside Becky's Blazer on the parking pad Kenny poured and jerks his brake. He reaches for his door, then stops. Sets his hands back on the wheel. Kenny crows tirelessly about how nothing nor nobody in the world will ever make him sell his place, but the truth is—nobody's offered to buy it.

Becky meets him at the bottom of the deck steps. "Oh, Dell, I thank ye. I thank ye, and I'm sorry, I am so sorry." She has an old denim coat of Kenny's thrown over her shoulders, and she's rubbing her fists on her thighs in fret. "I feel so bad about you missing your little Amanda's birthday, but where else can I turn? Where else can I turn?"

Dell knows sorry for him is about the least of her worries right now. "It's all right," he says. Kenny found her at a church function a while back, and she is fifteen or twenty years younger, and not real bright. His sensible wife, Doria, left back at the beginning of this mess. Now Becky is blocking the front door, her hand on the knob. "He says he's gonna roll that wheelchair up on the mountain and suicide bomb 'em, and he's already tried to get out on the deck twicet."

"We'll get him settled down," Dell says. "We'll get him settled down."

He works his shoes off in the little entrance hall. Kenny always insisted on that, and it used to annoy hell out of Dell. The ancient poodle with the stained under-eyes slingshots out of somewhere to harass his pants cuffs until she recognizes him and retreats, snuffling, to one of the big floral-patterned armchairs. Dell takes a breath. Then he follows the dog into the living room.

Kenny sits at attention in his wheelchair. Ironed jeans, steel-toed boots, a paisley pajama top. The chair is pulled up to the picture window, and under Kenny's right arm is snugged the black plastic case of a student-model guitar. The neck of it follows Kenny's fore-arm. The tip is pointed at the pane. Dell clears his throat.

"Hey, buddy." The bellow in his own voice catches Dell off guard, even though it's how he usually talks to Kenny now. "What's going on up here?"

Kenny snaps his head around. As if he's not watched Dell all the way up the drive, didn't have him and Becky at the end of the gui-tar case when they stepped up onto the deck. Kenny stares at Dell a hard five seconds, working a little his mouth. His eyes ringed dark, his face caved so the bones stand in peaks, and his silver hair slicked, he reminds Dell of a chicken-coon cross. The eyes slide off Dell's. Kenny pivots back to his vigil.

"Done got that side." He swings his free hand to the left. "Done got that side." Flings it past his face to the right. "Done got all that behind, and now they're coming after the front side, too. Gonna burn me and her out and blast right up under the house."

Behind Kenny's back, Becky raises her eyebrows and nods, See? Dell ignores her. He saunters across the persimmon-colored carpet into the kitchen, where he takes a place at the table so he can watch Kenny across the living room. Everything Dell does, he does nois-ier than usual, including an exaggerated sigh of contentment when he settles into the chair. Kenny does not turn around.

"Can I get you a cup of coffee, Dell?" Becky asks, like she always does, her overloud too. At least she's quick enough to remember her lines.

"Oh, yes, please." Dell booms. "Don't mind if I do."

"Black, right?" Becky asks.

"Black's right," says Dell. "Like my pap always said, 'Drink it black, or don't drink it at all.'"

On the little TV next to the microwave, Rachael Ray's whipping up some kind of Mexican dish. Dell thanks Becky for his coffee, and she sits across the table with her own, sugaring it heavy enough for a cake. Then they commence the pretending-to-watch the show, each sipping slow, now and again making a comment to each other for normalcy's sake. Both with an ear, an eye, constant-cocked to Kenny.

Dell can remember when Kenny's whole family had to live in this one room, the kids doing their homework on sawhorses. How Doria'd hung Christmas decorations on the insulation the December before they got the drywall up. Kenny built the house little by little, whenever he had the money, and Dell'd helped him off and on until he'd get sick of being bossed and take a break for a while. He always came back, usually after Kenny called and asked him to drive up and see some new tool or piece of equipment he'd got, which was as close as Kenny could come to an apology.

Dell sneaks a full-on look at Kenny. He can feel that it's still too soon.

Becky refills his cup. He'd had to ask Jason many times to show him the houses that he built before Jason finally did, one time about a year ago. A subdivision, Jason explained, an old horse farm split up. He and Jason glided in Jason's new Ford Explorer over fresh-paved streets through acre after acre of immaculate vacant homes, bulked up and bulging on undersized lots. The streets deliberately unstraight, snake-tailing into dead ends that made no sense, the area everywhere treeless, hill-less. Until Dell, despite how he'd looked forward to this, despite his pride in what his boy did—build things—started to get carsick for the first time in sixty years. He had to ask Jason to stop. By this time, they'd reached the outermost ring of the maze, where houses still under construction stood half-naked in their pressed woodchip skins, their Tyvek wraps. Dell stepped out and breathed deep: odor of raw lumber, fresh-poured concrete, and something chemical he could not name. He looked over his shoulder, expecting Jason behind him. Jason sat in the Explorer, fooling with his cellphone.

Dell hits the bottom of his second cup. Usually that signals that the wait's been long enough. He glances at Becky. She opens her hands in an I-don't-know. So Dell reaches toward Kenny, not with his body, not with his hands, but with the how-long-he's-known-Kenny—that's what he uses to catch where Kenny's at. But still Dell can't tell, and if he starts too early, Kenny won't play. Dell goes on and risks it.

"Hey, Kenny," he calls, forcing a casualness in his tone. "I hear you all been getting some real bad shakes up here." Dell waits. Kenny does not move. Dell swallows. "I don't see no cracks, though."

He waits again. The poodle tumbles off the chair and disappears. Then Dell does feel it off Kenny—a stiff ripple up his back, a prickling above his ears. Without turning from the window, without the slightest stir of his head, Kenny sneers, "Ha. Look there. Above the refrigerator. See there?"

Dell lifts his face, squints, and frowns, even though the cracks are as visible as the grandchildren's coloring book pages on the freezer door. "Huh. I can't see nothing," Dell says.

For some seconds, the only sound is Becky's fist, a sushing against the denim of her thigh. Then Kenny blurts breath in disgust. He thrusts the wheelchair back and heaves himself to his feet, hobbles a step or two, unstiffening. Then he stomps across the living room without a limp.

"Right there, you blind ole sumbitch. Right there. See where I tried to patch it up, bought that stuff from Lowe's? See what a sorry job I did, trying to patch it together?"

Becky vanishes like the poodle. Dell squints deeper. "Oh. Okay. Yeah." He nods slowly. "I see it." He gets to his feet, Kenny right up beside him now, wagging the guitar case back and forth from his waist, and Dell can smell the aftershave heavy on him. Dell reaches up on tiptoe, gritting his teeth against the old pain that lightnings down his right leg, and runs his fingers along the splits. "That is sorry."

"You never seen such shaking, buddy, the night that ceiling busted open." And now Kenny is going. "Here we was, just setting eating supper, had a big pitcher of ice tea there in the middle, and they set one off"—he leaps back, throws out his arms, the guitar case slamming into the door frame—"blew that pitcher clear up off the table. And she didn't tip, boys, she didn't tip, but tea sloshed out all over ever'thing. Spoilt our spaghetti." He swings the guitar case at the back wall. "Got them windows, too, that time. But I done replaced those."

"It's terrible." Dell shakes his head, freshly mournful and shocked, as though they've not already had this exchange eight times, ten. "It's just terrible." Then he cocks his head, studies the cracks more intently. He spreads his thumb and first finger to take the measure of one. "Huh. But I think I seen bigger cracks than these down at Charlie's." He nods thoughtfully. "Yeah. Believe I did. And over at Miz Reynolds', too, come to think of it."

Kenny starts working his mouth, his teeth rabbitting his bottom lip. The eyes seem to steam; Dell can see the wet glow. Finally Kenny snorts. "You did, huh? You did?" He reels away, the case grazing Dell's arm, and marches into the hall. "Well, you follow me. You just follow me."

Dell does. Kenny is heading for the fractures behind the photos in the hall, skipping both the living room and the garage. The tour is going so fast that Dell wonders, like he did last time—that tour shortened, too—how much Kenny is truly led on and how much he's performing, exactly like Dell and Becky are. "See here? My sheetrock?" Kenny has unhooked the picture of his son Roger in his high school football uniform, and the one of him and Becky getting married, and he thumps the wall with his palm. "Here how I tried to paper it back over?" "Yeah," Dell is commiserating, "I see what you mean, them ones are deeper than Charlie's," and as he says that, he's cramming down the other, what he dares not think in words but what boils up anyway, forcing itself through the cracks: that maybe, just maybe, the tour will shorten and shorten, until . . .

Then Kenny speaks again, his voice dropping to a husk: "And I got something else to show you, buddy. Here in the bedroom." He twitches his shoulder back toward the kitchen, and for the first time all morning, he grins. "Not even she don't know yet,"

The half hope drops out of Dell like a trapdoor in his gut. His face heats, his fists curl—he did think it, did jinx—but still he follows. He tails Kenny into the room, the air close and slept-in, Dell cringing with the queasiness he always feels in other people's rooms with beds unmade. Kenny is already in the closet, thrusting aside clothes on their hangers, and he calls, "Lookee there, Dell."

Dell looks. A dim, cream-colored wall.

"I don't see nothing, Kenny." He says it in his normal voice. Not the pumped-up playacting one. Not the one that goes along.

Kenny drops the guitar case, whips his free arm up, and jerks a cord. A bare bulb in the ceiling snaps on. "See there?" Kenny's voice is both soft and shrill. He is looking past Dell, to make sure, Dell knows, that Becky has not sneaked in. "Them scorch marks on the wall."

The wall shines bare in the harsh light. Dell does not speak.

"That's where they got it set. They test-runned her the other night, just to see how it worked. Left them marks there." Kenny lowers his arm, the hangers clashing back into place, picks up the case, and shuts the closet door, gently. He leans forward from his hips toward Dell's ear. Dell's arms pimple. "They got a three-mile-long fuse, Dell. End of it laid right under my bedroom."

Dell feels himself falling away. Kenny shrinking before him, although neither of them has moved, the distance widening, a rushing noise come in. Kenny seen across a featureless gray field. For twenty years, they strip-mined together—contour jobs, peeling the sides off hills. They'd both worked underground first. And after years in tunnels, what it meant to get up on top, nothing about to fall on you, the machines doing all the heavy work, no more black dust. To be up out of the dark. And they'd been proud of what they did, they made America's electricity, they kept on the lights. The money they earned raised their kids comfortable, like they deserved—way beyond how him and Kenny'd come up— refurbished Dell's old company house to modern, built Kenny's from the foundation up.

But to blow the top off a mountain. *It wasn't like this here.* Still, by now Dell understands the little hole inside him, boring down, down, farther than he knew he went, yearning always to be plugged. And all Dell can do is pull a screen across it.

Then the distance dissolves, and Kenny is regular-sized before him again. Dell hears himself speak.

"How's your bathroom holding up, buddy?"

Dell closes the door at the end of the hall behind them. He squeezes past Kenny and sags down onto the lip of the tub, twists on the spigots and lets the water run hard, his hand in the gush. Kenny's clapped the commode shut and dropped his guitar case again, which skitters against the metal trash can and drives it into Dell's leg. The temperature right, Dell stops the drain and sits studying the vinyl tile on the wall. He can feel Kenny behind him almost as certain as a touch, sitting on the toilet unlacing his boots—thinking what, Dell never knows. Only when the tub's full and Dell cuts off the water does Kenny stand and start to fumble with his clothes. The soft plomp on the floor, the clank of the belt buckle. Like he always does, he comes to the tub edge with his boxers still on.

Dell rises and takes Kenny's upper arm, a little rough. A helping hand, not a petting hand, not a comforting one. Kenny gets his leg over the rim, and Dell eases him down until he sits slumped in the water, his arms around his knees. All the muscle in his back has fled to a pile of sags at his waist. His skin is colored like a speckled cold grease.

That time Dell'd visited Jason a year ago, the time they'd gone out to the construction site, Kenny hadn't stopped him before he left, but Dell'd had to cut a five-day stay two days short. Becky'd called at eleven at night, swearing she'd spent since noon trying to get Kenny to himself, oh, she was terribly sorry, but where else could she turn? Dell had to sleep first. He was way too old to make an eight-hour drive in the middle of the night after playing with his grandbabies all day. He had set his alarm for four.

When he woke, he feared at first he'd overslept, light as it was outside, until he understood it was the condo complex's security lights. He'd never driven in northern Virginia before dawn, and as he loaded the Metro under floodlights, there stirred in him an uneasiness mingled with awe. Then he was passing under the streetlights that canopied the suburb's four-lane main drag; the gas stations, office buildings, stores, sidewalks, and the street itself were completely peopleless, him the single car, and all of it, everywhere, lit bright as an emergency room.

Dell's shoulders were hunched, the wheel was dampening under his hand—when, suddenly, the light turned to sound. The strip malls first—they burst into roar, a crowd in his head—and then the box stores, Target and Home Depot and Sam's, them louder yet, squalling and hollering bald blares of light. Among them the fast-food places, Wendy's, Burger King, Taco Bell, Sonic, each shrieking light, and then the quaint and quietful places—coffee shops, boutiques. Dell heard them, too, hissing their squander of light.

He was speeding now, his eyes cramped to just enough pavement to let him safely drive, his body braced, his heart held. And then he was out and onto the highway, hurtling south and west, toward home, his body easing, his breath coming catch-up in his chest—when he heard, from the near distance in what used to be fields, the wailing flare of subdivisions, each one, he knew, either uninhabited or asleep. Yet each one haloed in a great conflagration of light.

In the corner of the tub sits a tall plastic Go-Mart cup Becky keeps there for the purpose. Dell reaches for it, sinks it into the bath, and lifts it full, water dribbling into his pushed-up sleeve. He looks at Kenny's back, and for a second, Dell knows the chill of Kenny's bare skin, and for that second, a tenderness spears him. Dell banks it down. He tips the cup. Water sluices over Kenny's spine. Dell dips again, lifts, and pours. Again. And again. Sloshed water dabbling his knees, an old hurt wrenching his shoulder. Until Kenny starts to come back to himself.

Ann Pancake is a native of West Virginia. Her books include the short story collection *Given Ground* and the novel *Strange as This Weather Has Been.*

ANITA NOWACKA

*A*rsonists" *was inspired by the mysterious burning in the late 1990s of a town below a mountaintop removal mine in Logan County, West Virginia, and an interview an activist from North Carolina and I did with a retired coal miner. This man's home was surrounded on three sides by a mountaintop removal mine, and although his intestines had been ruined by his runoff-poisoned well, his mind was sound. I sat there on his couch drinking black coffee with a chihuahua named Cupcake huddled behind my back and marvelled at the blast cracks on his ceilings and walls. He looked at me and said, "It's like living with a gun to your head and you never know when the man's gonna pull the trigger." I thought about what it'd do to your brain if you lived like that too long.*

Aaron Gwyn

DRIVE

(from *The Gettysburg Review*)

They were driving back from Wewoka Lake on the narrow stretch of blacktop east of town. They'd been fighting all morning, and she'd been drinking all morning, and now she was drunk. He didn't think she was pretty when she was drunk. Her face turned red and rigid. She was sitting in the passenger seat of the Charger, staring out her window, and he'd turned the radio off so he could think. All his thoughts were mean and desperate. He couldn't get them to stop circling. They hit the straightaway right after the curve by the brick plant, trees on both sides, the black oaks leaning so that the road seemed like a tunnel, and the light inside it a strobe of shadow and sun.

His hands were twitching. He was sober. He didn't think he'd been more sober, and looking at things, clear headed as he was, he felt like it was finished. They'd never have kids, get married. They'd never have a lot of things, and when he thought about starting over with another one, something inside him seemed to fall. He didn't know what it was. His sternum felt frozen. There was a cool ache in his throat. He tried to clear it, but he couldn't.

The sun seemed to dim.

A van met them and slipped past. Then a pickup and trailer. He could see the sun reflect off the glass of another about half a mile away, coming their direction, and when the glint of it hit his eyes, he went cold and numb. He couldn't feel his fingers or face. It was like his hands belonged to someone else. They gripped the wheel at ten and two, and he watched them tighten and the knuckles go white, and then he watched, as if on a monitor, them steer the car into the oncoming lane. Jill didn't seem to notice. She probably thought he was trying to pass. But then he started accelerating, up from sixty to seventy to eighty-five, and right before the truck coming toward them began flashing its lights, she glanced up, and then over.

She said, "Jesus Christ, Jimmy! What in the fuck?"

He looked at her. He felt very calm.

When he looked back to the road, the truck coming toward them had begun to brake, and they were about a hundred yards away. He bore down on the pedal and clenched his jaw. He could feel his back teeth grinding. He didn't know what he wanted. He felt like he was floating or coasting. He felt like his mind was stripped bare, low to the ground and gliding fast. Right as Jill began to scream, the approaching pickup swerved into the opposite lane and went past in a blur of paint and chrome and a Dopplering of horn blasts and squealing tires.

She was saying, "My God." She was saying it over and over. She wouldn't look at him, and when he glanced at her, her face was completely drained of blood, and she was shaking.

He pulled into the right-hand lane, and when he turned into the driveway ten minutes later, feeling had returned to his hands and face, and he could sense his body. Jill was motionless, mute. She was staring at the console in front of her, the glove compartment. In it was a signature series Dan Wesson .357, five of the chambers loaded with Black Talons. She knew he kept it there. He leaned over and hit the compartment release, took out the gun and holster, and then got out and went up the walk to the house. He fumbled with the lock a moment and then he was inside and through the living room and up the hallway to the bedroom. He walked over to the dresser on his side of the bed, opened the drawer, and buried the pistol under a pile of socks. He sat there and tried to think. His skin was tingling. He decided he'd put the gun back before work in the morning. He decided he needed something to drink.

He went back down the hallway to the kitchen. Jill was standing in the living room. He hadn't heard her come inside. She was short and petite and darkly complexioned: dark eyes and hair and skin. She was twenty-seven years old, and she looked, of a sudden, twenty-one. The years had been burned out of her face. She looked like she'd gotten in from a run. He leaned against the wall a moment and stared at her. She was standing very still in her cut-off shorts and bikini top, her hair pulled into a ponytail, wisps of hair trailing around her ears. She stared at the carpet just in front of her. She had her hands held out to either side as though to steady herself.

She looked up and noticed he'd entered.

Then she started toward him.

One moment she was standing motionless, and the next she was moving, faster then he'd seen her move, and he thought she was going to hit him.

But she didn't hit him.

She came up, and he turned her and pressed her against the wall, and somehow she wrapped herself around him, climbed up, and was at his neck and ears and face. Her body gave off a strange heat. It almost hurt to touch. He held her very tightly, and they were kissing in a way that seemed vicious and fierce. He carried her down the hall toward the bedroom, but they didn't make it to the bedroom. They made it as far as the bathroom, and as he carried her, she came. She squeezed into him and screamed, and her entire body convulsed. It had never happened like that. They were both still clothed. He'd not even touched her there.

Then they were in the bathroom, and she was seated on the counter with her legs around his waist. His belt was off, and he was inside her. She was weeping and grabbing his hips and pulling him into her harder.

She said, "Motherfucker."

She said, "Kill."

She said other things.

She said something that sounded like *grate*.

Afterward, they lay atop the covers of their bed with the air-conditioning prickling their skin and her against him as though she'd wear him for warmth. He didn't understand what had happened, and he thought he loved her very much.

She turned at one point and kissed him gently on the cheek.

She said, "Don't ever do that again."

Of course, he did it again.

Why wouldn't he do it again?

He felt she wanted him to, and it wasn't something she could ask with words. She had to ask other ways. It was something he had to know.

Two weeks and they were coming back from the city after meeting friends for dinner. They'd made the Earlsboro exit and were driving past the county dump. It was just dark, and the stars were swarming up above them, and the trees beyond the bar ditch at either side of the road reflected moonlight in shades of green. Theirs was the only car on the highway. Jill reached over and brushed her nails very lightly against his arm, and he knew at once what she was thinking. She didn't have to say a word. He thought that they'd found something outside sex or speaking. He pressed down the accelerator, and the night began rushing past.

Her breath quickened. The time before, she'd been angry, but this was something else. When they topped the hill and descended the final stretch of blacktop before the 270 intersection, there were headlights in the distance.

They didn't speak. Her nails grazed his arm. She was making a loose fist and then releasing it, making a fist and releasing, letting her nails trail across his skin. The headlights were a mile off, and he gave the Charger more gas and watched the needle on the speedometer track up to 110. The front end trembled. Her nails stopped moving. They stopped moving and settled and then started to dig in. He pressed the pedal to the floor and steered across the center line.

The headlights were closer. They seemed to hesitate and twitch. You couldn't know what the other driver was thinking, and Jimmy didn't care. He wasn't doing it for the other driver, and he wasn't, he thought, doing it for himself. Something had opened up. He was nearer than he'd ever been. He didn't wonder about losing her. He didn't worry she'd disappear. They'd discovered something on the road by Wewoka Lake, and when you discovered something, there wasn't any going back. He didn't even see why you'd want to or how you could. They were going forward, fully forward, faster and faster like the car in which they traveled, on toward the lights that seemed to have stopped moving. They were running at 116 miles an hour with the engine whining in fifth gear and her nails clawing his skin and the two of them like one thing, watching, the Charger passing the motionless car, and not even honking this time, no telling what they thought, just wind moving past and the bright blur of the headlamps and the night rushing back to darkness as he eased off the accelerator and allowed the car to coast.

They started calling them *drives*. He'd turn and ask if she wanted to drive, and she'd know what he meant. There were drives that weren't *drives*, but more and more that were. He couldn't come out and say that's what they were doing. If it was a *drive*, he'd have to pretend it wasn't. She needed it to be like that. She'd ask it with her eyes.

She'd ask with her eyes and her cheeks and the way she'd tilt, to him, her face. She'd incline it just so, and he knew she was asking him to ask it.

And he would.

A week later, they pegged out the Charger on the flat stretch of highway headed toward Norman, traveling west. Sundown. Cool and cloudless. Jimmy steered into the passing lane going up a hill, no cars coming, but you couldn't see to know. Anything could suddenly crest out and come barreling into your teeth. When they topped the incline and looked down to see nothing on the road below them, he glanced over to the passenger seat, and she was grazing her nails along her thighs then reaching with one hand to caress her neck.

She sucked her top lip between her teeth.

Her eyes fluttered.

Then the Tuesday following. This time running slower and at dawn, a fog rising from creek bottoms along 99, and the car pushing through mists and trailing behind it two vortices of turning vapor. You couldn't see anything twenty yards ahead. Jimmy behind the wheel with love and terror churning inside him and thinking, as they parted the morning haze, that the territory into which they traveled was a territory of adoration and fear. Both drew them closer, pressed them, no distance and one mind watching, the old primal mind, reptilian.

And always afterward, after they pulled back into the drive, morning or evening, the two of them having at each other like teenagers, and with the same sense of wonder, and panic, and awe.

Her body was changing. She was changing inside it.

At first it was Jimmy who had changed, or Jimmy who had acted, and the action changed him, and her, changed them together, though somehow at different speeds. She was going faster than him now. She was accelerating, faster and faster. She was astride him, seated atop his hips with her shins braced against his thighs, not bouncing, but actually *riding,* the way a jockey will a horse, faster than bouncing, more controlled, her knees on the bed at either side of him, and now leaning forward, both palms braced against the center of his chest, turning her head as though looking back to someone, someone not in the room, and her eyes clenched and teeth bared, crying out, and him little more than a stump or post, because, in her velocity, she must have forgotten him entirely. He must have disappeared beneath her because now when she comes and quivers and collapses onto him, her body feels like there is no skeleton inside to sustain it, and he is not Jimmy, he is the thing onto which she's crumpled, boneless, and she just lies like that, heaving slightly and out of breath, and without looking or touching, she rolls off him and onto her side of the bed, and then pulls him to her, uses him to cover herself.

They would lie in the dark in the hours after. He had begun to feel the creep of something. Something very different.

"You awake?" she whispered.

"I'm awake," he said.

They lay there.

The air-conditioning clicked off.

The room was cold.

"Are you hungry?"

He said he wasn't.

"I'm hungry," she said.

"Eat something."

"I'm hungry all the time."

He could feel her toes against his ankle.

"You look like you lost weight."

"I have lost weight."

"You look good," he said.

"I've lost six pounds. It's like I can't get enough to eat. I'll eat, and then, ten minutes later, I'm hungry again."

A minute passed. He thought she'd fallen asleep.

"Do you still love me?" she asked.

He turned his head on the pillow and tried to see her in the dark.

"What?" he said.

"Do you?"

"Of course."

"Say it."

"I love you," he said.

"Say it again."

"I love you."

"Again."

"Jesus," he said. "I love you: I love you, I love you, I love you."

She reached out and touched his shoulder the way someone would to check the burner on a stove.

She said she loved him too.

"Are you going to get something?"

"Get what?" she asked.

"To eat."

"I don't know."

"Are you hungry?"

"Yes."

"Then eat," he said.

She said she wasn't sure.

He almost told her to let him sleep, but he didn't. It used to be something he would've said, not worrying whether it might sting. The drives had changed that, and now he did worry. They engaged twice a week in a ritual that could kill them instantly, and now he worried he might hurt her feelings if he asked to let him sleep.

"You think we'll keep this up?"

"Keep what up?" he asked, knowing exactly.

"You know," she said, and this time her hand on his shoulder was a caress. "The way we've become."

He coughed into a hand and cleared his throat. "I try not to think about that," he said.

She was silent for a time. He couldn't tell if what he said had satisfied her or if his lying had caused her to try a different approach.

"I want us to get married," she said. "I want a family."

He opened his mouth to respond, but he couldn't. He'd wanted that too, at one time, but now he couldn't conceive of that from her, and he realized it was finished.

"Baby?" she said.

"Yeah."

"Did you hear me?"

"Mm-hmm."

"What are you thinking?"

"I just—we talked about that all last spring."

She scooted across the bed and pressed herself against him. "It was different then. I don't think I was ready."

"And you feel like now you are?"

She seemed to be thinking about that. She said that now she felt she needed to be. Without it, she didn't feel safe.

He didn't know what to say. He pulled the covers off his chest and kicked them to the foot of the bed.

"You're hot?" she asked.

"A little."

"I'm cold."

"Here," he said, pulling the sheet back up. "Sorry."

She pressed herself tighter against him, laid her head on his shoulder, and in several minutes, her breathing had relaxed, and he could feel her face slacken against his skin.

Jimmy laid there. He was frightened in a way he didn't understand.

He thought he needed to try something to get them out of this.

Then he realized he already had.

The drives ended. He decided to leave. A month and a half ago, he'd almost killed them in a head-on collision because he thought she might move out. And now, just like that, he had to get away.

It was his house they lived in.

It had taken him most of his twenties to pay off, working pipeline jobs in Alaska and out West.

He thought he'd just let her have it and go.

He began to remove items from the den and place them in storage. Fall was coming into the air, and before she woke in the morning, he'd take his grandfather's pair of antique Persian pistols, or his suitcase of baseball cards, or an old photograph album with pictures of his nephews and nieces, take these in the Charger and pull in among the rows of identical aluminum-sided cells—each with a door that scrolled upward like the door on a garage—slip them into one of the cheap trunks he'd purchased, not knowing why it was these items he'd chosen and needed to protect. Standing in the morning cool with the sun not yet fully up, trying to hide his life and reassemble it.

He stood under the shower with his hands trembling.

He watched her as she slept.

Everything about her frightened him. Everything was strange.

He tried to think where he'd be when he told her. He considered moving to another town, going back West. He considered having a lawyer present, though he didn't know what for.

He thought about discussing it with a friend, but this was not something he could discuss. He couldn't disclose their drives. He couldn't allow another in on that.

And she was getting suspicious. She sat across the car on their way to get dinner, sat squinting and with her arms folded as they circled the drive-through, then sat quietly on their way home, staring out at the road with a look on her he'd never seen.

The sun was down.

The light was failing.

"James," she said, "you're not even here."

He drew a breath and let it slowly out.

"Where am I?" he asked.

"Don't be cute."

"What?"

"Don't get smart."

"I'm not getting anything," he said, braking slightly and slowing the car. "I don't know what you're talking about."

She turned to look out her window. The bag of burgers and fries in her lap and the smell of it made him nauseous. He didn't think he'd be able to eat. They started up the hill toward the airport, the city limits about a mile away.

"Why are you going so slow?" she asked.

"I'm driving the speed limit."

"You never drive the speed limit."

"I do on hills. Patrols set up all through here."

She turned back to face him. "You're worried about a ticket?"

He cleared his throat.

His chest felt thick.

He said he'd just as soon not get stopped.

She looked at him, and her eyes narrowed.

"You're breaking up with me," she said.

"What?"

"Don't lie to me, Jimmy." Her voice was almost a whisper. "Be a man, for God sakes."

"A man," he said. "Two months ago, you were ready to break it off yourself."

Her eyes started to tear. She shook her head. She wiped her face and back-handed the wet from her cheeks and said she thought they were getting married.

He focused on breathing. He watched the road.

She said, "Is there someone else?"

"No."

"Were you going to say something?"

He shrugged and shook his head. "I didn't know what to say."

She leaned back, and Jimmy thought, at that point, the fight was over. He thought he'd been impetuous moving things out of the den.

She sat slumped in her seat, almost lying.

Then she kicked the dash.

It happened quickly. She kicked with both feet, cracking an air-conditioning vent, and then she kicked the center console and shattered the face of the clock.

He had one arm out trying to push her back. He was saying her name and telling her to calm down.

She began screaming. She released a wail that seemed to come from all the way inside her. She doubled forward, and he was trying to press her back against her seat, and that was when she turned sideways and struck him with her fist.

He hadn't expected that. He raised an arm to fend off a second blow and swerved the car and checked the rearview mirror. He could feel a knot beginning to swell on his temple. She'd hit him very hard.

They passed the city limits. They began to pass construction supply and storage facilities, offices of the various production companies quartered in Perser.

There were a few moments of silence.

She began to shiver.

"Why," she told him, "don't you speed this thing up?"

He glanced at her.

"I'm not going to do that," he said.

"Why don't you give it a little gas?"

"I'm taking you home," he said. "I'm taking you to your mother's."

Her eyes cut sideways and then back to the road, and she pressed her palms together and held them. Then she drew a leg back as if to kick, but she didn't kick. She raised up in the seat and thrust her leg across the column and tried to snake her foot down on top of his and the accelerator.

He managed to push her back. He managed to keep them on the road.

"Speed up," she was saying, fast and barely coherent. "Speed it up."

She tried the thing with her leg again, and again he pushed her back. He was telling her to quit, she'd cause them to have a wreck, and she said she'd show him a wreck and tried it once more.

This time he pushed her harder and with more force than he intended and as she fell backward, her neck whipped, and her head cracked the passenger-side window. The lamination held, but the glass was shattered, spider-webbing from the point of impact so that the pane behind her was a nimbus of shattered glass.

"Jill," he said, "Jesus," and he reached for her knee, groping air.

She stared at him from beneath her brows, her eyes liquid and trembling. After the first drive she'd looked younger, but now she looked childlike and wounded. Outraged. Confused.

They drove half a mile. He reached to turn on the lights.

Something peculiar happened. Something strange came into the air. It was almost a scent and almost a breath, and it very nearly had a temperature and taste. It came from God knew where, and it was palpable, sudden. It wasn't there, and then it was. A scent and a breath and a flavor, almost, and also none of these. Jimmy thought immediately of the glove compartment and then thought, by thinking that, he'd bring it to her mind. He tried not to glance over, and then glancing, tried not to move his head.

He thought he should stop the car.

He thought again about the pistol, and this time, he did glance over, just barely turned his head, but it was too much, he knew instantly, and he knew, without any question, they'd been wired to each other or welded, fused in some permanent way, and he made for the glove compartment as quickly as he could.

Jill was faster. By the time his hand left the wheel, her fingers had already tripped the compartment release and gripped the pistol, and then she extended it, pressed the barrel to his temple, and cocked the hammer with her thumb.

It was fully dark now.

The blacktop clicked against his tires.

"Drive," she said.

Aaron Gwyn is the author of the story collection *Dog on the Cross,* finalist for the 2005 New York Public Library Young Lions Fiction Award, and the novel *The World Beneath,* published in 2009. His short fiction has been featured in *Esquire, McSweeney's, Glimmer Train, The Gettysburg Review,* and other magazines. This is his second appearance in *New Stories from the South.* He is an associate professor of English at the University of North Carolina–Charlotte, where he teaches fiction writing and contemporary American fiction.

EMILY BURGE

I wrote the first section of "Drive" pretty much as it appears in this anthology. Then I put it away. Almost threw it away. I thought the characters' behavior too extreme, bordering on implausible. The thing kept eating at me, though, and I picked it back up. As the writing progressed, I discussed the story with a woman friend. I read the first section to her, and when I paused she said, "A guy actually did that to me once," then went on to explain how, indeed, a guy had. I thought she was a isolated case. A few weeks later I read the section to another woman friend. She said, "You know, this guy I dated last year did that to me." It was their last date, she said. I mulled all this over, and then one day, at the coffee shop, I read the section to my friend, Adam. He nodded a few times and brushed a hand through his stubble. He said, "I actually did that to this girl one time." I realized I'd stumbled onto something.

Emily Quinlan

THE GREEN BELT

(from *Santa Monica Review*)

The dinner party started deteriorating when Barb burned her eyebrows off, but if every action has a reaction, then the fire resulted from the cognac, which resulted from the celebratory mood, which resulted from Leo's unexpected visit with a jujitsu belt in hand. He had taken the train down from Manhattan to Morocco, West Virginia, a thirteen-hour trip. He surprised his parents on the Fourth of July. Originally he had said that he wouldn't be able to make it down to the lake house for the holiday, but this was the way Leo created surprises and pleasure, by first creating disappointment. He brought his new girlfriend, Jiyoon, with him. Jiyoon ran an SAT prep academy in Manhattan. She was the one who had taught Leo jujitsu.

Dennis, Leo's father, bought some cognac, the good stuff, for drinking. Barb thought it was for cooking and the chicken was already skinned and crackling in the pot before Dennis thought about how he could snatch the bottle away from her. Barb was his sister-in-law; she was not a chef, not even really a decent cook, so *cognac de poulet* seemed doomed. When the column of flames shot up from the pot Barb screamed and sprung at the fire. She seemed to think that she could blow the flames out, as if the conflagration were one large birthday candle.

Dennis took the chicken out to the grill. He felt a little sick.

He thought that Barb's eyebrows were probably peppering all the breasts and thighs. His wife stood behind him while he grilled.

"Not yet," Pamela said, indicating that the chicken wasn't done. She said this a second and then a third time. She said it again when he brought the chicken inside on a platter.

"It's done," he said. "Trust me on this one. You don't even eat meat."

"It's still bone white," she said. "People like their meat charred. People like to see those grill marks."

What people? These people? "We're not feeding the world," he said.

She had begun to talk in terms of "people" quite a bit, even when it was just the two of them: "People don't understand how to use this food processor." "People need to throw these sheets in the washer." Dennis partially blamed the ladies' thespian group she had recently joined. They did plays in swimming pools, in bank vaults, in bowling alleys, in Dumpsters. The audience was required to remove their shoes and sit cross-legged on the ground. Once Dennis watched Pamela recite Ophelia's monologue while holding a pig's head. It was a real pig's head from the butcher. She had stayed up late the night before with plastic wrap, tin foil, garbage bags, and ice packs, trying to figure out the best way to transport the pig's head from the middle of their living room to the auditorium. It was the same finical care she used to take when packing the children's lunches.

Nobody ate much of the chicken. Everyone pushed it around on their paper plates. Jiyoon even served herself extra salad, only to use it in covering up her chicken. Maybe people did prefer grill marks, thought Dennis. Or maybe people believed that Barb's eyebrows were on the meat. He thought it was nice of Jiyoon to consider his feelings, though he didn't really care about the dinner—he was more excited about the dessert he had made. He smiled at Jiyoon and she frowned, as if she had caught him mocking her. He was glad to have all these people in one room together: Pamela, Leo, Jiyoon, Barb, who was Pamela's sister, Pluto, who was also

Pamela's sister, and Ray, Dennis's business partner. They owned a sink company together.

Pamela, Barb, and Pluto were fraternal triplets. When the flames had licked Barb she ran into the bathroom and shut the door. Everyone was alarmed. Pamela almost called for an ambulance. Barb screamed that she was fine. They heard water running. The door was locked. She screamed for someone to run out to her car and bring in her makeup bag. Pluto tried talking to her through the door, something about how she had gotten stoned once and set a fern on fire in Milwaukee. Now, after dinner, Barb sat on the deck in a rocking chair, pumping herself forwards and back a little viciously. The hood of her windbreaker was up and she held ice packs to her forehead. When Ray approached she let out a laugh like a hiss and said she was super and tightened the hood around her face. Dennis felt badly for Barb. She was fifty-two, built like a cabbage, and still had acne. She wore plaid jumpers with appliqués and holiday sweatshirts that played music when she touched a hidden button sewn into the sleeve. Pamela and Pluto were wispy. Pluto wore sandals with socks and smoked a pipe that used to belong to their father. Pamela was getting skinnier by the day. She wore ballet slippers everywhere and bought necklaces as big as boulders. Her favorite was an amber choker with little flies fossilized inside the beads, which Dennis found disturbing. He smiled again at Jiyoon. She crossed her arms and stared back at him.

Dennis looked at Ray, who was a good sport but always sat too far away from the table when he ate and dropped food on his slacks. Sink sales were pretty good. Neither of them needed to be at the store quite so often and Dennis had more time to spend in his garden. He called the Farmer's Weather Hotline every morning at four o'clock. He didn't grow any vegetables, but still—he liked to hear about humidity, the soil index, the rain water levels. His roses were doing especially well this year: Candied Girls, Angel Faces, and Blue Baby Climbers leaned in every direction. Last year he remembered how there had been a sudden cold snap and he and Pamela were up all night in headlamps, making newspaper teepees, heating bowls in the oven. They used straw, cordless hair-dryers, even their own warm breath to try and save the flowers. It felt good, working with Pamela like that. It felt good to be tired with her.

The sisters were getting drunk. They tried to experiment with infused vodka and shoved coffee beans, basil, and apple skins down the bottle necks. Pamela proposed swimming out to the float, two hundred feet away from the dock. Dennis said he didn't think it was a good idea to swim on a full stomach. Barb refused to wear her swimsuit when there was daylight out, but Pluto and Pamela tossed themselves into the water still wearing their clothes. They swam quickly and well, gulping the air with obscene sounds. Once on the float they started hooting and hollering and pounding their fists against their chests. Dennis was worried about them. He thought he should take the rowboat out with some life jackets. In the shed the jackets hung on nails. Their foam orange panels were spread wide, like mounted butterflies. There were the two large ones for Dennis and Pamela, and the three small ones, that Dennis had never bothered to replace with larger sizes. There was Leo's; there was Paul's, who lived in Boston and never visited; then there was Carrie's life jacket. Carrie, who was dead. Triplets ran in the family. It was hard to be a triplet! You couldn't blame anything on anybody. Always you were there, sitting right across from two copies of yourself who were doing correctly what you had just done wrong. A couple of shadows were on the heels of your mistakes, like someone taking caution to step over the slippery spot where you had just fallen down. He had gathered all this from watching his three children when they were young. He himself was an only child. Pamela said he could never understand.

It was ten o'clock before Dennis brought out the vanilla pudding cake in the shape of the American flag: strawberries and whipped cream for the stripes, blueberries and cream for the stars. They ate on the deck.

"Wow. This is terrific, Dad," said Leo. "Very festive."

Jiyoon looked skeptical. Pluto, shivering in a beach towel, stuffed tobacco into her pipe. Angela had showered and shampooed her hair, even put on some lipstick. Dennis jogged next door and invited the neighbor girl for dessert—he was trying to teach her how to garden but she killed everything in her path. Sometimes she popped rose heads off with her thumbnail just to watch them float on the lake. All she ever talked about was her sixteenth birthday, which was coming up in August. Pretty Virgo. Dennis called her this in his mind, though just Virgo to her face. Her real name was Gemma. When the girl asked for a second piece of cake he saw Pamela glance at Pluto who glanced at Barb who was peeking out from under her hood, finally having been coaxed to the table. He didn't know what they were communicating to each other. He used to be better at that, that knowing. These days he brought Pamela coffee when she wanted to sleep, tried to kiss her when she was dreaming of salad. While they ate the cake Leo talked excitedly about his jujitsu training. He looked at Jiyoon every few sentences for affirmation. They could see sparklers moving on the far shore across the lake. Purple and blue Roman candles shot through the sky.

"You've got to learn better time-balance," Jiyoon said to Leo solemnly. "You've just got to. I can still deliver a kuzushi kick to you in under six seconds." She went on to talk about her testing academy. She said that her training methods produced some of the highest SAT scores in the city, in all the boroughs. "The Bronx is getting close," she said with scorn. She explained how she wrestled with students who were tardy; she made those who forgot their homework push a Dumpster around a parking lot. A failed quiz resulted in wall-sits and push-ups.

They were all quiet.

"Well," said Pluto. "I guess somebody's got to love those kids an awful lot to put them through all that."

"Corporal punishment is illegal," Ray offered.

Jiyoon said it was only illegal if the students didn't want to be punished.

"Well," said Ray, "actually not. No."

She shrugged. "Why do we train a dog by shoving its nose in its own urine? Tell me that."

Ray began to glance around for his car keys.

During a strange moment when the liquor was gone and people were stretching and crumpling up their napkins, Jiyoon announced that she was pregnant. Leo smiled and started crying. It was the happiest Dennis had ever seen his son. Dennis thought it was strange that the green belt, not the baby, was the news they had shouted as they stepped off the train. Everyone hugged Jiyoon. Ray was drunk and clapped a little too loudly. Virgo was young and perfect, so she only wrinkled her nose—Dennis supposed that childbirth was grotesque to her.

Jiyoon and Pamela began talking about placentas, about water births, about how women used to have babies in a squatting position, hanging onto a tree limb and biting on wood. Apparently some parents buried the placenta in their yards, or even fried it and ate it.

"Say," said Dennis, "couldn't a baby drown during a water birth?"

They looked at him. Jiyoon blinked and Pamela began twisting her huge coral necklace around as if she were screwing off the lid to a jar. "Babies spend nine months in fluid," said Jiyoon patiently. "We were *meant* to be amphibious. A water birth is the only way that bond stays intact."

"You might have triplets," Pamela said.

Jiyoon nodded. "We've already thought about that," she said, indecisive, as if they had a choice in the matter.

Dennis went to get some citronella candles. "It's awfully buggy out tonight, folks. Bug City."

Nobody could fall asleep. They milled around the house, not talking, slamming in and out of the porch door. At midnight Pamela and Leo played one of their mother-son piano duets in the den. Dennis looked at how erect they sat on the piano bench, how he could see their spines stretch and move slightly under their clothes with the rhythm of the song, which he couldn't remember the name of. Jiyoon looked surprised. She said she didn't even know that Leo could play. People picked at the cold dinner that still sat on the table. The pieces of chicken were bald, unseeing, either under or over salad. They wouldn't let Ray drive home and so he sat at the water's edge with crossed arms and was petulant. Since they all forgot Virgo was there, nobody told her that she had better get home. She arranged her limbs on a lawn chair, her whole body splayed open towards the sky as if the sun were out.

At three o'clock Dennis called the Farmer's Hotline but there was no recording posted yet. He sat and dealt a hand of solitaire to himself. Pluto thought it would be funny to wake up her friend on the West Coast with a phone call. Barb swam in the dark and then drew some eyebrows on herself and fell asleep on the pull-out sofa. Pamela stood and watched Leo and Jiyoon wrestle in the yard. She turned the porch light on for them. Leo did a move where he brought his foot towards Jiyoon's jaw. Dennis gasped, but in the last second Jiyoon turned from him and drove a heel into his gut.

What had happened to Carrie was common, but also not. Nineteen years ago someone came into their house in the night and took her from her bed where she slept. A few days later, a few miles away from the house, her body was found in a wide green field, in a clear plastic bag that was sealed with packing tape. It was the summer she had refused to get into bed unless she was allowed to wear her blue bathing suit and her witch's hat.

"She *is* pretty," said Pamela, watching Jiyoon aim a roundhouse at Leo's ear, just before she sat on his back and twisted his arm behind him. A thin net of yellow pollen rose from the ground when they landed. Dennis didn't know if Pamela meant Jiyoon or Virgo. He hoped she meant Virgo—that would signify that she could read his mind.

He stood with his wife and watched the jujitsu. It didn't seem very fun to him, but competition was always good. It meant there was a prize. It meant there was something at stake.

———————

Emily Quinlan was born and raised in Morgantown, West Virginia. She received her MFA in fiction writing from the University of California, Irvine. Her work has appeared in *American Literary Review, Green Mountains Review,* and *Santa Monica Review.* She is finishing a novel and a collection of short stories and currently teaches English in Florida.

BROOKE QUINLAN

*T*his story, like most of my stories, is about family and violence. It is about both the large and the small crimes of our lives. "The Green Belt" started with Barb's singed eyebrows, a small injury. Next came the jujitsu belt, an equally small recovery. And so it went on: familial nicks and abrasions, then bandages and poultices. Finally, I realized that this family's efforts to heal themselves with holiday cakes and gardening lessons sprang from murder, from a loss that was very wide and very dark. And I have to say that growing up in a small town also influenced this narrative. Small towns have an intimacy, a collective complicity, that makes each onslaught of terror ring louder and longer. Oh, and I like funny things, too. A story has to be funny. A story should also include a lot of food.

Stephen Marion

THE COLDEST NIGHT OF THE TWENTIETH CENTURY

(from *Tin House*)

After the big snow a bright day came, so bright it hurt the eyes, and it was followed by a dusk so long and deep the earth seemed to be spilling into the sky. First it was light blue and then purple and eventually a lingering deeper blue again, and at the end of it everything was fixed and still. Even the snow, which was deep, went hard. It didn't take long to notice the cold. It was cold of a different kind than Marcus had ever felt. The surprise-meat sandwiches and even the big cart he had pushed them in on were extra cold.

It wasn't as bad in D Block as it was in solitary. When Marcus delivered their trays the two child abusers were bunnied up in the corner. Marcus looked at them and they blinked.

You shaved your head, said the one with fleshy lips.

Marcus didn't say anything.

How come you to shave your head? said the smaller one.

Marcus waited for a minute with his cart and watched them begin to eat. They had built a tent of blankets. The bread of the sandwiches themselves was chewy it was so cold. The child abusers chewed on it hungrily.

You be sorry you shaved off all of that hair, said the first one. Cold as it is.

Even among D Block it had gone quiet. The cold came right through the walls and hung around like a thick gas. Marcus didn't want to, but he went to the slot window and looked out. The jail made unusual popping and groaning noises. To him it was like a ship, or an ark, frozen in an antarctic sea. He wished he could get someone to realize what was happening, but no one did. Earlier while they were cooking breakfast somebody opened the side door and they got to see out. They saw the snow. The world was soft white and blue and black and it went all the way across the trees to the mountains, which were woolly white too. It was as if the mountains were right there in front of his face, instead of miles away.

If I had a camera, we would take that picture, said Sue, the cook.

Once the lights were out Marcus reached into his clothes, where he had hidden the panties, and they were still there. He brought them out as carefully as he would a baby animal. Each time he took them out Marcus liked to pretend it was the first time he had found them. He hadn't even told Lolly about the panties. Lolly was the mudman's name. He was lean, with a network of veins that wrapped all around his arms and went up his neck, even to his temples, where they pulsed softly when he ate or thought.

Lolly did the exact same things at the exact same times every day. But they had changed a little after he met Marcus. For instance, he had drawn his boat up next to Marcus's and they had started to talk at night.

It aint hard to figure out, Lolly said. He said this every night and repeated it seven or eight times in the way other people brushed their teeth or gargled. Lolly never slept. He did something else in which he talked to people who weren't there, and Marcus smelled his sweat and saw the flash of his arms gesturing in the dark.

If I hadn't of went to drinking, he said. Don't never go to drinking, Marcus.

Too late, said Marcus.

Lolly's wife had been going out on him for years and he never said a word about it until one afternoon he went over to the man's

house and emptied a .357 into his chest. The man had been mowing his yard. Everybody understood the simplicity. But to Lolly
it was of the complexity of a cut jewel. He held it up and turned
it around so different lights and colors formed and chanted to it.
At first Marcus tried to answer back to his questions because he
thought Lolly wanted a way out, but gradually he saw that the
jewel was impenetrable and precious to Lolly and that he wanted
to kill the man more now than he had been able to kill him before.
He was keeping Marcus awake. Marcus had become almost sorry
he had a friend, because life had been so much easier without one,
and he just wanted to be alone with the undiscovered panties.
Zoomer slept, and the others without friends slept, dreaming no
doubt of titties and checkbooks. Lolly pushed and reached and
shaped with his hands and arms with great strength as if he were
mixing mud, but no matter how hard he mixed it would always
come out to the same consistency.

Tonight Marcus had an idea.

Just lie, he said.

Huh? said Lolly.

In the blue light Marcus saw the same look out of Lolly's eyes
that he had seen in the dogs before the needle went in. Huh, said
Lolly.

Why don't you just tell a damn lie.

Lolly sat up on his boat.

If I hadn't of went to drinking, he said.

Marcus turned over. He could see his own breath, but he could
see it in a new way, such that it came out of his mouth or nose and
wavered around and stayed in the air a long time. He was afraid
the panties would lose their feeling. If he kept them out too long,
they did, like bubblegum. But they would always regenerate. He
could put them up and take them back out later. Probably it was
the depth of the cold. Everybody was buried in big army coats. The
sheriff had brought them in, a pile of them so big they couldn't
even see who he was until he dumped them on the concrete table
in the dayroom.

May hurt the rhubarb tonight, said the sheriff. Think the frost will hurt the rhubarb, Mr. Brabson?

He was talking to Lolly. The sheriff called him Mr. Brabson.

Think it will do it good, Sheriff, said Lolly.

The sheriff began to size them up. You need you a big one, he said to Sykes. Sykes looked as if he had taken offense. He was big and round and soft with black-rimmed plastic glasses. Sykes always took offense. He lived to fight. When he couldn't fight a person he fought air. He called fighting taking it to the road. By God, he would say, we'll take it to the road. Early on Marcus thought he was the only one Sykes had chosen to hate. By God what are you looking at? was the first thing he said to Marcus. By God I asked you a question. You by God answer me. But Marcus saw that he threatened everybody. It is on, he said. It is by God on right now, big boy. Marcus had figured he was in jail for killing somebody, or several people, but it was only for felony failure to appear.

I remember, said the sheriff. I remember how sometimes I didn't have no winter coat when I was a boy. We was lucky if we even had wood cut.

He cocked one skinny lean leg up on the concrete bench at the table. I always did look forward to thrashing time too. They had this big old machine that come around that done the thrashing. Daddy always had wheat. I looked forward to that because it meant I'd get me a new bed pillow. I'd get a new bed pillow and a new straw tick. That always did feel good to me. Get in them coats, boys. I done told you how cold it is going to be.

Everybody had put on a coat except Purkey and the sleeper. Purkey didn't want a coat. But he did have on a shirt, which was unusual for Purkey. The sheriff threw a coat over the sleeper. Marcus didn't know who the sleeper was because he slept all the time. After the sheriff left, Marcus lay on his boat. The lights went out but the blue light of the snow was brighter than the yellow light of the lights had been.

Your coat has got more fucking pockets, said Sykes, standing over Marcus's boat.

Take my fucking coat then, said Marcus, making as if he would take it off.

This was how you dealt with Sykes.

Take my fucking coat right, Marcus kept saying.

I don't want it now, said Sykes. They done give it to you, big boy. It has done got all your shit on it.

He shut up for a second, but then he said, But all's I don't understand is how come they give you one with more pockets.

Because he is special, said Zoomer.

He will be special, said Sykes, too softly. At the road he will. Mine is ripped, too.

But he hushed. If you talked too much, the cold got into your mouth and slurred the tongue and hurt the teeth. It was as if it had already frozen the concrete, and it was coming up through the boat and its mat directly into Marcus's side and his limbs. It was hardening his face. Marcus tried to cover up. He imagined that he was on a straw tick, whatever that was. And he had straw for his pillow. That had to be awful scratchy. He held the panties against his face and imagined that it was not his warmth in them but hers. He smelled the fabric, trying to differentiate it from the jail's cabbagy smell of years of prisoner habitation. He felt its weave, which smelled of the dryer and slightly of cigarettes but of something else too, something more marvelous. In his mind Marcus ran through seeing the girl again, and when he came to the end he would rewind and run it again with the softness and warmth of the panties on his cheek. This was the way, exactly the way, they had felt on her own skin. From the panties Marcus thought he could tell what she washed with and ate and how her voice sounded when she thought nobody could hear the sound of her voice. He could remember how she walked. She had a kind of float to her as if her hipbones were filled with a lighter substance.

When something woke him up he was sure it was daylight. The light was bright, coming through the slot windows, and several men were standing around him. But it was still only the blue light of the snow that had brightened as the night went on. It was bright enough to see that one of them had the panties. Lolly was talking even more persuasively.

What are you doing? Marcus asked.

At first they didn't say anything. Then Zoomer said, Having us a party.

Marcus started to get up and realized his feet were numb from cold. His ears were numb too. A few of them started pitching the panties around in such a way that made Marcus feel as if his heart had been pulled out. Zoomer started screaming. Marcus had heard Zoomer scream before and it was awful. It rang against the walls. Marcus was certain the jailers would hear it and be in there in a second, but they stopped pitching and Zoomer calmed down. He had the panties and was smoothing them carefully on the table.

Respect, said Zoomer. Have a little.

But he didn't even know the first thing about handling panties. Marcus wished he could kill Zoomer and kill everybody in the room and have the panties back. He was trembling on top of his shivering, but it was best not to let on. Everybody else, except Lolly, was in a festive mood. The whole dayroom was filled with mirth and moonlight. They were stomping and squeezing themselves and if they passed in front of a slot window a lingering smoke came out of their nostrils.

Is it always this cold? Marcus asked.

I aint never seen it like this, Lolly said.

Zoomer was passing out the cups. He had worked hard on them. It had taken effort to amount up nine plastic cups from the kitchen. The cups were an attractive golden plastic. Zoomer distributed one to each. Kimsey was sitting on the table dangling his legs and holding his cup out, and Purkey was going from man to man pushing the way football players used to do before a game in high school. Marcus wished he never had quit football or high school. Zoomer brought out his container, which he had patched together out of various containers, and it was bigger than Marcus had heard. It was full too. Each prisoner, including Marcus and Lolly, held out his cup, and Zoomer poured and everybody bitched about somebody else getting more and Zoomer shushed everybody.

Sykes gave a sign that wrestlers give before a move.

Nobody's going to hear nothing, he said.

Marcus looked at him. How do you know? he said.

Because of the tragedy, said Zoomer.

What tragedy? said Marcus.

The sheriff's tragedy, he said. He held up his cup. His wife is dead. Zoomer swirled his drink. She is very extremely dead.

How come?

Because that is often what happens, said Zoomer, when you get run over by a damn car.

Sykes laughed. He made a move on an imaginary opponent.

He didn't say nothing. We just now seen him, said Marcus. He was pointing as if to prove it.

People don't say nothing about something like that, said Zoomer.

He was probably crazy right then, said Purkey. I was crazy right after that woman died.

But you killed her, said Zoomer.

Marcus felt for the sheriff, if it was true. He thought back on it and something had been wrong with him, the way he acted about the rhubarb and the straw pillow. Once everybody had a drink Zoomer brought out the Lysol. Everybody cheered softly when he held it up. Zoomer went around and sprayed a good spray of Lysol in each cup. Marcus started to smell it and Zoomer slapped him.

Do not smell it, Zoomer said. If you smell it you won't drink it. Oh, God, do not smell it.

The slap didn't even sting, but it had popped loudly.

I wouldn't let him slap me like that, said Sykes.

One thing about it, Zoomer said. They won't be no germs in here.

They all looked at him. All drank. After they drank there was a great deal of muttering and swearing and some choking and somebody said, God-damn Zoomer that is nasty, and then a pause before they started drinking again. Zoomer sipped and smacked his lips as if it were delicious.

Even old mudman is having him some, said Zoomer.

It got quiet. Everybody stared at Lolly holding his cup.

Boys, said Lolly, you gone turn it loose. You don't be careful you gone to.

Everybody thought about that. It sounded like a warning, but how could it be much of a warning when Lolly had a drink in his hand too?

I like the sound of that, said Zoomer.

It was quiet again, as if things could go either way now.

I thought you didn't drink, said Marcus.

I do in a pinch, said Zoomer.

Is it a pinch? asked Purkey.

It is a pinch, Purkey, said Zoomer.

Marcus realized that Zoomer looked different because he didn't have on his glasses. He had big watery eyes. Marcus thought that was because he spent so much time reading the books and magazines his parents brought him. Zoomer would not share his books and magazines. He would not share the candy they brought him either, except for some of the hard ones and even then no strawberry. Zoorner's parents thought very highly of him. He was their only child. Marcus tried to stay off to himself because he saw it had started. Marcus was young but he still knew that it didn't matter what anybody did, because when it needed to start, it started. Even the sleeper had risen. He had not risen fully but he was far enough up to drink. The sleeper had freckles all over him. Marcus drank more. It was no time before the top of his head began to tingle and the angel hole opened up. The taste was very bad. His body began to hum. Marcus looked over at Lolly, who was sipping. The vein of his temple winked. Marcus felt the angel hole slip a little wider. It was nothing but air, an air hole. Marcus wished Lolly would do something. He realized he had been counting on Lolly to steer, but when he thought of what there was to steer he didn't want to think of Lolly steering it.

Everybody was lightening up. Some had even taken off their coats. Purkey got excited. When he got excited, he jumped up and down and wrung his hands as if they were wet. He did that for a few minutes and then he had to puke. He made it to the toilet and puked several times.

It's gone, he said, the toilet bowl magnifying his sobs. I can't get it back.

A lot is already in your bloodstream, said Zoomer. Besides, it aint been flushed yet.

Purkey began to lap from the toilet like a dog, but he stopped and puked again.

Purkey is pukey, said Zoomer. Pukey little Purkey. Have you ever read that book about the pukey little Purkey?

Zoomer poured more for Purkey. He poured with one hand and Lysoled with the other.

I gave you a extra spray, he said to Purkey. Everybody liked Purkey.

Fuck you, Zoomer, said Purkey through his tears.

Marcus had seen Purkey before they both got in jail. He was hard to miss because he rode a bicycle around all the time. Not that many people in Alexander County rode bicycles anymore, but Purkey did. He was wiry, with stringy hair. He had strangled a woman to death with her bra. It was a woman he barely knew from a plant where they both used to work until Purkey got fired. His lawyer tried to tell them that Purkey was retarded but Purkey wouldn't have any of that. He pleaded guilty and before long he was going to Brushy, soon as they had a bed. Everybody thought a lot of Purkey. He was always doing something funny. One day they were waiting to be signed back in from work and somebody said, Old Purkey, he's a good one, and somebody else said, You wouldn't think he'd of done nothing like they said he done. Everybody got quiet and concerned and didn't know what to say. Finally Zoomer spoke up. Why, he said, he was wanting that pussy. That's how come him to do it. And everybody cheered up and agreed that must have been true.

Marcus lay back on his boat. His feet and ears never had gone back to feeling, but now he didn't mind. It was like springtime. He could smell the grass somebody was mowing. He could smell his baptism water again. Marcus reminded himself that the panties after all were only panties. They weren't the girl. But he still waited for a chance to take them back. He felt funny. It was something additional to drunk. It was good, but not good enough. It was a little sad to realize that even something additional to drunk was not enough. Marcus wondered how additional he needed, and it seemed to be very very much.

Purkey had the panties over his head. He had them such that the two leg holes were on each side of his face and his mouth was right there in the crotch. Marcus could see his lips moving through the cloth. It sickened him and he was afraid he would puke too.

Okay, said Zoomer, pointing to Purkey's mouth and unzipping his fly. I'm sinking it in.

Purkey jerked the panties off and laughed as if that were the funniest thing ever and wrung his hands in the air. Zoomer had sat down on the table and was studying the Lysol can. It was a big industrial one. A radio played.

Lysol Brand Disinfectant Spray kills viruses and bacteria on environmental surfaces in your home and in public places, read Zoomer. He had the can right up in front of his large, watery eyes, each of which seemed to look around one side of the can. It eliminates germs and odors on hard nonporous surfaces that you come in contact with every day

Zoomer paused, turned the can around, and sprayed a long spray right into his mouth. He licked his lips.

Use Lysol Brand Disinfectant Spray in empty garbage cans, in pet areas, in sick rooms, under sinks. He paused, choking a little. Lolly stopped laughing. He had been laughing at everything Zoomer read, and even when he stopped he waited expectantly, ready to laugh some more. His laughter was disappointing to Marcus.

Wonder what it feels like to kill somebody, said Zoomer. I wonder what the natural high is like. What is it like, Lolly?

Lolly shook his head and laughed a little more softly

It has to be an adrenaline rush, Zoomer said. God. What's it like, Purkey?

What, said Purkey.

Killing somebody. What does it feel like? Is it a rush?

Purkey stared at Zoomer as if he had crossed a line.

In diaper pails, resumed Zoomer, in empty hampers, on doorknobs, around toilet areas. Fast easy effective.

Kimsey swung down from the ceiling pipe and without looking up Zoomer said, I am not involved in that.

What he was not involved in was the vent grate that Kimsey had removed and had been sticking back on with little things he made out of toothpaste. Kimsey would take a running start and leap up the wall and hang on a pipe and swing over to the grate. Tonight he had his light brown hair slicked back. He had a big plan and it seemed that tonight, since God had sucked all the warmth out of the world, all big plans were being put to work. Kimsey had it to the point where he could disappear into the duct with only the bottoms of his feet hanging out. He was developing a way to F Block and once he was in there, he was going to fuck every female in the jail and then run, he had told Marcus. Run so fast nobody would ever catch him.

Don't tell nobody, Kimsey said to Marcus. But my girlfriend is in jail. She wouldn't want nobody to know she was in jail.

Kimsey and the girlfriend had a stormy relationship. He was known for exploits with her and for running. Kimsey was the fastest runner in Alexander County. Nobody could catch him and many had tried. In high school they tried to get him to run track and he did for a little while but when they got to the meet and put him in the 880 he cut across the football field, jumped over the chain link fence, and kept on going. Marcus had seen it. He was practicing football. Another time the girlfriend was holding a birthday party for Kimsey in a stolen pickup truck and he was allegedly putting birthday cake all up in her pussy when the law put the lights on them. Kimsey fled and some of them stayed behind in wonderment over the cake. Others took off after him in the dark but he was gone. The girlfriend was smart. She said she didn't know nothing about no Kimsey and they wanted to know what was that big K on the cake and she said she thought it stood for Ken.

Kimsey's girlfriend was a screamer, they said. This was why the cops pestered him so much, because what could they desire more than a screamer?

Use on finished surfaces in basements, Zoomer continued. Closets, attics, laundry rooms, storage areas, vacation homes, boat interiors, shower stalls, and recycling bins.

Excellent! he called out. He started holding the can like a microphone. He would look at its text, memorize it, and then hold the can up and speak, or nearly sing, into it. Zoomer had a fine, clear radio voice. Excellent for controlling mold and mildew on mattresses, pillows, and shower curtains. He held up the can. Damn. Excellent.

Purkey had laid out the panties on the table and was humping them slowly, about one hump every fifteen seconds. The sleeper called out, Bring them over here. You been on them all night. He had a high voice. Lolly stayed next to Marcus and sipped his cup. He kept looking at Marcus with expectation. Marcus wondered if Lolly would back him up if he piled onto Purkey. But it seemed to be happening from a distance. Everything would have been so bad if it hadn't been so good.

It is unlawful, said Zoomer, to use this product in a manner inconsistent with its labeling. Hold container upright six to eight inches from surface. Nine or ten inches, by God, and your ass is in jail.

He stopped and listened. They could hear the rat of Kimsey scratching in the ceiling. The rat moved quickly away and they heard his voice as if from a great distance.

Shit, said Purkey. F Block. Apparently Kimsey had shared his plan with Purkey too. Purkey tried to scamper up the wall like Kimsey had, but his hands slipped off the pipe and he fell on his back. Uh, said Purkey. He started having convulsions and while he was having them Marcus got the panties back and put them down in his clothes. Lolly stood in front of him and blocked their view as he did it. All of a sudden Marcus felt like crying.

Something had happened to the pipe. It had crumbled into pieces and what remained lurched and ejaculated a long sliver of ice, which shattered on the floor. It was followed by some air and then water. It was a good-sized pipe and the water came out fast. For a few minutes they just watched, enjoying the water because it was warmer than the air. It must have been more than a few minutes, because some of the boats had turned into boats. They had to stand on the table and there wasn't room for everybody on the table.

The drain, said Zoomer. Somebody unstop the drain.

Purkey, on his knees, sloshed in the water feeling for the drain. He had turned wet and white, with his wild stringy hair pasted to his skull and his teeth chattering. Purkey sucked air through his chattering teeth and called out, due to the coldness of his wetness, which Marcus remembered from his baptism. Zoomer made everybody get down off the table and wait in line, though he had to push some of them and they fell with loud splashes and came up blowing spit and hollering. He stationed Sykes atop the table and Sykes leaned down and invited each man onto his shoulders and lifted him up the vent, but when it was his turn Lolly refused.

Stay here and be drownded then, said Zoomer.

Lolly climbed on Sykes's back and pulled himself into the vent with the smoothest strength Marcus had ever seen. Marcus went after him. He climbed into the vent, through which frigid air was moving as in a cave. The vent was big enough to crawl in, but it was slick on the bottom and every so often had sharp things and was pitch black dark. The sound of prisoners rumbling through the vent was so loud Marcus was sure they would be caught. It was almost a relief because he wished somebody would stop them. Something would, he thought. Didn't it always? He was moving as quickly as he could into the nothing but in a second a rumble came up behind him and something grabbed his leg and came over him with a bunch of elbows and knees. Marcus knew it was Purkey from the smell of the puke. Purkey weighed enough to make the vent flex and for a second they were wedged in it with Marcus screaming, but Purkey got over him and went on. It was only a second until they came to the place where everybody was all bunched up. Marcus heard a great deal of breathing and he could smell them but he wanted to draw up closer from the cold, but Purkey's big ass was between him and Lolly. A distance ahead Kimsey was pecking on a vent.

Hello, said Zoomer's voice. Hello, ladies.

There was no answer from the females.

Who is that? said a female voice, but it was Sykes making a female voice.

It aint nothing but the boys of D Block, said Zoomer. We have come to fuck you.

Everybody started laughing and that led to hollering and shoving, and Kimsey was apparently beating on the vent with something because in a second it gave and then the whole contents of D Block started dumping through it, each one pushed out by the one before him though some came out in twos. Everything was open again and it was dark in F Block but it had females in it because Marcus could hear them screaming and see their shadowy forms running around wrapped in blankets. It seemed as if the males were trying to herd them into a corner but they wouldn't go. It was terrible the fucking that was about to be unleashed. Marcus tried to help corner them but his ankle hurt. As he limped alongside Purkey Marcus saw him get kicked in the balls by one of the females. It was not a tentative, feeling kick, but rather a sweeping karate one that struck with a sound like a good deep punt, erasing all herding instinct from the room. Even before Purkey hit the concrete it had fallen quiet enough to hear his scream, which wasn't even a scream at all but just air from his throat. It made everyone shield himself, some with both hands. Marcus tried to fix his eyes on the woman who did it. She was short and wide, with

long hair that disappeared into her blanket, and he still could not
believe her leg would go that high.

That is for what you done to my friend, said the woman, who
seemed to be their leader the way Zoomer was D Block's. Then she
said, They are all drunker than hell.

What did you expect, honey? said Zoomer.

We wanted somebody to fix the fucking heat, said a female voice
other than the leader's. When she said it her teeth chattered.

Zoomer looked around.

Marcus is a roofer, he said. Do you know anything about heat,
Marcus?

We don't need no fucking roofer, the woman said. We need heat.

It was so good to hear the word fucking and even roofer out
of a female mouth that Marcus forgot about Purkey for a second.
F Block rolled around in his vision, locking down every second
or two.

Where is ours at? said another female voice.

Your what? Marcus said.

Our liquor, dumbass.

Marcus tried to pick out which one it was. The females had all
gathered together on the concrete table with some of them facing
one way and others the other way so nobody could sneak up on
them. The males were all walking around slowly trying to walk
off bruises and rubbing at various areas of their legs. Sykes was
trying to stop some bleeding. Everybody was soaking wet. Lolly
had backed up against the wall. Marcus could tell the women had
already unified. They were only about six or seven, plus the leader.
Some had articles of clothing tied around their heads. In the blue
light Marcus could see their breaths fogging out.

We aint drunk, said Sykes, licking his blood.

It sounded as if he had said it before.

The women laughed.

We smell it, said the leader.

We smell it too, said Zoomer.

You, the leader told Zoomer, aint nothing but a sleazy-ass junkie.

The females all laughed at that too, obscuring Zoomer's response. In the laughter Marcus tried to move cautiously away from where Purkey lay. Purkey's body had started jerking back and forth, still screaming the same way without sound, such that it was traveling gradually across the floor like a dismembered grasshopper leg. Marcus held onto the panties beneath his clothing but now the panties felt like a foreign growth. Backing up, he tripped on a boat in the corner. He caught himself before he fell, but all the women on the table and even the leader were looking at him such that he felt embarrassed and flattered for a second, but he realized they were looking at the boat instead of him.

Look it! one of the women at the table said. She had her hand over her mouth.

It was Kimsey on the boat, and he had his forehead against the back of the woman's neck, as if he were holding her still, the way Marcus had seen cats do. Blankets and clothes were piled over them, as if they had tried to hide, but they were definitely doing it. The whole room fell quiet and the women on the far side of the table came around to see better. Marcus felt them checking each other to see who it was and as soon as they figured it out they began to talk among themselves. Knowing her, he heard one of them say, he is probably up her ass.

No, said another, he is probably doing it that a way to keep from having to look at her face.

Have you ever looked at her nose? She thinks she is the best thing that ever pissed through hair.

They laughed again.

Hey, the leader called out. Stop it.

But Kimsey didn't stop. He kept going. And she wasn't screaming. Not far away, Purkey kept going too. Zoomer had walked over closer.

The thrill of victory, said Zoomer, nodding toward Kimsey. And the agony of defeat.

It was silent.

You all aint nothing but a bunch of old whores, said Sykes.

You all are drunk, hollered the female leader.

Zoomer made a motion as if tipping his imaginary hat. Kimsey had stopped and the other females were laughing a low wicked laugh, but the males were kind of ignoring it. Kimsey wrestled his way out from under the blankets and clothes, pressing down too hard on the girlfriend, but she never moved and kept her face turned to the wall. Marcus was surprised that Kimsey still had his clothes on. Kimsey jumped over Purkey and leapt onto the concrete table, scattering females, one of whom screamed. Several lost their headdresses. He grabbed the pipe and swung himself back and forth until he could fly back into the vent. It was about halfway up the wall. They heard him go thundering away in it.

Damn, said Zoomer. What an exit.

Everybody followed Kimsey, except for the agony of defeat, who still lay twitching on the floor next to the thrill of victory and her mound of clothes and blankets. A part ran down the hair on the back of her head. Marcus waited a minute before he climbed into the vent because he thought she was crying. He thought the mound of clothes and blankets was moving in the way it would with sobbing, but Sykes had him by the back of the neck and was trying to stuff him into the vent. Marcus wondered why their vent had been in the ceiling when the females had it on the wall. Once they had gone a ways in the duct and everybody was clotted up, breathing and stinking, they heard what sounded like screaming and bawling, but the sound was squeezed down smaller, as if it were very far away.

I think that would of went a lot better if we would of brought them something to drink, said Marcus.

The screaming increased and died back.

What did you ever expect from a bunch of jailbird bitches? said Zoomer.

Marcus had the urge to run. He felt as if that were the only response to what they had opened up, but it was hard to run in a vent. They reached a ninety-degree turn straight up. Marcus could tell because blue light was descending through it and somewhere way up were the sounds of voices and scratching as prisoners squirreled up it. Also, something was flowing down the vent pipe across his face and his arms and the rest of his body Marcus couldn't figure out what it was at first. He thought maybe it was water, but it was lighter than water, though it still stayed clammed all over him. As he tried to scramble up the vent the way the others had he realized it was nothing but cold. It was cold on top of cold, because he was already numb to the elbows and ankles and his face was a mask down to his neck and where the neck attached to the chest. It was a new kind of cold that didn't wait on anything. It was trying to stick his face to the vent pipe.

In a few seconds his feet started working and he went right up the pipe as if the world were sucking him out. The higher he got the more the cold became the opposite of itself. It was like a blanket, except the opposite of a blanket, one that wrapped you up immediately and sank down into your bones with its cold instead of warmth, but Marcus kept paddling and reached the top and Zoomer pulled him out and dropped him in some hard snow. Marcus jumped up. They were on top of the jail. The top of the jail was a large level plain of snow with various pipes emitting steam and little motors and shiny hoods jutting up around them. The cold was awful. It worked its prisoners like puppets, running them toward the edges of the snowy plain beneath the beautiful blue light, and the moon was waiting far above the trees in the very sharply starry sky: No one knew just then that it would be the coldest night of the twentieth century in East Tennessee. Marcus sure didn't. If he had of known, things might have been different. But right now he ran, or at least moved, because he could not feel his footsteps. It seemed like they were running from jail and running from jailbird bitches, running from everything that could be run from, and some of them hollered with freedom as they went.

On the edge of the jail one body had already sailed off and was rolling two times in the soft snow below. It was Zoomer. On the way down his coat winged open and fluttered. Right now he was cussing and had snow all over his face and he was clutching at it as if it really stung, and the figure of Kimsey was fifty, a hundred yards away, running with huge, floating strides. Sykes was dropping too but he got too far forward and belly flopped in the snow louder than if it had been water. Marcus tried to get Lolly to go with him at the same time, but Lolly shook his head and gestured and wouldn't go.

Come on, Lolly, Marcus hollered out, and it was interesting how clear his voice was.

Lolly shook his head. Marcus always remembered Lolly's face. The look on it was like the day he was baptized, as if it were asking a big question, except this time he realized the question only had one possible answer. But he realized it on the way down, and on the way down Marcus was amazed at how quickly the air moved around him, and despite his numbness he felt freer that he ever had before, with the big dark block of the jail stuck in the earth, bobbing in the cold, and him flying off it.

Stephen Marion's stories have appeared in four editions of *New Stories from the South*. He is a native of East Tennessee, where he lives and works as a journalist. Marion's fiction has appeared in *Tin House*, *The Oxford American*, and *Epoch*. His novel, *Hollow Ground*, was published in 2002.

EUGENIA MARION

In January 1985, the temperature where I live in East Tennessee dropped to twenty-seven degrees below zero. As luck would have it, several guys escaped from the county jail that night, and a wild series of events occurred. I had gone to school with one of the guys who escaped. He was one of the ones who ran back and knocked on the front door of the jail wanting to be let in. Another of the guys I had only met briefly. He had come by my house intending to rob it (he and his brother were on an armed robbery spree at that moment) but for some reason decided not to after asking me if I knew anybody who wanted to sell a bird dog. I had always wanted to tell his story, as I imagined it at least, out of gratitude for sparing me. He didn't actually have a Lysol party, however. That occurred later in the same jail, and it involved different people, but it still caught my eye.

CRY FOR HELP FROM FRANCE

(from *Subtropics*)

Robert Crumb has retired to south France. My toilet is from Paris. A coward is full of bluster about living well. A coward is terrified of even being alive. He may be also afraid—and this is congruent with the more popular visions of cowardice—of the opposite, both in its extreme, final expression (death), and in its less acute expressions (injury). But fear of injury or death, running from battles or fistfights etc., is just shallow cowardice; in fact it may not be cowardice at all. It may be mere anxiety, and usually rather rational at that. Who is to be faulted for preferring not to have his nose broken or not to die on the ground in the dirt without any painkillers or a girl to wipe one's brow? No, that is cosmetic cowardice. True cowardice would embrace a broken nose or the spectacle of one's guts flying while being afraid of buying a new car or getting married or having a child or changing jobs or selecting this coat over that coat or eating at a restaurant that is too expensive or one that is not expensive enough. A true coward knows the phrase *Go for it* and he deigns not go for it. Going for it scares him to death. He is so far from going for it that he does not even conceive what is to be gone for. This is why he does not perceive, usually, that he is a coward. Excuse me, I've been writing this, just now, and I'll admit to bearing down a bit to try to get my meaning correct, and clear if it is correct, and I fancy at this point it is clear but not yet correct—when a fat boy skipped by on the street, trying to skip, so uncoordinated that it lent the impression that his bones were soft, or even possibly bending. A goofy, happy, or let us say perhaps an unhappy boy trying to be happy, badly skipping down a sunny street in France. It is likely, in my imagination, at first, that this boy is not a coward. Then I immediately correct: he is likely not yet a coward. He does not know. He is still at the level of trying to see if his overfed and underused soft body will respond to a command he gives it, which command should be fun to obey. He has gone around the corner, gone with his early unconscious exploration into cowardice, and I now sit here with my later investigations. I am at a good oak table. I have coffee. It is quiet in this nice house in France. Send me some money, you people. I am just like Robert Crumb, except he can draw.

Padgett Powell has written several books, among them *The Interrogative Mood*.

I wrote "Cry for Help from France" sitting in a house in France crying for help. Mary Margaret Chappell, a nice girl from Richmond, had lent me her house in Cancale so I could properly execute a sabbatical. I sat in it hiding from having to speak badly with Frenchmen and admitting, finally, after studying French every day with the Peter Capretz of Yale method and lusting for the heroine of the lessons, that the only way I would ever possess a foreign language would be were the Language Fairy to put one under my pillow. I avoided conversations I could not script in advance.

One day a heavyset Frenchman came to the door collecting money for the handicapped, and the conversation got immediately off any script I could control. And then I saw another fat French boy skipping by the house. I wished that Mary Margaret Chappell, who speaks impeccably and who indentured herself in France to become a pastry cook, would come and teach me if not French then how to bake tasty sweet things, but she did not. I felt forsaken and started issuing cries for help.

I also had what the doctor finally called "an intestinal weerus" that I think I got from Africa, that nearly killed me, that made me locate Jesus beside me as a boon companion, and that months of diagnostics for which cost me about $250 — to include stool analysis, every blood test there is, and a sonogram, so do not tell me there is something wrong with "socialized medicine," please.

Kenneth Calhoun

NIGHTBLOOMING

(from *The Paris Review*)

I was told they found themselves retired and so they said,
Now's finally the time to form a band! You should see the
instruments they fished out of attics and basements. Not so much
the instruments themselves—horns haven't changed much over
the years—but the cases. Some are covered with flesh-tone leather,
boxes made of wood with rusty hinges, lined with red velvet.
When they crack them open, it looks like they're pulling metal
bones from the insides of a body.

The dudes are severely elderly, these Nightblooming Jazzmen.
They wear white belts and bow ties, polyester pants pulled up
high. Our angle is we're old, they say. So you have to dress the
part if you're going to be our pulse, drumbo. They got me wearing
plaid pants and bowling shoes. A couple of them have moustaches
and they're serious about them. I paste one on for the big gig just
to fit in around the face. Bleach my eyebrows and stick that silvery
fringe under the nostrils, pop on a straw hat.

They have the coolest names. There's Clyde and Chet and Wally
and Ernie and Horace. Do you believe that? When I first met up
with them, when I told them my name was Tristan, they said, Ho,
ho, what kind of name is that? Some of them thought I said Chris-
tian. I said I didn't know what kind of name it was, how should I
know? I wasn't there when I was named.

They said, Where are your people from?

My people? Sounded like they were talking about tribes. But I didn't have an answer for them. I'm from nowhere, around, all over.

You can't use a name like that, they told me. We'll think of a new one.

After my audition, Clyde and Horace came over to my car when I was packing up my drums. They told me I got the gig but from now on they were calling me Stanley and if I didn't like it I could take my twenty-two years of living and go sit on a dick.

They were grinning when they said it.

The big gig is under the elms in a lonely old park. The bandstand is covered with graffiti and the tennis courts have tattered nets and faded lines. A crowd of old people and a few of their grandkids look on from folding chairs. Everyone's eating. I watch them bite at deviled eggs and salted watermelon from behind my cymbals. The fans of the Nightblooming Jazzmen drink wine from Styrofoam cups. They eat cheese logs and grapes resting atop green Coleman coolers. Seeds are spat into the grass.

Clyde puffs into the mic and says, Good afternoon, ladies and germs. Then we're off and running. We cook up a carousel of sound with our hands, with the wind in our chests. Me and a gang of senior citizens just tearing up the place.

We're marching the saints and balling the jack. And, damn, these Nightblooming Jazzmen can bring it. Chet is coaxing sad wah-wahs out of his t-bone, muting with a toilet plunger. Clyde noodles out golden lassos on the clarinet and Wally burps wetly along on the tuba. I buzz the rolls and grab the crash. I stir the soup with brushes. I do all the stuff I never get to do—that no one plays anymore. Stuff I learned from my dad.

We play the Charleston and people are grabbing at their knees and head dancing. We stir up a flock of jazz hands.

The sun tilts through the trees and everywhere are shafts of dust. We're just a speck in the grand whirling scheme, but at least we're making noise.

We close the set like landing a plane, bouncing along a little then rolling to a stop. The guys are breathing heavy. They empty their spit valves into the lawn.

People applaud, then stand and fold up their chairs.

I'm tearing down my set and a kid comes over, starts asking me questions. How come there's a Rush sticker on my snare case? How come I'm not old but I play old music?

How do you know I'm not old? I ask.

Your elbows, he says. Too smooth.

I'm waiting for Clyde to cut the checks, sitting in my car smoking some reefer. I can see some of the guys standing by their van, arguing about something. Me? I'm mellow. It was just as good a gig as any. Better in some ways because there's nowhere to hide in this kind of sound. No smokescreens of distortion or feathered edges of reverb. You have to give these guys their due. They put it down precisely where they want it, dotted notes and all. I thought they were going to be a drag. I figured I'd play this one time and score the check, then ditch them. But I don't know. That gig was pretty sweet.

Clyde and Horace come over. I stash the nub of weed and step out. Great job, they tell me. You can swing, by God. How'd you learn it?

My dad, I explain. He loved Krupa.

Did he play?

Yeah. That's all I say, recalling his old Ludwig drum kit. His traps, he would call them. The shells were as thin as lampshades and the cymbals were brown and dull. I pawned it all a few years after he died, after I changed the skin on the floor tom and found some blood down in the crease under the ring. He threw up his guts during a gig once. He shouldn't have been playing in that state. They carried him home and put him to bed in his bloody T-shirt. He was a welder by profession. Health insurance was like a Rolls-Royce—both things he knew he'd never have.

Clyde gives me my check. His hand's all shaky when he signs his name.

Horace says, I tell you what, we met some nice old ladies and they've invited us over for a visit. Up for joining us?

What the hell, I say. It's not like I have anywhere else to go.

Horace rides with me as we caravan over. He tells me more about the band. What happened was that they used to be a big band, all Glenn Miller, Tommy Dorsey, Benny Goodman. They had a good run for a while, playing locally. You can't tour with a big band unless you have serious, Sinatra-sized bank. Costs too much to put all those guys in hotel rooms. But they did their thing often enough around town. Fellas started dying though, Horace says. Not because they whooped it up or got in car wrecks—the way the young bands die. These guys just died from staying in the world too long. Cancer mostly. Heart attacks and strokes. One after another.

So much for the big band. They tried to roll with it, calling themselves the littlest big band, but they couldn't draw a crowd. So Clyde, who's basically the leader, said they were going Dixieland and did anyone have a problem with that. Horace tells me one guy walked out, kicked over a music stand and flipped them the bird, grumbling that Dixieland was for Disneyland. Everyone else stayed put, even though Wally and Chet are starting to get flaky, Horace says.

He looks out at the yards sliding by. It's a crazy thing to say you're going to stick with something until you die, Horace tells me. You pick two or three things you feel that way about and life organizes itself for you.

He winks and it's a little spooky how he's talking right into me, how his words are driving into my head like pennies dropped from eight miles up.

The ladies are sisters, widows, some of them twice over. Three of our guys are widowers. Chet and Ernie are married, but Ernie's wife is an invalid. Doesn't give me an excuse to fool around, he says glumly.

What about you, they ask me before we go in.

We're standing in the street of some shady neighborhood—shady meaning it's leafy, not ghetto. The sidewalks are old and broken where the roots of oak trees push up. There's a dove cooing somewhere. A sprinkler hisses a few houses down. I see the blue haze of mist in the evening light.

They're waiting for an answer and I don't know how much to say. You can't tell people about your loneliness without adding to it. No one wants to hear how you're somewhere between the beat with people, never finding the count.

I'm in between, I say.

A pair of legs? Clyde asks, grinning. He has a square jaw and a Charlie Brown curl of gray hair on his big, blotchy forehead.

Between girlfriends.

Oh! Ménage à twat, Horace says.

Not like that, I say.

Now they're all grinning.

You guys are some dirty grandpas, I tell them.

They laugh. Good band name, they say. They slap me on the back. Clyde makes like he's strangling me. His hands are rough at my throat. You're a good kid, he says. He pulls me aside. You're not a cock-blocker are you?

I shake my head. Me? I'm thinking.

No one likes a cock-blocker, Clyde says. He's patting me hard on the back, like he's burping a baby.

The women are waiting. They've laid out a happy-hour spread. There's a green ceramic serving dish with pretzels and Ritz crackers. The dish has a built-in bowl that they have filled with some kind of white creamy dip. There's another plate of cheese and grapes and a can of roasted peanuts. I start attacking the snacks, standing over the low table, raining down crumbs.

Horace says, Easy, Stanley.

The women laugh. Someone's hungry!

They say, You boys should take a seat, waving us over to the long, avocado-colored couch. I sit down with a handful of crackers and line up cubes of cheese on my leg and start the assembly line. As I cram it all in my mouth, I take in my surroundings. The colors are green and yellow. A massive organ sits in the corner, its wooden pedals like a ribcage on the floor. There are plastic plants in the corners and hook rugs on the wall—shag tapestries of trees with red leaves, clouds over an island, an owl with furry eyes clutching a real piece of driftwood. There are shelves lined with little owl statues made from glass and clay. Someone likes owls. This is an owl house.

The women gather up and introduce themselves. They have cotton-candy hair and foggy eyes. There's more than one brooch and bracelets all around, so they jangle when they move. Shiny pants and small knitted vests; clown collars, nurse shoes. I have to say, these are some good-looking old ladies. The Jazzmen really scored. The ladies smell nice, too. I can smell them from across the room: it's all baby powder and flowers. They deliver their names like they're performing a song. Ruth and Ethel and Nancy are sisters, we learn, and Betty is an old friend from the neighborhood. Great names, I say. Some cracker crumbs fly from my mouth and Clyde gives me a look.

The women tell us how much they loved the music.

Ethel says her fingers are sore from snapping. The guys chuckle at this.

I hit the peanuts, throwing a handful in my mouth. I watch their lips move through the grinding in my head. When I swallow, I hear Betty say, So many of the summer concerts are such disappointments.

Ruth recalls a terrible rap act and they all shudder.

Wally says, That's not poetry, what they're doing. I don't buy it.

They look to me, expecting an opinion, I guess. Rap sucks, I say as I reach for some more cheese.

You have the most unusual eyebrows, Nancy says.

I don't understand, then I remember that I had bleached them.
Goes better with the moustache, I say.

Everyone laughs because, at the moment, my moustache is curled up on the dashboard of my car.

How's that for commitment? Clyde says. The kid lands a gig and he goes the extra mile to fit in. You didn't tattoo our name on your backside, did you?

I shake my head, because my mouth is full.

Stan the man can swing, Clyde says, reminding me of my new name. His smile has something like pride in it. They all look at me, smiling warmly.

I feel like I'm eight years old—a little kid with a whole army of grandparents. I never knew my real grandparents. My dad was already old when I was born and my mom never told her parents about me. One day she told me her father had finally died. That was all I had ever heard about them.

Wally slaps his thighs. Say, how about some drinks? Clyde says to Chet, You bring in your kit?

Chet says, Get yours.

The way he says it is kind of harsh. Clyde looks at him and there's a quiet little stare down before Clyde whistles through his teeth and heads out.

When Clyde comes back he has a small black box with a handle. It's like a square suitcase. He puts it on the dining room table and opens it up. I go over to check it out and he tells me not to get crumbs all over the place. I peer inside the case and see its shimmering contents. The inside is lined with black velvet. Held in places cut into the walls of the box are stainless-steel tools—shaker cups, some tongs and long spoons, a strange coil of spring, and, behind a secret panel, he shows me that it holds a blue bottle of gin and another bottle of tonic water. It's an incredible thing. I like cases and gear and kits. That's one reason I love the drums. I like how everything collapses, folds up, and has its place to go. It looks professional, just like Clyde's kit looks professional, even a little religious.

Would you ladies like to try a fine gin and tonic? Clyde asks. When they seem to hesitate, Clyde reminds them that the gin and tonic was invented as a health drink. Everything about it is designed to keep you alive. British troops in India came up with it, he explains. The tonic water has quinine, which cures malaria. Add gin for its cleansing quality and a lime to fight scurvy and you have yourself a good glass of medicine.

No, insists Betty. You're pulling our leg.

Nancy says, It's true, Betty. I heard that somewhere before.

Ethel and Nancy head to the kitchen to get glasses and ice while Clyde goes to work. Not everyone wants gin and tonics, but the ladies also have scotch and rum. There's no wine or beer, just hard liquor.

The party chugs forward, with the ladies pumping on the organ and some of the guys playing along on their horns, with stories of wars and coming West to pick citrus, more nuts being poured, more cheese being cubed and tossed like dice.

In the kitchen, a roast sits smoldering like a meteorite in the old car-sized oven. Nancy is sitting in the breakfast nook, telling a story about how she was the only sister brave enough to go barnstorming with a crazy carnival pilot, spinning low over the long-gone orchards and vineyards and looping over the fairgrounds, so close to clipping the Ferris wheel she could hear the riders scream. She's staring into space as she tells about it, like she's watching it happen on an invisible screen.

After the dishes are done, they start dancing to records. Ethel's on the turntable, spinning Rosemary Clooney and Louis Armstrong. Horace thumbs through a dead husband's stacks and finds Bob Wills and His Texas Playboys. He insists on "Sittin' on Top of the World" and it calls for pushing back the coffee table and pairing up. I watch, still hitting the crackers and nuts, even though

Nancy had served up roast beef and potatoes, hot buttered rolls and Jello salad, cottage cheese on a leaf of lettuce. Wally sits next to me, watching Clyde dancing with Betty.

Wally hums along. His ears are big and floppy. Hair creeps out of them.

He turns to me and says, Why don't you cut in?

Cut in?

You never cut in?

I don't know what you're talking about, Wally.

Cutting in? You know, you just go up to a fella who is dancing with the gal you want to dance with and you tap him on the shoulder and say, I'd like to cut in. Then he has to stand aside and let you take over.

Why?

It's just that way.

What if he doesn't want to give up the girl?

He won't want to, but he has to.

Who says?

No one says, it's just the way it is. Go on and see.

I can't dance to this kind of music.

Sure you can. It's just a box step. Go cut in.

I look over the dancing couples. The lady who catches my eye is Nancy. I notice the way her hands rub at the back of the guy she's dancing with. She just keeps them moving in slow circles on their back. She's doing it to Chet now. He has his head bowed and I can see the age spots on his neck. That looks like it would feel pretty good, just to have her rubbing that way. So I stand up and a bunch of nuts fall from the folds of my shirt. I'm a little buzzed from Clyde's gin and tonics, so I knock into Horace as I make my way to Nancy and Chet. Clyde sees me and frowns over Betty's shoulder, but lightens up when I move past him. I tap Chet on the shoulder and tell him I want to cut in. It works just like Wally said it would. Chet kind of puts Nancy's hand in mine with a little bow. Up close it's a small hand with swollen knuckles and purple veins, but it's warm and softer than it looks. Nancy smiles and even looks a little flattered. She moves in close as Chet stands back with his arms crossed.

I don't know how to dance to this music, I say.

Just follow my lead, Nancy says. She starts pushing me around the floor. I step on her foot once and she winces, but her smile climbs right back onto her face. She has waxy skin and bright red lips. Her hair is a cake of white curls. Her face sits behind a veil of wrinkles and creases, but the smile shines through it. She's light in my arms and I take care not to crush her. She's saying, Step and step and step and step. I smell the gin on her breath and I like it.

When I finally get the step, she says, Atta boy!

Her hands are rubbing at my back. I feel it in my chest, this feeling of almost burning warmth. It's been a long time since I felt it. It's how my body responds to kindness. I used to feel it at school, when a teacher would lean over me and show me how to draw cursive letters. Or when an older kid showed me how to fly a kite. I thought I had outgrown the ability to have that feeling. I had forgotten about it. But here I am, feeling it again as Nancy rubs my back.

I'm lost in these thoughts when Chet taps me on the shoulder and asks to cut in. I surrender Nancy like a real gentleman, transferring her hand like it's a parakeet that has to hop from my finger to his. He says, Thank you kindly, sir, and pretends to tip a hat.

No problem, sir, I say.

What a classy bunch of fellas, Nancy says, eyes rolling.

Looking out from the haze trapped in my car, I can see them, silhouettes jitterbugging in the rosy window. The music is faint, but I tap along on the steering wheel. Maybe it's sad to say, but it's been just about the best party I've ever attended. Through the window they look like a movie flashed on a wall, hanging in space with no connection to time. It seems impossible that I stepped out from it, or that I could get back in. It's like a soap bubble you try to put in your pocket.

I pick up the moustache, which has curled up from the heat, and

I smooth it under my nose. It still has some stick. From across the street, I hear a song end and everyone shouts out, More!

That's all I need to be called back. I cross the dark street and walk up the curvy brick path. I finish the joint leaning against a massive pepper tree, listening as I press at the moustache.

They're laughing in waves, singing harmonies. Someone's mixing drinks, shaking ice like a maraca. Someone's slicing meat with an electric knife. Why couldn't I have met them a long time ago, and played their music and eaten their cheese and crackers and drank their gin? But they didn't exist a long time ago, I know. Not as they are now. They only exist now and not much into later.

My dad didn't talk much. In the time I knew him, he only said one religious thing. He said, You know why people like beats? Because they tell you what's going to happen next. I've thought about that a lot. I think he was talking about patterns, about loops. And it's true that once you hear a measure or two of the beat, you know what's going to happen next and what to do when it happens. And the part that makes me think everything still has a chance—always has a chance—to work out is that you never know when the beat has completed a full cycle. This means everything in life that seems so random could actually be part of a beat. We just don't know yet. The full measure hasn't been played.

The door opens and one of the ladies peers out. It's Nancy.

There you are, Stanley! she says when her eyes lock in on me.

I wave, thinking I should probably tell her my real name.

Don't think I don't recognize you behind those handlebars.

I touch the moustache and smile.

She shuffles toward me and I offer my arm.

Got you right where I want you, she says.

She slowly leads me around to the other side of the pepper tree.

Whoops. Tipsy, she says when she trips on a root.

We step out on the lawn under the massive dark canopy. I can see a rope slicing down from a high branch, catching light from the house. I follow it down with my eyes and see that it is weighted on the end with a tire swing. Nancy pulls me to it.

We have this here for the grandkids, but they've outgrown it, she explains. It needs a muscle man to get it going and here you are. Lift me?

Before I know it, she has both her arms around my neck and she's hanging off me like a human necklace. I scoop up her legs and slide her into the tire. All I can say is, Really? You want to swing?

Swing, baby, swing, she says. Be-dap bap bap!

I look up at the rope. It looks solid, but it's dark so who can tell. I stand back. There's a buzzed eighty-year-old woman hanging a couple feet off the ground in front of me, jewelry jangling, white hair slightly aglow.

Come fly with me, she sings, Come fly, we'll fly away!

I'll swing her a little, I think. Why not?

I push her gently forward again. She's shaking her head.

Come on now, she says. Put some muscle into it! We're not going to get off the ground if that's your idea of swinging.

I give her a good push and she swings out over some of the yard.

That's better!

She swings back into me and I grab on to the tire and throw it out into the darkness. She goes with it, saying, Atta boy. Now really put your back into it!

She comes back at me and I sidestep her like a bullfighter, but as she passes by again, I throw my weight into a push that drops me to my knees. I watch her sail up and away, then reach the top of her arc, ease to a point, then fall back at me. She's yelling, Woohoo!

I roll out of the way and get to my feet in time to add to her momentum as she swings by. I watch her flying upward, now higher than the roof of the house. So high, her feet are up above her and her head aimed at the ground. The rope is creaking. The tree is moaning, shuddering when she hits the end of some slack.

All the way, honey! Loop the loop! Loop the loop!

I stand back and watch her moving past me like the arm of a metronome. She's keeping time but losing the beat with every pass, slowing more and more, until I come in and use everything I have to get her back on the beat, to hold the time steady. It will only slow down if I let it. I step in after her as she jangles by and try to send her over the top.

Glorious! she shouts as she sails up into the darkness.

Then I hear the guys yelling inside. Something crashes and someone screams. Be right back, I tell Nancy, giving her another shove into space.

Inside, I find the living room a mess. The coffee table has been knocked over and crackers and peanuts cover the ground. The guys are trying to pull Wally and Clyde apart as they grapple on the floor. I push in and pick up Wally.

Clyde comes with him, then lets go and falls to the ground with a grunt. The others pull Wally away as Horace helps Clyde to his feet. Clyde makes a big show of dusting himself off.

Hey, guys, I say. Chill out!

You're lucky this kid came along, Clyde says. I was close to murdering you.

You see what you did, you son of a bitch! Chet is yelling at Clyde. You see?

Chet points at Wally's ear, which is ripped a little by the lobe. Blood runs down into his collar. Wally dabs it and looks at his fingers. He rushes at Clyde but I push him back and he falls onto the couch.

You're all a bunch of assholes, Horace says, swatting at the air. You're all bent on ruining a good thing.

What's going on? I say.

Everything has to end, Wally says. It's the way of the world. You think you can escape that?

At first, I think they're talking about the party, the ladies. But what I soon realize is that they're talking about the band. They're talking about breaking up the band.

I sit down on the couch. Well, goddamn.

You said it was over when Abe died, Wally tells Clyde.

Then they're all shouting about Abe, who I learn was the drummer who just died. Abe was their meter man, their beat. It seems that Clyde promised Abe on his deathbed the band was kaput.

But you just got to keep going with the charade, Chet says. Look at us, for Christ's sake, we're down from fifteen guys to just the five of us.

I count the guys and it's clear that Chet isn't counting me. I'm six. If they want me, I'm six.

You think anyone cares about what we're doing? Chet yells.

They argue on, shouting in each other's faces. Ruth comes in and says if they don't leave she's calling the police, but they ignore her as they bring up old complaints about each other: Horace is losing his ear and he's hitting a lot of clinkers. Wally's lip is shot. Chet can't make it through a song without getting dizzy.

It's DOA, Wally is saying. It's DOA.

I reach up and pull off the moustache and smooth it out on my thigh, then crumple it up in my hand and stuff it in my pocket. Outside, I can hear a woman's frail voice, calling for someone named Stanley.

Kenneth Calhoun is astonished to realize he has lived in the South for ten years. During this residency, his short stories have appeared in *The Paris Review, Fence Magazine, Fiction International, Quick Fiction, Salt Hill,* and other publications. He has also won the Italo Calvino Prize for fabulist fiction and the Summer Literary Seminars/*Fence Magazine* fiction contest. He currently resides in the International Pavilion at Elon University, where he teaches interactive media.

ANYA BELKINA

A year out of high school, I made a living as a drummer. I taught lessons, did some theater, and played in two bands. One was a wedding band. The other was a post-punk, neighbor's nightmare called Hemingway Shotgun. We played all the hot clubs and bars. Only we played them on

Tuesday night. Around that time, my grandfather used to invite me to a concert-in-the-park series to hear Dixieland, which I secretly loved. Most of the musicians were pretty elderly, but they could still tear it up. Sitting in front of the bandstand with a crowd of senior citizens, carving at the inevitable cheese log with a fistful of crackers, I'd sometimes entertain myself with an absurd fantasy in which the ancient drummer would keel over and I'd have to fill in, saving the day. All this was nearly forgotten until my dad joined a Dixieland band after retiring. Most of his bandmates were in their seventies and beyond. It wasn't long before members started dying off and the band began to shrink. The fantasy of filling in came back to me, and this time I did something with it.

Marjorie Kemper

DISCOVERED AMERICA

(from *Southwest Review*)

In the fall of 1963, before John and I left California on what we were billing as our "Discover America Trip," people warned us we might hit bad weather. And there was some snow in the Rockies, but most òf the heavy weather turned out to be inside the car; elsewhere, the fine Indian summer seemed destined for a long run. We went all the way north to Canada. Even there they were still enjoying summer. They wore light clothes and surprised expressions. Then we turned south.

In Kentucky, at an abandoned rock quarry, John and I made love for what turned out to be the last time. Under sycamores which blazed red and gold. Driving south to Memphis, John began to itch and scratch.

"It's poison oak, or poison ivy, I can't tell which," he said.

It was poison oak, but I didn't see any particular reason to tell him. And it was serious, because John was one of these people who swell up like the Goodyear Blimp if they're bitten by a bee. We drove through Kentucky and into Tennessee. While John drove I scratched his shoulders for him.

"I can't wait to get home," he said, his voice hoarse, even the membranes of his throat were now irritated and swelling.

"I *am* home," I said, meaning the South, where I had lived my whole life until I'd gone away to college in California and met John.

"You know what I mean. I'm looking forward to it being just you and me again, in our own house. Jesus, I wish you knew how to drive! You're getting your license the day we get back."

Of course, it hadn't been just "you and me" in our house for a long time. But I wasn't supposed to know that.

John had been enthusiastic about seeing the America that lay beyond California, and so long as we had been in the north he seemed to like what he saw. But starting in Tennessee, John became more and more critical. Even the scenery irked him. He'd been outraged by the shacks on the edges of fields.

"Look at all those abandoned places," he said. "Why doesn't somebody pull them down?"

"They're not abandoned," I said. "They're sharecroppers' houses."

"You call those houses?" John asked angrily, as if I'd personally refused the occupants plumbing and whitewash.

"I'm only saying they're occupied."

"I don't know how you people live with yourselves."

I didn't say anything. John was the first person I'd ever had any difficulty living with.

By the time we made Memphis, and my Aunt Louise and Uncle Harold's house, John was turning a bad color.

The next morning, he was so swollen, his neck disappeared; it looked like his head was sitting on his shoulders. Calamine wasn't going to get it. Not an ocean of the lotion could have prevailed. My young cousins, five and eight, stared at John openly.

"John's head ate his neck," Teresa said.

"John's as red as my fire engine," Paul said, holding up this vehicle next to John's face for comparison.

"Go away," John croaked.

My aunt called the doctor she used for emergencies, usually having to do with Paul and Teresa—two congenital hellions who were forever splitting their lips, gashing their knees, and knocking out teeth—their own or each other's. Dr. Grueber's office was in his house ten minutes away, Louise told us. He'd see us right away, and it was better than sitting for hours in the emergency room at the hospital.

The house was just on the edge of town. On the verge of a black suburb. Actually, it wasn't a suburb, it was plain old outskirts. Some of you may remember outskirts. A light-skinned black woman let us in and showed us to the kitchen. This was my aunt's doctor's office: a kitchen in a run-down frame house with torn screens on the outskirts of Memphis. I wish I could say I was surprised.

Two little coffee-colored, red-haired boys were running in and out at the back screen door. Clearly, they were the doctor's own. And that did surprise me, because my aunt's views on "miscegenation" were broadcast regularly and well-known to us all. Perhaps the doctor and this woman had a grand passion, which had put convention in the shade for my aunt. But from the way they spoke to one another, not even that. Still, Grueber was a doctor. He had a diploma from Heidelberg University, hanging on his kitchen wall over wallpaper decorated with bunches of grapes.

When we'd pulled up, Dr. Grueber had been working on a GM van in his driveway. He was middle-aged—I couldn't help thinking he was the right age to have worn a German uniform during World War II. He washed his hands at the sink with Borax. He dried them on a towel hanging off the kitchen stove.

"So! Poison ivy!"

"Right," John whispered. John's head had eaten his neck; John was the color of Paul's fire truck, he was in no condition to question his new doctor's credentials, his diagnosis, or his living arrangements.

"Cortisone," the doctor said briskly. "Some epinephrine for good measure, I think," he added, eyeing John.

Dr. Grueber opened the fridge and batted around in it. A family-size bottle of ketchup fell out on the floor. The doctor kicked at it, and it lodged beneath a baseboard that had never seen a scrub brush. He called to the woman in German.

She was leaning against a counter and answered him in English. He found what he was looking for in the door. Where she'd said it was.

"Roll up your sleeve," he said. But John's arms were so swollen that his sleeve had to be slit with a bandage scissor before the doctor could administer the injections. At least John didn't faint, as he had when we got the blood tests for our marriage license. That had surprised me because John was a research chemist and did far worse things to rabbits all day long than draw their blood.

The doctor listened to John's chest with a stethoscope and took his blood pressure. I think he was vamping. He was giving the drugs time to work. Gradually John began to look more human. He cautiously cleared his throat.

"So," Dr. Grueber said, "you're starting feeling better?"

John nodded and smiled.

"You are traveling the country, your aunt told me."

John began to tell him about our trip, haltingly at first, but as his throat cleared, he achieved his usual pedantic stride. John delighted in maps, in gas mileage, in alternate routes, so he had a great deal to say. He made no mention of the rock quarry.

The doctor's wife continued to lounge against her kitchen counter. She looked angry. Or maybe just tired. I thought she might be as sick of Dr. Grueber as I was of John. Our eyes met only once, and then by accident, we both dropped our gaze at the same exact moment.

"Lorraine, let's have some coffee and kuchen."

Lorraine filled the kettle and put it on the stove with a thump.

As I'd known he would, John began to tell the doctor that as a child he'd lived in Germany. The doctor naturally asked him if he spoke German. *Ja.*

I had been struggling through my language requirement at Scripps when John and I met. John was an assistant professor at Caltech. Back then I'd been impressed by his gift for languages. I'd thought it a proof of culture and refinement.

John and Dr. Grueber spoke in German. My German was not

equal to following much of what they said. They both spoke with Bavarian accents; it didn't even sound like the German I had tried to learn. When the coffee was ready, the doctor switched to English, and the subject changed to race relations.

It was November 1963. All of my relatives, and now it seemed their peculiar doctors as well, were furious with President Kennedy and "that turncoat Johnson." Already that morning at breakfast this topic had come up.

"I guess you and your folks are happy now that Jack Kennedy's in the White House," my aunt had said, her merry eyes sparkling with malice.

We were, actually, but I demurred. My relatives had always baited Mother and Daddy and me about our liberal politics. I'd learned long ago not to react. In the absence of any spirited defense from me of Jack Kennedy, Louise told her stock of Kennedy family jokes—some of which were quite funny—and I didn't bother not laughing, though I was grateful that John hadn't come down for breakfast, because he was not inured by either time or blind love to the mean-spirited prejudices of some members of my family. He had never had to come to grips with loving people wholly, and helplessly, who, had they been anyone else, it might have been one's moral duty to shun. John was not capable of that kind of love. Nor did he approve of it.

Dr. Grueber expressed himself with greater sophistication than my aunt perhaps, but his opinions were familiar enough: black people were different than we were. No blame attached. No judgments made. Vive la différence.

Lorraine refilled our coffee cups.

The doctor could and did make the irrefutable claim that he knew blacks better than we did. As he should have. His companion and his children, after all, were, by the societal norms of the day, black. However, he did not raise this subject directly. I believe he said that he had "lived among them." Like Christ, one was left to infer.

Now, at the doctor's kitchen table, John's throat was opening to utter the doctrines of brotherhood and interracial harmony he had recently and rather incoherently embraced. But the doctor waved them away with one hand—the fingernails of which, I noticed, were still grimy.

"You Americans," he said, "misunderstand your own Constitution."

I stirred at my coffee. Let the doctor break John in. Better him than my vivacious aunt or my amiable uncle. Easier to listen to a German doctor who could, and did, quote Nietzsche, than a woman like my Aunt Louise who could say the most terrible things and still have you choking on suppressed laughter. Easier to hear the news from this Dr. Mengele than the sweetest man on earth, my Uncle Harold. At least the sound fit with the picture. The kuchen was very good. I sipped my coffee while John, his voice now returned to normal—always a little too loud—argued his case. Lorraine had turned her back on us and now leaned against the sink, watching her children play in the side yard.

A young woman came walking up the driveway. I watched her through the woody camellia that grew by the back door. Lorraine let her in. The woman carried a grocery sack, neatly folded over in half. She didn't look at us. Lorraine took her into the living room. I heard Lorraine say, "You can wait here."

I'd suspected that Grueber was an abortionist from the minute we drove up in front of the house and John had parked our car beneath the doctor's diseased maple. Now I was sure of it. Poison ivy cases and childhood accidents were strictly a sideline. I'd known because my abortionist's house—in a little foothill community in Los Angeles—had had this same forlorn air of neglect. Abortionists don't, as a rule, have green thumbs. Their lawns have bare patches. Their camellias invariably drop off in the bud stage. For reasons more obscure to me, their window screens are always in bad repair.

The two men still talked. Grueber didn't have to worry about keeping his next patient waiting. She had nowhere else to go. And she was lucky to have him. My abortionist hadn't had a degree from Heidelberg. Or anywhere else. John didn't know I'd aborted his baby.

The civil rights debate continued. John, who had grown up in a California suburb and in Europe, had never known a black person until he befriended Charles Reed—who taught music at Scripps—shortly before we married. And Charlie, who was a Californian too (his father taught at Caltech), didn't actually seem to know any black people either. Not counting his parents and his sister Clara, that is.

So John came late to the Good Fight. In all fairness, he'd only just discovered there was one going on, and in a flurry of militancy, he joined CORE, and then, I assumed, to turn word into deed, he asked Charlie to be best man at our wedding. John had closer friends, not to mention a perfectly presentable brother. It was not strictly necessary to put Charles in our wedding party.

"What is John thinking?" my mother asked me when she learned this. Not because she was a bigot, because she wasn't, but because the wedding photos would have to be sent to family. My parents were about to leave the country. They'd come out to California from Dallas for my wedding and would leave from there for Beirut, where my father, a petrochemical engineer, had been transferred.

This was, of course, back in the days when Beirut was "the Paris of the Mediterranean." Though when I look back now, I see that our family has had a predilection for cities that later would bear a stigma: Dallas, Memphis, Beirut.

In my first foray into standing by my man, I took a tone with my own mother. A woman who'd done more to fight racism than John will if he lives another fifty years. I implied that her objection to a black man in my wedding party proved that deep down she was a racist. Years of southern white guilt did the rest. She didn't say another word about Charles being best man. She made no explanations or apologies to the family either.

But John's interest in rights didn't extend to women's rights. Oh, he would have said it did. He is probably somewhere right this minute saying it. (Something inane like: The best man for the job is a woman.) But I am the one who should know, and I'm telling you it is purely talk. John was lucky to find me. Nobody but me could, or ultimately did, live with him six months hand-running.

I'd been brought up to defer to men. I knew never to tell a man bad news or raise an unpleasant subject until you'd fed him a good supper and had served him dessert and coffee. I knew when a man asked, "What are you thinking about?" there was only one right answer: "You, darling." So, thanks to this background, John and I had done pretty well. But that day, though John didn't know it yet, we were at an end.

The beginning of the end had dawned with my neighbor, Linda Bingham. I'd never been friends with anyone like Linda before, but an early marriage and student loans and an assistant professor's salary are great social levelers. I was lonely, and she was friendly, and it wasn't long before I was helping her with the fabric flowers she made for a nickel apiece in her living room to swell the family income. Dan Bingham was a dry-waller. (I never learned exactly what that was. I only knew it created a great deal of laundry.) I missed Dallas and my parents, and John was working longer and longer hours at the lab, and I was grateful for Linda's cheerful company. For her part, Linda was glad of someone to instruct. She had graduated young from the school of hard knocks and was eager to pass on what she had learned.

She taught me how to get out red-wine stains from upholstery; she taught me how to make something called tamale pie; but most importantly, she taught me how to tell when your husband was cheating on you—something of which she had considerable experience. You could tell, she said, when they started wanting it every night. That was the good news. But there were other signs that were not so felicitous—like late-night hang-up-calls and locating unfamiliar ladies' underwear shoved down behind the back seat of the car.

Linda was even the one to give me the news that I was pregnant. I'd come over for coffee at eight thirty when John left for school, when suddenly, sitting on her couch, and without warning, I threw up. I was appalled. And dizzy. And suddenly overcome by the smell of the hair spray that Linda used a can of every week.

"Oh-oh," she laughed. "How long is it?"

"How long is what?" I asked. I hadn't the slightest idea what she was talking about.

I knew from the start I couldn't take a chance on having John's baby. To have it was to be stuck with John forever because that's the way I am. And by then I believed that a woman had a right to a life not patched together from mistakes she'd made when she was too young or too dumb to know any better—like marrying a Yankee who talked too loud and didn't like her mother; a man who got midnight hang-up-calls and wanted it every night. (I never bothered hunting for her underwear.)

And it was Linda who found the abortionist. Not that she would have done it herself, as she told me several hundred times. She was pregnant too. She had a three-year-old and the incorrigible, dry-walling Dan, and yet she seemed overjoyed at the prospect of bringing another baby into their tiny house and their confused, overheated domestic life. But she had a friend who had a friend who'd had an abortion. Everybody had these friends in those days. And in your turn, you became the friend and were called up by friends of friends.

Then you knew for certain what kind of woman you were. You were the woman that somebody nice had for a friend. They kept track of you, just in case. That was, to my total surprise, the woman I'd turned out to be: a woman who needed to keep her options open so badly she would, like her president, "Pay any price, oppose any foe, to assure the survival and success of liberty." I had paid that price. I had opposed the tiny foe. All to keep a precarious handhold on my own liberty.

So I'd known I might have to divorce John even before we left on our trip. You may say, well, what were you doing in the rock quarry with him then? Why were you visiting your family, representing yourself to be a young, happily married woman?

My answer is, why not? We were married. I was a young woman, not particularly happy, but happiness is not a big tradition with us. In the beginning, I'd thought the trip might bring us together. I thought if I could get John away from her, whoever she was, I could win him back. And it seemed to be working. Until Kentucky. Which is where I discovered the identity of John's lover. It was Clara Reed, Charlie Reed's sister. It seemed that chief among the civil rights my husband was upholding so strenuously that year was a black woman's inalienable right to sleep with married, white assistant chemistry professors. This, it turned out, was John's real contribution to civil rights. I supposed that Clara was the reason Charlie had been John's best man. Though it may have been the other way around. It didn't really matter.

Either way, the whole time I'd thought I at last had John's full attention, he had been writing Clara postcards from our trip. I'd found one already stamped and addressed in the breast pocket of his jacket, when I'd reached in for the Mobil card to pay for gas—while John was in the men's room.

"Clara, Pushing for Memphis to visit more of Miriam's hillbilly relatives. Exhausted. How is it that a grown woman never learned to drive? Baked possum, anyone? Open a bottle of Châteauneuf-du-Pape and drink a glass for me. John."

Like I didn't know anything about good wine. It just happens I don't drink. As for driving: why drive when you can ride?

I'd decided not to have it out with John until we got back to California, because from Memphis we had planned to go to Dallas, to spend Thanksgiving with my grandparents, and then home. Thanksgiving with my grandparents could not be cancelled. They had been expecting us, counting on us. I'd called them before leaving California. They'd spoken on separate extensions: over and under one another—just as they did in person.

"Kennedy's going to be in town," Grandfather said. "You and John can go downtown and wave at him."

My grandparents hated the Kennedys. Grandfather hated their politics, and Grandmother was censorious because she thought they were bad Catholics. But since I was a bad Catholic too (just how bad, Grandmother could never have imagined), and since Grandmother was looking forward to my visit, and because my mother, another bad Catholic, was abroad and we both missed her terribly, Grandmother had planned a big, old-fashioned Thanksgiving and invited relatives from three states. "Like the old days," she had said.

"Christ Almighty!" Grandfather protested. "Not the old days. I'm too damn old for the old days. Too goddamn many people."

"You'll love it," Grandmother said shortly.

Grandmother didn't ask Grandfather for much. But what she asked for, she got—in return for Grandfather having everything exactly as he liked it the rest of the time. It struck me now that John was quite a bit like Grandfather. But I wasn't enough like Grandmother to make the equation workable. Grandmother would have let John keep Clara on the condition that she never had to learn to drive. Grandmother had struck many and many a bargain of this nature with Grandfather.

I couldn't hear myself think with John and Grueber talking over my head. I asked Lorraine if I could use the bathroom. She took me through the living room where the young woman still waited on a green, threadbare sectional sofa, staring at her shoes. She looked up quickly when we came in.

"The end of the hall," Lorraine said.

The bathroom was tiny. You couldn't have swung a cat. I sat down on the lid of the toilet, which was entirely swathed in violet chenille, which matched the violet chenille rug, which picked up the violets on the shower curtain—drawn across the grubby tub. I took an emery board out of my pocketbook. I shaped my nails and thought about our Discover America trip.

It had seemed important that we make it when we'd begun. And who knows, had I not found John's postcard to Clara we might have made a new beginning. Several times I'd felt we were on the brink of it. While we were driving across beautiful, empty Utah picking up faraway radio stations from Chicago and New

Orleans (all of them playing "Blue Velvet"); when we were eating hot roast beef sandwiches in diners with Gentleman Jim Reeves's piano tinkling from jukeboxes. Sometimes at night, when John's profile was silhouetted in the dash lights, he'd looked so young and so handsome I'd thought I could put up with anything. More than once I had seriously considered forgiving him everything. I had been very seriously considering it.

When my nails were perfect ovals, I examined my face in the medicine cabinet mirror. I was young and I had a level gaze and an honest face. I could still pass for a nice person. I turned on the tap and let the water run. There was a violet soap in the soap dish. There was a rust stain in the sink like the rust stain in my sink at home. It seemed neither Dr. Grueber nor John had ever heard of washers.

I stood on tiptoe to look out the high window at our car, parked under the maple—oozing sap. I liked that car; it was a red and white Ford wagon. Grandfather had bought it for us for a wedding present. I couldn't believe it had brought me here to this place. It was ironic of course, and had he known the whole story, John would have been the man to appreciate it. John claimed to love irony. It's never done a thing for me.

I opened the door and went back down the hall. The young woman looked up. Like she was seeking a sign: if I spoke to her, she'd go ahead with it; if I didn't, she'd leave—something childish like that. I hate it when people try to make me a party to their business. I didn't look at her.

Back in the kitchen, Dr. Grueber was fishing some pharmaceutical samples from a drawer. When he saw me he said, like he was just noticing my existence—which I think in a way he was, "Is there anything I can do for you, little lady?"

"No, thank you," I said. "May I have the keys, John, I need something from the car."

John handed me the car keys and turned back to Dr. Grueber to propose that, genetically speaking, a mixture of races made for a stronger species. I looked at the little boy with the runny nose who was now hanging on Lorraine's skirts, and at the two scientists sitting at the Formica table.

"Be right back," I said, for all the world as if anybody in that room cared. I walked out the front door and across the patchy yard to the car and got in behind the steering wheel. I sat there a minute, adjusting the seat and the mirrors, finding a good radio station and taking deep breaths—long enough to see Dr. Grueber's patient come out the front door too and walk away briskly up the street, swinging her paper sack, not glancing once at her shoes.

With your automatics, I found driving a car is not that big of a deal. *D* is for drive. That's pretty much it. I had no need of reverse. The worst part is you can't close your eyes crossing bridges. I drove to Dallas.

John was furious. He called at least ten times over the next two days; I never spoke to him. Grandfather finally told him to fly back home from Memphis and to keep in touch. I got my hair cut very short and bought a new wardrobe at Neiman's, where my charge plate was still good. I applied for a Texas State Driver's License and passed my driving test.

I wore my new skirt with the poplin blouse and red plaid jacket to wave at Jack and Jackie Kennedy. That was at Love Field. Before everything happened. They waved back. I remember thinking as I stood at the cyclone fence, being jostled by parochial school girls in plaid jumpers, *Too bad for you, John. You'll be sorry you missed this!*

Thanksgiving was so subdued not even Grandfather could complain of it. On television—which, after the assassination, was never off—I had seen that there was snow covering many parts of the America that John and I had discovered together.

I pictured our rock quarry under its white blanket. Even the poison oak—which of course I'd seen, but having just read John's postcard to Clara, I'd decided, strictly speaking, I was no longer under any obligation to mention. There would be crows in the trees we'd lain under, just as there had been that day, punctuating the now frozen silence with their loud warnings.

I'd told John at the time: "Always listen to the crows. Crows are the only creatures to concern themselves with human affairs."

He had laughed. And I had laughed too. I'd thought the crows were warning John of his immediate peril, and that once again, John was not listening. But I supposed now, as I lit the candles at either end of Grandmother's dining table, that the crows had been speaking more generally, and to all of us.

But we'd none of us listened, and now it was too late. Death was on television like a beauty pageant; it was in my grandfather's familiar cigarette cough; it was enthroned triumphant in my empty womb; it was depicted on the front page of every newspaper, morning and afternoon, which each new day hit the porch with sickening thuds.

The family was seated at the table. Grandmother's canary, Billy Boy, was singing up a storm in the kitchen—now a tropical zone from the heat of the oven. We bowed our heads. It was time to give thanks for our blessings. Of which, I still believed, I had many.

———————

Marjorie Kemper died on November 12, 2009, in Southern California, where she lived most of her adult life. She was born April 28, 1944, and grew up in Texas and Louisiana. Marjorie's short fiction recently appeared in *Alaska Quarterly Review*, *Ploughshares*, *Southwest Review*, and *The Sun*. She received an O. Henry Prize in 2003 for "God's Goodness," which was published by *The Atlantic Monthly*. Marjorie's novel *Until That Good Day* was published in 2003. She recently finished another novel, *Between the Devil and Mississippi*.

MICHAEL KRAMER

*E*lements of "Discovered America" are "true:" That sweet old red and white Ford wagon was named Gratia, after Marjorie's favorite great aunt, who lived halfway from town up the road to Grand Ecore, a big bluff above the Red River near Natchitoches, Louisiana. We did make such a trip. Both of us got poison oak from our romp by the quarry. We did visit a long-winded old German quack in Memphis. For years my nickname was Loud Man. From there the story takes off into that rich vein of imagination in which writers find the truth that makes great fiction. Marjorie said that when that process took hold, the characters—very much alive within the parallel universe of Marjorie's mind and heart—told her the story that she typed. And then sculpted to something close to perfection.—Gary Kemper

Elizabeth Spencer

RETURN TRIP

(from *Five Points*)

It was during a summer season Patricia and Boyd were spending together in the North Carolina mountains that Edward reappeared. He left a message on the answering machine predicting arrival the next afternoon, saying not to give a thought to driving into Asheville for him, that he would rent a car and come out, if at all welcome.

"At all welcome" sounded more than slightly aware that he might not be. Yet, of course, Patricia thought at once, they were going to say, "Come ahead, we'd love to see you," whether it was true or not. And for me, she thought, it really is true, though she doubted it was for Boyd. Edward had a charming way of annoying Boyd, she thought, though Boyd wouldn't say charming.

Patricia stood out on the porch of the cottage (rented for the summer) and looked out at the nearest mountain, thinking about Edward. Boyd soon joined her. "Wonder what he's got in mind."

"Oh, he won't be a bother. He'll probably be going on someplace else."

She could have asked, but didn't, just what it was Boyd thought Edward had in mind. Money used to be a problem for him, but family business might also be involved. Boyd never cared for him; she knew Edward was acknowledging that.

"Maybe he just wants to see us," she offered.

"Why not a dozen other people?"

"Those, too. He has affection. And God knows after what's happened he needs to find some."

"Nobody on the West Coast has any?"

"Well, but that girl died. Outside of that—"

"You'll ask."

"Certainly I'll ask. He'll tell me."

"But then you won't know either."

She whirled around, annoyed. "Don't brand him as a liar before he even gets here."

Boyd apologized. "He's your cousin," he allowed, adding, "Certainly not mine."

Patricia said what she always said, "But we're not close kin. In fact, hardly at all." Boyd had learned that just as there were complicated ways Mississippians took of proving kin, so there were also similar ways of disproving it. "God knows," he once remarked, "All of you down there seem to be kin." They dropped the subject of Edward.

Boyd spent the afternoon picking up fallen tree limbs from the slope back of the house. There were pine cones too. He built a fire every night, pleased to be in the mountains in mid-summer and need one. Boyd was from Raleigh, in flatter country, but he loved the Smokies. "My native land," he crooned to Patricia, "from the mountains to the sea." Patricia said she liked to look at them, but never ask her to climb one. She wasn't all that keen on driving in them either, though the next afternoon would find her whirling down the curves to Asheville. "I've got to go in anyway, to pick up groceries, oh, and mail off Mama's birthday present, else she won't get it in time."

"And pick up Edward," Boyd said.

"You won't mind," she said. "He'll be nice. I'll cook something good, you'll see."

But she had hardly made it out to the car when she heard the hornet buzz of a motorcycle coming up the Asheville road. It banked to pull in their drive and under the helmet and goggles she recognized her son. Oh Lord, thought Patricia. Why now? Then she was running forward to embrace him and hear about why now and calling to Boyd and finally getting into the car, leaving father and son to their backslapping and Whatderyaknows. A long weekend away from school. He might have told them. Boyd's shout of "Wonderful surprise!" followed her down the swirl of the mountain.

And all the way she wondered if the mystery could possibly come up again. They had been over it before and decided it was just a joke of nature, unfortunate, but only extended family to blame for their son looking so much like Edward.

Airport.

The heat in Asheville had about wilted her. She entered air-conditioning with a sigh and headed for the ladies' room to repair her makeup and make sure she looked her pretty best.

But before she could get there, a voice said, "Hey wait up, Tricia," and there he was when she turned, Edward himself, standing still and grinning at her.

"Oh!" He came forward and planted a sidewise kiss. But even those few feet of distance had let her notice that he didn't look so great. Older, and not very well kept up. Scruffy shoes, wilted jacket, tee shirt open. The blond hair was mingled with gray, but the smile, certainly, was just as she remembered.

He was carrying only a light satchel. "I checked the big one." He caught her arm. "We're heading somewhere right away and we're going to eat something edible. I nearly choked on dry pretzels."

She managed to find an ancient restaurant, still there from former days, dim and uncrowded, a rathskeller. She sat across from him, her questions still unasked.

Boyd was fine, she told him. Mark had just appeared. For a minute, she could plainly see, he didn't recall just who Mark was. Then he remembered. "Oh great!" he said. A silence.

Food ordered. Time for confidence.

Yes, his love had died. Yes, she said; she had heard and was sorry.

He had taken up with Joclyn in Mexico, followed her out to Pasadena, knew all along she didn't have long to live. Why do it at all? Patricia had wondered then, now wondered again. Love was what he said. It was reason enough. That was Edward.

"Oh, yes, Joclyn's gone," he said. "I tried but I simply couldn't stay on out there after losing her. I began to think, Where else is there? I mapped out a plan. Friends in Texas, a covey of cousins in Chicago. Brother Marvin in Washington. You here. I picked you first. And then, possibly, back to Mississippi. It's always there. Maybe not the happiest of choices. But there is where Mama used to be. But she's gone, too, and so is the house."

"And Aline?" She had to be mentioned sometime, especially if she was also gone.

"Oh, Lord," said Edward. "The eternal Aline. Don't ex-wives ever go away?"

"What do you mean? Die?"

"Or something."

"I always liked her," Patricia murmured.

"Spare me," said Edward.

Suddenly, Patricia felt terribly much older.

Boyd was showing Mark around the cottage.

"Isn't it a good place?" he enthused. "It's owned by Jim Sloan at the office. They couldn't take it this summer. You can bunk in here. Pat will make up the bed and so forth. And the bathroom's here. But now come on out and look at the view. We can see the New River. And the nights . . . ! Breathe in the cool. How's the new course?"

"I need to talk to you. I may be changing majors."

Boyd groaned. "Not again. Well, we'll discuss it. Meantime, do you remember Edward Glenn?"

Mark, thin but sturdy, often called handsome, given to pleasing smiles, looked puzzled.

"Cousin of Mother's?" he finally said. "Didn't she—?"

"Didn't she what?"

"I don't know, Dad. I just thought I remembered something."

"You better disremember it," Boyd grumbled. He was not given to subtlety, but he felt he was in a situation where such was required. "He just called up and said he was coming. Uninvited. She went down to meet the plane."

Mark's young brow wrinkled. "I thought of what I remembered—or what I couldn't remember. Didn't Mama date him or something?"

Boyd whirled on him so sharply he startled him. "Do me a favor? When he comes, act like you never heard anything about him."

"If that's how you feel." He concentrated, then said: "But why?"

Boyd was irritable. "I'll tell you later. After he leaves. Promise. Okay?" Outside in a flat side yard, Boyd explained he was trying to set up a fish pond. "Sort of kidney-shaped," he said. "Something to leave for the Sloans. They insisted on leaving us the house. Just the utilities to pay, though I guess if the roof blew off . . ."

"But do they really want a fish pond?"

"No trouble in summer. Just stock it. Feed 'em. Winter comes, scoop out the fish, drain it, leave it. We can start it while you're here." Mark had a look he got when something sounded like work. But then he got on better with his father when they worked together. Quarrels came when they pulled in opposite ways. He knows that, too, thought Mark. That's why he'd brought this up. Mark knew he had to ease his father into his new plans. Boyd went to a tool shed and produced two shovels. With a plastic measuring cup, he dribbled lime to mark the outline. He stood looking for a moment before he took up a shovel. A sudden thought. "Have you eaten?"

"I'm okay," said Mark and drove his shovel in the turf.

In Asheville, Edward and Patricia sat in front of a large house that was half burned down, surrounded by guard ropes and evidences of reconstruction, which was not at the moment proceeding. It was the remains of My Old Kentucky Home, the house

Thomas Wolfe had lived in and wrote about. Though why Edward had to see it, she wasn't quite clear.

"It's for my soul," he explained. "Tricia! I've got to live again. Every little bit helps."

She was wondering what little bit Thomas Wolfe had to offer.

"Didn't Wolfe have to put up with an awful family," Edward recalled. "I wonder how he stood it. We were luckier than that."

"Are we getting into family?" She was tentative.

"It's what we share," said Edward.

"Boyd's family . . ." she began again.

"What about them?"

"I've managed somehow. I even get on with his mother." She switched the subject. "You met Joclyn in Mexico."

"Yes, and I knew even then she was dying by degrees. After that she went back to Pasadena. I followed. Then there was chemo, all sorts of cures. But through it all she was happy. We were happy."

"Was that your reward?"

"Umm. The trouble now is, she was terribly rich. I didn't know how rich. It was some family legacy. Who's ever going to believe I didn't do it for that? Didn't even know a lot about it. Who'd believe it?"

"Nobody in Mississippi," she was quick to say.

Edward laughed. "Right on." A pause, then, "How did this house burn?"

"If I knew I've forgotten. Old houses just burn, I guess."

"I read Wolfe long ago. You learn something from other people's bad times."

"Like what?"

"How to get through your own."

"Edward?"

"Um."

"It's Mark. My son Mark."

"Of course. What about him?"

"Well . . . I better tell you." She laughed a little nervously. "He looks a lot like you."

"Poor kid . . . only . . . Well, now you've said it." He sat quietly, slowly digesting the implications. "I thought that was a dead issue. . . . Want me to leave?" He was only half-joking.

She was silent.

"Tricia . . . what if he does? Nothing happened. . . . We both know that. We've been all over it. I don't even think about it, haven't for ages." He stopped again, realizing he was getting off on the wrong track. "Let the past go."

"Boyd might not be the friendliest in the world."

"Maybe we can charm him with a drink or so."

"Just play it straight and we'll be okay. He's such a nice guy. At this moment you need us . . . need me. You said so. Besides, nothing happened."

"Tricia, nothing did happen."

"Right."

"Think of all Wolfe's talent in that one house . . . Busting to get out. And it did."

She started the car and backed away. Grey, old-fashioned, rambling and unsavory, the house had still managed to assert itself. The long-ago meetings, quarrels, seductions, and heartaches of that big, lumbering man's life, the family's torments, had all smoked up right out of the windows and porches to sit on the backseat of the car, leaning awkwardly over, speaking in their ears. So time to let it back out and then move on. Patricia thought she would read his book again. *Look Homeward, Angel.* Wasn't that it?

Later than it should have been, they pulled up to the cottage. Boyd and Mark were out on the terrace, drinking beer and admiring the view. But the stunning moment soon arrived, as Patricia and Edward appeared. All they did, naturally, was shake hands, then stood there, boy and newcomer, look-alikes, though not really carbon copies. Patricia removed herself hastily to the kitchen to stash away groceries, while Boyd turned and looked out down the mountain. The talk was perfunctory—weather, national news. Edward to Mark: "So what are you into at the university?" Mark to Edward: "It was history, but I'm trying to switch. I came home to talk about it." Boyd, disgruntled: "He's switched once already. Not good to keep on switching." Mark: "Computer science is a must these days." Boyd: "History is a great base. You can always take up the computer stuff when you finish that." Mark: "That's postponing." Edward: "I shouldn't have asked." Silence.

Patricia appeared with drinks. Bourbon for Edward with a little splash of water. Scotch straight for Boyd. Another beer for Mark. She had changed and smelled fresh. She settled into a lounge chair with gin and tonic.

"We started the fish pond," said Boyd.

"You can see the New River," said Patricia.

"It wasn't so much that I didn't like history. Old Douglas was interesting about the Greeks."

"The Greeks are important," said Boyd. "Ask Edward."

"So I'm told," said Edward.

"You all always knew each other," said Mark. "Funny, but I don't even remember kids I knew growing up."

"Well, being kin . . ." Edward began. "It makes a difference."

"Always at Aunt Sadie's," Boyd said with a shading of contempt, but maybe he was only recognizing their nostalgia for those youthful days. Patricia doubted it. She was bound to remember that one last evening. And so was Boyd. And so was Edward. And so soon after getting married too. Which made it worse.

She had often replayed it. Scene by scene, like a rented movie, its sequence never varied.

Edward was drunk and turning in. Boyd was drunk and staying up. Patricia was drunk and had gone to bed.

A house party given at Aunt Sadie's for Patricia and Boyd, bride and groom. What a glorious afternoon it had been! They had spent it walking to familiar places on the big property: the garden swing out near the lily pond, the winding path down to the stables, now empty, the old tennis court. Aunt Sadie, widowed but content these past years, with two gardeners to help, kept it all up. She had Lolly, too, a wonderful cook. Late as usual, Edward had appeared.

"Well, it's about time," Aunt Sadie scolded. "We'd about given you out. Where's Aline?" "Home with a headache." Edward's code response, everyone knew. He and Aline were famous for pitched battles. Aunt Sadie gave him a drink. The guests were trooping in. It had turned black and was about to rain. Thunder grumbled. They all crowded inside.

"We'll play games," somebody suggested, trying to ignore the weather threat, though the sky had turned purple and looked low enough to touch. They were setting up a table for bridge when the lightning flash crashed right into the room and the lights went out. "Too dark to see aces," Patricia said. Edward declared it was too dark to do anything but drink.

"We could all go to bed," said Boyd, provoking laughter to acknowledge his honeymoon state of mind. Aunt Sadie said no, they could eat, as everything was done. She began looking for candles.

By the time they sat down everybody had taken a drink too many. They alternated between silly remarks, some known only in the family, and gossip about absent relatives. Both subjects made Boyd cross. Patricia could sense this, but didn't see it was so important or why they should stop having fun. The family didn't get together that often. He could stand them this once.

Somebody (must have been Aunt Sadie's big son Harry) also sensed the unease. He said to Boyd, "You can see what a crazy family you've got into."

"Well," Patricia chimed in, just being funny, "you ought to see Boyd's family."

That remark didn't work the agreeable way Patricia had hoped, but by then it was pouring rain. She was never sure why he was so angry. He put down his napkin and got up from the table. Everybody tried to look like maybe he was just going to the bathroom. They ate steadily on, as though nothing was wrong but the weather. Edward tried to get Aunt Sadie to make a fourth for bridge. Everybody had another drink, which they didn't need. No lights came on. Patricia finally groped up to bed with a flashlight thinking she would find Boyd, but nobody was there. He couldn't be out in the rain, she thought, undressing, but as soon as her head hit the pillow, she went out like a light. So when the body landed in bed, it hardly registered, if at all.

It seemed scarcely a minute later but must have been an hour or so that she started straight up wide awake with the lights blazing and Boyd in the middle of room, yelling, "What the hell you think you're doing!" And ohmigod, it was Edward saying, "Huhuhuh," rubbing at his head and straightening up from where he was sprawled out next to her. Patricia had always maintained he was fully clothed, though why she had to maintain it was the real question.

"You'd have to see he hadn't even undressed," she kept saying to Boyd, as they drove away that very morning, hardly saying good-bye.

"Yes, all right," said Boyd, "but what was the bastard doing in my bed in the first place?"

"It was always his room when he came to Aunt Sadie's." Patricia had said it so often she was about to shriek.

"We won't discuss it," said Boyd. And wouldn't. Period.

But slowly it dawned on her that the reason he shut her up was that he didn't care for any of them, especially Edward. *He wants to get rid of all of us!* Such was the thought that kept hanging around like a bad child or a smelly stray dog, no matter how many times she told it to go away.

Now the thought had followed them all the way into the mountains. Patricia was so annoyed she actually considered leaving them before dinner, with nothing to eat. But staying, she had to face it that the only really difficult person was Boyd. Edward was grieving over his loss. Mark was worrying about changing majors. But Boyd was sinking into a mood of long ago. Yet when she came in with a smoking casserole, everyone seemed amiable, even smiling. Talking college days.

"What's Pasadena like?" Boyd wanted to know.

"I thought it was pretty nice. People out west aren't made like us. You had to make efforts to know them. Then it might not even register. They don't get into the politeness routines. Of course, Joclyn had friends, family too."

"I wish I had known her," Patricia said.

"It's what I mean," Edward said, half to himself. "Out there, nobody would say a nice thing like that." He smiled at her. Their kinship came back.

"We stopped by the Wolfe house," Patricia said, leaping to a subject.

Boyd looked blank. "The what house?"

"Oh, you know, Boyd. The Old Kentucky Home. Thomas Wolfe's mama kept a boarding house. It's in Asheville."

"Of course, I know that. Insured with the firm. When it caught fire, we had a struggle over payments."

"Did somebody set it?"

"The facts kept dodging us. It could have been some sort of family jealousy coming out that way."

Mark said brightly, "If you get mad in a family, it just goes on and on. There's this boy at school can't see his daddy because—" He stopped.

"So what will you do next?" Patricia asked Edward.

"When my round of visits are over you mean? I'll have to sit down and think about it."

Boyd regarded him as though he might be a half-wit. For a grown man just not to know what to do next seemed hard to believe.

Edward said, "I'd move back home if it weren't for Aline."

"That's his first wife," Patricia told Mark. "He doesn't like her."

"She wouldn't be all over the state," Boyd said.

"Yes, she would," said Edward. "She's got a talent for it."

"Word gets around," Patricia laughed. "We never knew what to make of Aline. But we tried."

"I tried too," said Edward.

"Do you remember that evening when you had gone fishing and came in to Aline's dinner party with a string of catfish, when she had made up this important meeting you had to attend?" Starting that story made Patricia choke on laughter.

But Boyd was getting stiff. "All that family stuff. . . ."

Patricia retreated. "I won't start it," she vowed. "I promise, cross my heart, hope to die."

Boyd laughed. He suddenly decided to be a good host. He went to work at it, asking if they had passed a highway project on the way from the airport. "Funny thing," he started out, and went into the funding, the business deal, the election that interrupted it, knocking out a campaign promise. He got them interested. His facts were certain to be correct. Boyd always said that to be funny you didn't have to exaggerate, just tell the truth. He said it was one thing Mississippi people knew very well. He said that now.

"Going to Mississippi is what I'd like to do," said Mark.

"It's not like it used to be," said Patricia. "All changed."

"Changed how?"

Boyd explained: "They don't have these big properties kept up by old ladies with lots of black help kowtowing and yesma'aming."

"Aunt Sadie was wonderful at it," Edward recalled, half to himself.

"She was getting dotty," said Boyd. "That's all I remember."

"She did her best," said Patricia fondly. "Right to the last."

"Was she my aunt, too?" Mark wondered.

"Great aunt, I guess," Patricia allowed, then asked about football.

Mark was their only child. In spite of efforts, she had never conceived again.

In the dark evening on the terrace they sat listening to a faint whispering of nighttime creatures, an occasional splash from the river.

"We could get the canoe out tomorrow," Mark said. "Is it still down there?"

"I haven't checked," said Boyd. "I'm sure they wouldn't have taken it to Europe."

"Maybe I'll go abroad," Edward mused.

"Ever been?" Patricia asked.

"Once with Joclyn. It was interesting, but we moved around too much. It might be nice just to find some place and sit in it."

"Wondering what to do next?" Boyd asked.

"Right," Edward agreed.

"Well," said Boyd, who was commencing to feel control, "you could go some place like Sweden. I always wanted to go there, but I never found the time."

"What would I do?"

"You said you would just like to sit," Boyd pointed out.

"The summers are too short."

"Try Mexico. That's summer all year round."

"I did try Mexico. It's where I met Joclyn."

"Oh."

Edward was silent. He seemed to have faded into the night shadows. He had declined dessert and coffee, wanted no more to drink. He came up out of his silence to say: "It was a pretty place."

Patricia knew he meant Aunt Sadie's place and she saw, as if it was actually there, the slope of the yard in the twilight and down beyond the drive the myrtle hedge and the fireflies.

"Lightning bugs," said Edward, echoing her own thought exactly. "Remember the time that—"

"I'm going to bed," said Boyd.

But when he left Mark wanted to know what time he meant.

"I bet he means the time about the pig," said Patricia, guessing. She was right.

"She made a pet of it and wanted it in the house," said Edward.

On they went, laughing and remembering, until Mark left for bed. Edward, finally rising, crossed to Patricia and kissed her on the forehead. She threw her arms up to him, and he was gone.

•••

While still at morning coffee, Boyd and Patricia saw Mark outside with Edward, bending intently over Mark's motorcycle. Straightened upright and started, it gave a nasty cough and snarled. Mark shut off the motor while Edward speculated. He seemed to know what was wrong. Mark came in with a grease smear down one cheek. "We need to go down to the store. Can we take the car?"

"What do you want?" Boyd asked.

"It's something to clean the gas line. They'll know at the filling station. Edward says he can tell them."

"I had one in Pasadena," Edward explained.

Boyd gave his consent. The two got in the car and went away.

Patricia finished in the kitchen and came out to the terrace. Boyd joined her.

"They're gone," she said.

Nobody had ever doubted that Boyd was right for Patricia. She had had a definite wild streak which she explained by saying nobody understood her. There had been escapades in the sorority at Ole Miss, sneaking out with that Osmond boy who wasn't the right kind, and then that wild night in the cemetery. Several had got expelled. It was said she escaped because of her good family. But then her own mother had run her out of church for showing up at Easter service in a low cut silver dress with spangles. Yes, Boyd Stewart was the right one. For one thing he had a no-nonsense approach. He corrected her right before the whole family. "That won't do, Pat," and once he just said, "Hush up!" The remarkable thing was she minded him. And after a year or so, remarked on in stages by home visits, she "settled down."

As for all the running around during those years that she and Edward had done—if nobody exactly minded, it was because they were kin, or near kin, thought of that way.

Boyd made money. He took life seriously. Insurance was a complicated business. He was still learning, he said. "But he must be fun, too," Aunt Sadie remarked. "How come?" her daughter Gladys asked. "Patricia wouldn't have had him if he wasn't fun."

They pondered over what the fun might be. They accepted Boyd. When he visited, he unpacked and hung his clothes up carefully. Driving away with Patricia after that first visit, he had remarked, "They're going to lose that place." "How come?" she asked. He laughed and said in his brushing-off way, "They drink too much." That wasn't what he meant, and a few years later, they had to sell. By then Patricia had had her baby and then she settled down even more.

Patricia and Boyd had lunch alone. Boyd wondered if he should call the filling station. Patricia giggled. "Maybe they went back to 'My Old Kentucky Home.'"

"Why do that?" Boyd asked.

"To look for Thomas Wolfe's ghost."

Boyd went out to work on the fish pond. At three o'clock he came in. The sky had thickened darkly. He was sweaty; his shirt and trousers smeared with dirt. Patricia was checking the weather station on TV. He stood in the door and announced: "I do love you, Pat." He sounded angry. "Why, honey," she said, "of course, you do."

Something was happening, but where it was happening, they didn't know. The first thunder rumbled.

Patricia came to Boyd. "And we both love Mark." Impulsively, they hugged. There was a rush of rain and closer lightning. They ran around closing windows and troubling about Mark and Edward, who did not come.

At twilight with the rain over and Boyd tired of ringing up with queries, they heard the car enter the drive and leaped up to see.

It was Mark.

"Gosh we were worried," Boyd reproved.

"It was just raining. We thought you'd know. We had a couple of beers."

"Where is Edward?"

"Oh, he's gone. He said you'd understand."

Patricia felt the breath go out of her, permanently, it seemed. "Why?"

"He said just throw away the stuff in that little bag. He had a big one checked at the airport. He took a taxi into Asheville. I offered to drive him but he said no."

"Well," said Boyd. "I guess that's that." Relief, unmistakably, was what it was.

Patricia went inside.

At dinner nobody talked but Mark, and he talked his head off. He had been to drink some beer with Edward! Edward was great to talk to! Mark could tell him things! He listened!

"About what?" Boyd asked.

"Everything. Girls and school and all. I could really talk to him. I'm sorry he went away."

Patricia got up to clear but Boyd said, "Don't worry, honey. I'll do all this. You go on out on the porch. It's cool out there. Look for the lightning bugs."

She sat in the dark and heard them quarreling. "If you think like that, son, just go on back to school and don't ever listen to me." They could say it was about school, but it was really about Edward. There was no way possible she and Edward could have done anything at all that long ago night, both drunk as coots. No, it wasn't possible.

Patricia got up from the porch and walked in the dark down to the New River. She kicked off her shoes, sat on the boat pier and put her feet in the cool, silky water. It was then she heard the Mississippi voices for the first time. She knew each one for who it was, though they had died years ago or hadn't been seen for ages. Sometimes they mentioned Edward and sometimes herself. They talked on and on about unimportant things and she knew them all, each one. She sat and listened, and let the water curl round her feet.

Elizabeth Spencer was born in Carrollton, Mississippi. She received an MA from Vanderbilt University in 1943. Her first novel was published in 1948; eight other novels followed. Spencer has published stories in *The New Yorker, The Atlantic,* and other magazines. She went to Italy in 1953 on a Guggenheim and met her future husband, John Rusher. In 1986 they moved to Chapel Hill, where Spencer taught writing at UNC until 1992. Her other titles include *The Voice at the Back Door, The Salt Line, The Night Travellers,* and *The Light in the Piazza,* which was made into a movie in 1962 and was premiered as a musical production on Broadway in spring 2005. It received very good reviews, and won six Tony Awards in June 2005. Spencer's writing has received numerous awards, including the Award of Merit from the American Academy of Arts and Letters. She is a member of the Academy and a charter member of the Fellowship of Southern Writers. In 2007 she received the PEN/Malamud Award for Short Fiction. Her latest award is the Lifetime Achievement Award from the Mississippi Institute of Arts and Letters. Her most recent book, *The Southern Woman: Selected Fiction,* has recently been released as a Modern Library trade paperback. Please see her Web site, www.elizabethspencer.com, for more information.

The story "Return Trip" is the result of a return trip of my own to Mississippi, my home state, two years ago. I have written both a play, For Lease or Sale, and two other stories centering on an enigmatic char- acter, Edward Glenn, who seems to wander around a lot, a sort of displaced person from Mississippi, showing up either there or elsewhere—Mexico, Pasadena, and in this case North Carolina. He is a gentleman and carries with him his own disturbing qualities. I now live in North Carolina and was invited once with my husband to a house in the mountains near the New River. I will always remember that house, that weekend, and it was easy to set a story there, which convinced me that it could have happened there. But the Mississippi memories were stirred by my recent return to home base.

Tim Gautreaux

IDOLS

(from *The New Yorker*)

Julian was living in a sooty apartment next to an iron foundry in Memphis when he received a letter announcing that his great-grandfather's estate had finally been cleared up. He stood in the doorway of his peeling duplex, his hands shaking as he read the terms. Most of the property had been sold off to satisfy liens and lawyers' fees, but the old country house and six acres remained, along with twenty-eight thousand dollars. Julian was a thin man of sixty-three, balding, a typewriter repairman who worked out of his spare bedroom and kept to himself. The one time he'd seen the grand old home was when he was eight, riding past it on a gravel road with his mother, back when she could afford a car. The mansion was surrounded on three sides by rows of cracked Doric pillars, its second-floor gallery missing many balusters, its windows patched with cardboard. Back then, it had been occupied by a glowering family of squatters who'd slouched on the porches and stared after his mother's black Ford as it crawled past the fence. For all he knew, they were still there.

He went inside, out of the late-June heat, and sat in a duct-taped recliner to reread the terms of his good fortune. The only extra money he'd ever had was a hundred-dollar win on a scratch-off ticket. Before his mother died, he'd spent two years at a tiny local college and considered himself at least wealthy in knowledge, more so than the shopkeepers and records clerks he dealt with. Normally, he disparaged people who owned large houses, yet deep in his heart he'd stored the memory of the old mansion, the only grand thing in his family's history. It had shamed him to long for the house, and now he owned it.

The thought of inflicting pain on unlucky people bothered Julian, so instead of personally telling the impoverished family who lived in the house that they would have to leave he asked the county sheriff to evict them. He spent a month emptying his apartment of derelict Selectrics and Royal 440s, then got into his twenty-year-old Dodge and drove southeast, into the scrub-pine flats of northern Mississippi. After an hour, he left the wide state highway for a snaky blacktop road, and deep in the woods he made a left turn down a gravel lane that ran as straight as a railroad for ten miles. At one point, he came upon a five-strand run of barbed wire healed into the bodies of live oaks, and he slowed, took a breath, and stopped the car. The lawn was a weave of waist-high weeds and fallen limbs punctuated by the otherworldly pink domes of thistle blooms, and rising beyond was a mildewed temple. Patches of plaster had fallen away from the main walls, showing orange, wind-wasted brick. Julian pulled past the end of the fence, got out, and sat on the car's hood. His now dead mother, whom he'd found hard to bear, pretentious for a poor woman and full of outdated airs, had talked about this house as though it proved something about her ancestors, the Godhighs. "They were noble and powerful people," she'd told him the day they'd driven by the place. "And we have their blood." He straightened his back so that he could stare over the wiry brush at the soaring columns, the brooding eaves, and felt that he deserved this inheritance, had deserved it all his life. He walked up the flag steps, through the unlocked door, and into a broad hall. It was an echoing house of frighteningly tall rooms that smelled of emptiness and mouse droppings. The place hadn't been painted in many decades, though the last occupants had left it relatively clean. The lightless kitchen, something added a hundred years after the place was built, contained a gassy-smelling stove and a badly chipped sink. Upstairs, four vast rooms opened off a wide hall, and a door led up to an attic crossed with naked cypress beams. Above that perched a glassed-in belvedere, unbearably hot, where he could look out over long flat plots of woods that had once been cotton fields. He imagined pickers dragging their bags slowly across the steaming landscape and understood whose labor had built the house. The roof was iron, and it looked to be sound, though storm-dented and running with rust. After inspecting the outbuildings, he drove six dusty miles to the town of Poxley, where he bought, on time, a bed, some chairs, a couple of tables, and a dinette set. Mr. Chance Poxley, a soft, liver-spotted gentleman in a white shirt and a skinny tie, also sold him a small used refrigerator.

"You can't live without no icebox," Mr. Poxley told him. "You'll leave a can of potted meat out too long on the windowsill and think you can eat it the next day. Then you'll get to throwin' up all over the place. You'll get the sick headache." Mr. Poxley raised a blue-veined hand to his forehead.

"All right," Julian snapped. "I'll take the damned thing."

"You better," he said.

"When can you deliver my items?"

"Where you live?"

He told him and watched for his reaction.

"Law. Is that old place still standin'?"

Julian sniffed and raised his chin. "Not only is it standing, I'm going to restore it the way it was."

Mr. Poxley scratched the back of his head and squinted. "What way was it? Ain't nobody alive ever seen a drop of paint on that place."

"That'll change soon," he said, plucking his receipt from the old man's fingers.

"You ought to get you a nice little brick house on a half acre, somethin' you can keep up. I don't think you understand how much that place'll cost to fix."

"The house is part of my family's history."

Mr. Poxley seemed to think about this a moment. "Well, I hope history can keep you out of a draft."

The next day, the old man and two high-school boys delivered Julian's purchases. Upstairs, Mr. Poxley stared at the sagging bedroom ceiling. "Say, what you do for a livin'?"

"I sell and service typewriters on a business route in Memphis."

"Typewriters," Mr. Poxley repeated, as if Julian had said buggy whips or steam engines. "We threw our last one out ten years ago."

"Some places need reliable old models to fill out forms and such." Julian spread open a sheet over his new mattress. "Antique shops want rare models restored."

The old man gave the house the once-over, looked down the flaking hall, across the warped pine flooring, gazed up at the cloth-covered wires snaking along the ceiling. "For your sake, I hope typin' comes back in style."

For the next three weeks, Julian scrubbed down the rooms and galleries and thinned out the fallen limbs in the yard, the end of each day finding him tired unto sickness. He bought an electric saw and some lumber to patch the second floor gallery, but every time he was halfway through a board a fuse would blow in the spider-haunted circuit box in the kitchen. The first time he fired up his double hot plate, the fuse-box door was open and he witnessed a cerulean flash and a rattail of smoke, the first of four fuses it took to fry one egg. He had no idea how to upgrade the wiring, and in the following days he began to eat his food cold.

Every day, he wandered through his rooms, calculating how long it would take to patch the fractured plaster, paint the blotched walls, and glaze the windows.

Julian understood that he would have to hire cheap help, a broken-down old carpenter desperate for work, or some rehabilitating wino or mental case, and the thought elevated his spirits, as if such servitude would echo the history of the place. There was an ancient kitchen house in the back yard, left over from the days when kitchens were built separate from the main houses in order to prevent fires, and the hired fellow could stay there as part of his salary. The rural living and the hard work would bring the man back to health, so the job would be like granting a favor.

He drove in to see Mr. Poxley, who, as usual, was standing at the end of his business counter, his left elbow holding him up. "What can I do for you, Mr. Typewriter Man?"

Julian frowned at the greeting. "I need to find somebody to do electrical work, simple carpentry, and painting."

Mr. Poxley's eyebrows flew up. "So do I."

Julian crossed his skinny arms. "But I can offer a place to live."

"You say you want this worker to live out there with you? What on earth for? You'll have to feed him, and he'll have lots of chances to bum money. After a few months on the place, he'll be the same as a brother-in-law."

"I want an employee, not a relative."

Mr. Poxley flapped his limp hand at him. "You want a sharecropper, son. Them days is over, gone to history."

Julian suspected that Chance Poxley had little grasp of history. He was just a desiccated old man who specialized in opinions. Still, he probably knew everyone in the county. Julian leaned in and lowered his voice. "I thought maybe I could find someone with a weakness. You know how people go out of circulation because they gamble too much or drink."

"Oh, you want a drunk sharecropper," the old man said.

"No, no. Maybe somebody just down on his luck. I could help turn him around."

"He gets drunk enough, he'll turn around plenty." Mr. Poxley slapped his leg and bent over laughing.

Julian had little patience with uneducated people and turned to walk out. He caught sight of a large corkboard tacked over with hand-printed messages, a community bulletin board. "Can I at least put up a little notice there?"

"Hep yourself." The old man limped off toward the restroom as Julian searched along the counter until he found pen and pad.

"Wanted: handyman to live on site and repair house. Ask Mr. Poxley for directions." Succinct, that was the way to be, Julian thought. He looked back toward the restroom, and added, "No drunks." He chose a black thumbtack out of a pile in an ashtray and stuck the note in the middle of the board, next to one offering a free rattlesnake to a good home.

The following Monday, Julian was outside on the lower gallery, cleaning up a geriatric Underwood on a plank table he had dragged from an outbuilding. In each room of the house, a single bulb hung from the ceiling, and the big spaces drank up all the light, so he'd begun to work outside in the morning sun, weather permitting. Around ten o'clock, he sensed movement in the periphery of his bifocals and raised his head to see a man standing in the heatstruck privet at the roadside, watching him. Julian called out, and the fellow struggled through the weeds and came up to the house. He seemed about fifty, a lean, fairly tall fellow wearing triple-seam blue jeans and a matching heavy denim shirt with the sleeves cut to the armpits. His baseball cap was of the same material, a plain-billed dome with no inscription. Julian had never seen a cap with nothing written on the front of it. "Where did you come from?" Julian asked.

"Town. I seen your note."

"What? Oh, yes." He stood up and began to look him over.

The man's yellowed eyes darted up the side of the building. "I can carpenter good. My name's Obadiah, but people call me Obie. It used to rile me when they called me that, but nowadays I just go along."

Julian studied him, looking for signals. "Can you paint?"

"Your name."

"What?"

"You ain't told me your name."

"Julian Godhigh. Right now it's Smith, but I'm going to change it to my ancestral name when I get a chance."

"Some men can change like a porch lizard switches colors," Obie said, focussing on Julian. "And some cain't." The man leaned off to the side and his skin was a cloudy blue-gray, as though he were ill in some exotic way. "I can paint a wall like a artist."

Julian smirked. "Really. Like Michelangelo?"

Obie looked away. "I reckon. Only I use a roller."

"What about electrical repairs?"

"It ain't nothing I cain't pick up. I can do one thing as good as another." He spat into the grass.

When the man turned, Julian glimpsed part of a tattoo, half a spider crawling out of the collar of his shirt. Again he saw that the skin on his arms was a smudged cyanic color, mottled in incoherent patterns, as if the flesh had been cooked all over. "Are you from around here?"

"Over in Georgia."

"Can't find work there?"

"My wife and me been havin' trouble, so I was stayin' in my cousin's travel trailer. Except now he wants to sell it."

The men walked around to the wasp-haunted kitchen house and forced open the cocked door. Julian said he would buy a cot and the man could sleep there. They would try a working relationship for a few days. The one-room building contained a table with a porcelain top and a hide-bottomed chair, both sitting under an unfrosted lightbulb hanging from the ceiling on a long cord, and Obie went in and scraped dust and fallen dirt-dauber nests off the table with the side of his hand. Julian returned to the big house and brought back bread, block cheese, and lunch meat, and they came to terms.

Obie stepped over to a window. He rubbed a hand over the cloudy glass and cleared a view out toward a collapsing shed. "You ever been married?"

Julian suddenly wanted a drink, and he sat down on the single chair. "One time. It lasted about four years, and then it was time to leave."

Obie reached over his shoulder to scratch his back. "I married a religious woman and did all I could to please her. I even got saved and tithed out of what little pay I made. She run me off even though I done things for her no other man would of." Obie looked down at the floor as though contemplating a scene of great sorrow. "It was a mystery why I did it."

Julian bobbed his head. "Mine asked me to make more money, but I wanted to keep doing what I was doing. A manual typewriter and I were made for each other. I can make the big old Smith Coronas tap-dance like Fred Astaire."

Obie looked up. "You left her, or she left you?"

"I think the motions were mutual."

Obie leaned against the beaded-board wall. "You traded a woman for typewriters."

At first, Julian felt insulted, but the way Obie made the comment suggested that he understood, that he himself had made some unusual trades in his time.

"I needed to follow my talent."

Obie nodded. "I know about what a man thinks he needs." And with this he began unbuttoning his shirt. "You think you need to make a statement in life. But it don't seem like nothin' you do gets taken serious."

Julian felt a slight rush of panic as Obie opened his shirt wide to reveal a tattoo of a tailless dragon over his liver and one of a disarmed battleship across his hairless chest. Below the vessel was a dolphin jumping out of the sea, but its fin and its eyes were blurred, as though by an industrial accident. All the skin from his shoulders down to his waistband was fine-line tattoo work partially eaten away, the flesh abraded and inflamed. "It's a sight, ain't it."

"What in the world happened to you?"

"My tattoo collection. I'm gettin' it burnt off. I got my arms did already. I found a cut-rate Indian doctor to do it over in Poxley, but those treatments still cost like the devil and I'm about tapped out. It's why I got to go to work."

"What changed your mind about those things?" The colors, he noticed, were garish and the designs incongruous.

Obie stood up and looked out the door toward the big house. "Maybe I don't need 'em no more. Get a little older, you need less and less."

Julian jabbed a finger at what was left of the dolphin. "Well, there's enough work around here so you can afford to burn yourself white as toilet paper."

The night was warm and Julian turned in his damp sheets, waking briefly at gray dawn and hearing someone walking, inside and out. When he got up at eight and made coffee, Obie came to the big house's kitchen door and waited outside the screen looking in, as if knocking were beside the point.

"I got a startin' list for you."

Julian looked up from his coffee. "A list of what?"

"Of things to fix the house."

"Come in here." He took the smudged sheet where he sat at the wobbly table. "Good God, this is over a thousand dollars' worth of stuff. Where'd you get the prices?"

"I borried the phone in the hall."

He shook his head. "That's too much."

"Delivery is free above a thousand dollars. It'll save you seven per cent, man said."

Julian saw that Obie was looking at the ceiling, already working in his mind. "Well, what's on the schedule first?"

"Electric wire. Then low-lustre paint for a couple of these rooms." He smiled, showing big, evenly spaced teeth. "Hide the cracks and raise the spirits."

After the Poxley Lumber Company truck left, Obie began work. By Saturday, the difference in the place was palpable. In the kitchen, he installed a new gray breaker box, and two walls in

Julian's room were patched, sanded, and painted an airy antique white. Julian paid Obie in cash on the next Saturday morning and drove him to Dr. Setumahaven's office in Poxley, dropping him off and then going shopping. When he picked him up after the treatments, the expression Obie wore was that of a martyr, his eyes misshapen and dark with pain.

"You look like a boiled lobster," Julian told him.

Obie gently lowered himself into the passenger seat. "I got my money's worth today, all right."

They rode along the dusty road without talking, and Julian imagined that he could smell the laser burn.

That day, Obie mixed mortar and began patching the first-floor exterior wall. The next week, he worked on the downstairs bathroom, and the rest of the month he repaired the sewer line out to the septic tank and installed a cheap air conditioner in Julian's room. The men tolerated each other and ate supper together on a card table set on the creaking floor of the big dining room. One rainy day, they sat under the wavering glow of a shorting light fixture while Obie feebly complained about how little Julian was paying him.

"Yeah, but you're getting cheap room and board."

Obie glanced up at the dusty brass disk holding a circle of twenty-five-watt bulbs. "I got to share it with the squirrels and the rats. You ought to charge them half the rent."

Julian motioned to Obie's neck, where Dr. Setumahaven's laser had reduced the spider to a dim blue shadow. "You're still making enough to get rid of your collection."

"If you paid me more, I could get 'em burnt off faster."

"I don't understand why you bother at all. I mean, who cares? The doctor's gotten rid of all the ones people can see."

Obie rubbed his narrow face, his whiskers crackling like coarse steel wool. "I used your phone to call my wife. She said she might could take me back if I got rid of all my idols. She calls 'em idols."

"Take you back?" Julian gave him a startled look. "Didn't you tell me that woman beat you with a broom?"

Obie looked down at his plate and smiled a faraway smile. "Aw, she's just a woman. Can't hurt a man unless she buys a gun."

Julian stood up and began to clear the table. "Next time you go see Setumahaven, tell him to stick that laser in your left ear. Light up your brains."

Obie watched him leave the room and called after him, "Ain't you never lonesome for some company?"

Julian came back in and stood behind his chair. "I've got to the point where I can live alone. I've built up my business, and now I've got this big house to keep me busy and give me a place in the world."

The light fixture made a futzing sound, and Obie blinked. "So this here place makes you feel important?"

Julian threw his arms wide to the echoing room. "I *am* important. What do you say to that?"

Obie turned toward the window, where the antique glass distorted everything beyond. "I say I need another box of roofin' nails so I can fix the tin on top of your importance."

The work went on through September, and Obie slaved over the corroded wiring and the slow-running plumbing. He ran his hands over every board in the building, finding where thousands of square nails had pulled free from the shrunken lumber. After Julian had gone to bed one night, he heard the back door to the main hall scuff open. Figuring Obie had come in for a drink of ice water, which was all he allowed him to have from the refrigerator, he dropped off to sleep. Soon, he was awakened by talking, just parts of words bouncing up the stairs to his single bed. He crept to the head of the stairway and heard Obie use a soft and rhythmic voice he had never heard before. He listened hard and heard him say, "Save me, O God, for the waters threaten my life; I am sunk in the abysmal swamp where there is no foothold." Julian walked down until he could see Obie seated at the old phone table, a flashlight shining down on an open Bible. He wondered if the call was long-distance, if he should yell out to stop reading Scripture into the phone at twelve cents a minute. Someone on the other end of the line must have said something, for Obie's voice stopped, and then said, "I'm workin', but I ain't able to save much. He cusses me and charges me for everthing. Sent me to town in his car to get tar and took the gas out my pay. What? Read Psalm 64? It'll cover him, will it?" Julian coughed, and Obie shined the flashlight up to the dark landing. "I got to go now. I'll call you fore long." He hung up and raised his face.

Julian's voice sliced down on him. "Was that that woman in Georgia?"

"It was."

"You planning on reading the whole Bible to her?"

"No."

"I'm glad to hear that, but when I get the bill I'll let you know the charges."

Obie turned his head toward the back door and looked as if he might speak, but the only sound that drifted up to Julian was the click of the flashlight and then the invisible creaking of the hallway's boards.

On Wednesday, he drove to Chance Poxley's store to buy a night table. Mr. Poxley leaned on the end of the counter and watched him walk in the door. The old man screwed up his face as though he smelled carrion.

"Do for you?"

"I need a small inexpensive table to put beside my bed."

"Uh-huh. That Parker boy still workin' for you?"

"He is, slowly."

"How much you payin' him, anyhow?"

Julian turned his head toward the store's cheap furniture, then looked back. "Has he been complaining to you?"

Mr. Poxley focussed on Julian's eyes. "That boy's a good worker. I believe he can fix a broke horse."

"He's all right."

"What you payin' him?"

"That's between me and him. He ought to pay me just to put up with his spooky ways."

"You bring him into town today?"

"He's over at Setumahaven's."

"I heard he had them on the bottoms of his feet. That must hurt like fire to have one took off there."

"I don't think about it."

Mr. Poxley blinked. "What *do* you think about, Mr. Typewriter Man?"

Julian looked at him. "What do you think I ought to think about?"

"How about payin' somebody does good work a livin' wage."

"Look, I admit he's a good worker and not bad to have on the place, but he doesn't bear the expense of commuting or of owning a car. Again, has he been complaining?"

Chance Poxley swung his head away. "That one won't complain."

"Well, by damn, show me a table, then."

He finished at the furniture store long before he was supposed to pick up Obie at the doctor's office. He parked his Dodge, angrily thought over Mr. Poxley's criticisms, and then went into the red brick city library, where he found a small Bible and walked into the stacks with it lest someone see him. He turned to Psalm 64 and read:

Hide me from the conspiracy of the wicked,
From that noisy crowd of evildoers,
Who sharpen their tongues like swords
And aim their words like deadly arrows.

He slammed the book shut, holding the cover down as though it might spring back open accusingly. Between two musty stacks of dog-eared history books, he waited for the words to have some effect, but he felt not a thing, no change at all, though he couldn't resist touching his tongue to the roof of his mouth.

When Obie climbed into the Dodge that afternoon, he was bent forward with pain. Julian looked at him intently. "I wouldn't give anyone money to hurt me. If I were you, I'd have saved up for an automobile instead."

Obie closed his eyes and leaned his head against the cracked window. "What do I have need of a automobile, with no place to go?"

"Which one did they finish up today?"

"The battleship. Feels like he dug it out of me with a pocket-knife."

Julian checked his rearview mirror before backing up. "Will you be able to work on the upstairs porch?"

"Gimme a couple hours. I'll see."

He drove into Memphis the next day, delivering refurbished typewriters and picking up dirty, nonfunctional machines from three behind-the-times businesses and two antique shops. He collected a few accounts and added up his money. The weather had been unseasonably warm, and he considered buying Obie a small electric fan but decided against it, because it would just make him unhappy if he ever had to live without one again. It was cruel, he thought, to make things too comfortable for someone going down in life.

Two weeks later, Obie walked up to Julian where he was working on an old gray Royal on the front porch and told him that he had an appointment with the doctor on Wednesday.

"I'm not going into town that day."

"It's important. I got to get the big one on my back burnt off."

He put down a slim screwdriver. "You have one on your back? What for?"

"It's a long story."

Julian straightened up in his tin chair. "Let me see it."

Obie unbuttoned his denim shirt and let it down and turned.

Julian put a hand to his chin. "Good Lord, it's Jesus."

"He cost me a lot."

He adjusted his glasses. "It's a good job for such a large image. Too bad I can't skin it off you and frame it or something."

Obie jerked up his shirt and began buttoning It. "Can you take me to town Wednesday or not?"

"Maybe so. If you pay my gas." Obie stared at him and Julian wondered how he could be such a mooch, expecting him to ride him around like a free taxi. "Now, what do you think about that railing up there?"

"I reckon it ought to be changed," Obie said, tucking in his shirt. "You might lean on it and fall and break your neck."

Julian waited outside the doctor's office, dozing behind the wheel, dreaming of tall gleaming pillars and him standing between them in an immaculate white suit. When the door on the passenger side opened, he woke up feeling sore and sour. He looked at his watch and frowned. "What did your red-dot doctor think about erasing God off you?"

Obie sat with his back away from the seat. "He only took him off the outside," he whispered.

"Are you sure he didn't replace him with Buddha?"

"Can we go on to the house?"

"Aw, can't you take a joke?"

Obie rolled his burning eyes toward him. "Do you have any aspirin?"

"There's a tin in the glove compartment. But don't ask me to stop and buy you a Coke."

In late October, the money finally ran out. Julian announced that he couldn't pay Obie anymore, but he would let him live on the place for free if he painted the outside. Obie walked out onto the front lawn under the two-hundred-year-old oak and stared. Julian stood between a pair of crazed pillars, watching him. After two minutes he called out, "What are you thinking?"

"I'm figurin' it would take me sixty gallons of primer and paint and a full year to do it myself. It needs to be sanded, washed, and scraped, and I'd have to live here three years past the end of the job to take the value out in rent."

Julian stepped into the yard and looked up at the complex eaves, the paint-sucking galleries. "We can work something out."

"No, we cain't. I'm finished with my treatments. Setumahaven give me some fading chemical, and Monday I'll go to that tanning parlor by the cornmeal plant."

Julian took a step backward, startled. "What are you talking about? You can't leave."

Obie spread his arms like a gaunt bird ready to take flight. "The old me's gone. The new me's got to move on down the road."

Over the next several days, Obie's color changed from a mix of blood and ink to a mildly unhealthy skim-milk hue, and after several sessions at the Red Bug Tanning Salon his skin turned an even, rosy manila. One night, Julian decided that Obie might stay and work for him if he went into his meagre retirement savings and paid him a real salary.

The next morning, Julian got out of bed and fried a ham steak for breakfast, Obie's favorite. After the table was set, he went out into the yard, and his heart skipped a beat when he saw that the door to the old kitchen was wide open. Inside, the cot was empty, and Obie's duffel bag, always in the same spot under it, was gone. He began to panic and stared up at his sickly house, which loomed over him, leprous and crippled. He raced into Poxley, but no one at the bus station had seen him, and Dr. Setumahaven's office was closed. After driving around the town's narrow streets for half an hour, he parked and went into Chance Poxley's store.

The old man came out of his office and squinted at him. "What?"

"I can't find my hired man."

"Well."

"He just left without a word."

Mr. Poxley leaned over and pressed the Clear button on his adding machine. "That so?"

"Have you seen him?"

The old man shook his head. "It's been a while. He did tell me he'd finished up with the skin doc. I don't think he had much need of your job anymore."

"He told me he used to stay with a cousin. Where's he live?"

"He's not there. That boy pitched him out to begin with."

Julian stared at the store's broad plate-glass windows, emblazoned with shoe-polish lettering: CASH TALKS. "I've got to find him."

"Unless I miss my guess, you can't afford him anymore."

"What are you saying?"

Mr. Poxley looked down and his voice softened. "What do you need him for, anyway?"

Julian's mouth fell open a bit and he focussed on a new gas range to the right of the counter. He could fix a typewriter, but nothing else in the world, and he didn't know if he could continue living in the old mansion, unable as he was to keep it nailed together. But the real problem came upon him as suddenly as thunder. He'd be alone. The house and its canyon rooms would swallow him up, the only sound would be his own footsteps thrown back in his face, and when he stopped moving he'd meet a silence as vast as night.

In the middle of November, a freakish weather pattern set in— howling wind with ice in its teeth. Julian was adjusting a Royal 440, and around sundown his hands began to shake. The single-pane windows and the shrunken doors shivered in their frames. There was no insulation anywhere and what little residual heat there was soon leaked through the ceiling lath. He put on sweaters and two jackets and remembered that the house had no functioning heating system. The squatters had used tin trash burners, running the stovepipes through the windows, but all that had been thrown out. Obie had told him that the fireplace flues were no longer safe, that the chimneys were falling apart in the attic. He climbed into bed under every sheet and quilt he owned, deciding that the next night would be warmer.

The next night brought a whip-cracking gale, and a weatherman on his car's radio announced that a solid week of unusually cold temperatures was on the way. Julian drove into town and bought an electric heater, but under the fifteen-foot ceilings the device was like a spark at the North Pole. The third night, he slept in his car with the motor running, but, when he checked the gas gauge on waking, he knew he couldn't afford to do that again. He got out of the backseat cursing the oil industry and the whole Middle East and loaded up five repaired typewriters for delivery in Memphis.

The fourth night, he became ill and for two weeks suffered through a cold, which turned into influenza. After a teasing warm spell, December's weather came back mortally cold, and he moved out of the mansion into Obie's little kitchen house. The electric heater and the old wood-burning range together would keep the room at fifty degrees, and he could sleep. But it was a miserable place to stay, its attic full of manic squirrels, its floor a dull smear of ground-in soot and dirt, its walls impregnated with the oily emanations of ten thousand meals.

One day in mid-December, there was a knock at the kitchen-house door and he found Chance Poxley standing in the tall dead grass, wearing a small tweed fedora, shading his eyes with one hand.

Julian held the door open only a little. "What can I do for you?"

"Can I step in? This wind is about to freeze me female."

He backed into the room, and the old man came up the three wooden steps. When his eyes adjusted, he looked around. "My God, you're livin' like a jailbird in here."

"Next year I'll arrange to keep the big house warm."

Mr. Poxley shook his head. "I hear in the old days it took three servants workin' full time to keep all the fireplaces going with coal. You can't even buy coal anymore."

"Did you come out here to discuss my heating problems?"

"No." The old man handed him a sheet of paper.

"What's this?"

"You're two months behind on your payments."

Julian reddened. He stood staring at the invoice for a long time as the squirrels began chasing one another above their heads. "Are you sure I haven't paid these?"

"If you can show me the cancelled checks, we'll know, won't we?"

"I'll examine my records, and if they indicate that I've missed paying you I'll mail you a check."

Mr. Poxley put out a hand. "I'd appreciate a check right now."

"But I can't do that. I might wind up paying you twice."

The old man lowered his arm and looked over at the smoking stove. "Let me tell you some facts. People that take over a place like this have a lot of money. They can afford to hire a bunch of contractors to do a proper restoration."

"My dream is to do just that."

"At the rate you're goin', it'll take you a hundred years just to make the place look second-rate. And if you stay out here it'll kill you."

Julian folded his arms. "It's my heritage."

"There's people that'll pay a bit of money for this property. With what you sell it for, you could get a tight little house with a shop out back."

"And you'd get your money for the refrigerator and the air conditioner."

Chance Poxley fixed him with his watery eyes and said in a low voice, "Look, if you don't at least make up the payments, I'll have to put a lien on the place. So will the folks down at the lumberyard, who I hear tell have advanced you considerable supplies on credit."

Julian opened the door and pointed outside. "You'll get your money."

The old man looked into the weedy yard. "Well, I got to admit I've never been throwed out of a worse place than this." He eased down the steps and turned around. "You know, I didn't come here to cause you any trouble. But I got to tell you, when the sheriff found out an owner was on this property he checked into the tax records and told me he don't care what the lawyers say, you owe county tax on this place back to 1946." The old man's hat blew off and his thin white hair was torn by the wind. "I didn't want to be the one to tell you."

Julian waved him away as though he were a stray dog. "Get off my property," he yelled. "I can buy and sell every damned one of you." He didn't know where this cutting voice had come from, its load of arrogance perhaps conjured up out of the red dirt around him, the dead fields and parched lumber of his inheritance.

Julian sat down that night to balance his checkbook and found that he'd have to transfer money from his tiny emergency fund at the bank in Memphis to hold off his creditors for a week or so. After that, he was bankrupt.

One night of gun-blue sky, the temperature went down to nine degrees. Julian had stuffed the cookstove with scrap wood he'd scavenged and the stovepipe was glowing red halfway up to the flimsy ceiling. An old Remington manual was set up on the table and it refused to move when he hit the Tab key, the fresh oil on its parts turned to gum by the cold. At about eleven o'clock, he had to go to the bathroom, so he put on padded slippers and all the clothes in the room and opened the door to the night. The wind was a black punishment, and his bones were rattling by the time he reached the back door of the big house. As soon as he stepped inside, his feet began to sting, and when he turned on the hall light he could see water running deep on the floor. He splashed over to the foot of the stairs and looked up at a ladder of water coming down, a scrim of ice on the edges like a mountain stream. Upstairs, he found that a frozen toilet had shattered and fallen away from the wall, snapping off the feed line at floor level, and water was jetting up to the ceiling. He had no idea where he could turn the water off. And only one person could tell him.

He sat next to the phone table in the hall and hooked his feet on a chair rung to keep them out of the water. Pulling out his service receipts from the drawer under the phone, he studied the column of calls until he found a number in Georgia. He had done so much for Obie that the man should at least tell him where a valve was. Looking up, he watched lines of icicles forming where water sluiced through cracks in the plaster.

After many rings, someone in Georgia picked up the phone, and he asked to speak to Obie Parker. "This is his former employer," he shouted into the receiver. "And I need to ask him a question."

A woman's reedy voice answered, sounding self-righteous and glad to be so. "Do you have any idea a-tall what time it is?"

"Yes, I'm sorry, but this is important."

"Obadiah is asleep, and a workin' man needs all the rest he's due, so I'm not a-goin' to roust him out of a warm bed, Mister."

Julian's voice rose in pitch. "But I've got a broken water pipe and—"

"A broke pipe, you say? Mister, there's people in the world got a whole lot worse than that wrong in their lives. They got the cancer, they got children sellin' dope, they got trailers blown apart by the tornado wind that leaves them standin' in the yard starin' up at the stars. But you know what? Ain't a one of them callin' me up at twelve-ten at night to whine about no broke water pipe."

"It's eleven-ten."

"Mister, you caught up in your own little world so much you think the rest of God's universe is in your time zone. It's twelve-ten in Georgia."

A piano-size raft of plaster detached from the ceiling and fell at his feet, covering him with a surf of freezing water. "Good Lord, lady, I've *got* to talk to your husband."

"People in Hell *got* to have strawberry shortcake, but they don't get it." She hung up.

He lowered the buzzing receiver and looked down the long, swamped hall toward the front of the house that was his glory. He knew everything about it, and at the same time nothing at all. The wind flattened the tall dry grass next to the pillars in a dead shout that told him not a thing that would help. Suddenly, he was startled by the jangling phone.

"Hello?"

"Hey. It's Obie. I heard my wife a-talkin' to you."

The voice was like a warm, comforting hand, but Julian couldn't help shouting, "Where the hell's the water valve to the house? I'm flooded out, here."

"If you got water on the floors, don't go after that pump switch in the panel box. It'll knock you into the next world. Look under the sink and turn that third valve to the right."

He sloshed to the kitchen and did as he was told. With a house-shaking crash, the dining-room plaster fell all at once. Shivering, he ran back to the phone, wet up to the knees, and climbed onto the chair. "What do I do now, Obie? All the plaster in the place is coming down."

The voice drifted in from Georgia, sleepy and soft. "You can't afford no plaster crew, that's for sure." After a pause, he said, "Might be time to sell out."

"Never," he yelled into the receiver. "I'll never leave here in a million years."

"One time, I said I'd never give up my tattoos."

"Thanks, but I don't need your moralizing lesson. I need you to come back and fix things."

"I'm sorry, Mr. Smith, but it sounds like things is past fixin'."

Something dropped onto the kitchen floor like a truckload of gravel. "What can I do about the plaster?"

"That plaster's the least of your problems."

"What do you mean?"

"Well, if you don't know I can't tell you."

The light fixture above Julian's head filled with water and popped off in a shower of blue sparks, and he dropped the phone. He was blind and trembling in the watery dark, and he began to struggle down the hall toward his outbuilding, desperate for the warmth of the red-hot stove. When he opened the back door, he saw that the old kitchen house had turned into a windblown orange fireball, streamers of flame running toward him through the grass. He stumbled outside and began stamping at the brush until he understood that with its brick porch and pillars the big house would probably not catch fire. Through a sidelight at the rear door he watched the flames race in the wind, flowing under his car and fanning out to light the corncrib, the smokehouse, and the big sagging barn, which went up in a howl of crackling lumber and dried-out hay. At one point, he tried to call the Poxley volunteer fire department, but the creosote pole that supported the telephone wire had already gone up like a torch, taking his service away. In ten minutes, the fire circled the house, and he climbed up to the belvedere to track its progress as it burned to the ditches surrounding his tract, taking out the pump house and a tractor shed, and incinerating his Dodge, which burned hot and high, killing most of the foliage of the live oak shading it.

At dawn, he could see that but for the roadside oaks everything was gone, burned off the face of the earth as if by a powerful beam of light, the house standing naked and singed in a field of white ash. He stayed up in the belvedere, hoping the new sun would warm him, but daylight brought a shrill wind crying like the voices of all the families, wealthy and destitute, who had lived in his house, who, each in turn, had given it up through death or duress and left it to falter. He stood unshaved and burning with fever, dressed in sopping house slippers and several layers of old robes and cotton jackets, waiting—for what, he wasn't sure. But in a few minutes he heard a car on the gravel road, looked down through the bubbled glass, and saw them. Even from a distance, he could tell that Mr. Poxley's mouth had fallen open at the sight of the guttering outbuildings. He and a big deputy stepped out of the police car and walked to the roadside fence. Each man held down his hat with one hand and bore a folded piece of paper in the other, liens and tax bills that would take the place away, and Julian felt house and history shrink to nothing beneath him—a void replaced by a vision of himself, dressed in borrowed clothes and defeat, spirited away that very evening on a lurching bus bound for Memphis and sitting next to some untaught, impoverished person, perhaps even another long-suffering and moralizing carpenter.

Tim Gautreaux's fifth book, *The Missing,* is a tale of child abduction and human loss set on the Mississippi River in the 1920s. His fiction has appeared in *The New Yorker, Harper's, The Atlantic Monthly, GQ,* and university textbooks. He is currently working on a new collection of short stories. He taught creative writing for over thirty years and retired from Southeastern Louisiana University.

*O*ne time I got a letter from a grammar school student who'd read my short story "Welding with Children" and wanted to know what happened to the characters after the tale ended. I was happy that the student thought the short story seemed real enough to trick her into believing it was true. To be honest, I've thought this way myself, wondering about the lives of fictional characters beyond the last pages of their capturing works. Then a friend called and asked me to write a story that showed Flannery O'Connor's influence, and I decided to find out if one of her famous characters could be "continued," so to speak, carried beyond his set narrative. In early draft I saw this was not enough, was too simplistic, so I borrowed an opposing O'Connor character as well and had the two interact, contrast, and arrive at different destinies. Well, that's the story.

Laura Lee Smith

THIS TREMBLING EARTH

(from *Natural Bridge*)

The baby was a little different to begin with. Hard to love. He had a strange, high-pitched cry and dark circles under eyes that were neither blue nor brown, but rather an indiscriminate muddy gray. Long limbs, a brittle appearance. His name was Ethan.

I was there for the delivery. Kristen, my daughter, thrashed in the hospital bed and cried for the epidural long before it was time. She was eighteen. In the delivery room, she held my hand and begged me to make the pain stop, but I only said, "I can't make it stop, baby. The only way out of it is through it."

Outside, the air was thick and salty with smoke. "Look at that," I said, pointing to the window, where billows of smoke trailed through the hospital's parking lot. "I swear, I think all of Georgia's burning," though it was only a wildfire in the Okefenokee, some ten miles away.

Kristen wept. She vomited in a little plastic tray, and then the doctor came in and gave her the epidural. An hour later, Ethan was born. "It's a boy," the doctor said, and I couldn't help it, I thought of Ty, my boy, my almost-man. Once, he was a baby, too. Now he was twenty, which made me forty, which was something I had yet to get my head around.

When Kristen's baby cried out, his small voice was abrasive, and the rest of the room fell silent. Even when the nurse brought him to Kristen and she put him awkwardly to her breast, no one spoke.

I took a week's vacation to help with the baby. I'm a bailiff for the Charlton County courts, which means that, among other things, I'm the one to hold the Bible up in front of the defendants and witnesses when they take the stand, ask them if they're ready to tell the whole truth, so help them God. Almost always they look at me, scared, and they sort of mumble when they say "I will," and you know they will, damn straight, because that's a pretty power-ful thing, a woman standing with a Bible in her hands calling on the power of God. But sometimes they're calm, and don't seem afraid, and they stand a little to the side and don't look straight at me when they answer, and those are the ones I know are fixing to lie. There's nothing I can do about that. I'm an honest woman myself, but there's nothing I can do about a person who's destined to be a liar.

There was no father, in case you are wondering. The man who impregnated my daughter, the married, middle-aged discount gro-cer in Folkston who saw an easy mark and went for it, denied the baby was his. He actually sat in my living room and denied it, with Kristen sitting on the couch across from him weeping and shak-ing her head. "You got the wrong man, sister," he said. "You are sadly mistaken." He drove a Dodge Magnum past our house every day on his way to work. Of course there are DNA tests now, but Kristen said to leave him alone, so we did. I thought very seriously about killing him, but I did not know how to go about it, and I was very busy, because I had other people to look after.

We had to leave the hospital the day after Ethan was born. Kristen cried again and said she wasn't ready. "Tell it to the gov-ernment, honey," the nurse said. "That's Medicaid for you." She patted both of us on the arms. "You'll be OK, darlin'. Y'all got each other." She leaned close to me and whispered loudly. "Sometimes they ain't got nobody. No husband, no mama, nobody to help. At least she's got you."

I helped Kristen into the front seat of the car. She was slow and sluggish and walked gingerly. She was still wearing maternity jeans and a pilled cotton top with yellowish stains under the arms. Even before the pregnancy, she'd been stout, mulish. Now she was bloated and doughy, her face resembling a quilted, overstuffed pillow. She had a raised, brown mole at the corner of her mouth. On some girls, it might have been considered attractive.

I buckled the baby seat into the back of the car. Ethan started screaming as soon as we pulled out of the parking lot, but Kristen sat silently, slumped against the passenger door, biting her nails.

We drove into the smoke. In Folkston, we stopped at the Krystal. I leaned over the seat and bobbled a pacifier against Ethan's lips, but he would not take it, so I carried him into the restaurant, wrapped tight in a blue-and-pink hospital receiving blanket and still crying. I bought a sack of burgers and three orders of fries. I was thinking of Ty at home, how he would be hungry.

"That's a little one," said a fat man with no teeth. "Look at that bitty one." He reached out a dirty finger to touch Ethan's face. "Whatchoo cryin' about, little one?" he said. I jerked the baby back before the man could touch him. "He's sick," I said, which was not true, of course, but I wanted the man to leave us alone. "You could catch it." The man backed away. Then we drove on, the afternoon sky darkening through the haze. When we pulled up in front of the house—a bruised thing, damp cedar shingles and a spindly wooden deck all around—I saw a quick movement at the window, Ty, as though he'd been watching for us.

My house is on the eastern lip of the Okefenokee Swamp, the place the Seminoles called "trembling earth" for the way the dry land, what little there is, will yield to the pressure of natural gasses, shift and dislodge into thick islands, which float like massive lily pads through the tannin water. The swamp is a national preserve, but that doesn't mean much to those of us who have always lived here, like Ty, who can wander in and out of the preserve's boundaries without a thought, the way you wander from one room of your house to another when you're feeling restless. Ty grew up in the swamp. He knows its secrets. I always thought he should have been a park ranger. They make money. Ty could have been anything. He just chose not to. Or maybe he didn't. I don't know.

Ty's seen foxfire in the swamp, probably a dozen times or more. He used to tell me about it—the way the light glows through the palmetto scrub, faint at first so you think you're seeing just a reflection of the moon, then stronger, so you think you've lost your bearings and you're coming out on a road and catching sight of some car's headlights, then so bright and blinding and beautiful that you know it's foxfire—swamp gas, some call it. Ty said it was like a gift, to be allowed to see it. I'd never seen it, not in all my years near the swamp. But I looked for it—I looked for it all the time.

I brought the car seat into the kitchen and set it on the table, then went back to help Kristen into the house. When we returned, Ty was there, staring at the baby, who had suddenly, finally, fallen silent.

"So here he is, huh? He made it, huh?" Ty said. He lit a cigarette.

"You idiot. Don't smoke near him," said Kristen.

He snorted. "Like it makes a difference. Whole world filled with smoke."

"Mom," said Kristen.

"Mom," he mimicked.

I lifted the baby from his carrier. "Go on and lay down for a bit, Kristen," I said. "Food there," I said to Ty, nodding at the bag on the table. I carried Ethan into the living room. Ty followed.

"Hey, Mom. You got a few bucks I can borrow?" he said.

"Jesus, Ty. I just got home. We got a baby here, can you see that?"

"Yeah, I see it. It's just that I need a few bucks." His eyes moved quickly around the room. He scratched his head, squeezed his hands together, swung his arms. He paced. He had a habit of running his fingers through his long hair and flipping it out of his eyes. His skin was pale, and his eyes were a deep green, the color of moss. He was tall and thin, unlike Kristen. She took after her father; he took after his.

"You want to hold him?" I said.

"No."

"Why not?"

"I'll just look."

"I think he looks like you, Ty," I said. That was a lie. "He reminds me of you when you were a baby." I stared at the baby's face and thought of the first time I saw Ty. I'd been so young myself, like Kristen, lying in a hospital bed, but with no one there to hold my hand. That was before Ray, Kristen's father, who'd married me even though I had a toddler, but who didn't stick around long enough to see his own daughter learn to walk. When Ty was born I'd struggled up on my elbows to look at him the minute he was out, with the doctor still wiping all the muck away from his face. He was hot and wriggling, and had, even then, an air of discomfort about him, of restlessness. He was like something wild. But he was mine. And he was beautiful. I was unprepared for how beautiful he was. I'd felt a tingling in my breasts, something faint, like a memory.

Ethan started to cry again, his thin voice bleating and raw. Ty's eyes grew wide as he shook his head, did a little backward dance across the room.

"Holy Jesus, that's scary. Can't you make him stop that?"

I tried to slip the pacifier in the baby's mouth, but he refused it. I stood up, paced around. Kristen did not come.

"Go get your sister," I said, but Ty walked back through the kitchen and made no move toward Kristen's room.

I held Ethan up to my shoulder, patted him softly on the back, trying to quiet his screams. When he paused to draw a breath, I heard a series of noises in the kitchen and knew Ty was reaching into my purse. Then a rustling of the bag as he took the Krystal burgers. The back door slammed and Ty's truck started, and then he was gone.

"Shhhh," I said to Ethan. "It's all right. It's all right." Kristen's door remained closed.

The baby would not nurse. He shook his head from side to side in impatience at Kristen's breast, sucked viciously for a few seconds at the tip of the nipple but would not latch on. Kristen was despondent, her breasts growing flaccid with each passing day. "Come on, baby, come on," I said, tickling his lips with my finger and urging Kristen to try again, try again, but Kristen only sulked and said it hurt. Eighteen, maybe you couldn't expect much more. The baby cried incessantly. Ty slammed out of the house each night, looking for quiet, he said. He returned in the mornings and left his boots, caked thick with mud, on the bathroom floor.

Ty was a rattlesnake hunter. I didn't like it. It wasn't honest. He'd sleep during the day and then head out at dusk to haunt the swamp, dragging a burlap sack and a heavy plastic can filled with gasoline. He'd pour the gasoline down into the burrows made by gopher tortoises; the gas would flush out any snakes sharing the burrow. When he'd return the next morning, the sack was filled with live diamondbacks, and the can was empty. The tortoises would die, but Ty, he didn't care about that.

It was competitive, he told me. The snakers fought for territory. They sat out in the swamp drinking all night, waiting for dawn, when the snakes were more active. They sold the snakes to the rattlesnake roundup over in Whigham. I don't know what Ty did with the money he made. But I didn't like it. It wasn't honest. I may not be much, but I've always been an honest person.

On the third morning after we came home from the hospital, I got scared about the baby not nursing, so I drove to Winn-Dixie to buy formula. I wouldn't go to that damn discount grocer's if it killed me, even though he was closer by two miles. Ethan took the bottle immediately, sucking in the warm liquid like he'd been suffocating and it was air, exhaling though his tiny nose after each swallow. Kristen threw away her nursing bra. "Thank you, Jesus," she said, and then she flopped on the couch next to me and stared at Ethan.

"Here, you take him. You feed him," I said.

"You're doing fine." Her face was slack, her eyes blank.

"Kristen."

"Mom."

But she took the baby, holding him awkwardly on her knees with the bottle straight out in front of his face.

"Like this," I said. I repositioned Ethan into the crook of Kristen's arm. "There you go." The baby's hands clenched, unclenched, clenched again. Her face was flat and empty as she regarded him.

I left them and went to the kitchen window. Outside, in the fading light, the smoke from the wildfire in the swamp cast a strange haze behind the trees. Ty's truck was gone. A raccoon walked across the yard. He saw me in the window and stopped for a second, but then he continued, brash, making his way up the steps to the bowl of cat food on the porch. His hands were black and leathery, like little gloves. I could have chased him away, but I didn't. He'd only be back. Wild things; they don't change for anybody.

After a week, I had to go back to work. I'd used up all my vacation. I called home two, three, four times a day to check on Kristen and the baby. Once, I had to leave the courthouse to run home and deliver more diapers. I'd found Ethan screaming in his crib, Kristen asleep on the couch.

Ty emerged from his bedroom while I was changing Ethan's diaper. The baby had begun to quiet, his small face flushed and mottled, his lips trembling. Ty was shirtless and barefoot, a pair of ripped jeans clinging to his hips. His face was chiseled stone.

"Can't sleep with that damn kid screaming," he said. "She won't shut it up."

A pair of small wings beat in my stomach. I held them down. I fastened the diaper tapes, picked up the baby, went to get a bottle. Ty followed. "I mean, Mom. She won't do anything. I swear to God."

"He can't help it. The doctor said he has colic," I said. I was making that up. I don't know what made that baby cry so much, but I wanted to give Ty a reason.

He shook his head, then made a thick, grunting sound, turned on his heel and slammed his fist into the kitchen wall. The drywall buckled and a small pile of dust filtered to the floor. Kristen sat bolt upright on the couch, her mouth gaping. Ethan renewed his cries.

"Ty," I said, staring at him.

His hands shook, and the one that had hit the wall was bleeding across the knuckles. A bead of sweat tricked down his face, though the house was cool and still.

"She needs to keep that kid quiet," he said. He jerked his head, flipped his hair off his face. "I can't sleep, didn't you hear me?" Then he tucked his hurt hand under his arm, walked back into his bedroom, and closed the door.

Kristen and I stared at each other until she lowered her head into her hands and began to weep. My God, I thought. More crying. When do I get to be the one to cry? I held the baby to my chest, bounced on my heels until he quieted. I placed him in his car seat. I waited as long as I could before placing the car seat at Kristen's feet.

"Kristen," I said. She looked at me, red-eyed. "Keep him close to you. Do you understand? If he cries, take him out in the stroller for a walk. I'll be back in a few hours."

On the way back to work, the wings began to beat in my stomach again, but I held my breath and pinched myself on the wrists until they stopped. "Okay," I said to myself. "Okay. Okay. Okay."

They say a mother can never have a favorite child, but I don't know if that's true. There is guilt in the name that springs to your lips, in the face that forms in your mind, when you hear the words "favorite child." There is culpability. I know about words like that.

There is a balance sheet in your head of all the things you did, and didn't do, for your children. There are debts that will never be paid. There are little things over-done, small excesses of affection, slight deficits, tiny omissions. There is the looking away from one child to watch for the other's approach. There is the tender touch on the head. There is the slap on the cheek. There is the impatience and the frustration and the tolerance and the forgiveness, and there are the times when they are not evenly distributed. These things add up, over the years, and there will come a day when you hold yourself accountable. If you are a mother, then you know what I mean.

The sheriff's deputy came the next day. It was Saturday. I'd gotten Kristen to take a shower and to eat some breakfast, but after that she'd fallen asleep again on the couch. I'd given Ethan a bottle and put him into his swing.

Ty was not home. He'd left the house at dusk the night before.

He'd said nothing about the hole in the wall. He'd simply pulled on his muddy boots and walked out the door, white tape wrapped tightly around his right hand.

Now, I stood at the door and looked at the deputy, a tall black man with gloom in his eyes. I'd seen him before, at the courthouse, but I didn't know his name. He'd left his car running. A second cruiser idled in the driveway.

"Do you know where he is?" he asked.

"No."

"You don't have any idea?"

"No."

"Do you know when he'll be back?" he said.

"No. What is this about?"

"I need to ask him some questions."

"About what?"

"About a snaker in Folkston," he said. He paused for a moment, narrowed his eyes. "Fourteen stab wounds, one to the throat. Hanging on by a thread. We got another guy says your boy done it. You know anything about that?"

The wings were back, beating wildly in my stomach. I stared straight at him. "No," I said.

The sheriff rolled his eyes, tired of mothers like me. He handed me a card. "Your boy comes back, you have him call me," he said. "A heap of trouble only gets bigger you don't face it. You know what I'm saying, mama? You have your boy call me."

Behind me, in the living room, Ethan began to cry. The deputy stretched his neck to see behind me. "That your grandbaby?" he said. "Your boy the daddy?"

"My daughter's," I said.

He turned away, looked out over the yard, where the smoke from the swamp hung thick. "We ever gonna get this smoke cleared out?" he said. "Them fires ever gonna stop burning?" Something crackled through the radio at his hip, and he looked at me once more before walking to his car.

"You have him call me," he said.

Before dawn, I woke to Ethan's cries and went to him. His cheeks burned with fever. I fixed a bottle and poured a dose of Motrin in with the formula. I sat at the kitchen table with Ethan. His hair had begun to come in, blond and downy, and by the glow of the moon shining through the kitchen window, his small head was crowned with light. I stroked it. Kristen slept. Ty had not yet returned. The deputy had called twice the day before, asking if I'd seen him.

The house was silent. We sat together, Ethan and I, until the bottle was empty and his skin had begun to cool. His cheek rested against my breast through my nightgown, and he studied my face, silently, seriously, his small fingers closed around the thumb of my right hand. Then the corners of his mouth twitched into something like a smile.

I heard Ty's truck pull into the yard. He walked into the kitchen and flipped on the light before realizing I was there. I blinked in the sudden brightness, and Ethan flinched.

"Sorry," Ty said. He left the light on. His left eye was swollen shut. He wore no shirt, but his pants were stiff with something that could have been mud, could have been blood. A man's smell

came to me from across the kitchen, which always surprised me.
Ty had grown up so fast. Ethan began to cry.

"Oh, Jesus, here we go," Ty said.

I stood up, held Ethan up to my shoulder, started pacing.

"Well, if you hadn't turned the light on," I said. "Where have
you been?"

"We got anything to eat?" he said.

"Where have you been?"

"Whigham."

"You look like you been in the swamp."

"That too."

"What happened to your face?"

His hand reached up, touched the swelling around his eye. Then
he turned away. "I fell on a stump," he said. "Dumbest thing. I
just fell right over and landed on a cypress stump. We got anything
to eat?"

Ethan screamed. My arms ached from holding him, and I had
an impulse to fling him down, take Ty in my arms instead, rock
him on my shoulder and let him sleep. Instead, I called him a
liar.

"Bullshit," I said. "You been in a fight."

Ty opened the refrigerator, leaned in. "I told you I fell."

"Deputy came, Ty."

He stood up straight, closed the refrigerator, looked around the
kitchen.

"Where the fuck is Kristen?" he said. "Why are you always the
one taking care of that baby?"

"Did you hear what I said? Deputy came."

His chin was up, but his face was pale, and as he reached for a
bag of potato chips on the counter, his hand shook.

"He was looking for you."

"So?"

"Said a guy's been stabbed. He's in the hospital. Half dead."

"So?"

He wouldn't look at me.

"So, they think you did it."

He snorted, looked out the kitchen window, to where the first fingers of dawn had begun to reach through the limbs of the oaks. Ethan was relentless, his volume intensifying. I switched shoulders, bounced up and down, patted him on the back.

"Did you?"

Ty stared at the wall, chewing potato chips, but a red flush had begun to creep up from his neck into his face, and when he finally turned to look at me his eyes were wet, and wide, and bright green.

And that was all I needed, and then I knew. The thing in my stomach exploded.

"If he dies, you'll be wanted for murder," I said.

Ethan's cry stretched itself thin and then stopped, and for a moment the kitchen was silent as his lungs emptied themselves and he contracted to draw another breath. Ty blinked.

"Oh, Jesus, Mama," he said, his voice soft. "Ain't no way he's gonna live."

The Okefenokee Swamp sprawls through the southeastern corner of the state of Georgia. Our town, Folkston, is to the east, and on the other side, across twenty-five miles of thick pinelands and nearly impenetrable marsh, trails the Suwannee River, which you could canoe as far as Fargo before picking up a ride on 94. If you made it as far as Valdosta, you could go on to Thomasville, and then drop down to Tallahassee, which is an easy place to pick up a lift on I-10 West and ride it as far as you can go. You could even get within striking distance of Mexico.

But first, if you know the land, if you're good with a gun, if you're young and strong and scared, you can lay low in the swamp for weeks, months if necessary.

We took every piece of food in the kitchen and flung it into plastic bags. We packed water, matches, bug spray, hand tools. We found a tent, a lantern, a rusted camp stove. Ty loaded his rifle.

We moved quickly, not speaking, and when the phone rang we ignored it and went outside to load the canoe onto the roof of my car. Through all this, Kristen slept.

I drove fast as the sun rose, toward the smoke, until we could see the soft glow of the fire in the distance. Ty sat in the passenger seat. Ethan, quiet at last, rode in his car seat behind us.

"Go in my wallet," I said to Ty. "Take whatever cash is there, and take the credit card."

He did as I said.

"Don't go into the preserve," he said. "There's a guard. Keep driving straight, and I'll show you where to pull over."

The smoke was thicker than I'd ever seen it, and it was becoming difficult to breathe. "Pray for rain," I said.

"I don't pray for nothing," he said.

He lit a cigarette, drummed his fingers on his knees.

"Down there," Ty said, pointing to a dirt lane off the road.

I pulled the car in until it was no longer visible from the road. Through the brush to our left, the land receded sharply into marsh, the still, silvery water just visible between thick reeds. When I closed the car door, something heavy moved in the brush and splashed into the water.

"You can skirt the fire?" I said. "You're sure?"

"Don't worry," he said. "I know where I'm going. Fire's in the north—you can see it from here. I go south, I'm OK. And ain't nobody gonna come into it looking."

He pulled the canoe off the top of the car and dragged it through the palmettos until the nose was in the water. Then he came back to the car.

"I'll call," he said.

"No," I said. "They'll find out."

The smoke stung my eyes and left a charred taste in my mouth.

"You go now," I said. "The only way out of it is through it."

He hesitated, then ducked his head and leaned into me. I put my arms around his back, drew him to me. His body was thin and taut, and his chest rose and fell against mine. When he pulled away I felt the separation of our bodies as clearly and as physically as I had on the day he was born.

Still strapped in the back of the car, Ethan began to cry.

"Well," Ty said. "I guess you better get him out of the smoke."

He stepped into the canoe and crouched down to clear the low-hanging branch of a cypress tree. I waited until he was completely out of sight, until the smoldering swamp had swallowed my son whole, and then I climbed behind the wheel of the car, and Ethan and I, we cried until the sun had cleared the tops of the tallest pines.

The deputy was at my house with three other cops when I got home. He said the boy died. I told him I didn't know anything. He looked at my red eyes and at the baby in my arms, shook his head, and walked away.

And now we are three again, and we are doing the best we can. Kristen is better. She is back at work at AutoZone. Ethan goes to day care, and when we all come home at night we cook dinner together and watch reruns of Judge Judy, and most days the only one crying in the house is me, but I do it alone, after dark, where nobody has to see.

I know Kristen will do very little with her life. She will do even less than me, and for this, I must forgive her. She will raise Ethan, with a great deal of help from me and from the Charlton County public school system. She will be an adequate but never exemplary employee. She will always be forty pounds overweight. She will be a chain smoker. She will complain about things over which she has no control. It is all she was meant to do. It is all that is within her power.

I don't look for foxfire any more. I stay away from the swamp, even now that it's winter and the fires have gone out and the air is crisp and clear and you could see for miles in the swamp, if you wanted to, out across the open spaces, toward the pine stands and the tupelo and the titi shrubs. But I don't look.

Laura Lee Smith lives in St. Augustine, Florida. Her fiction has appeared in *The Florida Review, Natural Bridge, Bayou,* and other journals and received the 2006 Snake Nation Press prize for short fiction. She teaches creative writing at Flagler College and works as an advertising copy-writer.

JUDY COOK

*S*pringsteen's *"Highway Patrolman"* is about *a cop who makes a decision to let his criminal brother escape. The song was on my mind when I started playing with this character, a lonely mother of two disappointing children. I knew that the introduction of a noisy, sickly baby could easily upset the tenuous balance of this small dysfunctional family. The decision to set the story in the Okefenokee came later, when I went back to the swamp after many years and was reminded of its beauty and mystery. And the final element, the ever-present fires, came from a period in 2008 when it seemed that all of north Florida and south Georgia was ablaze—acres and acres succumbed to wildfires, and the smoke hung everywhere. I fought hard against this story becoming too fatalistic, too dark. But in the end, it is what it is, and the story took its own turns. The hopelessness of the situation could not be resolved. I let it go.*

Brad Watson

VISITATION

(from *The New Yorker*)

Loomis had never believed that line about the quality of despair being that it was unaware of being despair. He'd been painfully aware of his own despair for most of his life. Most of his troubles had come from attempts to deny the essential hopelessness in his nature. To believe in the viability of nothing, finally, was socially unacceptable, and he had tried to adapt, to pass as a believer, a hoper. He had taken prescription medicine, engaged in periods of vigorous, cleansing exercise, declared his satisfaction with any number of fatuous jobs and foolish relationships. Then one day he'd decided that he should marry, have a child, and he told himself that if one was open-minded these things could lead to a kind of contentment, if not to exuberant happiness. That's why Loomis was in the fix he was in now.

Ever since he and his wife had separated and she had moved with their son to Southern California, he'd flown out every three weeks from Mobile to visit the boy. He was living the very nightmare he'd tried not to imagine when deciding to marry and have a child: that it wouldn't work out, they would split up, and he would be forced to spend long weekends in a motel, taking his son to faux-upscale chain restaurants, cineplexes, and amusement parks.

He usually visited for three to five days and stayed at the same motel, an old motor court that had been bought and remodelled by one of the big franchises. At first the place wasn't so bad. The Continental breakfast included fresh fruit and little boxes of name-brand cereals and batter with which you could make your own waffles on a double waffle iron right there in the lobby. The syrup came in small plastic containers from which you pulled back a foil lid and voilà, it was a pretty good waffle. There was juice and decent coffee. Still, of course, it was depressing, a bleak place in which to do one's part in raising a child. With its courtyard sur-rounded by two stories of identical rooms, and excepting the lack of guard towers and the presence of a swimming pool, it followed the same architectural model as a prison.

But Loomis's son liked it, so they continued to stay there, even though Loomis would rather have moved on to a better place.

He arrived in San Diego for his April visit, picked up the rental car, and drove north on I-5. Traffic wasn't bad except where it al-ways was, between Del Mar and Carlsbad. Of course, it was never "good." Their motel sat right next to the 5, and the roar and rush of it never stopped. You could step out onto the balcony at three in the morning and it'd be just as roaring and rushing with traffic as it had been six hours before.

This was to be one of his briefer visits. He'd been to a job inter-view the day before, Thursday, and had another one on Tuesday. He wanted to make the most of the weekend, which meant doing very little besides just being with his son. Although he wasn't very good at doing that. Generally, he sought distractions from his ineptitude as a father. He stopped at a liquor store and bought a bottle of bourbon, and tucked it into his travel bag before driving up the hill to the house where his wife and son lived. The house was owned by a retired Marine friend of his wife's family. His wife and son lived rent-free in the basement apartment.

When Loomis arrived, the ex-Marine was on his hands and knees in the flower bed, pulling weeds. He glared sideways at Loomis for a moment and muttered something, his face a mask of disgust. He was a widower who clearly hated Loomis and refused to speak to him. Loomis was unsettled that someone he'd never even been introduced to could hate him so much.

His son came to the door of the apartment by himself, as usual. Loomis peered past the boy into the little apartment, which was bright and sunny for a basement (only in California, he thought). But there was no sign of his estranged wife. She had conspired with some part of her nature to become invisible. Loomis hadn't laid eyes on her in nearly a year. She called out from somewhere in another room, "Bye! I love you! See you on Monday!"

"OK, love you, too," the boy said and trudged after Loomis, dragging his backpack of homework and a change of clothes. "Bye, Uncle Bob," the boy said to the ex-Marine. Uncle Bob! The ex-Marine stood up, gave the boy a small salute, then he and the boy exchanged high fives.

After Loomis checked in at the motel, they went straight to their room and watched television for a while. Lately, his son had been watching cartoons made in the Japanese anime style. Loomis thought the animation was wooden and amateurish. He didn't get it at all. The characters were drawn as angularly as origami, which he supposed was appropriate and maybe even intentional, if the influence was Japanese. But it seemed irredeemably foreign. His son sat propped against several pillows, harboring such a shy but mischievous grin that Loomis had to indulge him.

He made a drink and stepped out onto the balcony to smoke a cigarette. Down by the pool, a woman with long, thick black hair—it was stiffly unkempt, like a madwoman's in a movie—sat in a deck chair with her back to Loomis, watching two children play in the water. The little girl was nine or ten, and the boy was older, maybe fourteen. The boy teased the girl by splashing her face with water, and when she protested in a shrill voice he leapt over and dunked her head. She came up gasping and began to cry. Loomis was astonished that the woman, who he assumed was the children's mother, displayed no reaction. Was she asleep?

The motel had declined steadily in the few months that Loomis had been staying there, like a moderately stable person drifting and sinking into the lassitude of depression. Loomis wanted to help, find some way to speak to the managers and the other employees, to say, "Buck up, don't just let things go all to hell," but he felt powerless against his own inclinations.

He lit a second cigarette to go with the rest of his drink. A few other people walked up and positioned themselves around the pool's apron, but none got into the water with the two quarrelling children. There was something feral about them, anyone could see. The woman with the wild black hair continued to sit in her pool chair as if asleep or drugged. The boy's teasing of the girl had become steadily rougher, and the girl was sobbing now. Still, the presumptive mother did nothing. Someone went in to complain. One of the managers came out and spoke to the woman, who immediately, but without getting up from her deck chair, shouted to the boy, "All right, God damn it!" The boy, smirking, climbed from the pool, leaving the girl standing in waist-deep water, sobbing and rubbing her eyes with her fists. The woman stood up then and walked toward the boy. There was something off about her clothes, burnt-orange Bermuda shorts and a men's lavender oxford shirt. And they didn't seem to fit right. The boy, like a wary stray dog, watched her approach. She snatched a lock of his wet black hair, pulled his face to hers, and said something, gave his head a shake and let him go. The boy went over to the pool and spoke to the girl. "Come on," he said. "No," the girl said, still crying. "You let him help you!" the woman shouted, startling the girl into letting the boy take her hand. Loomis was fascinated, a little bit horrified.

Turning back toward her chair, the woman looked up to where he stood on the balcony. She had an astonishing face, broad and long, divided by a great, curved nose, dominated by a pair of large, dark, sunken eyes that seemed blackened by blows or some terrible history. Such a face, along with her immense, thick mane of black hair, made her look like a troll. Except that she was not ugly. She looked more like a witch, the cruel mockery of beauty and seduction. The oxford shirt was mostly unbuttoned, nearly spilling out a pair of full, loose, mottled-brown breasts.

"What are you looking at!" she shouted, very loudly from deep in her chest. Loomis stepped back from the balcony railing. The woman's angry glare changed to something like shrewd assessment, and then dismissal. She shooed her two children into one of the downstairs rooms.

After taking another minute to finish his drink and smoke a third cigarette, to calm down, Loomis went back inside and closed the sliding glass door behind him.

His son was on the bed, grinning, watching something on television called *Code Lyoko*. Loomis tried to watch it with him for a while, but got restless. He wanted a second, and maybe stronger, drink.

"Hey," he said. "How about I just get some burgers and bring them back to the room?"

The boy glanced at him and said, "That'd be OK."

Loomis got a sack of hamburgers from McDonald's, some fries, a Coke. He made a second drink, then a third, while his son ate and watched television. They went to bed early.

The next afternoon, Saturday, they drove to the long, wide beach at Carlsbad. Carlsbad was far too cool, but what could you do? Also, the hip little surf shop where the boy's mother worked during the week was in Carlsbad. He'd forgotten that for a moment. He was having a hard time keeping her in his mind. Her invisibility strategy was beginning to work on him. He wasn't sure at all anymore just who she was or ever had been. When they'd met, she wore business attire, like everyone else he knew. What did she wear now? Did she get up and go around in a bikini all day? She didn't really have the body for that at age thirty-nine, did she?

"What does your mom wear to work?" he asked.

The boy gave him a look that would have been ironic if he'd been a less compassionate child.

"Clothes?" the boy said.

"OK," Loomis said. "Like a swimsuit? Does she go to work in a swimsuit?"

"Are you OK?" the boy said.

Loomis was taken aback by the question.

"Me?" he said.

They walked along the beach, neither going into the water. Loomis enjoyed collecting rocks. The stones on the beach here were astounding. He marvelled at one that resembled an ancient war club. The handle fit perfectly into his palm. From somewhere over the water, a few miles south, they could hear the stuttering thud of a large helicopter's blades. Most likely a military craft from the Marine base farther north.

Maybe he wasn't OK. Loomis had been to five therapists since separating from his wife: one psychiatrist, one psychologist, three counsellors. The psychiatrist had tried him on Paxil, Zoloft, and Wellbutrin for depression, and lorazepam for anxiety. Only the lorazepam had helped, but with that he'd overslept too often and lost his job. The psychologist, once she learned that Loomis was drinking almost half a bottle of booze every night, became fixated on getting him to join A.A. and seemed to forget altogether that he was there to figure out whether he indeed no longer loved his wife. And why he had cheated on her. Why he had left her for another woman when the truth was that he had no faith that the new relationship would work out any better than the old one. The first counsellor seemed sensible, but Loomis made the mistake of visiting her together with his wife, and when she suggested that maybe their marriage was kaput his wife had walked out. The second counsellor was actually his wife's counsellor, and Loomis thought she was an idiot. Loomis suspected that his wife liked the second counsellor because she did nothing but nod and sympathize and give them brochures. He suspected that his wife simply didn't want to move out of their house, which she liked far more than Loomis did, and which possibly she liked more than she liked Loomis. When she realized that divorce was inevitable, she shifted gears, remembered that she wanted to surf, and sold the house before Loomis was even aware it was on the market, so he had to sign. Then it was Loomis who mourned the loss of the house. He visited the third counsellor with his girlfriend, who seemed constantly angry that his divorce hadn't yet come through. He and the girlfriend both gave up on that counsellor because he seemed terrified of them for some reason they couldn't fathom. Loomis was coming to the conclusion that he couldn't fathom anything; the word seemed appropriate to him, because most of the time he felt as if he were drowning and couldn't find the bottom or the surface of this murky body of water he had fallen, or dived, into.

He wondered if this was why he didn't want to dive into the crashing waves of the Pacific, as he certainly would have when he was younger. His son didn't want to because, he said, he'd rather surf.

"But you don't know how to surf," Loomis said.

"Mom's going to teach me as soon as she's good enough at it," the boy said.

"But don't you need to be a better swimmer before you try to surf?" Loomis had a vague memory of the boy's swimming lessons, which maybe hadn't gone so well.

"No," the boy said.

"I really think," Loomis said, and then he stopped speaking, because the helicopter he'd been hearing, one of those large twin-engine birds that carry troops in and out of combat—a Chinook—had come abreast of them, a quarter mile or so off the beach. Just as Loomis looked up to see it, something coughed or exploded in one of its engines. The helicopter slowed, then swerved, with the slow grace of an airborne leviathan, toward the beach where they stood. In a moment it was directly over them. One of the men in it leaned out of a small opening on its side, frantically waving, but the people on the beach, including Loomis and his son, beaten by the blast from the blades and stung by sand driven up by it, were too shocked and confused to run. The helicopter lurched back out over the water with a tremendous roar and a deafening, rattling whine from the engines. There was another loud pop, and black

smoke streamed from the forward engine as the Chinook made
its way north again, seeming hobbled. Then it was gone, lost in
the glare over the water. A bittersweet burnt-fuel smell hung in
the air. Loomis and his son stood there among the others on the
beach, speechless. One of two very brown young surfers in board
shorts and crewcuts grinned and nodded at the clublike rock in
Loomis's hand.

"Dude, we're safe," he said. "You can put down the weapon."
He and the other surfer laughed.

Loomis's son, looking embarrassed, moved off as if he were
with someone else in the crowd, not Loomis.

They stayed in Carlsbad for an early dinner at Pizza Port. The
place was crowded with people who'd been at the beach all day, although Loomis recognized no one they'd seen when the helicopter
had nearly crashed and killed them all. He'd expected everyone in
there to know about it, to be buzzing about it over beer and pizza,
amazed, exhilarated. But it was as if it hadn't happened.

The long rows of picnic tables and booths were filled with
young parents and their hyperkinetic children, who kept jumping
up to get extra napkins or forks or to climb into the seats of the
motorcycle video games. Their parents flung arms after them like
inadequate lassos or pursued them and herded them back. The
stools along the bar were occupied by young men and women who
apparently had no children and who were attentive only to one another and to choosing which of the restaurant's many microbrews
to order. In the corner by the restrooms, the old surfers, regulars
here, gathered to talk shop and knock back the stronger beers, the
double-hopped and the barley wines. Their graying hair frizzled
and tied in ponytails or dreads or chopped in stiff clumps dried by
salt and sun. Their faces leather brown. Gnarled toes jutting from
their flip-flops and worn sandals like assortments of dry-roasted
cashews, Brazil nuts, ginger root.

Loomis felt no affinity for any of them. There wasn't a single person in the entire place with whom he felt a thing in common—other

than being, somehow, human. Toward the parents he felt a bitter disdain. On the large TV screens fastened to the restaurant's brick walls surfers skimmed down giant waves off Hawaii, Tahiti, Australia.

He gazed at the boy, his son. The boy looked just like his mother. Thick bright-orange hair, untamable. They were tall, stemlike people with long limbs and that thick hair blossom on top. Loomis had called them his rosebuds. "Roses are red," his son would respond, delightedly indignant, when he was smaller. "There are orange roses," Loomis would reply. "Where?" "Well, in Indonesia, I think. Or possibly Brazil." "No!" his son would shout, breaking down into giggles on the floor. He bought them orange roses on the boy's birthday that year.

The boy wasn't so easily amused anymore. He waited glumly for their pizza order to be called out. They'd secured a booth vacated by a smallish family.

"You want a Coke?" Loomis said. The boy nodded absently. "I'll get you a Coke," Loomis said.

He got the boy a Coke from the fountain, and ordered a pint of strong pale ale from the bar for himself.

By the time their pizza came, Loomis was on his second ale. He felt much better about all the domestic chaos around them in the restaurant. It was getting on the boy's nerves, though. As soon as they finished their pizza, he asked Loomis if he could go stand outside and wait for him there.

"I'm almost done," Loomis said.

"I'd really rather wait outside," the boy said. He shoved his hands in his pockets and looked away.

"OK," Loomis said. "Don't wander off. Stay where I can see you."

"I will."

Loomis sipped his beer and watched as the boy weaved his way through the crowd and out of the restaurant, then began to pace back and forth on the sidewalk. Having to be a parent in this fashion was awful. He felt indicted by all the other people in this teeming place: by the parents and their smug happiness, by the old surfer dudes, who had the courage of their lack of conviction, and by the young lovers, who were convinced that they would never be part of either of these groups, not the obnoxious parents, not the grizzled losers clinging to youth like tough, crusty barnacles. Certainly they would not be Loomis.

And what did it mean, in any case, that he couldn't even carry on a conversation with his son? How hard could that be? To hear him try, you'd think they didn't know each other at all, that he was a friend of the boy's father, watching him for the afternoon or something. He got up to leave, but hesitated, then gulped down the rest of his second beer.

His son stood with hunched shoulders, waiting.

"Ready to go back to the motel?" Loomis said. There was plenty of light left in the day for another walk on the beach, but he wasn't up to it.

The boy nodded. They walked back to the car in silence.

"Did you like your pizza?" Loomis said when they were in the car.

"Sure. It was OK."

Loomis looked at him for a moment. The boy glanced back with the facial equivalent of a shrug, an impressively diplomatic expression that managed to say both "I'm sorry" and "What do you want?" Loomis sighed. He could think of nothing else to say that wasn't even more inane.

"All right," he finally said, and drove them back to the motel.

When they arrived, Loomis heard a commotion in the courtyard, and they paused near the gate.

The woman who'd been watching the two awful children was there at the pool again, and the two children themselves had returned to the water. But now the group seemed to be accompanied by an older heavyset man, bald on top, graying hair slicked against the sides of his head. He was arguing with a manager while the other guests around the pool pretended to ignore the altercation.

The boy and girl paddled about in the water until the man threw up his hands and told them to get out and go to their room. The girl glanced at the boy, but the boy continued to ignore the man until he strode to the edge of the pool and shouted, "Get out! Let them have their filthy pool. Did you piss in it? I hope you pissed in it. Now get out! Go to the room!" The boy removed himself from the pool with a kind of languorous choreography, and walked toward the sliding glass door of one of the downstairs rooms, the little girl following. Just before reaching the door the boy paused, turned his head in the direction of the pool and the other guests there, and hawked and spat onto the concrete pool apron. Loomis said to his son, "Let's get on up to the room."

Another guest, a lanky young woman whom Loomis had seen beside the pool earlier, walked past them on her way to the parking lot. "Watch out for them Gypsies," she muttered.

"Gypsies?" the boy said.

The woman laughed as she rounded the comer. "Don't let 'em get you," she said.

"I don't know," Loomis said when she'd gone. "I guess they do seem a little like Gypsies."

"What the hell is a Gypsy, anyway?"

Loomis stopped and stared at his son. "Does 'Uncle Bob' teach you to talk that way?"

The boy shrugged and looked away, annoyed.

In the room, his son pressed him about the Gypsies, and he told him that they were originally from some part of India, he wasn't sure which, and that they were ostracized, nobody wanted them. They became nomads, wandering around Europe. They were poor. People accused them of stealing. "They had a reputation for stealing people's children, I think."

He'd meant this to be a kind of joke, or at least lighthearted, but when he saw the expression on the boy's face he regretted it and quickly added, "They didn't, really."

It didn't work. For the next hour, the boy asked him questions about Gypsies and kidnapping. Every few minutes or so, he hopped

from the bed to the sliding glass door and pulled the curtain aside
to peek down across the courtyard at the Gypsies' room. Loomis
had decided to concede that they were Gypsies, whether they really were or not. He made himself a stiff nightcap and stepped out
onto the balcony to smoke, although he also peeked through the
curtains before going out, to make sure the coast was clear.

The next morning, Sunday, Loomis rose before his son and
went down to the lobby for coffee. He stepped out into the empty
courtyard to drink it in the morning air, and when he looked into
the pool he saw a large dead rat on its side at the bottom. The rat
looked peacefully dead, with its eyes closed and its front paws
curled at its chest as if it were begging. Loomis took another sip
of his coffee and went back into the lobby. The night clerk was still
on duty, studying something on the computer monitor behind the
desk. She only cut her eyes at Loomis, and when she saw he was
going to approach her she met his gaze steadily in that same way,
without turning her head.

"I believe you have an unregistered guest at the bottom of your
pool," Loomis said.

He got a second cup of coffee, a plastic cup of juice, and a couple
of refrigerator-cold bagels (the waffle iron and fresh fruit had disappeared a couple of visits earlier) and took them back to the room.
He and his son ate there, then Loomis decided that they should
get away from the motel for the day. The boy could always be
counted on to want a day trip to San Diego. He loved to ride the
red trolleys there, and tolerated Loomis's interest in the museums,
sometimes.

They took the commuter train down, rode the trolley to the
Mexican border, turned around, and came back. They ate lunch
in a famous old diner near downtown, then took a bus to Balboa
Park and spent the afternoon in the air-and-space museum and
the natural-history museum, and at a small, disappointing model-
railroad exhibit. Then they took the train back up the coast.

As they got out of the car at the motel, an old brown van, plain and blocky as a loaf of bread, careened around the far comer of the lot, pulled up next to Loomis, and stopped. The driver was the older man who'd been at the pool. He leaned toward Loomis and said through the open passenger window, "Can you give me twenty dollars? They're going to kick us out of this stinking motel."

Loomis felt a surge of hostile indignation. What, did he have a big sign on his chest telling everyone what a loser he was?

"I don't have it," he said.

"Come on!" the man shouted. "Just twenty bucks!"

Loomis saw his son standing beside the passenger door of the car, frightened.

"No," he said. He was ready to punch the old man now.

"Son of a bitch!" the man shouted, and gunned the van away, swerving onto the street toward downtown and the beach.

The boy gestured for Loomis to hurry over and unlock the car door, and as soon as he did the boy got back into the passenger seat. When Loomis sat down behind the wheel, the boy hit the lock button.

"Was he trying to rob us?" he said.

"No. He wanted me to give him twenty dollars."

The boy was breathing hard and looking straight out the windshield, close to tears.

"It's OK," Loomis said. "He's gone."

"Pop, no offense"—and the boy actually reached over and patted Loomis on the forearm, as if to comfort him—"but I think I want to sleep at home tonight."

Loomis was so astonished by the way his son had touched him on the arm that he was close to tears himself.

"It'll be OK," he said. "Really. We're safe here, and I'll protect you."

"I know, Pop, but I really think I want to go home."

Loomis tried to keep the obvious pleading note from his voice. If this happened, if he couldn't even keep his son around and reasonably satisfied to be with him for a weekend, what was he at all anymore? And (he couldn't help but think) what would the boy's mother make of it, how much worse would he look in her eyes?

"Please," he said to the boy. "Just come on up to the room for a while, and we'll talk about it again, and if you still want to go home later on I'll take you, I promise."

The boy thought about it and agreed, and began to calm down a little. They went up to the room, past the courtyard, which was blessedly clear of ridiculous Gypsies and other guests. Loomis got a bucket of ice for his bourbon, ordered Chinese, and they lay together on Loomis's bed, eating and watching television, and didn't talk about the Gypsies, and after a while, exhausted, they both fell asleep.

When the alcohol woke him at 3 A.M., he was awash in a sense of gloom and dread. He found the remote, turned down the sound on the TV. His son was sleeping, mouth open, a lock of his bright-orange hair across his face. Loomis eased himself off the bed, sat on the other one, and watched him breathe. He recalled the days when his life with the boy's mother had seemed happy, and the boy had been small, and they would put him to bed in his room, where they had built shelves for his toy trains and stuffed animals and the books from which Loomis would read to him at bedtime. He remembered the constant battle in his heart those days. How he was drawn into this construction of conventional happiness, how he felt that he loved this child more than he had ever loved anyone in his entire life, how all of this was possible, this life, how he might actually be able to do it. And yet whenever he had felt this he was also aware of the other, more deeply seated part of his nature that wanted to run away in fear. That believed it was not possible after all, that it could only end in catastrophe, that anything this sweet and heartbreaking must indeed one day collapse into shattered pieces. How he had struggled to free him-self, one way or another, from what seemed a horrible limbo of anticipation. He had run away, in his fashion. And yet nothing had ever caused him to feel anything more like despair than what he felt just now, in this moment, looking at his beautiful child asleep on the motel bed in the light of the cheap lamp, with the incessant dull roar of cars on I-5 just the other side of the hedge, a slashing river of what seemed nothing but desperate travel from point A to point B, from which one mad dasher or another would simply disappear, blink out in a flicker of light, at ragged but regular intervals, with no more ceremony or consideration than that.

He checked that his son was still sleeping deeply, then poured himself a plastic cup of neat bourbon and went down to the pool to smoke and sit alone for a while in the dark. He walked toward a group of pool chairs in the shadows beside a stunted palm, but stopped when he realized that he wasn't alone, that someone was sitting in one of the chairs. The Gypsy woman sat very still, watching him.

"Come, sit," she said. "Don't be afraid."

He was afraid. But the woman was so still, and the expression on her face he could now make out in the shadows was one of calm appraisal. Something about this kept him from retreating. She slowly raised a hand and patted the pool chair next to her, and Loomis sat.

For a moment, the woman just looked at him, and, unable not to, he looked at her. She was unexpectedly, oddly attractive. Her eyes were indeed very dark, set far apart on her broad face. In this light, her fierce nose was strange and alarming, almost erotic.

"Are you Gypsy?" Loomis blurted, without thinking.

She stared at him a second before smiling and chuckling deep in her throat.

"No, I'm not Gypsy," she said, her eyes moving quickly from side to side in little shiftings, looking into his. "We are American. My people come from France."

Loomis said nothing.

"But I can tell you your future," she said, leaning her head back slightly to look at him down her harrowing nose. "Let me see your hand." She took Loomis's wrist and pulled his palm toward her. He didn't resist. "Have you ever had someone read your palm?"

Loomis shook his head. "I don't really want to know my future," he said. "I'm not a very optimistic person."

"I understand," the woman said. "You're unsettled."

"It's too dark here to even see my palm," Loomis said.

"No, there's enough light," the woman said. And finally she took her eyes from Loomis's and looked down at his palm. He felt relieved enough to be released from that gaze to let her continue. And something in him was relieved, too, to have someone else consider his future, someone aside from himself. It couldn't be worse, after all, than his own predictions.

She hung her head over his palm and traced the lines with a long fingernail, pressed into the fleshy parts. Her thick hair tickled the edges of his hand and wrist. After a moment, much sooner than Loomis would have expected, she spoke.

"It's not the future you see in a palm," she said, still studying his. "It's a person's nature. From this, of course, one can tell much about a person's tendencies." She looked up, still gripping his wrist. "This tells us much about where a life may have been, and where it may go."

She bent over his palm again, traced one of the lines with the fingernail. "There are many breaks in the heart line here. You are a creature of disappointment. I suspect others in your life disappoint you." She traced a different line. "You're a dreamer. You're an idealist, possibly. Always disappointed by ordinary life, which of course is boring and ugly." She laughed that soft, deep chuckle again and looked up, startling Loomis anew with the directness of her gaze. "People are so fucking disappointing, eh?" She uttered a seductive grunt that loosened something in his groin.

It was true. No one had ever been good enough for him. Not even the members of his immediate family. And especially himself.

"Anger, disappointment," the woman said. "So common. But it may be they've worn you down. The drinking, smoking. No real energy, no passion." Loomis pulled against her grip just slightly, but she held on with strong fingers around his wrist. Then she lowered Loomis's palm to her broad lap and leaned in closer, speaking more quietly.

"I see you with the little boy—he's your child?"

Loomis nodded. He felt suddenly alarmed, fearful. He glanced up, and his heart raced when he thought he saw the boy standing on the balcony, looking out. It was only the potted plant there. He wanted to dash back to the room, but he was rooted to the chair, to the Gypsy with her thin, hard fingers about his wrist.

"This is no vacation, I suspect. It's terrible, to see your child in this way, in a motel."

Loomis nodded.

"You're angry with this child's mother for forcing you to be here."

Loomis nodded and tried to swallow. His throat was dry.

"Yet I would venture it was you who left her. For another woman, a beautiful woman, eh, *mon frère?*" She ran the tip of a nail down one of the lines in his palm. There was a cruel smile on her impossible face. "A woman who once again you believed to be something she was not." Loomis felt himself drop his chin in some kind of involuntary acquiescence. "She was a dream," the woman said. "And she has disappeared, poof, like any dream." He felt suddenly, embarrassingly, close to tears. A tight lump swelled in his throat. "And now you have left her, too, or she has left you, because"—and here the woman paused, shook Loomis's wrist gently, as if to revive his attention, and indeed he had been drifting in his grief—"because you are a ghost. Walking between two worlds, you know?" She shook his wrist again, harder, and Loomis looked up at her, his vision of her there in the shadows blurred by his tears.

She released his wrist and sat back in her chair, exhaled as if she had been holding her breath, and closed her eyes. As if this excoriation of Loomis's character had been an obligation, had exhausted her.

They sat there for a minute or two while Loomis waited for the emotion that had surged up in him to recede.

"Twenty dollars," the woman said, her eyes still closed. When

Loomis said nothing, she opened her eyes. Now her gaze was flat, no longer intense, but she held it on him. "Twenty dollars," she said. "For the reading. This is my fee."

Loomis, feeling as if he'd just been through something physical instead of emotional, his muscles tingling, reached for his wallet, found a twenty-dollar bill, and handed it to her. She took it and rested her hands in her lap.

"Now you should go back up to your room," she said.

He got up to make his way from the courtyard, and was startled by someone standing in the shadow of the Gypsies' doorway. Her evil man-child, the boy from the pool, watching him like a forest animal pausing in its night prowling to let him pass. Loomis hurried on up to the room, tried to let himself in with a key card that wouldn't cooperate. The lock kept flashing red instead of green. Finally the card worked, the green light flickered. He entered and shut the door behind him.

But he'd gone into the wrong room, maybe even some other motel. The beds were made, the television off. His son wasn't there. The sliding glass door to the balcony stood open. Loomis felt his heart seize up and he rushed to the railing. The courtyard was dark and empty. Over in the lobby, the lights were dimmed, no one on duty. It was all shut down. There was no breeze. No roar of rushing vehicles from the 5, the roar in Loomis's mind cancelling it out. By the time he heard the sound behind him and turned to see his son come out of the bathroom yawning, it was too late. It might as well have been someone else's child, Loomis the stranger come to steal him away. He stood on the balcony and watched his son crawl back onto the bed, pull himself into a fetal position, close his eyes for a moment, then open them. Meeting his gaze, Loomis felt something break inside him. The boy had the same dazed, disoriented expression he'd had on his face just after his long, difficult birth, when the nurses had put him into an incubator to rush him to intensive care. Loomis had knelt, then, his face up close to the incubator's glass wall, and he'd known that the baby could see him, and that was enough. The obstetrician said, "This baby is very sick," and nurses wheeled the incubator out.

He'd gone over to his wife and held her hand. The resident, tears in her eyes, patted his shoulder and said, for some reason, "You're good people," and left them alone. Now he and the child were in this motel, the life that had been their family somehow dissipated into air. Loomis couldn't gather into his mind how they'd got here. He couldn't imagine what would come next.

Brad Watson has spent most of his life so far in Meridian, Mississippi; Tuscaloosa, Alabama; and the Alabama Gulf Coast, where he dispatched many newspaper stories about dwindling water supplies for the coast's rapid development as well as the lack of adequate sewage treatment plants. It was fascinating work, and no doubt he wouldn't be the writer he is today if he hadn't dispatched so many stories about salt-water intrusion and floating solids. Later, he spent five years in Boston, teaching at Harvard. Then, he knocked around for a while, brooding. Now he's spent five years in Wyoming, where he's discovered true winter, teaching at the University of Wyoming MFA program. A more intimate biographical note would reveal that he is, unfortunately, supremely qualified to write a story like "Visitation."

LINDSAY BEAMISH

I wrote "Visitation" after spending a number of years commuting to visit my own young son in similar circumstances. I wrote it in longhand in the backyard of our house in Laramie during the summer of 2008, while I was enjoying a blessed and too-rare long-term visitation from him in my own home. It was such a relief from the motel-dad life that I was able to look back on those years with some remove and write about the experience with the necessary detachment and invention. Which is usually when the darker emotional experience of it all comes back to you with a power that needs some outlet. You find a way to ground yourself and let the current pass through. Into a story is good.

Wells Tower

RETREAT

(from *McSweeney's*)

Sometimes, after six or so large drinks, it seems like a sane idea to call my little brother on the phone. Approximately since Stephen's birth, I've held him among the principal mother-fuckers of my life, and it takes a lot of solvent to bleach out all the dark recollections I've stashed up over the years. Pick a memory, any memory. My eleventh birthday party at Ernstead Park, how about? I'd just transferred schools, trying to turn over a new leaf, and I'd invited all the boys and girls of quality. I'd been making progress with them, too, until Stephen, age eight, ran up behind me at the fish pond and shoved me face-first into the murk. The water came up only to my knees, so I did a few hilarious staggers before flopping down, spluttering, amid some startled koi. The kids all laughed like wolves.

Or ninth grade, when I caught the acting bug and landed a part in our high school's production of *Grease* playing opposite a girl named Dodi Clark. We played an anonymous prancing couple, on stage only for the full-cast dance melees. She was no beauty, a mousy girl with a weak chin and a set of bonus, overlapping canine teeth, but I liked her somewhat. She had a pretty neat set of breasts for a girl her age. I thought maybe we could help each other out with our virginity problems. Yet the sight of Dodi and me dancing drove Stephen into a jealous fever. Before I could get my angle going, Stephen snaked me, courting her with a siege of posters, special pens, stickers, and crystal whim-whams. The onslaught worked and Dodi fell for him, but when she finally parted her troubled mouth to kiss him, he told me years later, he froze up. "I think I had some kind of primeval prey-versus-predator response when I saw those teeth. It was like trying to make out with a sand shark. No idea why I was after her to begin with."

But I know why: in Stephen's understanding, nothing pleasant should ever flow to me on which he hasn't exercised first dibs. He wouldn't let me eat a turd without first insisting on his cut.

He's got his beefs, too, I suppose. I used to tease him pretty rigorously. We had these little red toads that hopped around my mother's yard, and I used to pin him down and rub them into his clenched teeth. Once, when we were smoking dope in high school, I lit his hair on fire. Another time, I locked him outside in his underwear until the snot froze in scales on his face. Hard to explain why I did these things, except to say that I've got a little imp inside me whose ambrosia is my brother's wrath. Stephen's furies are marvelous, ecstatic, somehow pornographic, the equally transfixing inverse of watching people in the love act. That day I locked him out, I was still laughing when I let him in after a cold hour. I even had a mug of hot chocolate ready for him. He drained it and then grabbed a can opener from the counter and threw it at me, gouging a three-inch gash beneath my lower lip. It left a white parenthesis in the stubble of my chin, the abiding, sideways smile of the imp.

But give me a good deep rinse of alcohol and our knotty history unkinks itself. All of the old crap seems inconsequential, just part of the standard fraternal rough-and-tumble, and I get very soppy and bereft over the brotherhood Steve and I have lost.

Anyhow, I started feeling that way one night in October just after I'd crossed the halfway point on a fifth of Meyer's rum. I was standing at the summit of a small mountain I'd recently bought in Aroostook County, Maine. The air was wonderful, heavy with the watery sweetness of lupine, moss, and fern. Overhead, bats hawked mosquitoes in the darkening sky, while the sun waned behind the molars of the Appalachian range. I browsed the contacts on my phone, wanting to call someone up, maybe just deliver an oral postcard of this place into someone's voicemail box, but I had a reason not to dial each of those names until I got to Stephen's.

I dialed, and he answered without saying hello.

"In a session," he said, the last syllable trilling up in a bitchy way, and hung up the phone. Stephen makes his living as a music therapist, but session or not, you'd think he could spare a second to at least say hello to me. We hadn't spoken in eight months. I dialed again.

"What the fuck, fool, it's Matthew."

"Matthew," he repeated, in the way you might say "cancer" after the doctor's diagnosis. "I'm with a client. This is not an optimum time."

"Yeah," I said. "Question for you: mountains."

There was a wary pause. From Stephen's end came the sound of someone doing violence to a tambourine.

"What about them?"

"Do you like them? Do you like mountains, Stephen?"

"I have no objection to them. Why?"

"Well, I bought one," I said. "I'm on it now."

"Congratulations," Stephen said. "Is it Popocatéptl? Are you putting 7-Elevens on the Matterhorn?"

Over the years, I've made a hell of a lot of money in real estate, and this seems to hurt Stephen's feelings. He's not a church man, but he's big on piety and sacrifice and letting you know what choice values he's got. So far as I can tell, his values include eating ramen noodles by the case, getting laid once every fifteen years or so, and arching his back at the sight of people like me—that is, people who have amounted to something and don't reek of thrift stores.

But I love Stephen. Or I think I do. We've had some intervals of mutual regard. Our father came down with lymphoma when Stephen was four, so we pretty much parented ourselves while our mother nursed our father through two exhausting cycles of remission and relapse.

At any rate, the cancer got our father when I was ten. Liquor killed our mother before I was out of college, and it was right around then that we went on different courses. Stephen, a pianist, retreated into a bitter fantasy of musical celebrity that was perpetually being thwarted—by his professors at the Eastman School, by the philistines in his ensembles, and by girlfriends who wanted too much of his time. He had a series of tedious artistic crackups, and whenever we'd get together, he'd hand me lots of shit about how drab and hollow my life was.

Actually, my life was extremely full. I married young, and married often. I bought my first piece of property at eighteen. Now, at forty-two, I've been through two amicable divorces. I've lived and made money in nine American cities. Late at night, when rest won't come and my breathing shortens with the worry that I've cheated myself of life's traditional rewards (long closenesses, offspring, mature plantings), I take an astral cruise of the hundreds of properties that have passed through my hands over the years, and before I come close to visiting them all, I droop, contented, into sleep.

When no orchestras called Stephen with commissions, he exiled himself to Eugene, Oregon, to buff his oeuvre while eking out a living teaching the mentally substandard to achieve sanity by blowing on harmonicas. When I drove down to see him two years ago after a conference in Seattle, I found him living above a candle store in a dingy apartment which he shared with a dying collie. The animal was so old it couldn't take a leak on its own, so Stephen was always having to lug her downstairs to the grassy verge beside the sidewalk. Then he'd straddle the dog and manually void its bladder via a Heimlich technique horrible to witness. You hated to see your last blood relation engaged in something like that. I told Stephen that from a business standpoint, the smart thing would be to have the dog put down. This caused an ugly argument, but really, it seemed to me that someone regularly seen by the roadside hand-juicing a half-dead dog was not the man you'd flock to for lessons on how to be less out of your mind.

"The mountain doesn't have a name yet," I told him. "Hell, I'll name it after you. I'll call it Brown Cloud Hill"—my old nickname for the gloomy man.

"Do that," said Stephen. "Hanging up now."

"I send you any pictures of my cabin? Gets its power off a windmill. I'm telling you, it's the absolute goddamned shit. You need to come out here and see me."

"What about Charleston? Where's Amanda?"

I spat a lime rind into my hand and tossed it up at the bats to see if they'd take a nibble at it. They didn't.

"No idea."

"You split?"

"Right."

"Oh, jeez, big brother. Really? Wedding's off?"

"Yep."

"What happened?"

"Got sick of her, I guess."

"Why?"

"She was hard of hearing and her pussy stank."

"That's grand. Now look—"

Actually, like about fifty million other Americans, I'd been blindsided by sudden reverses in the real-estate market. I'd had to borrow some cash from my ex-fiancée, Amanda, an Oldsmobile dealership heiress who didn't care about money just so long as she didn't have to loan out any of hers. Strains developed and the engagement withered. I used the last of my liquidity to buy my hill. Four hundred acres, plus a cabin, nearly complete, thanks to my good neighbor George Tabbard, who'd also cut me a bargain on the land. The shit of it was I'd have to spend a year up in residence here, but I could deal with that. Next fall I could subdivide, sell the plots, dodge the extortionary tax assessment the state charges nonresident speculators, and float into life's next phase with the winds of increase plumping my sails and a vacation home in the deal.

"Anyway," I went on. "Here's a concept. Pry the flute out of your ass and come see me. We'll have real fun. Come now. I'll be under a glacier in six weeks."

"And get the airfare how? Knit it? Listen, I've got to go."

"Fuck the airfare," I told him. "I'll get it. Come see me." It wasn't an offer I really wanted to make. Stephen probably had more money in the bank than I did, but his poor-mouthing worked an irksome magic on me. I couldn't take a second of it without wanting to smack him in the face with a roll of doubloons. Then he said he couldn't leave Beatrice (the collie was still alive!). Fine, I told him, if he could find the right sort of iron lung to stable her in, I'd foot the bill for that too. He said he'd think it over. A marimba flourish swelled on the line, and I let Stephen go.

The conversation left me feeling irritable, and I walked back to my cabin in a low mood. But I bucked up right away when I found George Tabbard on my porch, half of which was still bare joists. He was standing on a ladder, nailing a new piece of trim across the front gable. "Evening, sweetheart," George called out to me. "Whipped up another *objet* for you here."

George was seventy-six, with a head of scraggly white hair. His front teeth were attached to a partial plate that made his gums itch so he didn't wear it, and his breath was like a ripe morgue. At this point, George was basically my best friend, a turn I couldn't have imagined ten months ago when life was still high. His family went back in the area two centuries or so, but he'd moved around a good deal, gone through some wives and degrees and left some children here and there before moving back a decade ago. He'd pretty much built my cabin himself for ten dollars an hour. He was good company. He liked to laugh and drink and talk about road grading, women, and maintaining equipment. We'd murdered many evenings that way.

A couple of groans with his screw gun and he'd secured the item, a four-foot battery of little wooden pom-poms, like you'd see dangling from the ceiling of a Mexican drug dealer's sedan. I'd praised the first one he'd made, but now George had tacked his lacework fancies to every eave and soffit in sight, so that the house pretty well foamed with them. An otherwise sensible person, he seemed to fear a demon would take him if production slowed, and he slapped up a new piece of frippery about every third day. My house was starting to resemble something you'd buy your mistress to wear for a weekend in a cheap motel.

"There we are," he said, backing away to get the effect. "Pretty handsome booger, don't you think?"

"Phenomenal," I said.

"Now how about some backgammon?"

I went inside and fetched the set, the rum, and a jar of olives. George was a brutal prodigy, and the games were dull routs, yet we sat for many hours in the cool of the evening, drinking rum, moving the lacquered discs around the board, and spitting olive pits over the rail, where they landed quietly in the dark.

To my surprise, Stephen called me back. He said he'd like to come, so we fixed a date, two weeks later. It was an hour and twenty minutes to the village of Aiden, where the airfield was. When George and I arrived, Stephen's plane hadn't come in. I went into the Quonset hut they use for a terminal. A little woman with a brown bomber jacket and a bulb of gray hair sat by the radio, reading the local newspaper.

"My brother's flight was due in from Bangor at eleven," I told the woman.

"Plane's not here," she said.

"I see. Do you know where it is?"

"Bangor."

"And when's it going to arrive?"

"If I knew that, I'd be somewhere picking horses, wouldn't I?"

Then she turned back to her newspaper and brought our chat to an end. The front-page story of the Aroostook Gazette showed a photograph of a dead chow dog, under the headline, MYSTERY ANIMAL FOUND DEAD IN PINEMONT.

"Quite a mystery," I said. "The Case of What Is Obviously a Dog."

"'Undetermined origin,' says here."

"It's a dog, a chow," I said.

"Undetermined," the woman said.

With time to kill, we went over the lumberyard in Aiden and I filled the bed of my truck with a load of decking to finish the porch. Then we went back to the airfield. Still no plane. George tried to hide his irritation, but I knew he wasn't happy to be stuck on this errand. He wanted to be out in the woods, gunning for deer. George was keen to get one before the weather made hunting a misery. Loading your freezer with meat slain by your hand was evidently an unshirkable autumn rite around here, and George and I had been going out about every fourth day since the opener three weeks ago. I'd shot the head off a bony goose at point-blank range, but other than that, we hadn't hit a thing. When I'd suggested that we go in on a side of beef from the butcher shop, George had acted as though I'd proposed a terrible breach of code. Fresh venison tasted better than store-bought beef, he argued. Also you were not out big money in the common event that your freezer was sacked by the meat burglars who worked the outer county.

To buck George up, I bought him lunch at a tavern in Aiden, where we ate hamburgers and drank three whiskey sours each. George sighed a lot and didn't talk. Already, I felt a coursing anger at Stephen for not calling to let me know that his plane was delayed. I was brooding heavily when the bartender asked if I wanted anything else. I told him, "Yeah, tequila and cream."

"You mean a Kahlúa and cream," he said, which was what I'd meant, but I wasn't in a mood to be corrected.

"How about you bring what I ordered?" I told him, and he got to work. The drink was bilious, vile, but I forced it down. The bartender told me, sneering, that I was welcome to another, on the house.

When we rolled back by the airport, the plane had come and gone. A light rain was sifting down. Stephen was out by the gate, on the lip of a drainage gully, perched atop his luggage with his chin on his fist. He was thinner than when I'd last seen him, and the orbits of his eyes were dark, kind of buttholish with exhaustion. The rain had wet him through, and what was left of his hair lay sad against his skull. His coat and pants were huge on him. The wind gusted and Stephen billowed like a poorly tarped load.

"Hi, friend!" I called out to him.

"What the shit, Matthew?" he said. "I just stayed up all night on a plane to spend two hours sitting in a ditch? That really happened?"

Of course, Stephen could have waited with the radio woman in the Quonset hut, but he'd probably arranged himself in the ditch to present a picture of maximum misery when I pulled up.

"You could have let me know you got hung up in Bangor. I shit-canned three hours waiting for you. We had stuff on our plate, but now George is drunk and I'm half in the bag and the whole day's shot. Frankly, I'm a little heated at you here."

Stephen bulged his eyes at me. His fists clenched and unclenched very quickly. He looked about to thrombose. "Extraordinary! This is my fault now? Oh, you are a remarkable prick. This is your fucking . . . region, Matthew. It didn't occur to me that you'd need to be coached on how not to leave somebody in the rain. Plus call you how, shitball? You know I don't do cell phones."

"Come get in the truck."

I reached for him and he tore his arm away.

"No. Apologize to me." He was red-eyed and shivering. His cheeks and forehead were welted over from repeated gorings by the vicious cold-weather mosquitoes they had up here. Right now, one was gorging itself on the rim of his ear, its belly glowing like a pomegranate seed in the cool white sun. I didn't swat it away for him.

"Mother*fucker*, man. Just get in the truck."

"Forget it. I'm going home." He shouldered his bag and stormed off for the airfield. His tiny damp head, and squelching shoes—it was like watching the tantrum of a stray duckling.

Laughing, I jogged up behind Stephen and stripped the bag

from his shoulder. When he turned I put him in a bear hug and kissed his brow.

"Get off me, you ape," he said.

"Who's a furious fellow?" I said. "Who's my little Brown Cloud?"

"Fucking asshole, I'll bite you, I swear," he said into my chest. "Let me go. Give me my bag."

"Ridiculous," I said.

I walked to the truck and levered the seat forward to usher Stephen into the club cab's rear compartment. When Stephen saw that we weren't alone, he stopped grasping for his bag and making departure threats. I introduced Stephen to George. Then my brother clambered in and we pulled onto the road.

"This is Granddad's gun, isn't it?" said Stephen. Hanging in the rack was the .300 Weatherby magnum I'd collected from my grandfather's house years ago. It was a beautiful instrument, with a blued barrel and a tiger-maple stock.

"Yes," I said, marshalling a defense for why I hadn't offered the gun to Stephen, who probably hadn't fired a rifle in fifteen years. Actually, Stephen probably had a stronger claim to it than I did. As kids, we'd gone out for ducks and rabbits with our grandfather, and Stephen, without making much of it, had always been the more patient stalker and a better shot. But he did not mention it.

"Hey, by the way," he said. "The tab comes to eight-eighty."

"What tab?" I said.

"Eight hundred and eighty dollars," Stephen said. "That's what the flight came to, plus a sitter for Beatrice."

"Your daughter?" George asked.

"Dog," said Stephen.

"George, this is a dog that knows where it was when JFK was shot," I said. "Stephen, are you still doing those bowel lavages on her? Actually, don't tell me. I don't need the picture in my head."

"I'd like my money," Stephen said. "You said you'd reimburse me."

"Don't get a rod-on about it, Steve-O. You'll get paid."

"Lovely. When?"

"At some future fucking juncture when I don't happen to be operating a moving motor vehicle. Is that okay with you?"

"Sure," said Stephen. "But just for the record, me being colossally shafted is how this is going to conclude."

"You little grasping fuck, what do you want, collateral? Want to hold my watch?" I joggled the wheel a little. "Or maybe I'll just drive this truck into a fucking tree. Maybe you'd like that."

George began to laugh in a musical wheeze. "How about you stop the car and you two have yourselves an old-fashioned rock fight."

"We're fine," I said, my face hot. "Sorry, George."

"Forget it," Stephen said.

"Oh, no, Steve, money man, let's get you squared away," I said. "George, my checkbook's in the glove box."

George made out the check, and I signed it, which hurt me deeply. I passed it to my brother, who folded it into his pocket. George patted my shoulder. "His name shall be called Wonderful Counselor, the Everlasting Father, the Prince of Peace," he said.

"Oh, suck a dong," I said.

"If there's no way around it," sighed George. "How's clearance under that steering wheel?"

"Fairly snug."

"A little later, how about, when I can really put my back into it?"

"That's a big ten-four," I said.

At all this, Stephen tittered. Then, after being such a childish shit about the check, he began a campaign of being very enthusiastic about everything going past the windows of the truck. The junky houses with appliances piled on their porches? "Refreshing" compared with the "twee fraudulence of most New England towns." Two hicks on a four-wheeler, blasting again and again through their own gales of dust, knew "how to do a weekend right." "Wagnerian" is how he described the storm clouds overhead. Then Stephen began plying George with a barrage of light and pleasant chatter. Had he lived here long? Ten years? Amazing! He'd grown up here, too? How fantastic to have escaped a childhood in the ex-urban soul vacuum we'd been reared in. And George had gone to Syracuse? Had he heard of Nils Aughterard, the music biographer on the faculty there? Well, his book on Gershwin—

"Hey, Stephen," I broke in. "You haven't said anything about my new truck."

"What'd you pay for it?"

"Best vehicle I've ever owned," I said. "V-8, five liter. Three-and-a-half-ton towing capacity. Carriage-welded, class-four trailer hitch. Four-wheel drive, max payload package. It'll pay for itself when the snow hits."

"So you and Amanda, that's really off?"

"Yeah."

"I'm so sorry, Matty," Stephen said. "You were so hot on her."

Stephen had despised her. Amanda was a churchgoer, and a Republican. They'd argued about the war in Iraq. Over dinner, Stephen had baited her into declaring that she'd like to see the Middle East bombed to a parking lot. He'd asked her how this tactic would square with "Thou Shalt Not Kill." She'd told him "Thou Shalt Not Kill" was from the Old Testament, so it didn't really count.

"Anyway, I'm sorry," he went on. "I know it's got to hurt."

I took a tube of sunflower seeds from the dashboard and shook a long gray dose into my mouth.

"To be honest with you," I said, cracking a seed with my back teeth. "I just don't see the rationale for anybody owning a vehicle without a carriage-welded, class-four trailer hitch."

In silence, we rode through bleary, rural abridgements of towns, down a narrowing vasculature of country roads, to the rilled and cratered fire trail that served as a driveway to my and George's land. High weeds stood in the spine of earth between the tire grooves, brushing the truck's undercarriage with a sound of light sleet. We passed George's handsome cedar-shake cottage,

I dropped the truck into four-wheel drive, and the Dodge leapt, growling, up the hill.

My home hove into view. I was ready for Stephen to bust my balls a little over George's fancy trim, but he took in the place without a word.

George ambled off to take a leak in the trees. I grabbed Stephen's bag and led him indoors. Though my cabin's exterior was well into its late rococo phase, the interior was still raw. Stephen gazed around the living room. I felt newly conscious of the squalor of the place. The floors were still dusty plywood. The drywall stopped four feet from the floor, and pink insulation lay like an autopsy specimen behind the cloudy plastic sheeting. The sheetless mattress I'd been sleeping on sat askew in the center of the room.

"Feel free to do a little embellishing when you send out the Christmas letter this year," I told him.

Stephen went to the window and gazed out at the wiry expanse of leafless trees sloping down the basin of the valley. "Hell of a view," he said. Then he turned away from the window and looked at the mattress. "You got a place for me to sleep?"

I nodded at a sleeping pad rolled up in the corner. "Top-of-the-line pad, right there. Ever get down on memory foam?"

"You didn't tell me we'd be camping."

"Yeah, well, if it's too much of a shithole for you, baby brother, I can run you back to the motor lodge in Aiden."

"Of course not," Stephen said. "The place is great. I think you're making real progress, Matthew. Honestly, I was expecting a modular chalet with tiered Jacuzzis and an eight-car garage."

"Next time you visit, I'll strip nude and wear a barrel, maybe get a case of hookworm going," I said. "You'll really be proud of me then."

"No, I'm serious. I'd kill for something like this," he said, reaching up to rub his hand along a smooth log rafter. "I mean, God, next month I'm forty. I rent a two-room apartment full of silverfish and no bathroom sink."

"That same place? You're kidding," I said. "What about that condo you were looking at?"

"Cold feet, I guess, with the economy and all. I figured I'd just get rooked."

"It's still on the market? You should've called me. I'd get you set up."

"No."

"But that money, your Gram-Gram cash? Still got it for a down payment?"

He nodded.

"Listen, you get back to Oregon, we'll find you something. Look around, send me some comps, I'll help you through it. We'll get you into a place."

Stephen gave me a guarded look, as though I'd offered him a soda and he wasn't sure I hadn't pissed in it first.

I wanted to get the porch wrapped up before dark, and I suggested that Stephen take a drink up to the summit, where I'd hung a hammock, while George and I nailed the decking down. Stephen said, "Why don't I help you guys? I'm acquainted with Manuel."

"Who?"

"Manuel Labòr," he said, and giggled.

So we unloaded the wood and he and George got to work while I stayed inside, slathering auburn Minwax on sheets of bead-board wainscot. Whenever I poked my head out the front door, I saw Stephen vandalizing my lumber. He'd bend every third nail, and then gouge the wood with the hammer's claw trying to correct his mistake. Water would pool in those gouges and rot the boards, but he seemed to be enjoying himself. Through the closed windows, I could hear George and Stephen chatting and laughing as they worked. I'd learned to tolerate long hours of silence in the months I'd been up here, to appreciate it, even. But it warmed me to hear voices coming from my porch, though in the back of my mind I suspected they were laughing about me.

•••

George and Stephen took until nightfall to get all the decking in place. When they were finished, we made our way down to the tiny pond I'd built by damming a spring behind my house. We shed our clothes and pushed off into the pond, each on his own gasping course through the exhilarating blackness of the water. "Oh, oh, oh, *God* it feels good," cried Stephen in a voice of such carnal gratitude that I pitied him. But it was glorious, the sky and the water of a single world-ending darkness, and we levitated in it until we were as numb as the dead.

Back at the house, I cooked up a gallon or so of beef stroganoff, seasoned as George liked it, with enough salt to make you weep. A run of warm nights was upon us, thanks to a benevolent spasm of the Gulf Stream, and we dined in comfort on the newly finished porch. Over the course of the meal, we put away three bottles of wine and half a handle of gin. By the time we'd moved on to brandied coffee to go with the blueberry pie George fetched from his place, the porch was humid with bonhomie.

"Look at this," Stephen said, stomping heavily on one of the new boards. "Man, I put this bastard here. Some satisfying shit. God bless 'em, there's 'tards I've worked with ten years and we still haven't gotten past chants and toning. But look—" he clogged again on the board. "Couple hours with a hammer. Got something you can stand on. I ought to do like you, Matty. Come out here. Build me a spot."

"Hell yeah, you should," I said. "By the way, how big's that wad you've got? What's it, twenty grand or something?"

"I guess," he said.

"Because look, check it out," I said. "Got a proposition for you. Listen, how many guys like us do you think there are out there? Ballpark figure."

"What's that mean, 'like us'?" Stephen said.

Then I began to spell out for him an idea I'd had on my mind lately, one that seemed rosiest after a wine-soaked dinner, when my gladness for the land, the stars, and the bullfrogs in my pond was at its maximum. I'd get to thinking about the paunchy hordes, nightly pacing carpeted apartments from Spokane to Chattanooga, desperate for an escape hatch. The plan was simple. I'd advertise one-acre plots in the back pages of men's magazines, put up a few spec cabins, handle the contracting myself, build a rifle range, some snowmobile trails, maybe a little saloon on the summit. In they'd swarm, a hill of pals, a couple of million in it for me, no sweat!

"I don't know," said Stephen, helping himself to another fat dollop of brandy.

"What don't you know?" I asked him. "That twenty grand, you're in for an even share. You'd be getting what the other investors are getting for fifty."

"What other investors?" Stephen asked.

"Ray Lawton," I lied. "Lawton, Ed Hayes, and Dan Welsh. My point is I could let you in, even just with that twenty. If you could kick that twenty in, I'd set you up with an even share."

"No, yeah, I like it," Stephen said. "It's just I need to be careful with that money. That's my whole savings and everything."

"Now goddammit, Stephen, I'm sorry but let me explain something to you. I *make* money, that's what I do," I said. "I take land, and a little bit of money, and then I turn it into lots of money. You follow me? That's what I do. What I'm asking is to basically just *hold* your cash for five months, max, and in return you'll be in on something that, guaranteed, will change your life."

"Can't do it," he said.

"Okay, Stephen, what can you do? Could you go ten? Ten grand for a full share? Could you put in ten?"

"Look, Matthew—"

"Five? Three? Two thousand?"

"Look—"

"How about eight hundred, Stephen, or two hundred? Would that work for you, or would two hundred dollars break the bank?"

"Two hundred's good," he said. "Put me down for that."

"Go fuck yourself," I said.

"Matthew, come on," said George. "Cool it."

"I'm totally cool," I said.

"No, you're being a shit," said George. "And anyway, your dude ranch thing isn't worth all this gas. Never work."

"Why not?"

"First of all, the county'd never let you do it in the watershed. The ten-acre buffer—"

"I already talked to them about a variance," I said. "Wouldn't be—"

"And for another thing, I didn't move back here to get among a bunch of swinging dicks."

"Due respect, George, I'm not talking about your land."

"I know that, Matthew," George said. "What I'm saying is, you carve this hill up and sell it out to a bunch of cock-knockers from Boston, I'd say the chance is pretty good that some night in the off-season, I'd get a few too many beers in me and I'd get it in my head to come around with a few gallons of kerosene."

George was staring at my with an irritating, stagy intensity. "Forget the kerosene, George—a hammer and nails'll do it," I said, turning and sweeping a hand at the wooden dainties on my gable. "Just sneak up some night and do a little raid with your scrollsaw. Turn everybody's camp into a huge doily. That'll run them off pretty quick."

I laughed and went on laughing until my stomach muscles ached and tears beaded on my jaw. When I looked back at George, he had his lips set in a taut little dash. He was evidently vain about his scrollsaw work. I was still holding my pie plate, and without giving it much thought, I flung it into the woods. A crash followed, but no rewarding tinkle of shattered crockery.

"Ah, fuck," I said.

"What?" said Stephen.

"Nothing," I said. "My life is on fire."

Then I went into my cabin and got down on my mattress, and before long I was sleeping very well.

• • •

I woke a little after three, hungover and thirsty as a poisoned rat, but I lay paralyzed in superstition that staggering to the sink would banish sleep for good. My heart raced. I thought of my performance on the porch, then of a good thick noose creaking as it swung. I thought of Amanda, and my two ex-wives. I thought of my first car whose engine seized because I didn't change the timing belt at 100,000 miles. I thought of how two nights ago I'd lost thirty dollars to George in a cribbage game. I thought of how in the aftermath of my father's death, for reasons I couldn't recall, I stopped wearing underwear, and of a day in junior high when the cold rivet in a chair alerted me to a hole in the seat of my pants. I thought of everyone I owed money to, and everyone who owed me money. I thought of Stephen and me and the children we'd so far failed to produce, and how in the diminishing likelihood that I did find someone to smuggle my genetic material into, by the time our little one could tie his shoes, his father would be a florid fifty-year-old who would suck the innocence and joy from his child as greedily as a desert wanderer savaging a found orange.

I wanted the sun to rise, to make coffee, to get out in the woods with George and find his trophy buck, to get back to spinning the blanket of mindless incident that was doing an ever-poorer job of masking the pit of regrets I found myself peering into most sleepless nights. But the sun was slow in coming. The montage wore on until dawn, behind it the soothing music of the noose, *crik-creak, crik-creak, crik-creak.*

At the first bruised light in the eastern windows, I got up. The air in the cabin was dense with chill. Stephen wasn't on the spare mattress. I put on my boots, jeans, and a canvas parka, filled a thermos with hot coffee, and drove the quarter mile to George's house.

The lights were on at George's. George was doing sit-ups and Stephen was at the counter, minting waffles. A very cozy pair. The percolator was gasping away, making me feel forlorn with my plaid thermos.

"Hey, hey," I said.

"There he is," Stephen said. He explained that he'd slept on George's couch. They'd been up late at the backgammon board. He handed me a waffle, all cheer and magnanimity, on his way toward another social heist in the Dodi Clark vein.

"What do you say, George," I said, when the old man had finished his crunches. "Feel like going shooting?"

"I suppose," he said. He turned to Stephen. "Coming with, little brother?"

"I don't have a gun for him," I said.

"Got that .30-.30 he can use," George said.

"Why not?" said Stephen.

Our spot was on Pigeon Lake, twenty miles away, and you had to boat out to the evergreen cover on the far shore. After breakfast, we hooked George's skiff and trailer to my truck, and went jouncing into the white fog that blanketed the road.

We dropped the boat into the water. With Stephen in the bow, I took the stern. We went north, past realms of marsh grass and humps of pink granite, which, in the hard red light of morning, resembled corned beef hash.

George stopped the boat at a stretch of muddy beach where he said he'd had some luck before. We beached the skiff, and trudged into the tree line.

My calamitous hangover was worsening. I felt damp, unclean, and suicidal, and couldn't concentrate on anything except the vision of a cool, smooth-sheeted bed and iced seltzer water and bitters. It was Stephen who found the first heap of deer sign, in the shadow of a pine sapling stripped orange by a rutting buck. He was thrilled with his discovery, and he scooped the droppings into his palm and carried them over to George, who sniffed the dark pebbles so avidly that for a second I thought he might eat them.

"Pretty fresh," said Stephen, who hadn't been out hunting since the eleventh grade.

George said, "Looks like he winded us. Good eyes, Steve."

"Yeah, I just looked down and there it was," said Stephen.

George went off to perch in a nearby stand he knew about and left the two of us alone. Stephen and I sat at adjacent trees with our guns across our laps. A loon moaned. Squirrels rasped.

"So Matty, you kind of put a weird bug in my ear last night."

"That a fact?"

"Not that ridiculous bachelor-campus thing. But this place is fantastic. George said he sold it to you for ninety bucks an acre. Is that true?"

"Market price," I said.

"Astounding. "

"You'd hate it out here. What about your work?"

"I'd just come out here for the summers when my gig at the school slacks off. I need to get out of Eugene. It's destroying me. I don't go out. I don't meet people. I sit in my apartment, composing this crap. I'm done. I could have spent the last two decades shooting heroin and the result would be the same, except I'd have some actual life behind me."

I lifted a haunch to let a long, low fart escape.

"Charming," said Stephen. "How about you sell me two acres? Then I've got twelve thousand to put into a cabin."

"I thought you had twenty."

"I *had* twenty-three," he said. "Now I've got about twelve."

"You spent it? On what?"

"Investments," he said. "Some went to this other thing."

"What other thing?"

Distractedly, he pinched a few hairs from his brow. I watched him put the hairs into his mouth and nibble them rapidly with his front teeth. "I've got a thing with this girl."

"Hey, fantastic," I said. "You should have brought her. What's her name?"

"Luda," Stephen said. "She's Hungarian."

"Far fucking out," I said. "What's a Hungarian chick doing in Eugene?"

"She's still in Budapest, actually," Stephen said. "We're trying to get the distance piece of it ironed out."

"How'd you meet her?"

"That's sort of the weird part. I met her online."

"Nothing wrong with that."

Stephen coughed and ripped another sprig from his brow. "Yeah, but, I mean, it was one of these things. To be totally honest, I met her on this site. Really, pretty tame stuff. I mean, she wasn't, like, fucking people or anything. It was just, you know, you pay a few bucks and you can chat with her, and she's got this video feed."

I looked at him to see if he was kidding. His face was grim and earnest. "You and like fifty other guys, right?" I said after a while.

"No, no. Well, yeah," Stephen said. "I mean, there is a group room or whatever, but if you want to, you can, like, do a private thing where it shuts out all the other subscribers and it's just the two of you. And over time, we started really getting to know each other. Every once in a while, I'd log in under a different name, you know, to see how she'd act with other guys, and almost every time she guessed it was me! A few months ago, I set up a camera so she could see me, too. A lot of the time, we don't even do anything sexual. We just talk. We just share our lives with each other, just stuff that happens in our day."

"But you pay her, Stephen," I said.

"Not always," he said. "Not anymore. She's not a whore. She's really just a normal woman. She's getting her degree in computer science. She's got a little son, Miska. I've met him, too. But, yeah, I try to help them when I can. I ought to show you some of her emails. She's very smart. A good writer. She's probably read more books than I have. It's not as weird as it sounds, Matty. We're talking about me maybe heading over there in the new year, and, who knows, just seeing where it goes from there."

"How much money have you given her?"

He took a breath and wiped his nose. "I haven't added it all up. Seven grand? I don't know."

I didn't say anything. My heart was beating hard. I wasn't sure why. Minutes went by and neither of us spoke. "So, Stephen—" I finally said. But right then, he sat up and cocked an ear. "Hush," he whispered, fussing with the rifle. When he managed to lever a round into the chamber, he raised the gun to his shoulder and drew a bead on the far side of the clearing.

"There's nothing there," I said.

He fired, and then charged off into the brush. I let him go. The shot summoned George. He jogged into the clearing just as Stephen was emerging from the scrub.

"Hit something, little brother?" George asked him.

"Guess not," he said.

"At least you got a look," he said. "Next time."

At noon, we climbed back in the boat. There wasn't another craft in sight, and the loveliness of the day was enough to knock you down, but it was lost on me. The picture of gaunt Stephen, panting at his monitor as his sweetheart pumped and squatted for him, her meter ticking merrily, was a final holocaust on my already ravaged mood. I couldn't salvage any of the low glee I've wrung in the past from my brother's misfortunes. Instead, I had a close, clammy feeling that my brother and I were turning into a very ugly pair of men. We'd traced such different routes, each disdaining the other as an emblem of what we were not, only to fetch up, together, in the far weird wastes of life.

The boat plowed on. No planes disturbed the sky. Swallows rioted above the calm green lid of the lake. Birch trees gleamed like filaments among the evergreens. I was dead to it, though I did take a kind of comfort in the fact that all of this beauty was out here, persisting like mad, whether you hearkened to it or not.

George steered us to another stretch of lakefront woods, and I went and hunkered alone in a blueberry copse. My hands were cold, and my thighs and toes were cold, and my cabin would be cold when I got back, and to take a hot shower I would have to heat a kettle on the stove and pour the water into the rubber bladder hanging over my bathtub. The shower in my house in Charleston was a state-of-the-art five-nozzler that simultaneously blasted your face, breasts, and crotch. The fun was quickly going out of this, not just the day, but the whole bit up here, the backbreaking construction hassles, and this bullshit, too—crouching in a wet shrub, masquerading as a rugged hardscrabbler just to maintain the affection of an aged drunk.

Off to my right, I could hear George coughing a wet, complicated, old-man's cough, loud enough to send even the deafest herd galloping for the hills. I leaned out of my bush to scowl at him. He sat swabbing his pitted scarlet nose with a hard green hankie, and disgust and panic overwhelmed me. Where was I? Three months of night were coming on! Stuck in a six-hundred-square-foot crate! I'd probably look worse than the old man when the days got long again! Sell the truck! Sell the cabin! Get a Winnebago! Drive it where?

The sun was sinking when George called out, and the three of us slogged back to the soggy delta where we'd tied the boat.

Glancing down the beach, I spotted something that I thought at first might be a driftwood sculpture, but which sharpened under my stare into the brown serrations of a moose's rack. It was standing in the shallows, its head bent to drink. Well over three hundred yards, and the moose was downwind, probably getting ready to bolt in a second. I was tired. I raised my gun. George started bitching at me.

"Goddammit, Matthew, no, it's too far." I didn't give a shit. I fired twice.

The moose's forelegs crumpled beneath it, and an instant later I saw the animal's head jerk as the sound of the shot reached him. The moose tried to struggle upright but fell again. The effect was of a very old person trying to pitch a heavy tent. It tried to stand, and fell, and tried, and fell, and then quit its strivings.

We gazed at the creature piled up down there. Finally, George turned to me, gawping and shaking his head. "That, my friend," he said, "has got to be the goddamnedest piece of marksmanship I've ever seen."

Stephen laughed. "Unreal," he said. He moved to hug me, but he was nervous about my rifle, and he just kind of groped my elbow in an awkward way.

The moose had collapsed in a foot of icy water and had to be dragged onto firm ground before it could be dressed. I waded out to where it lay and Stephen plunged along after me.

We had to crouch and soak ourselves to get the rope under its chest. The other end we looped around a hemlock on the bank, and then tied the rope to the stern of the skiff, using the tree as a makeshift pulley. George gunned the outboard, and Stephen and I stood calf-deep in the shallows heaving on the line. By the time we'd gotten the moose to shore, our palms were torn and puckered, and our boots were full of water.

With George's hunting knife, I bled the moose from the throat, and then made a slit from the bottom of the ribcage to the jaw, revealing the gullet and a pale, corrugated column of windpipe. The scent was powerful. It brought to mind the dark, briny smell that seemed always to hang around my mother in summertime when I was a child.

George was in a rapture, giddy at how I'd put us both in six months of meat with my preposterous shot. "We'll winter well on this," he kept saying. He took the knife from me and gingerly opened the moose's belly, careful not to puncture the intestines or the sack of his stomach. He dragged out the organs, setting aside the liver, the kidneys, and the pancreas. One strange hitch was the hide, which was hellish to remove. To get it loose, Stephen and I had to take turns, bracing our boots against the moose's spine, pulling at the hide while George slashed away at the fascia and connective tissues. I saw Stephen's throat buck nauseously every now and again, yet he wanted to have a part in dressing it, and I was proud of him for that. He took up the game saw and cut off a shoulder and a ham. We had to lift the legs like pallbearers to get them to the boat. Blood ran from the meat and down my shirt with hideous, vital warmth.

The skiff sat low under the weight of our haul. The most substantial ballast of our crew, I sat in the stern and ran the kicker so the bow wouldn't swamp. Stephen sat on the cross bench, our knees nearly touching. We puttered out, a potent blue vapor bubbling up from the propeller. Clearing the shallows, I opened the throttle, and the craft bullied its way through the low swells, a fat white fluke churning up behind us. We skimmed out while the sun sank behind the dark spruce spires in the west. The gridded rubber handle of the Evinrude thrummed in my palm. The wind dried the fluids on my cheeks, and tossed Stephen's hair in a sparse frenzy. With the carcass receding behind us, it seemed I'd also escaped the blackness that had plagued me since Stephen's arrival. The return of George's expansiveness, the grueling ordeal of the butchery, the exhaustion in my limbs, the satisfaction in having made an unreasonably good shot that would feed my friend and me until the snow melted—it was glorious. I could feel absolution spread across the junk-pit of my troubles as smoothly and securely as a motorized tarp slides across a swimming pool.

And Stephen felt it, too, or something anyway. The old unarmored smile I knew from childhood brightened his haunted face, a tidy, compact bow of lip and tooth, alongside which I always looked dour and shabby in the family photographs. There's no point in trying to describe the love I can still feel for my brother when he looks at me this way, when he's stopped tallying his resentments against me and he's briefly left off hating himself for failing to hit the big time as the next John Tesh. Ours isn't the kind of brotherhood I would wish on other men, but we are blessed with a single, simple gift: in these rare moments of happiness, we can share joy as passionately and single-mindedly as we do hatred. As we skimmed across the dimming lake, I could see how much it pleased him to see me at ease, to have his happiness magnified in my face and reflected back at him. No one said anything. This was love for us, or the best that love could do. I brought the boat in wide around the isthmus guarding the cove, letting the wake push us through the shallows to the launch where my sturdy blue truck was waiting for us.

With the truck loaded, and the skiff rinsed clean, we rode back to the mountain. It was past dinnertime when we reached my place. Our stomachs were yowling.

I asked George and Stephen if they wouldn't mind getting started butchering the meat while I put a few steaks on the grill. George said that before he did any more work he was going to need to sit in a dry chair for a little while and drink two beers. He and Stephen sat and drank and I waded into the bed of my pickup, which was heaped nearly flush with meat. It was disgusting work rummaging in there. George came over and pointed out the short ribs and told me how to hack out the tenderloin, a tapered log of flesh that looked like a peeled boa constrictor. I held it up. George raised his can in tribute. "Now there's a pretty, pretty thing," he said.

I carried the loin to the porch and cut it into steaks two inches thick, which I patted with kosher salt and coarse pepper. I got the briquettes going while George and Stephen blocked out the meat on a plywood-and-sawhorse table in the headlights of my truck.

When the coals had grayed over, I dropped the steaks onto the grill. After ten minutes, they were still good and pink in the center, and I plated them with yellow rice. Then I opened up a bottle of burgundy I'd been saving and poured three glasses. I was about to call the boys to the porch when I saw that something had caused George to halt his labors. A grimace soured his features. He sniffed at his sleeve, then his knife, then the mound of meat in front of him. He winced, took a second careful whiff and recoiled.

"Oh good Christ, it's turning," he said. With an urgent stride, he made for the truck and sprang onto the tailgate, taking up pieces of our kill and putting them to his face. "Son of a bitch," he said. "It's going off, all of it. Contaminated. It's something deep in the meat."

I walked over. I sniffed at the ham he'd been working on. It was true, there was a slight pungency to it, a diarrheal tang gathering in the air, but only faintly. If the intestines had leaked a little, it certainly wasn't any reason to toss thousands of dollars' worth of meat. And anyway, I had no idea how moose flesh was supposed to smell.

"It's just a little gamy," I said. "That's why they call it game."

Stephen smelled his hands. "George is right. It's spoiled. *Gah.*"

"Not possible," I said. "This thing was breathing three hours ago. There's nothing wrong with it."

"It was sick," said George. "That thing was dying on its feet when you shot it."

"Bullshit," I said.

"Contaminated, I promise you," said George. "I should have known it when the skin hung on there like it did. He was bloating up with something, just barely holding on. The second he died, and turned that infection loose, it just started going wild."

Stephen looked at the meat strewn across the table, and at the three of us standing there. Then he began to laugh. I went to the porch and bent over a steaming steak. It smelled fine. I rubbed the salt crust and licked at the juice from my thumb.

"There's nothing wrong with it," I said.

I cut off a dripping pink cube and touched it to my tongue. Stephen was still laughing.

"You're a fucking star, Matty," he said, breathless. "All the beasts in the forest, and you mow down a leper moose. God, that smell. Don't touch that shit, man. Call in a hazmat team."

"There's not a goddamned thing wrong with this meat," I said.

"Poison," said George.

The wind gusted suddenly. A branch fell in the woods. A squad of leaves scurried past my boots and settled against the door. Then the night went still again. I turned back to my plate and slipped the fork into my mouth.

———————

Wells Tower's fiction and nonfiction have
appeared in *The New Yorker, Harper's, GQ, The
Paris Review, McSweeney's, The Washington Post
Magazine, The New York Times,* and elsewhere.
The recipient of two Pushcart Prizes and the
Plimpton Discovery Prize from the *Paris Review,*
Tower was named Best Young Writer of 2009 by
the Village Voice. He is the author of *Everything
Ravaged, Everything Burned.* He lives in North
Carolina and Brooklyn.

SUZANNE BENNETT

*H*ere's a remarkable swindle: somehow I managed to persuade the
excellent and otherwise undupable people at McSweeney's to publish
"Retreat" two times. In the first go-round, the younger (and in that draft,
more sympathetic) of these two unhappy brothers was telling the tale, but
when it came time to revise it for publication in a collection, an emotional
niggardliness seemed to pervade the story. A brief synopsis might have read,
"A smug narrator perceives his brother to be obnoxious, and his perceptions
are ratified when his brother ultimately ingests a ration of possibly lethal
moose flesh." The story aspired to stingy ends, a kind of glib, just-deserts
satisfaction at best. So I took another stab at it, tasking myself with a mission
of greater narrative generosity, a more complicated balance of sympathies,
fewer cheap tricks. It struck me as a sadder and more interesting story if we
could get to know Matthew as a plenary human being, an aware, discerning
narrator who nonetheless can't stop alienating people despite what he believes
are his best intentions. Amazingly, McSweeney's took that version, too: the
old mechanic's hustle of doing a crappy job on somebody's head gasket and
then getting a second paycheck to fix your own shoddy work.

APPENDIX

A list of the magazines currently consulted for *New Stories from the South: The Year's Best, 2010,* with addresses, subscription rates, and editors.

AGNI Magazine
236 Bay State Road
Boston, MA 02215
Biannually, $20
Sven Birkerts

American Short Fiction
P.O. Box 301209
Austin, TX 78703
Quarterly, $30
Stacey Swann

The Antioch Review
P.O. Box 148
Yellow Springs, OH 45387-0148
Quarterly, $40
Robert S. Fogarty

Apalachee Review
P.O. Box 10469
Tallahassee, FL 32302
Semiannually, $15
Michael Trammell

Appalachian Heritage
CPO 2166
Berea, KY 40404
Quarterly, $25
George Brosi

Arkansas Review
P.O. Box 1890
Arkansas State University
State University, AR 72467
Triannually, $20
Janelle Collins

Arts & Letters
Campus Box 89
Georgia College & State University
Milledgeville, GA 31061-0490
Semiannually, $15
Martin Lammon

The Atlantic Monthly
600 New Hampshire Avenue NW
Washington, DC 20037
Monthly, $39.95
James Bennet

Bayou
Department of English
University of New Orleans
2000 Lakeshore Drive
New Orleans, LA 70148
Semiannually, $15
Joanna Leake

Bellevue Literary Review
Department of Medicine
New York University School of
  Medicine
550 1st Avenue, OBV-612
New York, NY 10016
Semiannually, $15
Ronna Weinberg

Black Warrior Review
University of Alabama
P.O. Box 862936
Tuscaloosa, AL 35486
Semiannually, $16
Nick Parker

Boulevard
6614 Clayton Road, PMB 325
Richmond Heights, MO 63117
Triannually, $20
Richard Burgin

Callaloo
Department of English
Texas A&M University
MS 4212
College Station, TX 77843-4212
Quarterly, $50
Charles H. Rowell

The Carolina Quarterly
Greenlaw Hall CB# 3520
University of North Carolina
Chapel Hill, NC 27599-3520
Triannually, $18
Matthew Luter

Cimarron Review
205 Morrill Hall
Oklahoma State University
Stillwater, OK 74078-4069
Quarterly, $24
E. P. Walkiewicz

The Cincinnati Review
Department of English and
  Comparative Literature
McMicken Hall
Room 369
University of Cincinnati
P.O. Box 210069
Cincinnati, OH 45221-0069
Semiannually, $15
Don Bogen

Colorado Review
Department of English
Colorado State University
9105 Campus Delivery
Fort Collins, CO 80523
Triannually, $24
Stephanie G'Schwind

Columbia
www.columbiajournal.org
Annually, $10
Alexis Tonti

Confrontation
English Department
C.W. Post Campus
Long Island University
Brookville, NY 11548
Semiannually, $10
Martin Tucker

Conjunctions
21 East 10th Street
New York, NY 10003
Semiannually, $18
Bradford Morrow

Crazyhorse
Department of English
College of Charleston
66 George Street
Charleston, SC 29424
Semiannually, $16
Anthony Varallo

Denver Quarterly
University of Denver
Denver, CO 80208
Quarterly, $20
Bin Ramke

Ecotone
Department of Creative Writing
UNC Wilmington
601 South College Road
Wilmington, NC 28403-3297
Semiannually, $16.95
Ben George

Epoch
251 Goldwin Smith Hall
Cornell University
Ithaca, NY 14853-3201
Triannually, $11
Michael Koch

Fiction
c/o Department of English
City College of New York
Convent Avenue at 138th Street
New York, NY 10031
Quarterly, $38
Mark Jay Mirsky

The First Line
P.O. Box 250382
Plano, TX 75025-0382
Quarterly, $12
David LaBounty

Five Points
Georgia State University
P.O. Box 3999
Atlanta, GA 30302-3999
Triannually, $21
Megan Sexton and David Bottoms

Fugue
English Department
University of Idaho
200 Brink Hall
Moscow, ID 83844-1102
Biannually, $14
Andrew Millar and Kendall Sand

Gargoyle
3819 North 13th Street
Arlington, VA 22201
Biannually, $30
Lucinda Ebersole and Richard
    Peabody

The Georgia Review
Gilbert Hall
University of Georgia
Athens, GA 30602-9009
Quarterly, $30
Stephen Corey

The Gettysburg Review
Gettysburg College
300 N. Washington Street
Gettysburg, PA 17325-1491
Quarterly, $28
Peter Stitt

Glimmer Train Stories
1211 NW Glisan Street, Suite 207
Portland, OR 97209-3054
Quarterly, $36
Susan Burmeister-Brown
    and Linda B. Swanson-Davies

Granta
12 Addison Avenue
London W11 4QR
United Kingdom
Quarterly, £45.95
John Freeman

The Greensboro Review
MFA Writing Program
3302 Hall for Humanities and
    Research Administration
UNC Greensboro
Greensboro, NC 27402-6170
Semiannually, $10
Jim Clark

Gulf Coast
Department of English
University of Houston
Houston, TX 77204-3013
Semiannually, $16
Fiction Editor

Harper's Magazine
666 Broadway, 11th Floor
New York, NY 10012
Monthly, $21
Ben Metcalf

Harpur Palate
English Department
Binghamton University
P.O. Box 6000
Binghamton, NY 13902-6000
Semiannually, $16
Fiction Editor

Harvard Review
Lamont Library, Harvard
    University
Cambridge, MA 02138
Semiannually, $16
Nam Le

The Hudson Review
684 Park Avenue
New York, NY 10065
Quarterly, $36
Paula Deitz

The Idaho Review
Boise State University
Department of English
1910 University Drive
Boise, ID 83725
Annually, $10
Mitch Wieland

Image
3307 Third Avenue, W.
Seattle, WA 98119
Quarterly, $39.95
Gregory Wolfe

In Character
John Templeton Foundation
Attn: In Character
300 Conshohocken State Road,
    Suite 500
West Conshohocken, PA 19428
Triannually, $18
Charlotte Hays

Indiana Review
Ballantine Hall 465
Indiana University
1020 E. Kirkwood Drive
Bloomington, IN 47405-7103
Semiannually, $17
Chad B. Anderson

The Iowa Review
308 EPB
University of Iowa
Iowa City, IA 52242-1408
Triannually, $25
David Hamilton

Iron Horse Literary Review
Department of English
Texas Tech University
Mail Stop 43091
Lubbock, TX 79409-3091
Semiannually, $15
Lee Martin

The Jabberwock Review
Department of English
Mississippi State University
Drawer E
Mississippi State, MS 39762
Semiannually, $15
Michael P. Kardos

The Journal
The Ohio State University
Department of English
164 W. 17th Avenue
Columbus, OH 43210
Semiannually, $15
Kathy Fagan and Michelle Herman

The Kenyon Review
www.kenyonreview.org
Quarterly, $30
David H. Lynn

The Literary Review
Fairleigh Dickinson University
285 Madison Avenue
Madison, NJ 07940
Quarterly, $18
Minna Proctor

Long Story
18 Eaton Street
Lawrence, MA 01843
Annually, $7
R. P. Burnham

Louisiana Literature
SLU-10792
Southeastern Louisiana University
Hammond, LA 70402
Semiannually, $12
Jack Bedell

The Louisville Review
Spalding University
851 South 4th Street
Louisville, KY 40203
Semiannually, $14
Sena Jeter Naslund

McSweeney's
849 Valencia Street
San Francisco, CA 94110
Quarterly, $55
Dave Eggers

Meridian
University of Virginia
P.O. Box 400145
Charlottesville, VA 22904-4145
Semiannually, $12
Aja Gabel

Mid-American Review
Department of English
Bowling Green State University
Bowling Green, OH 43403
Semiannually, $15
Karen Craigo and Michael
    Czyzniejewski

Mississippi Review
University of Southern Mississippi
Box 5144
Hattiesburg, MS 39406
Semiannually, $15
Frederick Barthelme

The Missouri Review
357 McReynolds Hall
University of Missouri
Columbia, MO 65211
Quarterly, $24
Speer Morgan

Narrative
narrativemagazine.com
Triannually, $57
Carol Edgarian and Tom Jenks

Natural Bridge
Department of English
University of Missouri-St. Louis
One University Boulevard
St. Louis, MO 63121
Semiannually, $10
Mary Troy

New England Review
Middlebury College
Middlebury, VT 05753
Quarterly, $30
Stephen Donadio

New Letters
University of Missouri–Kansas City
5101 Rockhill Road
Kansas City, MO 64110
Quarterly, $22
Robert Stewart

New Orleans Review
P.O. Box 195
Loyola University
New Orleans, LA 70118
Semiannually, $15
Christopher Chambers and
   John Biguenet

New South
Campus Box 1894
Georgia State University
MSC 8R0322 Unit 8
Atanta, GA 30303-3083
Semiannually, $8
Peter Fontaine

The New Yorker
4 Times Square
New York, NY 10036
Weekly, $39.95

Nimrod
University of Tulsa
800 South Tucker Drive
Tulsa, OK 74104
Semiannually, $18.50
Francine Ringold

Ninth Letter
Department of English
University of Illinois
608 South Wright Street
Urbana, IL 61801
Biannually, $21.95
Jodee Stanley

North Carolina Literary Review
English Department
2201 Bate Building
East Carolina University
Greenville, NC 27858-4353
Annually, $10
Biannually, $20
Margaret Bauer

Northwest Review
5243 University of Oregon
Eugene, OR 97403
Triannually, $22
Ehud Havazelet

Now & Then
Center for Appalachian Studies and
   Services
East Tennessee State University
Box 70556
Johnson City, TN 37614-1707
Semiannually, $15
Fred Sauceman

One Story
www.one-story.com
Monthly, $21
Hannah Tinti

Open City
270 Lafayette Street
Suite 1412
New York, NY 10012
Triannually, $30
Thomas Beller, Joanna Yas

Overtime
www.workerswritejournal.com
P.O. Box 250382
Plano, TX 7502-0382
Quarterly, $15

The Oxford American
201 Donaghey Avenue, Main 107
Conway, AR 72035
Quarterly, $24.95
Marc Smirnoff

Parting Gifts
3413 Wilshire
Greensboro, NC 27408-2923
Semiannually, $18

Pembroke Magazine
UNC-P, Box 1510
Pembroke, NC 28372-1510
Annually, $12
Shelby Stephenson

The Paris Review
62 White Street
New York, NY 10013
Quarterly, $48
Philip Gourevitch

The Pinch
Department of English
University of Memphis
Memphis, TN 38152-6176
Semiannually, $22
Corey Clairday

Pleiades
Department of English and
    Philosophy
University of Central Missouri
Warrensburg, MO 64093
Semiannually, $16
Phong Nguyen and Matthew Eck

Ploughshares
Emerson College
120 Boylston Street
Boston, MA 02116-4624
Triannually, $24
Ladette Randolph

poemmemoirstory
University of Alabama at
    Birmingham
Department of English
HB 217
1530 3rd Avenue, S.
Birmingham, AL 35294-1260
Annually, $7
Tina Mozelle Harris

Potomac Review
Montgomery College
51 Mannakee Street
Rockville, MD 20850
Biannually, $20
Julie Wakeman-Linn

Prairie Schooner
201 Andrews Hall
P.O. Box 88034
Lincoln, NE 68588-0334
Quarterly, $28
Hilda Raz

A Public Space
www.apublicspace
Quarterly, $36
Brigid Hughes

The Rambler
P.O. Box 5070
Chapel Hill, NC 27515
Semiannually, $24
Dave Korzon

River Styx
3547 Olive Street, Suite 107
St. Louis, MO 63103
Triannually, $20
Richard Newman

The Rome Review
P.O. Box 57013
Washington, DC 20037
Quarterly, $13.70
Tarek Al-Hariri

Salamander
Suffolk University
English Department
41 Temple Street
Boston, MA 02114
2 years, 4 issues, $23
Jennifer Barber

Santa Monica Review
Santa Monica College
1900 Pico Boulevard
Santa Monica, CA 90405
Semiannually, $14
Andrew Tonkovich

The Sewanee Review
735 University Avenue
Sewanee, TN 37383-1000
Quarterly, $25
George Core

Shenandoah
Washington and Lee University
Mattingly House
2 Lee Avenue
Lexington, VA 24450
Triannually, $25
R. T. Smith

The South Carolina Review
Center for Electronic and Digital
   Publishing
Clemson University
Strode Tower, Box 340522
Clemson, SC 29634
Semiannually, $28
Wayne Chapman

South Dakota Review
Department of English
414 Clark Street
University of South Dakota
Vermillion, SD 57069
Quarterly, $30
John R. Milton

Southern Humanities Review
9088 Haley Center
Auburn University
Auburn, AL 36849
Quarterly, $15
Dan R. Latimer and Chantel Acevedo

The Southern Review
Old President's House
Louisiana State University
Baton Rouge, LA 70803
Quarterly, $40
Jeanne M. Leiby

Southwest Review
307 Fondren Library West
Box 750374
Southern Methodist University
Dallas, TX 75275
Quarterly, $24
Willard Spiegelman

Sou'wester
Department of English
Southern Illinois University at
   Edwardsville
Edwardsville, IL 62026-1438
Semiannually, $15
Allison Funk and Valerie Vogrin

Subtropics
Department of English
University of Florida
4008 Turlington Hall
P.O. Box 112075
Gainesville, FL 32611
Triannually, $26
David Leavitt

Sycamore Review
Perdue University
Department of English
500 Oval Drive
West Lafayette, IN 47907-2038
Semiannually, $14
James Xiao

Tampa Review
University of Tampa
401 W. Kennedy Boulevard
Tampa, FL 33606-1490
Biannually, $22
Richard Mathews

Third Coast
www.thirdcoastmagazine.com
Biannually, $16
Daniel Toronto

The Threepenny Review
P.O. Box 9131
Berkeley, CA 94709
Quarterly, $25
Wendy Lesser

Timber Creek Review
8969 UNCG Station
Greensboro, NC 27416
Quarterly, $17
John M. Freiermuth

Tin House
P.O. Box 10500
Portland, OR 97296-0500
Quarterly, $29.90
Rob Spillman

TriQuarterly
Northwestern University
629 Noyes Street
Evanston, IL 60208-4210
Triannually, $24
Susan Firestone Hahn

The Virginia Quarterly Review
One West Range
P.O. Box 400223
Charlottesville, VA 22904-4223
Quarterly, $32
Ted Genoways

West Branch
Bucknell Hall
Bucknell University
Lewisburg, PA 17837
Semiannually, $10
Paula Closson Buck

Zoetrope: All-Story
The Sentinel Building
916 Kearny Street
San Francisco, CA 94133
Quarterly, $24
Michael Ray

Zone 3
P.O. Box 4565
Austin Peay State University
Clarksville, TN 37044
Biannually, $10
Amy Wright

PREVIOUS VOLUMES

Copies of previous volumes of *New Stories from the South* can be ordered through your local bookstore or by calling the Sales Department at Algonquin Books of Chapel Hill. Multiple copies for classroom adoptions are available at a special discount. For information, please call 919-967-0108.

NEW STORIES FROM THE SOUTH: THE YEAR'S BEST, 1986

Max Apple, BRIDGING

Madison Smartt Bell, TRIPTYCH 2

Mary Ward Brown, TONGUES OF FLAME

Suzanne Brown, COMMUNION

James Lee Burke, THE CONVICT

Ron Carlson, AIR

Doug Crowell, SAYS VELMA

Leon V. Driskell, MARTHA JEAN

Elizabeth Harris, THE WORLD RECORD HOLDER

Mary Hood, SOMETHING GOOD FOR GINNIE

David Huddle, SUMMER OF THE MAGIC SHOW

Gloria Norris, HOLDING ON

Kurt Rheinheimer, UMPIRE

W. A. Smith, DELIVERY

Wallace Whatley, SOMETHING TO LOSE

Luke Whisnant, WALLWORK

Sylvia Wilkinson, CHICKEN SIMON

NEW STORIES FROM THE SOUTH: THE YEAR'S BEST, 1987

James Gordon Bennett, DEPENDENTS

Robert Boswell, EDWARD AND JILL

Rosanne Caggeshall, PETER THE ROCK

John William Corrington, HEROIC MEASURES/VITAL SIGNS

Vicki Covington, MAGNOLIA

Andre Dubus, DRESSED LIKE SUMMER LEAVES

Mary Hood, AFTER MOORE

Trudy Lewis, VINCRISTINE

Lewis Nordan, SUGAR, THE EUNUCHS, AND BIG G. B.

Peggy Payne, THE PURE IN HEART

Bob Shacochis, WHERE PELHAM FELL

Lee Smith, LIFE ON THE MOON

Marly Swick, HEART

Robert Love Taylor, LADY OF SPAIN

Luke Whisnant, ACROSS FROM THE MOTOHEADS

NEW STORIES FROM THE SOUTH: THE YEAR'S BEST, 1988

Ellen Akins, GEORGE BAILEY FISHING

Rick Bass, THE WATCH

Richard Bausch, THE MAN WHO KNEW BELLE STAR

Larry Brown, FACING THE MUSIC

Pam Durban, BELONGING

John Rolfe Gardiner, GAME FARM

Jim Hall, GAS

Charlotte Holmes, METROPOLITAN

Nanci Kincaid, LIKE THE OLD WOLF IN ALL THOSE WOLF STORIES

Barbara Kingsolver, ROSE-JOHNNY

Trudy Lewis, HALF MEASURES

Jill McCorkle, FIRST UNION BLUES

Mark Richard, HAPPINESS OF THE GARDEN VARIETY

Sunny Rogers, THE CRUMB

Annette Sanford, LIMITED ACCESS

Eve Shelnutt, VOICE

New Stories from the South: The Year's Best, 1989

Rick Bass, WILD HORSES

Madison Smartt Bell, CUSTOMS OF THE COUNTRY

James Gordon Bennett, PACIFIC THEATER

Larry Brown, SAMARITANS

Mary Ward Brown, IT WASN'T ALL DANCING

Kelly Cherry, WHERE SHE WAS

David Huddle, PLAYING

Sandy Huss, COUPON FOR BLOOD

Frank Manley, THE RAIN OF TERROR

Bobbie Ann Mason, WISH

Lewis Nordan, A HANK OF HAIR, A PIECE OF BONE

Kurt Rheinheimer, HOMES

Mark Richard, STRAYS

Annette Sanford, SIX WHITE HORSES

Paula Sharp, HOT SPRINGS

New Stories from the South: The Year's Best, 1990

Tom Bailey, CROW MAN

Rick Bass, THE HISTORY OF RODNEY

Richard Bausch, LETTER TO THE LADY OF THE HOUSE

Larry Brown, SLEEP

Moira Crone, JUST OUTSIDE THE B.T.

Clyde Edgerton, CHANGING NAMES

Greg Johnson, THE BOARDER

Nanci Kincaid, SPITTIN' IMAGE OF A BAPTIST BOY

Reginald McKnight, THE KIND OF LIGHT THAT SHINES ON TEXAS

Lewis Nordan, THE CELLAR OF RUNT CONROY

Lance Olsen, FAMILY

Mark Richard, FEAST OF THE EARTH, RANSOM OF THE CLAY

Ron Robinson, WHERE WE LAND

Bob Shacochis, LES FEMMES CREOLES

Molly Best Tinsley, ZOE
Donna Trussell, FISHBONE

NEW STORIES FROM THE SOUTH: THE YEAR'S BEST, 1991

Rick Bass, IN THE LOYAL MOUNTAINS
Thomas Phillips Brewer, BLACK CAT BONE
Larry Brown, BIG BAD LOVE
Robert Olen Butler, RELIC
Barbara Hudson, THE ARABESQUE
Elizabeth Hunnewell, A LIFE OR DEATH MATTER
Hilding Johnson, SOUTH OF KITTATINNY
Nanci Kincaid, THIS IS NOT THE PICTURE SHOW
Bobbie Ann Mason, WITH JAZZ
Jill McCorkle, WAITING FOR HARD TIMES TO END
Robert Morgan, POINSETT'S BRIDGE
Reynolds Price, HIS FINAL MOTHER
Mark Richard, THE BIRDS FOR CHRISTMAS
Susan Starr Richards, THE SCREENED PORCH
Lee Smith, INTENSIVE CARE
Peter Taylor, COUSIN AUBREY

NEW STORIES FROM THE SOUTH: THE YEAR'S BEST, 1992

Alison Baker, CLEARWATER AND LATISSIMUS
Larry Brown, A ROADSIDE RESURRECTION
Mary Ward Brown, A NEW LIFE
James Lee Burke, TEXAS CITY, 1947
Robert Olen Butler, A GOOD SCENT FROM A STRANGE MOUNTAIN
Nanci Kincaid, A STURDY PAIR OF SHOES THAT FIT GOOD
Patricia Lear, AFTER MEMPHIS
Dan Leone, YOU HAVE CHOSEN CAKE
Reginald McKnight, QUITTING SMOKING
Karen Minton, LIKE HANDS ON A CAVE WALL
Elizabeth Seydel Morgan, ECONOMICS

Robert Morgan, DEATH CROWN

Susan Perabo, EXPLAINING DEATH TO THE DOG

Padgett Powell, THE WINNOWING OF MRS. SCHUPING

Lee Smith, THE BUBBA STORIES

Peter Taylor, THE WITCH OF OWL MOUNTAIN SPRINGS

Abraham Verghese, LILACS

NEW STORIES FROM THE SOUTH: THE YEAR'S BEST, 1993

Richard Bausch, EVENING

Pinckney Benedict, BOUNTY

Wendell Berry, A JONQUIL FOR MARY PENN

Robert Olen Butler, PREPARATION

Lee Merrill Byrd, MAJOR SIX POCKETS

Kevin Calder, NAME ME THIS RIVER

Tony Earley, CHARLOTTE

Paula K. Gover, WHITE BOYS AND RIVER GIRLS

David Huddle, TROUBLE AT THE HOME OFFICE

Barbara Hudson, SELLING WHISKERS

Elizabeth Hunnewell, FAMILY PLANNING

Dennis Loy Johnson, RESCUING ED

Edward P. Jones, MARIE

Wayne Karlin, PRISONERS

Dan Leone, SPINACH

Jill McCorkle, MAN WATCHER

Annette Sanford, HELENS AND ROSES

Peter Taylor, THE WAITING ROOM

NEW STORIES FROM THE SOUTH: THE YEAR'S BEST, 1994

Frederick Barthelme, RETREAT

Richard Bausch, AREN'T YOU HAPPY FOR ME?

Ethan Canin, THE PALACE THIEF

Kathleen Cushman, LUXURY

Tony Earley, THE PROPHET FROM JUPITER

Pamela Erbe, SWEET TOOTH

Barry Hannah, NICODEMUS BLUFF

Nanci Kincaid, PRETENDING THE BED WAS A RAFT

Nancy Krusoe, LANDSCAPE AND DREAM

Robert Morgan, DARK CORNER

Reynolds Price, DEEDS OF LIGHT

Leon Rooke, THE HEART MUST FROM ITS BREAKING

John Sayles, PEELING

George Singleton, OUTLAW HEAD & TAIL

Melanie Sumner, MY OTHER LIFE

Robert Love Taylor, MY MOTHER'S SHOES

NEW STORIES FROM THE SOUTH: THE YEAR'S BEST, 1995

R. Sebastian Bennett, RIDING WITH THE DOCTOR

Wendy Brenner, I AM THE BEAR

James Lee Burke, WATER PEOPLE

Robert Olen Butler, BOY BORN WITH TATTOO OF ELVIS

Ken Craven, PAYING ATTENTION

Tim Gautreaux, THE BUG MAN

Ellen Gilchrist, THE STUCCO HOUSE

Scott Gould, BASES

Barry Hannah, DRUMMER DOWN

MMM Hayes, FIXING LU

Hillary Hebert, LADIES OF THE MARBLE HEARTH

Jesse Lee Kercheval, GRAVITY

Caroline A. Langston, IN THE DISTANCE

Lynn Marie, TEAMS

Susan Perabo, GRAVITY

Dale Ray Phillips, EVERYTHING QUIET LIKE CHURCH

Elizabeth Spencer, THE RUNAWAYS

New Stories from the South: The Year's Best, 1996

Robert Olen Butler, JEALOUS HUSBAND RETURNS IN FORM OF PARROT
Moira Crone, GAUGUIN
J. D. Dolan, MOOD MUSIC
Ellen Douglas, GRANT
William Faulkner, ROSE OF LEBANON
Kathy Flann, A HAPPY, SAFE THING
Tim Gautreaux, DIED AND GONE TO VEGAS
David Gilbert, COOL MOSS
Marcia Guthridge, THE HOST
Jill McCorkle, PARADISE
Robert Morgan, THE BALM OF GILEAD TREE
Tom Paine, GENERAL MARKMAN'S LAST STAND
Susan Perabo, SOME SAY THE WORLD
Annette Sanford, GOOSE GIRL
Lee Smith, THE HAPPY MEMORIES CLUB

New Stories from the South: The Year's Best, 1997

PREFACE *by Robert Olen Butler*
Gene Able, MARRYING AUNT SADIE
Dwight Allen, THE GREEN SUIT
Edward Allen, ASHES NORTH
Robert Olen Butler, HELP ME FIND MY SPACEMAN LOVER
Janice Daugharty, ALONG A WIDER RIVER
Ellen Douglas, JULIA AND NELLIE
Pam Durban, GRAVITY
Charles East, PAVANE FOR A DEAD PRINCESS
Rhian Margaret Ellis, EVERY BUILDING WANTS TO FALL
Tim Gautreaux, LITTLE FROGS IN A DITCH
Elizabeth Gilbert, THE FINEST WIFE
Lucy Hochman, SIMPLER COMPONENTS
Beauvais McCaddon, THE HALF-PINT

Dale Ray Phillips, CORPORAL LOVE
Patricia Elam Ruff, THE TAXI RIDE
Lee Smith, NATIVE DAUGHTER
Judy Troy, RAMONE
Marc Vassallo, AFTER THE OPERA
Brad Vice, MOJO FARMER

NEW STORIES FROM THE SOUTH: THE YEAR'S BEST, 1998

PREFACE *by Padgett Powell*
Frederick Barthelme, THE LESSON
Wendy Brenner, NIPPLE
Stephen Dixon, THE POET
Tony Earley, BRIDGE
Scott Ely, TALK RADIO
Tim Gautreaux, SORRY BLOOD
Michael Gills, WHERE WORDS GO
John Holman, RITA'S MYSTERY
Stephen Marion, NAKED AS TANYA
Jennifer Moses, GIRLS LIKE YOU
Padgett Powell, ALIENS OF AFFECTION
Sara Powers, THE BAKER'S WIFE
Mark Richard, MEMORIAL DAY
Nancy Richard, THE ORDER OF THINGS
Josh Russell, YELLOW JACK
Annette Sanford, IN THE LITTLE HUNKY RIVER
Enid Shomer, THE OTHER MOTHER
George Singleton, THESE PEOPLE ARE US
Molly Best Tinsley, THE ONLY WAY TO RIDE

NEW STORIES FROM THE SOUTH: THE YEAR'S BEST, 1999

PREFACE *by Tony Earley*
Andrew Alexander, LITTLE BITTY PRETTY ONE
Richard Bausch, MISSY

Pinckney Benedict, MIRACLE BOY

Wendy Brenner, THE HUMAN SIDE OF INSTRUMENTAL
   TRANSCOMMUNICATION

Laura Payne Butler, BOOKER T'S COMING HOME

Mary Clyde, KRISTA HAD A TREBLE CLEF ROSE

Janice Daugharty, NAME OF LOVE

Rick DeMarinis, BORROWED HEARTS

Tony Earley, QUILL

Clyde Edgerton, LUNCH AT THE PICADILLY

Michael Erard, BEYOND THE POINT

Tom Franklin, POACHERS

William Gay, THOSE DEEP ELM BROWN'S FERRY BLUES

Mary Gordon, STORYTELLING

Ingrid Hill, PAGAN BABIES

Michael Knight, BIRDLAND

Kurt Rheinheimer, NEIGHBORHOOD

Richard Schmitt, LEAVING VENICE, FLORIDA

Heather Sellers, FLA. BOYS

George Singleton, CAULK

NEW STORIES FROM THE SOUTH: THE YEAR'S BEST, 2000

PREFACE *by Ellen Douglas*

A. Manette Ansay, BOX

Wendy Brenner, MR. PUNIVERSE

D. Winston Brown, IN THE DOORWAY OF RHEE'S JAZZ JOINT

Robert Olen Butler, HEAVY METAL

Cathy Day, THE CIRCUS HOUSE

R.H.W. Dillard, FORGETTING THE END OF THE WORLD

Tony Earley, JUST MARRIED

Clyde Edgerton, DEBRA'S FLAP AND SNAP

Tim Gautreaux, DANCING WITH THE ONE-ARMED GAL

William Gay, MY HAND IS JUST FINE WHERE IT IS

Allan Gurganus, HE'S AT THE OFFICE

John Holman, WAVE

Romulus Linney, THE WIDOW

Thomas McNeely, SHEEP

Christopher Miner, RHONDA AND HER CHILDREN

Chris Offutt, THE BEST FRIEND

Margo Rabb, HOW TO TELL A STORY

Karen Sagstetter, THE THING WITH WILLIE

Mary Helen Stefaniak, A NOTE TO BIOGRAPHERS REGARDING FAMOUS
   AUTHOR FLANNERY O'CONNOR

Melanie Sumner, GOOD-HEARTED WOMAN

NEW STORIES FROM THE SOUTH: THE YEAR'S BEST, 2001

PREFACE *by Lee Smith*

John Barth, THE REST OF YOUR LIFE

Madison Smartt Bell, TWO LIVES

Marshall Boswell, IN BETWEEN THINGS

Carrie Brown, FATHER JUDGE RUN

Stephen Coyne, HUNTING COUNTRY

Moira Crone, WHERE WHAT GETS INTO PEOPLE COMES FROM

William Gay, THE PAPERHANGER

Jim Grimsley, JESUS IS SENDING YOU THIS MESSAGE

Ingrid Hill, JOLIE-GRAY

Christie Hodgen, THE HERO OF LONELINESS

Nicola Mason, THE WHIMSIED WORLD

Edith Pearlman, SKIN DEEP

Kurt Rheinheimer, SHOES

Jane R. Shippen, I AM NOT LIKE NUÑEZ

George Singleton, PUBLIC RELATIONS

Robert Love Taylor, PINK MIRACLE IN EAST TENNESSEE

James Ellis Thomas, THE SATURDAY MORNING CAR WASH CLUB

Elizabeth Tippens, MAKE A WISH

Linda Wendling, INAPPROPRIATE BABIES

New Stories from the South: The Year's Best, 2002

PREFACE *by Larry Brown*

Dwight Allen, END OF THE STEAM AGE

Russell Banks, THE OUTER BANKS

Brad Barkley, BENEATH THE DEEP, SLOW MOTION

Doris Betts, ABOVEGROUND

William Gay, CHARTING THE TERRITORIES OF THE RED

Aaron Gwyn, OF FALLING

Ingrid Hill, THE MORE THEY STAY THE SAME

David Koon, THE BONE DIVERS

Andrea Lee, ANTHROPOLOGY

Romulus Linney, TENNESSEE

Corey Mesler, THE GROWTH AND DEATH OF BUDDY GARDNER

Lucia Nevai, FAITH HEALER

Julie Orringer, PILGRIMS

Dulane Upshaw Ponder, THE RAT SPOON

Bill Roorbach, BIG BEND

George Singleton, SHOW-AND-TELL

Kate Small, MAXIMUM SUNLIGHT

R. T. Smith, I HAVE LOST MY RIGHT

Max Steele, THE UNRIPE HEART

New Stories from the South: The Year's Best, 2003

PREFACE *by Roy Blount Jr.*

Dorothy Allison, COMPASSION

Steve Almond, THE SOUL MOLECULE

Brock Clarke, FOR THOSE OF US WHO NEED SUCH THINGS

Lucy Corin, RICH PEOPLE

John Dufresne, JOHNNY TOO BAD

Donald Hays, DYING LIGHT

Ingrid Hill, THE BALLAD OF RAPPY VALCOUR

Bret Anthony Johnston, CORPUS

Michael Knight, ELLEN'S BOOK

Patricia Lear, NIRVANA

Peter Meinke, UNHEARD MUSIC

Chris Offutt, INSIDE OUT

ZZ Packer, EVERY TONGUE SHALL CONFESS

Michael Parker, OFF ISLAND

Paul Prather, THE FAITHFUL

Brad Vice, REPORT FROM JUNCTION

Latha Viswanathan, COOL WEDDING

Mark Winegardner, KEEGAN'S LOAD

NEW STORIES FROM THE SOUTH: THE YEAR'S BEST, 2004

PREFACE *by Tim Gautreaux*

Rick Bass, PAGANS

Brock Clark, THE LOLITA SCHOOL

Starkey Flythe, Jr., A FAMILY OF BREAST FEEDERS

Ingrid Hill, VALOR

Silas House, COAL SMOKE

Bret Anthony Johnston, THE WIDOW

Edward P. Jones, A RICH MAN

Tayari Jones, BEST COUSIN

Michael Knight, FEELING LUCKY

K. A. Longstreet, THE JUDGEMENT OF PARIS

Jill McCorkle, INTERVENTION

Elizabeth Seydel Morgan, SATURDAY AFTERNOON IN THE
    HOLOCAUST MUSEUM

Chris Offutt, SECOND HAND

Ann Pancake, DOG SONG

Drew Perry, LOVE IS GNATS TODAY

Annette Sanford, ONE SUMMER

George Singleton, RAISE CHILDREN HERE

R. T. Smith, DOCENT

New Stories from the South: The Year's Best, 2005

PREFACE *by Jill McCorkle*

Judy Budnitz, THE KINDEST CUT

James Lee Burke, THE BURNING OF THE FLAG

Robert Olen Butler, SEVERANCE

Lucinda Harrison Coffman, THE DREAM LOVER

Moira Crone, MR. SENDER

Janice Daugharty, DUMDUM

Tom Franklin, NAP TIME

Allan Gurganus, MY HEART IS A SNAKE FARM

Ethan Hauser, THE CHARM OF THE HIGHWAY MEDIAN

Cary Holladay, JANE'S HAT

Bret Anthony Johnston, ANYTHING THAT FLOATS

Dennis Lehane, UNTIL GWEN

Ada Long, CLAIRVOYANT

Michael Parker, HIDDEN MEANINGS, TREATMENT OF TIME,
    SUPREME IRONY AND LIFE EXPERIENCES IN THE SONG
    "AIN'T GONNA BUMP NO MORE NO BIG FAT WOMAN"

Gregory Sanders, GOOD WITCH, BAD WITCH

Stephanie Soileau, THE BOUCHERIE

Rebecca Soppe, THE PANTYHOSE MAN

Elizabeth Spencer, THE BOY IN THE TREE

Kevin Wilson, THE CHOIR DIRECTOR'S AFFAIR (THE BABY'S TEETH)

New Stories from the South: The Year's Best, 2006

Guest edited by Allan Gurganus

Chris Bachelder, BLUE KNIGHTS BOUNCED FROM CVD TOURNEY

Wendell Berry, MIKE

J. D. Chapman, AMANUENSIS

Quinn Dalton, THE MUSIC YOU NEVER HEAR

Tony Earley, YARD ART

Ben Fountain, BRIEF ENCOUNTERS WITH CHE GUEVARA

William Harrison, MONEY WHIPPED

Cary Holladay, THE BURNING

N. M. Kelby, JUBILATION, FLORIDA

Nanci Kincaid, THE CURRENCY OF LOVE

Keith Lee Morris, TIRED HEART

Enid Shomer, FILL IN THE BLANK

George Singleton, DIRECTOR'S CUT

R. T. Smith, TASTES LIKE CHICKEN

Mary Helen Stefaniak, YOU LOVE THAT DOG

Daniel Wallace, JUSTICE

Luke Whisnant, HOW TO BUILD A HOUSE

Kevin Wilson, TUNNELING TO THE CENTER OF THE EARTH

Erin Brooks Worley, GROVE

Geoff Wyss, KIDS MAKE THEIR OWN HOUSES

NEW STORIES FROM THE SOUTH: THE YEAR'S BEST, 2007

Guest edited by Edward P. Jones

Rick Bass, GOATS

James Lee Burke, A SEASON OF REGRET

Moira Crone, THE ICE GARDEN

Joshua Ferris, GHOST TOWN CHOIR

Tim Gautreaux, THE SAFE

Allan Gurganus, FOURTEEN FEET OF WATER IN MY HOUSE

Cary Holladay, HOLLYHOCKS

Toni Jensen, AT THE POWWOW HOTEL

Holly Goddard Jones, LIFE EXPECTANCY

Agustín Maes, BEAUTY AND VIRTUE

Stephen Marion, DOGS WITH HUMAN FACES

Philipp Meyer, ONE DAY THIS WILL ALL BE YOURS

Jason Ockert, JAKOB LOOMIS

George Singleton, WHICH ROCKS WE CHOOSE

R. T. Smith, STORY

Angela Threatt, BELA LUGOSI'S DEAD

Daniel Wallace, A TERRIBLE THING

Stephanie Powell Watts, UNASSIGNED TERRITORY

New Stories from the South: The Year's Best, 2008

Guest edited by ZZ Packer

Karen E. Bender, CANDIDATE

Pinckney Benedict, BRIDGE OF SIGHS

Kevin Brockmeier, ANDREA IS CHANGING HER NAME

Stephanie Dickinson, LUCKY 7 & DALLOWAY

Robert Drummond, THE UNNECESSARY MAN

Clyde Edgerton, THE GREAT SPECKLED BIRD

Amina Gautier, THE EASE OF LIVING

Bret Anthony Johnston, REPUBLICAN

Holly Goddard Jones, THEORY OF REALTY

Mary Miller, LEAK

Kevin Moffett, FIRST MARRIAGE

Jennifer Moses, CHILD OF GOD

David James Poissant, LIZARD MAN

Ron Rash, BACK OF BEYOND

Charlie Smith, ALBEMARLE

R.T. Smith, WRETCH LIKE ME

Stephanie Soileau, SO THIS IS PERMANENCE

Merritt Tierce, SUCK IT

Jim Tomlinson, FIRST HUSBAND, FIRST WIFE

Daniel Wallace, THE GIRLS

New Stories from the South: The Year's Best, 2009

Guest edited by Madison Smartt Bell

Pinckney Benedict, THE WORLD, THE FLESH, AND THE DEVIL

Wendell Berry, FLY AWAY, BREATH

Kelly Cherry, BANGER FINDS OUT

Stephanie Dickinson, LOVE CITY

Cary Holladay, HORSE PEOPLE

Charlotte Holmes, COAST

Juyanne James, THE ELDERBERRIES

Tayari Jones, SOME THING BLUE

Katherine Karlin, MUSCLE MEMORY

Michael Knight, GRAND OLD PARTY

Stephen Marion, TOUCH TOUCH ME

Jill McCorkle, MAGIC WORDS

Rahul Mehta, QUARANTINE

George Singleton, BETWEEN WRECKS

Stephanie Soileau, THE CAMERA OBSCURA

Elizabeth Spencer, SIGHTINGS

Clinton J. Stewart, BIRD DOG

Stephanie Powell Watts, FAMILY MUSEUM OF THE ANCIENT POSTCARDS

Holly Wilson, NIGHT GLOW

Kevin Wilson, NO JOKE, THIS IS GOING TO BE PAINFUL

Geoff Wyss, CHILD OF GOD